SISTER WAKE

Also by Dave Rudden

Knights of the Borrowed Dark

Knights of the Borrowed Dark

The Forever Court

The Endless King

Doctor Who

Wannabes

Twelve Angels Weeping

The Wintertime Paradox

Origin Stories

Tales of Darkisle

Conn of the Dead

SISTER WAKE

DAVE RUDDEN

HODDERSCAPE

First published in Great Britain in 2026 by Hodderscape
An Hachette UK company

The authorised representative in the EEA is Hachette Ireland, 8 Castlecourt Centre, Dublin 15, D15 XTP3, Ireland (email: info@hbgi.ie)

1

Map illustrations by Dewi Hargreaves

A CIP catalogue record for this title is available from the British Library

Hardback ISBN 978 1 399 73261 1
Trade Paperback ISBN 978 1 399 73262 8
ebook ISBN 978 1 399 73263 5

Typeset in Baskerville by Hewer Text UK Ltd, Edinburgh
Printed and bound in Great Britain by Clays Ltd, Elcograf S.p.A.

Hodder & Stoughton policy is to use papers that are natural, renewable and recyclable products and made from wood grown in sustainable forests. The logging and manufacturing processes are expected to conform to the environmental regulations of the country of origin.

Hodder & Stoughton Limited
Carmelite House
50 Victoria Embankment
London EC4Y 0DZ

www.hodderscape.co.uk

For Sarah, *a chuisle mo chroí*

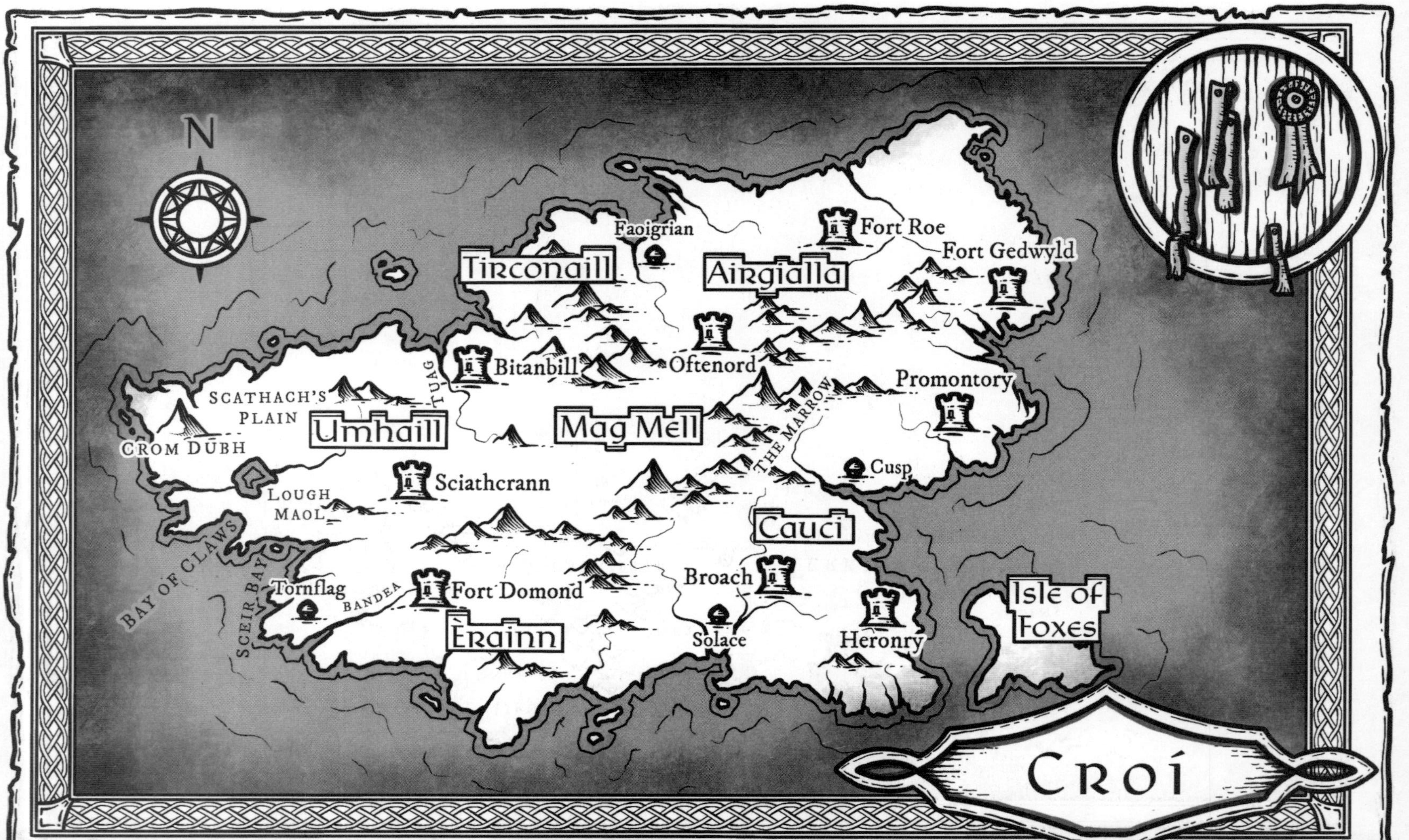
Croí
N
Tirconaill
Faoigrian
Airgialla
Fort Roe
Fort Gedwyld
Bitanbill
Oftenord
Promontory
Tuag
Scathach's Plain
Umhaill
Mag Mell
The Marrow
Crom Dubh
Cusp
Sciathcrann
Lough Maol
Cauci
Bay of Claws
Sceir Bay
Tornflag
Bandea
Fort Domond
Broach
Isle of Foxes
Èrainn
Solace
Heronry

The Answering
and Surrounding Territories
The Tattered Shore
The Contested Territories
The Unbeknownst Sea
The Stone Sea
Straits of Mearc
The New Territories
Croi
Druingill
Nimaedre
Cilkeld
Lindhord
Shetterling
Salinshrad
Salins
Wustamber
Sceppensceale
Ihankyle
Longreach
Sorbek
Urdur
Dollowport
Modigkaern
Modigmark
Idegeld
Dreodyrne
Lodemagan
Feondhall
Saergewinn
Rodeorand
N

The Irish for history is star.
The Irish for teach is moon.
The Irish for light is loss.
The Irish for secret is ruin.

'False Friends', Doireann Ní Ghríofa

Dramatis Personae

The Croí

Sister Wake – a saint

Brother Wight – her guardian, a Knight of the Hollow Eye

Mother Promise – a rebel

Creidne – a rebel

The Bear – a rebel *rí*

The Pious – a rebel *rí*

The Abacus – a rebel *rí*, dispossessed

Netha Tal-Aneririn – a *filí* in exile, with three colours to their cloak

The girls of the mountain

Brother Caid – a prick

The Answering

Mathilde – a child

Rubeo Medalwyn – King of the Answering

Offrian Medalwyn – Prince of the Answering, the King's only son

Kalifsena Medalwyn – Queen and second wife of the King

Talasa – Princess-Undynast and daughter of Kalifsena

Abelard Caudefoy – an aspiring naturalist, fourth son of Marquis Lukas Caudefoy of Modigmark

Armin Tell – Reeve Paramount of the King's Rationale
Hagan Meilyr – Lord Protector of Croí
Symon Aetsomne/MacGiolla – High Chieftain of the Cauci and Lord Seneschal of Croí
Lady Aetsomne – wife of the Lord Seneschal
Guilliam Baver – lord and Gentlemen of the Chamber
Welfin – lord and Gentlemen of the Chamber
Adger Gibb – lord and Gentleman of the Chamber
Master of the Elaborate – head of correspondence for the royal household
Daughter of the Elaborate – not an official title
Lieutenant Gabel – lieutenant of the kingscarls
Colby – Master of Secandeur House, a tutor
Stord – assistant archivist of Secandeur House

The Nemed

Anu – Queen of the Gods, Mother of Mysteries
The Cailleach – the Hag of Winter and Goddess of Death
Macha – Goddess of War and Sovereignty, the Red Mare, second of her sisters, the Proving Ground
The Warping Man – a demi-craithur
The Daughters Dearg
The Elk of Seven Tines

Before

IT'S A BEAUTIFUL morning to be a human sacrifice, the girl thought bleakly, trying to get the shackle off her leg.

It was the right thought to be having. It was the obedient thought.

'The gods were not miserly when they gave us this island.'

That was what Brother Caid had said. Kneeling at her feet. Fastening the manacle tight enough to bruise.

'We owe them.'

Worm lips moving in his worm head.

'*You* owe them.'

A familiar catechism. She and Da had uttered much the same every evening as they dotted honey on their little shrine to Queen Anu. That was what obedience had meant, before Brother Caid had dragged her from her bed. The kiss of honey. A prayer with Da before going to sleep.

And in fairness, this place would put obedience on you, if you hadn't it already. The mountain of Crom Dubh would have been spectacular even if it wasn't sacred – a hoary old grandfather of a peak, all black granite and stubborn scabs of snow, soaring up from the heathery plain of Umhaill like a thorn from the stem of a rose.

By itself, it would have been beautiful. But Crom Dubh was *holy*, and that made it oppressive in its splendour. This barren knob of a summit was where Anu, Mother of Mysteries, had first made herself known to her people. This was where Ogma had first shared the art of poetry, where Smithing Brí had taught the forging of swords.

In every way possible, Crom Dubh loomed. Children had nightmares about it. The girl certainly remembered hers. And now, from this wind-scraped holy place, she could see the whole island of Croí fall away before her, rumpled and patchwork as her father's *léine* on her back.

The dawn was spectacular too, not that it was much of a comfort. She'd had ample opportunity to observe it, huddled in the shadow of the altar, trying to keep the wind from freezing her dead.

That first blush of light on the horizon, like milk feathering in tea. The deep purple bowl of Scáthach's Plain below her filling up with golden light, the silver line of the Dunadhach the only flaw in the curve.

Brother Caid preached that the day and night were enemies, but the generosity in the dark's retreat reminded the girl of nothing so much as her parents navigating each other in the doorway, perfectly and lovingly aware of where one ended and the other began.

It was all, she conceded, very fucking beautiful. And yet her hands kept straying to the manacle and the chain.

Checking for weaknesses. That's all. That was another good and obedient thought to have, so she continued having it. Brother Caid had explained the significance of the ritual on the long walk up, and she hadn't been able to get the cloth gag out of her mouth to disagree with him.

It all had to be perfect. Queen Anu loved the dawn. Only the right and proper sacrifice would court her *tabharthas* – her blessing – for the harvest. Keep down the *crithir fola* in the sheep. Guarantee good births, presumably so they too could be sacrificed in their turn.

It was all so practised. So confident in the terms. A better harvest. A kinder winter. Not a wish but a ritual, not a hope but a bargain. Give and take. Conditions of sale, perfect and proper.

The girl's fingernails were split where she'd tried to prise a chain link away from itself. *And if I somehow manage to escape, then maybe conditions aren't perfect after all.*

And maybe I could just go home.

'Shit. Shit! Shitshit*shit* . . .'

The girl only realised she was shouting when a claggy knot of rust broke under her stamping heel and took some skin with it. The chain wasn't strong, and the fastening ring set into the anchor stone was rough and weather-gnawed, but it didn't matter. The chain didn't need to be strong. It just needed to be stronger than her.

She blasphemed a couple more times, half because it made her feel better and half because there was nobody to hear her but the mountain and the altar and the chain. The gale was plastering Da's *léine* to her collarbone, rolling around the sky like a miser scraping up soup. Grass rippled, grey-green in the half-light.

It could have been peaceful. It might have been beautiful. Except for the prickling knowledge that the sun was rising, and the girl began to imagine that she could see *it*, the actual point where the day began, coming towards her like an axe –

The altar. A white star of torcstone twice her width and half her height, named for the thick neck rings the old gods had worn. *One end in one world, one end in the other*, so they said. It wasn't finely carved or set with gold like altars in the stories, but it gleamed so bright against the black granite summit you could see it for miles around.

She could push it. Couldn't she? They must have gotten it up here somehow. *Unless it had been fucking Anu.* Maybe the grass was slick enough from dew that she could get it moving. The mountain's steepness would do the rest.

And maybe, just maybe, she wouldn't lose her leg.

Chain clinking, she approached the stone like a skittish horse, and then braced her knees and *pushed.*

Nothing. Not an inch. Not even when she strained until the terror came up her spine and out of her mouth in a scream that would have done *damage* to that fucker Brother Caid.

They had come for her in the night when Da was away, because he was big and strong, and she hadn't licked her disobedience off the turf. She hadn't screamed when they'd caved in the door. This was firstly because she was from the west, and screaming was not in the culture, and secondly because she had been in shock.

It wasn't that she didn't *believe.* The Answermen had outlawed worship of the old gods, but every Croí house had a hidden shrine and every Croí child knew the stories.

Sacrifice was important. The gods of Croí were a hungry lot. They drank and they feasted and they brawled through the stories, so you left out sloe wine and fresh bread and whatever clothes you could spare.

But then there were the hard winters. Failed crops. Answering tithes. And nobody in the village would say a thing if maybe, just maybe, you went up to the altar after the gods failed to appear and took back a loaf to feed your starving wains. What would be the point of doing otherwise? Surely the gods didn't want you to starve?

Ten years since Brother Caid last set foot in the *túath*. Ten years, because he had a hundred tiny villages up and down the coast to cover, and the Answermen to avoid as well. A Brother's scalp would get you a farm.

Old red stained the white stone. *If I live, I'll take his scalp for free.*

Oh, the girl was in the full tilt of blasphemy now, and who could blame her? In those ten years Brother Caid had become like the gods themselves. A story you told. A shrine in a window, worn smooth by touch.

But not *real*. Not something to fear, no more than you feared Macha of Summer, or Ragwort Laughing, or the Cailleach, who could kill with a look.

The stains on the stone were ten years faded. Everyone said the O'Cuain girl had just run away.

What story will they tell about me?

And then she felt the hands on her back.

'C'mon now, girleen,' Da said into her shriek, like he was offering her a mug of tea. 'We're going home.'

He had a hammer and chisel in his hand.

It was like permission. The girl had been braver alone. But Da had arrived, solid as the altar and tougher than the chain, and the first thing he did was swirl his thick *brat* around her and swaddle her in it like a baby. The gentleness of it took the lid off her terror, and suddenly it was all she could do to not take the chisel to the chain or her shinbone, whichever would give way first.

'You weren't there,' she babbled. 'You weren't there, and they *broke our door . . .*'

'I'll fix the door,' Da rumbled. She wasn't sure why she found that small invasion so upsetting. 'Or maybe we'll just leave, hah? Go down the coast to Érainn. Or become sailors. How about that? Head across the Unbeknownst Sea where there's no priests at all, and I'll wake you every morning with a song.'

'Please *don't*,' she said, but with a snuffling kind of laugh. 'What about Brother Caid?'

'I'll fix him too.' She hadn't heard that voice since Mam died. 'Watch me.'

Da bent down, chisel in hand, and the relief came out of the girl in sobs. Suddenly the mountain *was* beautiful. The wind was softening. The sun was rising, fierce and fast, and she could feel Da's heartbeat pounding through his shoulder as he sawed.

There was no bargain. There were no gods. It was just priests. Just men, men who liked stories and power and the sound of their own voices. That was all it had ever been. Girls with chain on their legs, and priests slaking a thirst for blood and sweet sloe wine.

'Nearly there,' Da muttered. 'Nearly . . .'

And then . . .

A quiver.

A tremble.

A sound beneath sound.

'Da?'

'Close your eyes,' he hissed. '*Now*.'

She obeyed without thinking, squeaking as his huge arms drew her close. The *brat* was suddenly stifling, scratching her forehead, making her twist and duck her head away.

Da's eyes were closed too. She could feel it in the tension of him. The heat and the fear.

Another rumble rang both their bones at once, mashing her further against the wool of the cloak. She struggled, pushing herself back so she could breathe, wondering at the impossibility of a mountain shaking under her feet.

Crom Dubh. That black and hateful spike. It *shook*.

Something was coming.

The gods. The words arrived so cold and clean they might have been Brother Caid's. There had been a promise. A contract. And now it was not Queen Anu who had come to punish her for it. The girl knew the sermons. She knew what happened when a bargain was broken.

Folded into the hugeness of her father, she opened her eyes to see the hot little cave between his chest and her nose fill with frosting breath. Winter's cold, on a summer dawn.

It was the Cailleach. The Hag of Winter, who dragged icy chains in her wake.

'Close your *eyes*,' her father whispered.

The Cailleach, who could kill with a look.

The girl could see nothing but Da, the wool pile of his cloak spiking and stiffening with unnatural cold. Could feel his heart through his *léine*, battering like a bird in cloth. Could hear the Cailleach perfectly, because nothing that enormous could be anything less than deafening.

The bellowing rasp of air through lungs.

The cold that beat off her in waves, cold so cold it had a *sound*, like the noise in your ears when you cricked your jaw.

The rattle and creak of freezing chains.

The gods *were* real.

The gods were real, and they had come for the girl.

'Da,' she said, suddenly, madly brave. *It's my mistake. My blasphemy.* Maybe there was a chance. A way to make things right. 'Let me go. It's me. I'm the—'

'Sacrifice,' he finished, taking the words out of her mouth. 'Fair enough.'

He lifted his head, and the tension in his arms went away.

'No!'

The heat in Da drained into her. The heartbeat stuttered out.

Perfect conditions.

One little change can make the whole world wrong.

Da fell backwards, and the girl looked up at the Goddess of Death.

It was as if someone had taken every single cruel story about an old woman, every mean and monstrous caricature, and stacked them thirty feet tall. The Cailleach's skin was as translucent as fly wings. Her remaining teeth were grey with mould. Her hair had the surprising beauty old women's hair sometimes possessed – a fine gauzy veil, covering her naked body like fog.

Her eye sockets were black and empty as kicked-in doors.

And it was scant comfort to see that Brother Caid had only gotten it half right. The Cailleach didn't drag chains. Her left arm *was* a chain – fat links of dirty ice, metre upon metre of them furrowing the earth behind her.

'Go on then,' the girl whispered.

The cold beating off the goddess was a physical weight. It pinched the sweat in the girl's armpits. Turned the tears on her cheeks tight and crunchy with frost. She could feel particles of it on her tongue when she spoke.

'Isn't that why I'm here?'

The Cailleach glared down at her silently, and the girl met that gaze because it was better than looking down at the body at her feet.

'Take me too.'

It was a plea. A prayer. And then the goddess moved, ponderous as a glacier, and stepped *over* the girl like she wasn't even there. She was so huge the girl could hear every creak of muscle, every sinew tense and release, as a hand came down, gripping the altar . . .

The chain.

. . . then picked it up and flung it hard.

Just a little tug to her ankle, enough to make the girl stumble. That was all. The chain must have been nearly cut through.

And then it was over. Dawn became day. Purple became gold. The goddess strode away up the slope, dragging her chain behind her, freezing the grass beneath her feet.

This was supposed to be a story.

The girl's knees gave way. Suddenly she was on the grass, and the frost in her eyes must have spread, because she could see nothing but the white fronds of her breath wisping away. *Thank you*, she thought. The Cailleach *had* killed her. It had just taken a little longer.

The prayer left her lips in a plume of smoking cold, and then the dawn took that as well.

I

A Good and Obedient Thought

1

Sister Wake

THE ATTACK WOULD happen today.

Sister Wake could feel it. She'd been awake for hours, listening to the army prepare outside the walls of her little wooden wagon. The smiths' hammers, the cough and clop of horses, the bellow of livestock and the constant, rattling mutter of thousands of men and women *being* men and women – there was no one difference to point at, but every note of the song had changed key. It was the difference between a conversation and an argument.

The attack would happen today.

Hissing at the early-morning cold, she wriggled out of her blankets and began to dress. First the black wool trews, before lifting up her arms and letting the long black *léine* billow down her short, compact frame. Then her half-tanned leather boots, a splash of frigid water from her little tin bowl, and two daubs of black ink under her kingfisher-blue eyes.

Finally, she settled the rough-red *brat* around her shoulders; a heavy square of a cloak that sat across back and chest like a breastplate, thick enough to turn a knife.

It was the only piece of clothing she'd brought from her old life into the new. The only thing she owned not clumsily dyed some shade of black. Brother Wight had told her it ruined the effect. She'd told him to fuck off. In the end, they'd agreed to disagree.

She was in the middle of scraping her short red hair into spikes with the last of her precious little bowl of beeswax when the knock came, loud and sharp. She let him wait, placing her meagre belongings into her shoulder sack one by one. There wasn't much – her beeswax, a knife, a couple of Answering half-scruples she'd picked up off a corpse. Everything that made Sister Wake useful was inside her own head.

Only when the sack was across her shoulder, and she'd taken a steadying breath, did Sister Wake reach out and open the wagon door. Beyond was a figure cast in silhouette by an achingly bright dawn.

'Bag,' said Brother Wight, holding it out. 'Now.'

Sister Wake put on the bag, gingerly resting it on her spikes. *At least they wash it*, she thought. Things could have been worse.

Find pleasure in small rebellions. That was what Mother Promise said, and as someone who'd spent their whole life rebelling, she should know. Sister Wake could have railed at her confinement. Three weeks in this wagon, rattling around like a bean in a jar, only leaving to stretch or piss or advise warriors who sweated with fear at the sight of her.

Three weeks of the bag. Of speaking only when spoken to. Of wondering would the cold ever leach out of her father's *brat.*

But admitting that weakness to these warriors was an honour they didn't deserve. Instead, Sister Wake stepped from the wagon like it was an Answering sedan chair and wished they could see that she was smiling.

It took a moment to adjust to the dark. Year's end was coming, and the morning was crisp. A breeze flattened the rough canvas of the bag against her cheekbones. Sounds felt distant yet magnified, a dull roar of competing noise punctuated by sudden clarity – shouts, yells, clatters, clanks. A boy cursing as he dropped his spear. Someone's boots fitting worse than the day before. Nobody liked a soldier called Maeg, and nobody ever would.

Everyone sounded very alive. Sister Wake liked that. By noon, they could all be dead.

It had taken a year to assemble this army. A year of threatening and cajoling and begging and bargaining, of hidden troop movements and training. Of rousing speeches in forest clearings and the back of barns, trying to convince farmers to leave their fields and herders their flocks. A year of forging and fletching in secret so at least a scattering of these souls would have weapons suited for more than slaying wheat.

Most of that had been before Sister Wake had been recruited. She was a latecomer to this war, insomuch as any Croí could be late to it, when it was all any of them had known for three hundred years. Maybe that was why it sat ill with her that, one way or another, how many died this morning was up to her.

That's my burden, she told herself. *My sacrifice.* And there was no sacrifice too great for the Rising. That was what Mother Promise said too. If the island of Croí was to throw off its oppressors, every man, woman and child would have to find their own ways to serve.

And though Sister Wake couldn't help but turn over everything the old woman said like a gardener looking for thorns, she also couldn't help but agree. It felt churlish to whine about a bag when surrounded by those who would do the actual fighting and the killing and the dying. If the army were so superstitious of the Cailleach's sight they had to put a bag on Sister Wake, they were welcome.

It didn't hide a jot. When an army marched, the first thing it murdered was the land.

Every blade of grass trampled underfoot. Every head of cattle butchered for the long march east. Every tree felled for kiln fuel and every stream emptied of fish. Even the squirrels the sons of the *ríthe* shot for sport. Despite her locked, windowless cage, Sister Wake heard every death.

The notes of a song sung just for her.

Even now, deaths burbled and nagged for her attention like conversations in another room. A warrior killed a grass snake with a boot knife. Somewhere above, a kestrel smashed a thrush out of the air. Sister Wake would not pick up a blade today, like so many of those around her, but sensing those deaths was her way to serve.

Sister Wake resettled her *brat* around her shoulders and stepped down onto the earth, holding her arm out stiffly for Brother Wight to take.

'Good morning.'

His only answer was a hard grip on her arm. He led her through the camp, Sister Wake trusting living obstacles to get out of her way and Brother Wight to lead her around everything else. She was a figurehead of this Rising. Appearances had to be maintained. It wouldn't do her air of eerie grace much good if she fell over a tent peg.

'Did you sleep well?'

Brother Wight slept under her wagon with one eye open in case someone tried to murder her in her sleep, and they both knew it. Not all Croí believed in the Rising. Some were so afraid of the boot on their neck they'd kill their own people to keep it there.

Sometimes Sister Wake could hear him, awake and listening on the other side of the wagon slats. The squeak of leather as he gripped his sword hilt. Sometimes, on cold nights, she thought she could feel the warmth of his breath.

'Would you rather a place in the vanguard?'

Another avenue of attack. Brother Wight did not respond to this one either.

'If so, I formally release you from your *geis*. You no longer need to serve me, Knight of the Hollow Eye. You can die in a fight of your choosing, covered in Answermen blood.'

Silence. Sister Wake formally released Brother Wight from his *geis* about five times a day. So far, it had not taken. His hand tightened on her arm to let a troop of warriors pass, close enough that she could smell the clean saltiness of their sweat.

She was blessed with more senses than the five with which she'd been born, but to picture Brother Wight in that moment, all she needed was memory. He'd been assigned to her along with her belongings – dark of hair and eye and mood, as if chosen to match the clothes they made her wear.

Maybe that was why she clashed with him so much, in the hope that she'd move his blunt and unlovely face to something other than simmering contempt.

'Go,' he murmured, his fingers hot on her skin. It was always her arm, or her wrist, or her shoulder, she noted. He never took her by the hand.

He had spoken, though. A minor victory. Sister Wake tried again.

'Do they look ready? The army, I mean. Do they look . . .'

There had been rebellions against the Answermen before. The Waxmelt Campaign, the Tumult of the Dál Riata – you were taught their names, and you were taught how they ended. In some places, the bodies still swayed.

Their weaving passage through tents became a straight line across firm, tramped ground. They were in a different part of the camp now. The wind was sharper, carrying with it the thick, warm smell of horses. The raucous shouting of warriors had been replaced by knots of quiet, urgent conversation. She could barely even smell middens any more.

'Have you eaten?' she continued, changing tack. 'I've heard warriors say they can't eat before a battle, but you should have something before—'

'Stop it.'

They must have been close to the *ríthe*. Sister Wake knew from experience that, were they alone, Brother Wight could ignore her for days.

'Stop what?'

'Trying to be friendly.'

'I'm naturally friendly,' she said airily. 'People don't know that about me because I so often have a bag on my head.'

Two hands then, gripping her elbows, and though Sister Wake could not see him, she knew Brother Wight was glaring at her so intently that the canvas between them could have flashed into flame.

'This moment does not *require* friendly,' he said flatly. 'This moment requires dignity. And reverence. And silence. If you know what that is.'

And then his hand was on her neck, gentle as his words were sharp, guiding her head under a trailing edge of fabric. The sounds of the camp became muted. Sister Wake shivered against his fingers.

It always felt like a ritual.

'My *ríthe*,' said Brother Wight, and suddenly his voice was rich and warm, in a way it never was when he spoke to her. That was his side of the performance. The other half of their strange duet. 'Attend upon Sister Wake, living saint of the Goddess of Death.'

2

Abelard

ABELARD CAUDEFOY'S ENTHUSIASM had survived a lot of things.

It had survived a life of being perpendicular to the uses his family wished to make of him. It had survived his schooling, which was no small feat either, and then two failed betrothals and three failed applications to the Ceolmund Academies at Fyren, Lofgeorn and Wlanc.

Maribeth Gonwald, the second of his betrothals and the one Abelard had actually quite liked, had told him he couldn't be faulted for a lack of enthusiasm. Later, when he had realised she had not meant it as a compliment, his enthusiasm had survived that too.

So of course, when he had found himself summoned to his father's chambers to be given, for the first time in his life, a position of trust and a task to complete, there was no question of the manner with which he would tackle it.

He rode into a wet and glassy morning, out and through the mist and dew-drenched hills of his family estate. His companion was a letter in his coat pocket and an unfamiliar warmth in his narrow chest. Abelard Caudefoy had no experience of being useful to his father. It surprised him how much, in the moment, it had meant.

Anfloga Dock was a morning's ride away; just an indentation in the wet and ragged shoreline, like someone had pressed their thumb into wet clay. Further up the coast there were the Mortigern Cliffs, bleak and heron-haunted, and to the south there were the watchtowers Victory and Resist.

Here, though, the land was mostly marsh and lichen, and the shore didn't so much end as give up. The only thing that made Anfloga's set of whitewashed warehouses and simple wooden piers notable was that it was a short twenty miles from the heartland to Croí.

And this morning, that narrow stretch of channel was crowded with ships.

Caravels split the iron-dark water with ease. Rowboats struggled against the waves. Barges, and flats, and tubby little fishing cogs; so many the strain and creak of them carried over the sea's hushing roar, so many that Abelard could imagine stepping deck to deck all the way to Croí.

He had only ever seen this many ships once before, during his childhood in the capital. As cogs and caravels made their august passage from Dreodyrne Port out to sea, he remembered thinking that there was something very *neat* about naval warfare – each ship a lacquered-wood island, tidy as the markers on a map.

But as the first of the boats neared Anfloga, he saw there was nothing neat about the heaving crowds crammed into each deck. There was nothing tidy about their fear.

'What do you mean,' the dockmaster whispered, '*evacuation*?'

He had a good face for exasperation; mostly eyebrow, with a short, square beard like the business end of a chisel and the permanent windburn that came from a life of facing the sea.

His office was as dark as a badger's sett, smelling of dead paper and frustration. Abelard had waited patiently as the man went looking for something that resembled a chair, and then accepted his defeat in the endeavour just as graciously.

'I'm sorry for this disruption,' he said, and then winced. *You promised yourself no apologies.* It was an effort for him, sometimes. Not for his brothers, of course. Hugh, Astor and Berrigan were all of an admirable piece – pale and proud with brows meant for glaring and jaws meant for steeling, like the statues of the First Among who had founded the Answering so long ago.

Abelard, in contrast, had the frame and constitution of a mayfly, and wore an old gamekeeper's coat because it had a hundred pockets for beetle jars and useful bits of string. He didn't resemble the First Among. He mostly resembled a paintbrush.

Today, though, he had made an effort. His red curls were bound with a ring of silver, his grey coat and trews were pressed, his boots practically squeaked with polish, and his long fingers, the only part of himself he actually liked, were laced behind his back as per the favoured portrait pose.

And then he had to ruin it all by *apologising*. Apologising to social inferiors was just about the most unbecoming thing you could do. You might as well eat with your hands.

'If we may return to the present matter . . .'

That wasn't perfect, but it was better than nothing.

'Of course, my lord. You were saying?'

This was safer territory. All Abelard had to do was repeat what he had been told. Father had written a monograph about this, one that had created delicious outrage in Dreodyrne. There was nothing, the monograph supposed, actually *different* between a king and a peasant. Nothing except blood, obviously. And education. And any standing men-at-arms. And a heritage that could be traced back to the First Among. Nothing *tangible*.

And yet, the understanding was that when you spoke to one of the Peerage, you were speaking to them all. They *insured* each other, to use base economic slang.

Abelard's shoulders instinctually stiffened. *As hard as it may be for some to believe*, the Marquis Lukas had murmured, *when they speak to you, they are, in some way, speaking to the King.*

Abelard might be a paintbrush, but he was also a Caudefoy, and this morning he had a job.

'If we may return to the matter at—'

The door opened hard enough to dislodge a veil of dust from the rafters.

'Captain Taber reporting, my lord,' the man said, and saluted, sharp as closing scissors. 'You. Dockmaster. Come with me.'

And he did. He just did. Abelard hadn't even gotten the letter out. By the time he drew himself together and emerged into the milk-pale sun, it was somehow too late. The hill was crawling with men in black trews and Caudefoy blue coatees, pitching tents and hammering posts. It was all very methodical and organised – Answering logistics at its best – which made it all the more galling that Abelard hadn't had a chance to actually organise it.

'I don't understand,' the dockmaster said, though Abelard could not help but notice he had spoken to Taber instead of Abelard himself. 'They're evacuating Cusp?'

Cusp was the seat of Answering government on Croí.

Taber scowled. 'It's not your place to—'

'Whiteseal,' Abelard said, and the dockmaster hissed between his teeth. Whiteseal was the province surrounding Cusp, named for the white wax that denoted a parliamentary communiqué. Outside Whiteseal, the patrols became fewer, the wax became thinner and rents were collected at the point of a sword. 'For starters.'

The ships were closer now. It was hard to talk *and* look at them, because every face was a story that froze the words in Abelard's throat.

There, a woman hefting her infant high because there wasn't room to hold it close.

There, a white-faced boy pressed against a railing, elbows braced in front of him so he could breathe.

There, three men half dead in exhaustion, snarling as they dragged at their oars.

'My lord?' The captain's voice was careful. He was watching the boats too. 'Perhaps I could liaise with the dockmaster over the finer details, and you could . . . oversee our efforts?'

'Yes,' Abelard said, relieved someone seemed to have a handle on how best he could serve. 'Good. Good! I'll just call out if I have any suggestions, shall I?'

Taber seemed to think about this quite carefully. 'Maybe it's best to bring those directly to me, milord. So as not to confuse the chain of command.'

That had been the last Abelard saw of him. It wasn't even that large of a dock.

He had retreated up the hill a stretch, as the first of the boats docked and soldiers began to funnel disembarking refugees away to make room for those behind.

They did not seem inspired by Answering punctiliousness overmuch either. Instead, each one trudged up the slope with a dead-eyed lassitude, swaying under their hefted bags, only stopping when halted by a hand or outstretched arm.

Watching made Abelard need to be useful again. He set off towards a flat, fat barge forcing up against the pier, visibly swaying in the water as a burden it was never designed for squirmed and shoved on its deck.

The pier crew had just reached out with hook and stave to pull it in when part of the deck's railing gave way with a *snap*. Half the crowd on the barge surged forwards, and the other half pulled back, like two limbs of the same panicking beast. People fell on the deck, disappearing under trampling feet. The barge rocked. The air rang with splashing and screams, and the dockmaster rushed forward, cursing.

'Get hooks,' he roared. 'Pull them out! Signal the other ships to hold!'

Abelard started forward as well, and then slowed as he realised that he had no idea what to do. Dockhands ran by or around him. One collided with him, nearly knocking him to the dirt, and turned around with fists raised before suddenly realising who Abelard was.

It took five minutes to stem the dockhand's frantic apologies. By that stage most of the refugees had been pulled from the water.

I'm not helping, Abelard realised, as the dockhand finally went back to his duties with one last terrified look at him. *I'm an active hindrance.*

Abelard's parents had gone straight to the fief capital of Modigkaern, of course, to co-ordinate and prepare the entire relief effort. There was another dock up the coast, he was sure, where Hugh Caudefoy was barking orders with curt, inspirational masculinity. Astor Caudefoy had no doubt redesigned Victory Watchtower's process of receiving refugees from the ground up. Berrigan Caudefoy was a soldier born – as good with speaking to men as he was at killing them.

All biological distillations of Father, in one way or another, the way you could rely on a spotted finch to produce a spotted finch, again and again and again.

And then there's me, Abelard thought, digging his hands into the pockets of his coat. *The runt of the litter.* No, worse than that. At least runts were the same species. There was a bird in the northern moors that laid its eggs in the nests of others. When the alien hatchling emerged, it was far larger and brasher than the real chicks, dominating the nest with ease. Abelard, somehow, was the reverse.

It wasn't that he didn't have skills. It wasn't that he didn't have *use*. He could tell kestrels from goshawks. He understood the mechanics of beehives and what nasal discharge meant on a cow's snout. One of the proudest moments in his life had been badgering his father to assess Ceph, one of their horses, because he'd noticed an odd timbre to its cough.

They'd managed to catch the case of stiffenrot before it spread to the other horses. Standing there in the sweaty confines of the stable, his father had almost shyly placed his hand on Abelard's shoulder in gratitude, before ordering him out so he could do what had to be done.

That had been a good morning. There hadn't been many between Abelard and his father, but that had been a good one.

The memory steeled him. Leading in times of crisis was what the Peerage of the Answering was for. This was what *he* was for, despite the beastly job he had so far made of it.

He reached up and pulled a graphite stylus from his ponytail. *Deciphering things*. That was what he was good at. Why not look to decipher this?

That the refugees weren't native Croí was an easy enough first deduction. Croí was the First Colony. The archetype, in a way. Much of what made the Answering the Answering had been learned in that coarse and pagan place.

And yet, despite the Answering's best efforts, civilisation had never quite taken. Modigmark was the closest heartland fief to Croí, the doorway to the west, and as pre-eminent lords of that domain, the Caudefoys had deep interests in the place. Abelard's father was fond of saying that *Croí wear the Answering like a poorly tailored coat.*

A flawed simile, Abelard had always thought, though of course he had never articulated that aloud. When a coat didn't fit you, you tailored it. You did not try to tailor the flesh beneath.

But it was clear to him that the people now spilling out of multiple vessels were not Croí but exemplars – settlers from all over the empire, from the balmy New Territories to the south to the Contested Territories in the east. Exemplars were the latest solution to the Croí problem – invited to accept parcels of land all over Croí to serve as an example of what was possible with compliance.

Now, it seemed, Croí had sent those settlers back, and as the morning soured towards afternoon, no one wanted to tell Abelard why.

He tried to be delicate. He worked out the questions beforehand in his little gesso table-book, weighing each word as he had seen Father do before speeches in the Rationale, excising phrases he deemed too callous or forceful.

That had taken him an hour, before he finally admitted to himself that he was stalling and made himself approach a miserable mother of two.

'Madam, if I may . . .'

She ran away from him. She actually ran away, grabbing her boys by the wrists and dragging them behind her. It took Abelard some minutes to find the courage for a second attempt.

That one was more successful, in that the group of exhausted, dishevelled men did not immediately flee, but before he could level even the first of his enquiries, a soldier called out for extra hands on a pallet, and Abelard was left with muttered apologies and no answers at all.

A good peer would just order them to answer, he found himself thinking, and then immediately felt ashamed.

Around him, the dock became busier. There was no end to the fleet of ships. Each one deposited its refugees and then ponderously departed, and as numbers grew, the great engine of Answering efficiency began to stick and grind.

The lines for water were growing. Hungry, angry people pulsed out over the pier like blood from a nicked vein. Fights broke out between settlers over space, and the Caudefoy soldiers had to wade in and break them up.

The day dragged on, the sun got hotter, and Abelard began to quietly and industriously despair.

Finally, he found someone. Caspar Maynard was a third-generation exemplar. A small man, rheumy-eyed, voice filtered through a dense mat of wrinkles and solemnity, he introduced himself like he was announcing the death of a relative, and the two of them sat down on a free patch of grass.

'I'm from Mornspiel,' the old man said eventually. 'I'm a cobbler. And the King has to do something.'

The three phrases came with the exact same inflection, and Abelard was again reminded of that unspoken contract. Caspar wasn't speaking to Abelard Caudefoy. He was speaking *through* Abelard to the highest authority in the land.

'Can you tell me what happened?' Abelard said, carefully balancing his table-book on his lap.

'It was a story,' Caspar said simply. 'A story, come to kill us or drive us away.'

This was not what Abelard had expected. 'What do you mean, a story?'

Caspar pointed at a spot a few metres down the slope. What Abelard had thought was a sack of belongings unfurled itself and glared at them both. 'My wife.'

'Hello, madam,' Abelard said politely. The old woman leaned over and deliberately spat.

'She's Croí,' Caspar said, by way of explanation. 'Doesn't have much time for Peerage, not that we've met too many.'

'That's quite all right,' Abelard said. The brash honesty of it had tickled him.

'She was the one who explained it,' Caspar continued. 'None of us knew, you see. We just thought it was . . . I don't know what we thought it was. Everyone was running. Screaming. Some people talked about finding weapons and trying to fight it, and my wife told us it wouldn't do any good. She recognised it, you see.' He gave Abelard a wary frown. 'Not that she's a pagan or anything. That's a hanging offence, it is.'

'Is it?' Abelard asked. 'I didn't know that.'

He'd had a book as a child, *Stories of the Hinterlands*, a collection of some of the more palatable stories from Answering colonies. It, just as much as his father's sketches or the great green fields of their estate, had inspired his constant, burning desire to *see* and *examine* and *know*. The stories had been quaint, the illustrations brightly coloured. Abelard wondered suddenly where its author was now.

'I don't know a lot about the Croí faith,' he said.

'It's mostly stories now,' Caspar said. 'Now that all the priests are dead.' His wife was still glaring at him. 'There're lessons too. Lessons about history. About places. About us, too.' A tired smirk. 'Challenges. Warnings. Don't go there, don't drink that. They put them in stories so you remember them.'

'I understand,' Abelard said. 'I think. Something happened to your home, and your wife told you a story to make sense of it?'

'No,' Caspar said, and gave him a look. 'She told us the stories are coming back to punish us. For taking Croí land. Devils from their blackest pagan stories have come to push us into the sea. That's what happened in Mornspiel. That's what happened in Redstone. That's what happened in Rasp and Founderhall and Bellworth.'

He didn't sound old any more. He sounded like a little boy. He sounded the age Abelard had been when he'd first read stories about bánánachs and eating-worms.

'A monster,' the old man said. 'We saw a monster.'

* * *

The dockmaster was berating two soldiers for dropping a pallet when Abelard found him.

'Be right with you, milord,' he said, between blistering curses. 'Now, you—'

'That ship unloading right now,' Abelard said, pointing. 'How long until it heads back to Croí?'

The soldiers took the opportunity to heft their pallet higher and make for safety, while the dockmaster frowned in confusion.

'Half an hour or so. Why?'

'I'm going to be on it.'

'What? *Why?*'

No one would have dared question Berrigan's choices, or Hugh's, and Astor's reasons, had he chosen to share them, would have been ironclad.

All Abelard had was enthusiasm. The memory of a hand on his shoulder.

And maybe, just maybe, a very specific kind of expertise.

'Because,' Abelard Caudefoy said firmly, in his best approximation of his father the Marquis, 'there's something I have to see.'

3

Talasa

'EVERYTHING IS CONNECTED,' Queen Kalifsena Medalwyn said in a voice like brushed silk. 'And everything has consequences.'

The single candle in the middle of the table flickered between her fingers, plucking only fragments of the audience from the gloom – a pair of eyes, a tremulous smile, a bead of unladylike sweat.

There were nine of them sitting around the table. Four men, five women, the best and brightest Dreodyrne society had to offer. Talasa had watched them file in – noting their silken finery, their iron postures, the measuring stares.

None had been in the least bit cowed by the Queen's presence. Why would they be? Lord-General Ainslei, with his regiments. High Reeve Hadder and his stranglehold on the Lodemagan voting bloc. They all had their own petty kingdoms. Each of them was royalty in their own lives, and with far better claim, some might argue, than Kalifsena herself – this newly married foreigner with her thick accent and strange ways.

Her station was a wedding gift. Not a birthright.

But that prejudice, that *confidence*, departed with each snuffed candle wick. In the darkness, the room became smaller. Hotter. More cramped. Men breathed more shallowly. The sigh of crinkled skirts and shawls became perishingly loud.

And in that silence, the waif-like Queen Kalifsena seemed to expand.

She did not move. There was no softening of that posture, no leaning forward in a cheap offer of intimacy. She let the darkness do that work for her, the single candle between her fingers the only point of light.

With no small sense of pride, Talasa watched her mother go to work.

'Consequences are a river, deep and violent as the flow of the Dreor. The current of the past gouges out the path of the present. Indeed, it is that principle on which our empire is based, for is not every luminary here a product of the choices made long ago? Past braveries. Past triumphs. All to make you what you are.'

Our empire. A subtle reminder. The candlelight quavered. The air held the faintest trace of brine.

'But if that is true, perhaps the current of the future can be anticipated as well.'

There was rustling. Heads turning this way and that. The Peerage of the Answering, Queen Kalifsena was fond of saying in private, were like the snow deer of their homeland; constantly, desperately aware of their surroundings. The only difference was that snow deer watched for predators, and the Peerage watched each other.

That was why the Queen liked them in the dark. So that every one of them would feel alone.

'Is it dangerous?' Kalifsena said liltingly, repeating a question no one had asked. 'Of course. Knowledge is always dangerous. But *you* . . .' At this, the light from the candle seemed to steady. Those fragments of faces became more distinct. Men straightened. Women sighed. '*You* are no strangers to consequence. You are makers and sufferers of larger fates. You may decide that it's worth the risk to know what battles lie ahead, how harvests will fare, such mysteries as—'

'Where the King is . . .' came a mutter. Dark smirks in the dark room. Talasa noted each and every one.

Superstition was a flaw, in the eyes of the Answering. But it was the worst-kept secret in the capital that King Rubeo Medalwyn had quite the fascination with the occult.

Depending on who you asked, the King had vaults full of heathen esoterica (including but not limited to owls' teeth, demon bones, and cadavers that told the future), libraries of ritual texts culled from a dozen heathen territories (written on human skin, obviously) and a penchant for vanishing in pursuit of the merest *rumour* of pagan practice or practitioners.

It was asked in somewhat quieter tones why he had thought fit to marry one.

'My husband seeks his own answers,' Kalifsena said coolly, and then she smiled too. 'But I will inform him of your concern.'

The smirks disappeared.

Haltingly, a young woman raised her hand.

'Nadene Borley,' Kalifsena murmured. The girl flinched at her name in a queen's mouth.

'Y-yes, your Majesty.'

Huge eyes. Chewed lip. Too much of her father the admiral in her features, as if not content with leading a fleet, he'd needed to stamp his authority on his daughter's face as well. Nadene had three years on Talasa's sixteen, but she seemed younger, and she'd been the first to arrive.

Telling. Everything was telling. Queen Kalifsena was fond of saying that too.

'Nadene, would you like to know your future?'

'Yes,' the girl whispered. 'Yes, I would. I am newly—'

The Queen's hand flashed in the shadows, pale as the underside of a spider.

'Do not tell me. That is not your role.'

Talasa fought a smile as annoyance flashed across Nadene's face. Even the least of the women here were not used to being spoken to in such a way.

The hand folded itself back into the velvet dark.

'You wish to know of your husband. Of the children you will have. What joys and sorrows await you.'

Some of the anticipatory heat left the room. The younger nobles were still sweaty and eager, of course. War and children, advancement, advantage . . . these were the secret sinews that pulled at every joint.

But there was disaffection now too, among the older attendees, the ones who had played this game enough to see more than a move or two ahead. They had attended out of curiosity, of course, and shallow courtesy to a queen they despised but had to appease.

But there had been a hope too. Talasa had seen it – dirty and furtive, as they'd waited outside. A desire to witness something magical.

Dashed now, of course. Queen Kalifsena wasn't some eerie witch plucking futures from the frigid winds of her homeland. She was a charlatan, at best feeding scraps of political forecast from her husband the King, and at worst predicting love and babies for delusional girls.

That familiar squeeze of fear in Talasa's chest. *And if they knew the truth . . .*

Nadene, of course, was rapt. 'I want to know. I need to know.'

'There is a cost,' the Queen added mildly, and the mood jaundiced further. Unsurprising, really. There was all sorts of speculation on what kind of demoniac knowledge and unsavoury practices the woman must have used to seduce the King, and now here she was again, trading secrets for affection.

'Your Majesty,' Nadene said hesitantly. 'Of course I will pay. But what could I have that you . . .'

Kalifsena's smile was the curve of the moon.

'I never said you were paying me.'

The growl came from everywhere and nowhere. Peers shrieked as warm breath slid across their necks. A man rose, making wildly for the door, until the Queen's soft voice froze him in his tracks.

'If you value your soul, stay still. They will take any who run.'

In another world, it might have been funny. The most powerful people in the Answering half standing in terror or huddling together as the breath of something huge fluttered their collars and plucked at their hair.

The air smelled like the inside of an animal – hot and close and salty. The growl came again, thick and wet and rough as fur.

And Nadene Borley made her father's face her own, fixing the hidden terrors with a glare worthy of a fleet.

'I will pay. Now, *tell me.*'

Later, when the lamps were unshuttered and light returned, the room seemed quite mundane.

The guests had struggled with the transition too. Desdemona Culzean had run her hand under the edge of the table as she passed. Several generals had rapped surreptitiously at the walls. All were blinking furiously, though their eyes must long since have adjusted.

Just another receiving room in the Palace; mahogany and brass and the ever-present tang of polishing oil. And Kalifsena was once again that pale, slight woman, receiving bows from peers who hated her – her dark eyes always fixed on a point through and beyond the back of their skulls.

It was only when the last of them were long gone that Talasa stepped out from behind the false wall, sliding it shut behind her.

The room had originally been used for private meetings between reeves. It hadn't taken much effort to convert it from a place where kings could spy to somewhere queens could perform.

Bellows screwed to hidden grates could huff warm breath at neck level. A succession of candles could provide scents of brine, flowers or the earthier smells of blood and meat. Smell went a surprisingly long way in a dark room.

'Did you see Ainslei's face?' the Queen said, offering Talasa a sugar lozenge and a cup of water.

Talasa took a long and grateful gulp, and then let out another burbling growl. It sounded less other-worldly in person than through the speaking tubes set into the walls, but it was still, she fancied, not what you'd expect from so small and skinny a girl.

'He's used to arguments at range, I think,' she said, and was rewarded with a distinctly unqueenly snort.

The Queen and her daughter worked in comfortable silence, placing their tools in a neat rosewood box.

'What did we learn?' Kalifsena said when all was done, casting one last look around the room. It was important to remember that the show wasn't over just because the audience had left.

Talasa related smartly who had sat with who, as well as their gossip. She was proud at how her voice no longer wavered as she shared each insult and slur. It had been a hard first year. There was a fine line between remembering what was thought of them and not letting it scar your heart.

They might have been mirrors of each other, the Queen and her daughter – both tiny, dark-haired dolls, their eyes sharp and their mouths precise. Both wore black. For Kalifsena, to better highlight the paleness of her skin against the darkness of an unlit chamber. For Talasa, to vanish in that darkness entirely.

'Do you think we convinced anyone of my dread powers?' Kalifsena asked.

'Nadene, certainly,' Talasa said. 'She'd die for you. Or the future you predicted, at least.'

'It was the spirits who predicted it,' the Queen said idly. 'And I don't need her to die. Just to remember there is value to her future, and her current actions put that in jeopardy.'

Something squirmed in Talasa's stomach, and she dug a knuckle into her side to root it out. What a luxury, to be nineteen in this city of vipers and in love with a tailor you were sure nobody knew about. The 'spirits' had been as kind as they could, and very careful not to reveal Nadene Borley's secret engagement so that anyone could use it against her.

Anyone but the Queen, of course.

'What if the Admiral doesn't realise it was you who dissuaded her?' Talasa said.

'Do you remember the first thing I told them?'

'That actions have consequences,' Talasa said promptly.

'That's the only lie I told today, Talasa. Actions don't have consequences.'

'They don't?'

'No. They have reactions. A subtle difference. I don't need Admiral Borley to *know*. I just need him to wonder. To question his good fortune at a scandal averted and a daughter suddenly brought into line. These seances aren't about convincing any of these hoary old gargoyles of anything. They're about uncertainty. A drop of hesitation so their reactions are slowed.'

'For what?'

'Snow deer watch,' the Queen said. 'All day, every day. They watch the horizon, and they sniff the air, and they live their lives on hooks waiting for the moment they need to bolt. Which is more dangerous – the snow deer or the leopards that hunt them?'

'The leopards,' Talasa said, knowing she was wrong and wanting to know why.

'A leopard will kill a deer, yes; but if enough deer escape its claws, the leopard is doomed. Deer kill a leopard by running. By surviving. By not being food. And a snow deer will always outrun a leopard

– unless the deer falters. Unless they are uncertain which way to turn. That is what allows the leopard to eat.'

'We are the leopards,' Talasa said. She liked the way it sounded.

'Yes, child. And we must watch. And learn. And remember.'

Kalifsena closed the lid of the box with a snap, but not before Talasa saw the minute tremble in her hands. The King had never been away from the capital this long before. Never so strenuously tested Dreodyrne society's oh-so-polite tolerance of his obsessions.

It made being one of those obsessions a dangerous role to play.

'Because we are alone.'

4

Sister Wake

THIS WAS THE life of a saint of death.

Sometimes *ríthe* wanted to see a monster, and so you clacked your teeth and fought your bonds and howled until grown men went white with fear. You wore the black leather armour with the cinder-etched runes and daubed your lips with dirt so they could imagine you worrying corpses out of the earth with your teeth.

Sometimes, *ríthe* wanted to be seduced, and so you spoke in mysteries, or whispered secrets Brother Wight had fed you the night before so you could appear to have the wisdom of a god.

Sometimes you just made things up, because the chieftains were Croí and the wants of any Croí, on the whole, were simple enough to predict. In that at least, Brother Caid had been correct. Health. Good harvests. The boot off your throat.

Believing in the gods is easy. That was what Mother Promise had said, the first day they'd met. *It's believing in victory that will be hard.*

The bag came off.

The tent had been looted from the Answering – a rich rectangle of calfskin dyed so crimson it turned the sunlight red. The earth had been strewn with straw to keep out the ground chill. A pallet piled in hides lay in the corner, a half-eaten meal on a copper plate beside it. *Someone can eat so*, she thought.

But it was the table that interested her, an Answering fold-away contraption now so mounded in parchment it looked to be wearing a magistrate's wig.

Sister Wake would have loved just an hour with those maps. Da had taught her some – she knew the six provinces, the shape of Croí to draw. But all she'd really had was the purblind cartography of childhood, where she could describe in detail every inch of her *túath* and very little beyond.

I haven't even seen the castle they've brought me here to break.

'Is it ready?'

Sister Wake had been so intent on the table she'd barely noticed the men around it. Now, starved of real landscapes, she mapped the *rí* who'd spoken instead.

The oldest was always the first to speak at these councils – fast and low and angry, resenting every moment wasted on idle conversation. Hunger radiated from him, in the twitch of his fingers, the rattle of the mail he wore for show. The most to gain, the most to lose.

The Answering had likely taken the castle from his grandfather's grandfather. All this man had ever owned were his grudges, his whole life spent a petitioner at the hearths of others. A beggar chief. An orphan lord.

The Abacus, she called him. She could count every tooth in his head.

'Show some *respect*,' snapped the Pious, wiping spittle from his weak mouth. 'She is god-sent proof. A blessing on this Rising.'

The Pious was the one Sister Wake liked the least. She could understand the Abacus's hunger. She was homeless too. But the Answering had spent three hundred years hunting Croí faithful and, like any crop grown in darkness, that had twisted their religion into queer and hungry shapes.

Her ankle itched where the manacle had bitten.

'Indeed she is,' Brother Wight interjected smoothly, and just like that he was handsome – the dull, staring alertness of a man who had been fighting his entire life transmuted to a flinty, admirable kind of charm. The right side of his scalp was shaved, the left a foaming wave of black. A gold ring drew his beard together, sharpening his pale and freckled cheeks.

The *ríthe* gathered before her were all known to the Answering. Permitted to rule, permitted to bear arms – both ceremonially, of course. Under their richly dyed *bratanna* their armour was heavy scale, and their swords gleamed for rarely being drawn.

Brother Wight, by contrast, was a warrior of the Croí faith and its long, doomed war, and was as different to them as a wolf to a hound. Most Croí had learned to live with three centuries of occupation, fighting it in small, survivable ways. Hedge schools. Old stories. Shrines hidden out in the woods where only the faithful could see.

But then there were those who resisted it with every breath, for whom the raw wound of invasion had not for a moment been allowed to heal. The men who lived wild in the hills and killed Answering couriers when they could find them. The women who hadn't waited for the Macha Laws to take up a sword.

Brother Wight wore no colours of a *túath*, for to do so was to invite the burning of your home and the slaying of your family, whether they had anything to do with you or not. No jewellery that could shine, no mail that could clink or rustle. His spear could have been anyone's spear. His knife could have been anyone's knife.

All that set him apart as a Knight of the Hollow Eye, the *geis*-sworn blade to a saint of the Cailleach, was the polished stolen wheellock pistol at his hip.

'We are ready to carry out their will,' he said to the *ríthe*. Sister Wake had once asked him where the ring had come from. He hadn't spoken to her for a week. Whatever its history, the gleam of it was a message. *No more hiding.* 'You do your part, and we will do ours.'

'Good,' said the Bear. The largest of the three *ríthe* always waited to speak until everyone had done their posturing. Sister Wake liked that. He wasn't expending any undeserved energy either. 'Because there's no turning back now.'

There was always some small rebellion happening – though *rebellion* was a grand word for a couple of torched granaries, or an Answering official caught too far from home with too few men. This morning was different. It had to be different.

This was the Rising that would work.

'You can see scurrying around the battlements,' the Bear said. 'They know we're here at last.'

He looked like the statues of Manannán Mac Lir that the Érainn put on their beaches – a hulking totem of a man in crimson-banded white, his olive skin turned rough by time. The Answering liked to mock Croí for their love of bright colours, for marking *túath* and family with saffron and blue and cockle-dyed purple. It was gaudy. Silly.

It didn't look silly on the Bear. It looked like blood and bone.

'We were lucky to get this close,' he said. 'It's as off-guard as we were ever going to catch them.'

'It wasn't luck,' Brother Wight responded. 'It was her.'

He never missed a chance to remind them that the gods were with them now. They were blessed. One of those blessings was sitting before them, nineteen years old and missing her breakfast, wishing she could reach up and make sure the bag hadn't fucked her hair spikes.

Three thousand men and women had made their way from three different *túatha*, and because three thousand men and women together would have made it less than fifty miles before being discovered and annihilated, they had come in bands of a hundred – covering their tracks, travelling light, skulking through the bogs of Umhaill where there were no Answering eyes to see.

It would have been impossible if not for Sister Wake – sitting in her wagon, using the *tabharthas* of the Cailleach to read the land and the many deaths that studded it like currants in bread.

'Thank you,' the Bear said.

Sister Wake fought to hide her surprise. He was looking at her – not past her to her *tabharthas* or through her to the Rising or down at the frostbite scars on her fingers that had never quite healed.

He was looking at *her*.

She opened her mouth, and then closed it again when she saw the expression on Brother Wight's face. The silence stretched for an instant, probably not long at all, and then the Bear cleared his throat and broke her gaze.

'The last bands have arrived. My household stands at nineteen hundred men.'

'And mine at eighteen,' the Pious said, with his own sickly smile. 'Ready to serve the saint.'

'Will it be enough?' the Abacus asked.

'If the saint does as you say,' the Bear said. 'Shieldwood Keep is—'

'Sciáthcrann,' the Abacus snapped. 'Shieldwood is the *Answering* name. The name they stamped it with when they drove my family out. It was Sciáthcrann then, and it will be so again.'

He spoke like the theft was a fresh wound. It would have been admirable, except that Sister Wake had felt the deaths from the hunting and felling that had been going on all morning. Armies needed to eat. They needed ladders and rams. Sciáthcrann would be paying the price of its own freedom for decades to come.

The Abacus wouldn't have cared. It wasn't the kind of thing he counted.

'Do not worry, brother,' the Pious said. 'You'll take your place once again. The gods are with us, and they will wreak glorious havoc upon the invaders before we throw them back into the sea.'

There were tears of rapture in his frog eyes. That was more and more common these days. A wild fervour had bloomed in the faithful now that their gods had turned out to not just be real but magnificently, distressingly present.

Macha the Red Mare – queen of war and sovereignty, her body a battlefield no man could cross. Ogma the Smiling – the liar, the secret-breaker, dragging around his enormous, ear-studded tongue. Cailleach of the Storm, turning summer into winter with every rattle of her chain.

The gods of the Croí were here, and they were angry, and the whole island was experiencing whatever was the reverse of a crisis of faith.

'They have artillery,' the Abacus said flatly. 'Can the gods answer that?'

The Bear beckoned them to the table before the Pious could counter. This was where the Abacus had shown his value – mapping the land for them, advising on proper approaches and dangers.

One diagram showed the settlement entire – the hexagonal walls surrounding the village and the keep at its centre. Six points were marked with red ink, and it was those the Bear tapped with a knuckle, one by one by one.

'Bombards would be my guess,' he said. 'I've seen them used.' He did not elaborate further. 'If our scouts are correct, the garrison seems understrength. We have three times their numbers, but none of that will matter if those things fire. They'll paint us across the grass before we get within a hundred feet of the walls.'

'Heathen technology,' the Pious said primly. The others ignored him.

Heathen was a good word. A powerful word. Good for morale. Much better than *invader*, and far better than *Answering*, a word designed to remind the oppressed that retaliation from the oppressor was never far away.

Heathen implied *uncivilised*. It implied *backward*. But it was a dangerous word too, because it neatly hid the fact that despite all the planning, despite all the secret training camps and carefully hoarded weapons and the Macha Laws putting swords in the hands of women and girls, these foreign *heathens* had the edge on the native Croí in every single way.

Except one.

Brother Wight traced the butt of his pistol. A little prearranged indication. It wasn't necessary. Sister Wake knew her cue when she heard it.

'The eye of the Cailleach is on this place,' she said dreamily, and watched the words take root in them like frost. 'If you want safety, go home. If you want long lives, live them far from here. Far from me.'

Sister Wake was not particularly good at rousing speeches. She understood that about herself. It had certainly been explained to her enough times, gently by Mother Promise and somewhat less gently by Brother Wight.

If he was glaring at her now, she chose not to see it.

'Flee, and it will buy you years. It will buy you a death on your back. A death in bed. A death at another man's hearth, begging for a bowl of soup.'

The Pious was swaying, eyes closed. The Abacus was chewing nothing in his mouth. The Bear had placed a thick brown finger over one of those red dots, as if running the path to the wall in his head.

'There are no good deaths,' Sister Wake said, thinking of an altar stone and long-faded stains. 'But there are deaths *for* something, and there are deaths for nothing at all.'

Did she believe what she was saying? She was living proof, after all, of what death could buy.

Besides, what she believed didn't matter. What mattered was that these men believed, because their deaths were in front of them and uncertain.

The only deaths that mattered to Sister Wake were behind her.

'I was a sacrifice,' she said, and bared her manacle scar. 'And the Cailleach made me a saint.' She smiled a dead smile. 'What will she make you?'

5

Abelard

ABELARD HAD NEVER been on a ship before. His stomach was responding enthusiastically.

Motion sickness occurs due to a difference between actual and expected motion, he told himself, pressing his throat gently into the railing in the hope the wood would tame his convulsing oesophagus. *Symptoms include nausea, vomiting, cold sweat and increased salivation.*

It was an old trick he'd picked up from a journal of medicine. Bloodlessly analysing symptoms distracted from them. That was the sciences for Abelard in general. If you understood something, you feared it less. Map something and you knew it. You controlled it.

He made a quick mental list of all the species of fish that frequented the King's Channel, and then the ship skewed lopsidedly through a swell and suddenly all he could do was offer silent apologies for polluting it.

Complications can include dehydration, he thought weakly. *Headaches. Lower oesophageal tears caused by an overabundance of retching.* Medically speaking, Abelard wasn't sure what constituted an 'overabundance' of retching. Frankly, any at all seemed too much.

He pushed away from the railing and made his careful way up the deck. *Channel's Cry* was a smart, narrow ballinger. Above him, sleek lateen sails thrummed like beating wings, and the wind was such that the oars had been stowed with no real cost to speed.

In more normal times, the low deck might have been crowded with perishable goods for trade, or messengers ranging from common couriers to the neat white-and-blacks of the King's Cursors. Now, it had been cleared of all but two tall stacks of tight-lashed barrels up by the prow, and Abelard could see the jumble of wet footprints still shining on the planks. Some of them were bare. Some were pathetically small.

This is adventure. This is having a pioneer spirit. This was how the First Among must have felt when they led their people out of the darkness of pre-civilisation and into the light of empire.

The unfamiliar rise and fall of the vessel beneath his feet, the earthy curses of the sailors – some of which he had written down in order to look up later – even the squirming nausea in his throat; this was *learning*.

And it was worth the risk. It had to be. Because if it wasn't, the Right Most Honourable Marquis Lukas Caudefoy would have an opinion on it.

The thought of it lifted Abelard's gorge back up his throat. *You wanted to be useful.* A fine notion. Except that *useful* and *useless* were appellations only his father had the judgement to bestow, and they were now separated by an increasing length of sea.

It wasn't that his father would lose his temper. The Right Most Honourable Marquis Lukas Caudefoy did not have a temper to lose. He employed people to lose their tempers instead. Sometimes, he employed entire battalions to lose their temper – violently and in formation.

No, Abelard's father had opinions. These opinions were not developed lightly, or quickly, but with precise and glacial deliberation. And like glaciers, they tended to leave countries in a different shape after they'd passed by.

At least they had, Abelard thought. Now, the Marquis shaped little more than the land of the estate, matters of local governance and the inside of his sons' heads.

Abelard had enjoyed a quiet life up until now precisely because his father didn't seem to have an opinion on him at all. The thought of him finally developing one made the vomit curdle at the base of Abelard's throat.

Ahead, the coastline of Croí should have been visible. Instead, the dreary sky and misty horizon had knotted themselves together, hiding the island beneath veils of grey.

In a story, Abelard thought to himself, *that would be an omen.*

A disorderly thought for a scientist to have. But that was the thing, Abelard mused, navigating his way along the deck through shouting sailors and juddering ropes. He was chasing stories. And he was doing it because, strange as it seemed, Caspar had reminded him of his father. Not in means or manners, certainly, but in *solidity*.

It would have been easy to dismiss the old man's words as the wild claim of a charlatan. People made false claims all the time, laypeople and academics both.

And though it was common knowledge that the King offered rewards for evidence of things outside the boundaries of known science, it hadn't *felt* like Caspar was lying. The old man had spoken in such a clear and mundane way that Abelard knew he didn't care whether he was believed or not.

A story, come to kill us or drive us away.

Abelard knew nothing about billeting refugees or sequestering ships, but the natural laws were an area in which neither Berrigan nor Hugh nor Astor Caudefoy could claim expertise. If there was an opportunity for his particular skills to finally be of use to his father, he meant to take advantage of it.

He'd made up his mind to make some enquiries of the captain when singing drifted across the deck. The sailors heard it too; heads rising, busy hands pausing a beat before resuming their work. For a moment, Abelard wondered was it some sort of shanty or work song, but none of the sailors around him joined in.

Just that single voice, low and funereal, sawing out from the prow, harsh and beautiful and challenging. Abelard found himself making his way towards it, clinging to the railing as the hull crested another swell.

The prow of the *Channel's Cry* was somewhat sheltered from the rest of the ship. Barrels and crates formed an artificial wall between it and the upper deck. As he rounded the wall, he counted six sailors – some in mismatched leather jerkins and slit-hemmed skirts, others naked to the waist. All were barefoot. Most were armed.

Their station and purpose were easy enough to discern. The figure they surrounded was a different prospect entirely.

Even a poor excuse for a peer like Abelard was expected to be able to make certain deductions from speech and carriage. The cut of a coat, the tint of powder, the tilt or freshness of a wig – such things were the code and currency of conversation among the gentle classes. Abelard had spent most of his tutelage in this regard sketching stamens and bird skulls, but even his father the Marquis might have struggled here.

They were tall and thin and perfectly bald, their skin the rich red-black of a calla lily. And they were the one singing – eyes closed, head ticking left to right as if following notation on the inside of their eyelids. There were words in that ululation, Abelard realised – drawn out so as to be unrecognisable, then delivered in short, dramatic punches of sound.

A Terod. The Terod Union covered the entirety of the great southern continent of Adake – a gargantuan network of satraps, principalities and minor kingdoms united under a single empress. An insular place, if you could use the word for somewhere so sprawling, and singularly uninterested in anything except the awesome task of keeping itself together.

Maps that professed to know the full extent of the Union were prized in the Answering, as were trade connections, particularly for the high-quality gravedust and guns that maintained Answering superiority in war. Many families had made their fortunes based on the Union's rare and priceless regard.

Abelard had never spoken to one before, but you saw them sometimes in the capital; diplomats and merchants mostly, sweeping imperiously ahead of trains of servants, their bright linen robes literally a world away from the neat solemnity of Answering dress.

This Terod, however, wore a battered topcoat that would not have looked out of place on Abelard himself – stains and all – over an untucked white smock and long red kirtle. Their neck and shoulders were swaddled in scarves; some of thick, sensible wool, others of light and airy silk.

A pair of old miner's boots completed the chaos, their tips a dented, dirty steel. Between the baldness and the motley, Abelard found himself casting around not just for class and station but for age and gender as well.

And then the song ended, and the stranger's eyes snapped open, as if waking from a dream. The last notes hung in the air before the slap of the water washed them away.

'A song of luck and victory,' they said into the silence, their voice as low and deep as stones rolling around a bowl. 'I can do one for you too, if you like.'

Someone had drawn a chalk circle on the deck, eight feet in diameter. A wrestling game, maybe? There were bands of scars on most of the sailors' forearms. Knots of pink on bellies and ribs. Abelard thought of the old stag that frequented the hills above the manor at home, and the accumulated trauma that came from a hard life in a wild place.

'Come on then,' the Terod said. 'I can do first blood, or third blood, or *enrek jol*, if you have that here, or this gentleman can throw a cloth in the air and we have until it hits the deck.' They smiled. 'Or you do.'

Abelard swore the ship dipped a little as the largest of the sailors stepped forward. He was taller than two barrels stacked atop each other, arms corded with tattooed muscle. The skin of one arm was utterly mangled, scarred a dozen different shades beneath his tan, and his eyes were huge and soft in a face of blunt bone and windburn.

When he advanced, everyone else stepped back, even the Terod, though Abelard noted they hid the movement behind a long, lunging stretch.

The brute stared down at the foreigner. When his fingers flexed, they could all hear it, like a bowman taking aim.

'Where,' he said, in gravelly tones, 'did you learn Croí songs?'

*   *   *

It was only after Netha Tal-Aneririn had begged off another encore that they and Abelard actually got a chance to speak.

This private little arrowhead of decking was a place for sailors to take a quick gulp of ship's spirits or wrestle or smoke, and the captain pretended he didn't know exactly where they were as long as the work got done.

For the duration of three songs, Netha had turned it into a barbican performance hall. The gathered seamen had looked like boys, somehow, arms locked, swaying back and forth, their eyes closed. Some had joined in, and their rough and unpolished voices had not taken away from Netha's but instead alloyed and strengthened it.

Now, the poet sat on a barrel, sipping water and clearing their throat. The other seamen drifted in and out of the cordoned space as their duties allowed, with the ease of men used to snatching time where they could.

'Do all poets fight in the Terod Union?' Abelard asked.

Netha harrumphed low in their throat. It felt like a ritual – a sip, a deep guttural cough, and then a speculative note or two, as if testing the fit between air and throat.

'The *filidh* of the Six-Coloured Court do not resort to crass physicality,' Netha said loftily. 'Except when we do, of course. Then we try and be very good at it.'

It was a voice meant for singing as much as speaking, the pause between each syllable wide and pronounced. *Fil-idh. Re-sort.*

They grinned, and Abelard found himself grinning too.

'You're a long way from home,' he said politely.

'Closer than I've ever been,' Netha said, easing at one of their boots.

'I'm sorry?'

'No apology required,' Netha said. 'I had heard that Answermen fail to take much interest in the history of the places they conquer.'

Abelard wasn't an expert in etiquette, but he knew that if your opponent broke the rules, you were generally allowed to as well, especially in the service of patriotism.

'Well, we conquer so much, you see,' he said, despite himself. His brothers might have been impressed. 'Though I cannot claim that we have ever done so to the Union. Unless you'd like to enlighten me?'

'I'm Croí,' Netha said simply. 'A *filí*, though the tradition no longer exists on that side of the misty horizon. Part of a caste of saga-speakers. Poem-smiths. Law-brokers too, and historians, and adjudicators of disputes. We crowned kings. Deposed them too, sometimes, when they forgot to treat us well.'

'Your ancestors were Croí?' Abelard asked, to hide his confusion.

Netha nodded. 'They travelled from *túath* to *túath*, province to province, mediating and sharing news and receiving good meals and hot water so we wouldn't sing about what a shit host you were. That bit would have been my favourite, I think. You're a noble, aren't you? I have that right?'

'Yes,' Abelard said. It felt strangely cosmopolitan to address it head-on. 'The son of one, at least.'

'And your family? Do they put on a good spread?'

He blinked. 'A spread?'

'For any visitors? Do they make sure they eat right?'

'Messengers . . . eat with the rest of the servants,' Abelard said, suddenly flushing. 'Is that bad?'

Netha ticked their tongue against their teeth. 'Depends on how you treat your servants, I suppose.'

'So that's what you do?' Abelard said. 'You write . . . insulting poems about people who don't treat you very well?'

'Well,' Netha said. 'We used to do a lot more.'

'Before the Answering came,' Abelard said. There was a prickling heat on the back of his neck, and he rubbed it to try to make it go away. 'They outlawed it?'

'Oh no,' Netha said. 'They made it punishable by death. That's why I'm of Terod birth. The Answermen came, and it was not enough to take the land and the trees and the meat and the bread, but you reached into us and cut out our laws and language as well.'

Their voice took on the pitch of ritual then, soft and applauded by the waves.

'No one lives free when their tongue has been taken.'

Abelard's cheeks burned.

'We brought schools,' was all he could think to say.

'We had schools. They just weren't the schools you wanted.'

Abelard remembered the look on the sailor's face when Netha had sung. Not hungry, but malnourished. When a lack of sustenance left a mark.

Netha followed his gaze. 'You can hear Croí accents as far away as the Cape of Flames if you know where to look. Children half a world away from here tell each other stories of otter kings and ossuary wolves and the Warping Man with his slavering head. Tales make an easy load. That's why the *filidh* were always given a good meal.'

'The Croí put stories to work,' Abelard said, suddenly desperate to proffer some sort of understanding.

'Yes. Law is just a story we tell ourselves. So is reputation. The *filidh* and our sibling orders were in charge of both – a neutral body. Literally, for many of us.' They slid a hand over their burnished scalp. 'He or she or they, the teller is as the story demands.'

'Sounds freeing,' Abelard said without thinking, and just as quickly, Netha's smile was back.

'You've no idea.'

They stood in an almost companionable silence for a while, Netha occasionally looking Abelard over unashamedly, in the same way Abelard might have peered at an animal he was studying. A stare that asked questions and made notes and prepared follow-up enquiries for later.

'Is being a *filí* still against the law?' Abelard said eventually, carefully navigating the word.

'Yes.'

'Is it not dangerous for you to go home?'

'Very.'

'Then why are you—'

'Do you know far it is?' Netha asked suddenly. 'From great and sprawling Khoan, Grandmother of Cities, to . . .' Their brow furrowed.

'Anfloga Dock,' Abelard supplied helpfully.

'Anfloga Dock,' Netha finished grandly. 'Do you?'

'No,' Abelard said.

'Eleven months,' Netha said. 'Eleven months since I set out from that white and spitting bay, through Tamesa, and Banwit, and the boiling plains of Moraso's Curse, singing for steerage or just stowing away. A long way. A long time. But nothing compared to how long I have been waiting to set foot on that soil.'

That look again. Starving for something they had never tasted.

'My arrow was loosed towards Croí three hundred years ago, and only now is it finding home. The question is – why are all these people trying to leave?'

Shouts began to rise before Abelard could answer. The captain had emerged from his cabin and was in furious argument with two of the crew. The word *panic* didn't suit such large, scarred men, but it was the word that came to mind.

'What's wrong?' Abelard asked.

Netha pointed wordlessly. Darkness was swelling through the horizon, filling the grey clouds with bruise-streaks of black. The wind was rising, and the flecks and sprats of sea spray had turned sharp and pelting. A storm was coagulating in the clouds ahead.

But between that and *Channel's Cry*, the sea had darkened too. Wreckage crowded the water. Planks bobbed and drifted. Sails spread and rippled like slicks of oil. Barrels very similar to the ones on which they sat formed little islands in the rolling waves.

Abelard felt sick in a way that had nothing to do with the ship's motion. A vessel, either on its way to Croí to pick up evacuees or . . . on its way back, packed to the gills with frightened bodies hoping to escape.

And something had torn it to splinters.

'Perhaps it is my part to find out,' Netha said.

6

Talasa

'ORDER IN THE Bicameral!' bellowed the Speaker over the din. 'This is his Majesty's Rationale, not a brothel at capacity!'

'Should I ask him how he knows the difference?' Kalifsena whispered, quiet enough that their grim escort of kingscarls couldn't hear. Talasa bit down on a smile. It was the little touch of medicine she needed before all this began.

The Bicameral Seat dominated Dreodyrne's skyline – the inner curve of its great grey dome ringed with galleries as snug as the segments of an orange in their skin. There was intentionality in everything in the Answering. As a girl spoken to by no one but the Queen, Talasa took every opportunity to listen to what the architecture was telling her instead.

Each of the cardinal fiefs of the Answering had its own gallery hung with heraldry – the burgundy of Idegeld, the blue of Modigmark – with the lesser fiefs relegated to the cobwebbed anonymity of the upper heights. Each cramped little stage was its own nation state, complete with high reeves, reeves, junior ministers, scribes, runners, sometimes even dedicated men-at-arms.

If this building truly was the heart of the Answering, it was a tight and crowded knot of muscle that required a physician's care and expertise to understand.

Normally, the entrance of a queen made some dent in the arguing, insult-trading, gossip-brandishing and base attempts at intimidation. Today, however, Talasa and her mother were invisible.

She'd always thought the Rationale a pompous name for a government. The First Among had not just been conquerors, despite the long and dreary list of victories shared by her history tutor, Master Colby. They had been *propagandists*, and just as Kalifsena peddled illusions and sold higher truths, so too had they in every naming convention.

An empire to answer petty internecine conflict, and a Rationale to direct it.

Now, though, rationality had been driven out. Reeves roared in each other's faces. Beat fists on railings. Individual arguments were hard to pick out, but two words peppered the air like grapeshot, hot with rage and contempt.

Croí. Shore.

'You embarrass yourselves before a queen, gentlemen!'

Speakers were chosen for their voices. By the time the last syllable landed, more than half the room had sat, whiskers twitching like scalded cats. A long glare from the Speaker did for the rest.

'It is perishingly rare that I enjoy looking upon this chamber,' he growled, pausing for a burble of amusement. 'But it is with great pleasure that I welcome Queen Kalifsena and Princess-Undynast Talasa to the Bicameral Seat to address his Majesty's Rationale.'

Kalifsena took the oak podium they called the Supplicant's Stand, and Talasa the seat beside. For a moment the Queen just stood. Even at the Rationale, where she was entitled to an official greeting and little else, there was a weight to the tiny woman that made her the hub of a wheel, the centre around which all else turned.

'Thank you, Speaker. And thank you, honoured reeves. I will endeavour not to waste too much of your time.'

The warmth in her voice when she mentioned the Speaker was not feigned. Talasa liked him too. Most nobles tripped over the *Princess-Undynast* – a title dug out from the vast tomes dictating the tangled mess of expectation, custom and tradition on which the Answering ran.

To be Undynast was to be acknowledged as royalty but be unable to continue it. To the Answering, who derived worth from their fathers and obsessed over what to leave their sons, there was no greater curse.

But the Speaker delivered the title with just as much respect as a king's, and that meant more than Talasa could admit to anyone but herself.

Besides, she thought, there were benefits to nobody quite knowing what to do with her. There was no official curtsey depth or schedule of social appointments for embarrassing bastards. The fact was, Talasa was more of a ghost in public society than she was behind a wall.

'Your Majesty. Prin . . . Princess-Undynast.'

But for his scarlet cheeks, you'd never have guessed Eorl Fostenden had been screaming his lungs out just a moment prior.

'On behalf of my fellows of Wustamber, namely, I, Eorl Fostenden, Lord Gegory, Sir Trost . . .'

Talasa discreetly tried to squirm some sort of comfort out of her seat as reeve after reeve delivered their official greetings. This part was always interminable. Feigned politeness. Acknowledgement of politeness. Feigned politeness in return.

You got used to it, apparently. And that was the point. If Talasa had a tenth the power of these men, she would have cut the pleasantries and replaced the chairs with ones designed for human spines. But that wasn't what was *done*.

The city of Dreodyrne was the centre of the Answering, and the centre of the Answering – depending on who you asked – was either the Palace or the Bicameral Seat. You didn't spend your life climbing the oiled ladder of influence to bring *change* to a place like this; you changed yourself, sacrificing your spine so you fitted into the rigid angles of the seating.

Like horses, or dogs, ministers were bred for the role. You had to be a man, of course. A man with money, or land, or a family that had once possessed money and land, because the Answering's memory was long, and could stand a family being temporarily embarrassed for a century or two.

Then there were the great academies, where sons with potential were sent to study law or philosophy, and those without were sent to study the sciences to keep them out of trouble. Schools where young men were taught words like *concatenation* and how to say *shame, shame* with a straight face.

There were schools for girls too. Mostly, it seemed to Talasa, they taught you how to be wives.

'Permission to interrupt, Speaker?'

Armin Tell, Reeve Paramount and the most powerful man in the Answering after the King himself, looked like he had skipped his lessons, possibly to be a pirate. Where the other reeves wore traditional black robes and powder, his giant frame was clad in a simple white shirt and trews. Where they slumped or squeaked around on the polished wooden seats like seals on a beach, Tell paced, or swooped like a hawk on those who weren't paying attention.

Were it not for his rich Feondhall drawl and deep brown skin, Talasa could have pictured Tell as a *zemlja*-lord from her homeland, the kind of man who fought in wars rather than salivated over them.

'There are thirty-two more official greetings to be had,' the Speaker said drily, sniffing his spectacles back up his nose. 'Am I to understand you wish to deny the Queen the pleasure of hearing them?'

Tell grinned, teeth shockingly white in his curly black beard.

'I would never deny our Queen anything, Speaker. I simply understand that her time is precious.' His smile vanished. 'And we have the crucial matter of—'

That set the reeves off again, and it took the Speaker a full minute of bashing his gavel and demanding silence before anything more could be heard.

When quiet did eventually fall, Kalifsena favoured the Reeve Paramount with a precise smile, as if no interruption had happened at all. 'You are too kind, my dear Armin. Alas, it is the province of queens to devalue the time of powerful men.'

They could have gone on like this for hours. The Queen and the Reeve Paramount shared a polite sort of distaste for each other. Armin Tell was a man who liked things tidy. Streets. Laws. Governments. Kalifsena represented disorder he could not unpick or tidy away.

'No powerful men here, your Majesty,' he said to quiet laughter. 'Just servants, eager to hear the voice of their master.'

Now the silence was expectant. There was only one reason the Queen attended these councils, after all. But the hunger in the air was something new. They had walked in on a Bicameral that did not just want the words of the King – they *needed* them for a specific purpose.

Or a choice.

Kalifsena's pale hand produced that slim little document cylinder, and Talasa felt, more than heard, a hundred men sigh with relief.

She made note of those who didn't, too. That was her function here. The Answering had little use for sixteen-year-old girls, let alone those who seemed to barely speak Answering, who sat in her rooms like a discarded hairbrush when she was not required, and trailed after her mother when she was.

They were right about one thing. Talasa rarely spoke. She just listened. And everything she heard, she remembered.

'Twelve weeks,' Tell said. 'Twelve weeks since his Majesty set out on another . . . pilgrimage. Twelve weeks, as the war with the Shore grinds on, consuming more men, more materiel . . .'

For as long as the Answering had existed, there had always been some sort of war with the nation states of Talasa's homeland. They ground against each other like ice floes, breaking off a settlement here, some farmland there. Some *zemlje* and townships had changed hands so often nobody remembered who had owned them in the first place.

That wasn't why Tell had said it, of course. The reeves didn't need reminding – they had clearly been stewing in bad news from the border all morning. He did it in case anybody for a second forgot who Kalifsena was.

'And now . . .' He raised his fist as if to thump it on his plinth, and then brought it gently to his chest instead. A lovely little bit of theatre. 'We hear of unrest in Croí.'

Mutters and mocking from the galleries.

'When is there not?'

'Hang a hundred, teach the rest!'

Laughter at that, until Tell waved them down. 'The Lord Protector has been hanging them,' he said drily. 'I don't believe he has ever needed much encouragement in that regard, and we who own stocks in rope are all very grateful.

'But he has been writing to me in a *froth* for weeks. There are organised forces at work.'

Men laughed or shook their heads in disbelief at the thought. *Croí. Organised.* Talasa only knew the Croí from a couple of pleasant enough maids and the cartoons in the periodicals, and the general belief was that organisation was as foreign to them as washing and pronouncing their 'r's.

Tell persevered.

'Grain shipments are under threat, gentlemen. If we lose access to the breadbasket that is Croí and the Mag Mell plain, our horses go hungry, and our men walk. To the east, more and more men flock to the banners of Cardinal Rokita and his Bloody Bulls, and to the south, the New Territories founder. We need *action*, and only our King may declare it.'

It wasn't hyperbole. Nobody presumed that the King had to stand over every filled pothole in Dreodyrne. But it had been twelve weeks. Twelve weeks since he had disappeared in the middle of the night with a couple of his favourite retainers and too few kingscarls, and the kind of hungry gleam in his eye that a more acceptable monarch might have reserved for women or wine.

And in his absence . . . Backbiting among reeves. Uncertainty in the military. The Tattered Shore eroding the eastern border like wood under a craftsman's plane.

That was the advantage of being a loose conglomeration of city states, Talasa mused, with uncharacteristic patriotism. Chaos was your natural condition. The Answering, on the other hand, had been bred to desire leadership, even the inattentive sort King Rubeo favoured.

And there were whispers that the King was soft on the matter of the Shore. Everyone knew his head could be turned by stories of witchery, but far more insidious, Talasa knew, were the stories that his head had been turned by a witch.

'We are bleeding,' Armin Tell said, in a voice that should have been too soft to carry as far as it did. 'And unless these wounds are staunched, we will weaken and fall. Deliver his words, your Majesty, and his answers on the many queries this seat has put to him in letters past.'

Talasa had seen those letters, sealed in their straining cases of red leather before being sealed with soft white wax and reverently dispatched to wherever Rubeo's obsessions had taken him. And yet, for all their pomp and ceremony, they hadn't a tenth the weight of the slim cylinder of paper in Kalifsena's hand.

The Queen turned the letter over, and another sigh breathed through the room at the sight of its pristine white seal. She broke it with a nail, unfolded it and—

'Wait!'

Reeves turned towards the doors. Some sort of commotion had broken out – not a fight, but a messy, shoving confusion. Kingscarls retreated towards the Stand as if under enemy fire, and in those harried movements Talasa recognised the quiet panic of soldiers suddenly realising just who they were trying to bar entry to.

The young man didn't spare a glance for the reeves as he stormed down the central aisle. He shared a likeness with his father – the height, the auburn curls, the penny redness of their skin. There was even that similar spark, the light Rubeo got in his eyes when an ambassador produced some trinket or folk tale the King had never come across before.

'Your Highness,' the Speaker said carefully. Angry murmurs had broken out in the galleries. First the Queen, then the Prince. How were the Rationale supposed to pretend they ran the Answering if the family who *did* run it kept showing up unannounced? 'May I ask—'

'For Father's letters, of course,' Prince Offrian Medalwyn said sharply. 'I trust someone was going to inform me that they were being presented?'

Armin Tell paused. There was no trace of amusement on his broad, bearded face, but Talasa had the distinct impression he let the silence drag on a beat too long.

'We are just learning of this ourselves, your Highness. Which is why I have suggested, *many* times, that his Majesty could communicate directly with the Rationale instead of—'

'I recognise the burden I represent for you, Armin,' Kalifsena interrupted lightly. 'But as always, gentlemen, I rushed here as soon as the missive arrived. It will be transcribed and shared as soon as we are finished here.'

She nodded indulgently at the furiously scribbling scribes, their cloaks the red-and-white dashwork of the Ceolmund Academies.

'As is appropriate,' the Prince said.

He wasn't half as good at keeping his tone neutral as Tell. Talasa was reminded of an effect she had once seen, where lights were placed behind a portrait of a man on thin-scraped vellum. With different lights, different aspects of the portrait came to the fore, making the man old, then young, angry, then sad.

Offrian was just eighteen, and strikingly well-made, but something shone sourly through him, tinting and tainting the good that was there.

'Well. Now that we're all here,' Kalifsena said, as if this were a garden terrace luncheon and the attendees didn't all hold each other in varying degrees of contempt. 'If I may continue?'

'Please,' Tell said.

It was rare that this chamber hung on the word of a woman. Kalifsena let the silence billow out like a sail until finally she unfolded the letter and began to read.

'*My dearest wife. Star of my soul. My everything. Your eyes are comets in the sky of my—*'

'My Queen?' Armin Tell said mildly.

'Yes?' Kalifsena said. 'Oh. Of course.'

She put down the first page. And the second. Tell raised a bushy eyebrow. Reeves muttered like crows. Talasa could hear Offrian's teeth grinding from across the podium. He hadn't looked at her once since entering the chamber. She couldn't blame him for being angry. His father the King had gone on a simple diplomatic mission and come back with a new wife and daughter.

She thought about him sometimes, though. How they held two pieces of the same man, and whether they would ever talk about the shape they made together.

'Ah,' the Queen said suddenly. 'Here we are.' She relaxed her iron-straight posture, ground both elbows into the podium and gave them all a speculating look. The effect was so like Rubeo that some reeves laughed, though many caught themselves when they realised.

Offrian didn't laugh. Neither did Tell.

'*Please relay to Armin that I understand his concerns regarding the loss of the fort at Cadslina and the routing of the Black Mirandas,*' Kalifsena read. '*Alas, if all your countrymen could be as elevated as you, my greatest love, Queen of my . . .*'

She looked up at the silent assembly, mock-embarrassed.

'It continues.'

Another rustle of pages.

'Ah. *However, he knows – perhaps better than I – that we are stretched thin as it is. The New Territories require. The Contested Territories require. We haemorrhage men and funds to ceaseless conflict and will continue to haemorrhage more if nothing changes.*'

A ghost of a smile crossed her face.

'*I can see Armin now,*' she read. '*Thumping the podium. Calling for action.*'

Tell smiled, suddenly in on the joke. That was the thing so easily forgotten about Rubeo – how *likeable* he was. How he didn't make you feel like you were a subject or a resource to be spent, but as if you were conspiring together to make the Answering a better place.

There was a reason an interest in spiritualism and the occult was sweeping the nation, despite the best efforts of rhetoricians to maintain appropriate rationale.

Kalifsena resumed. '*I have read his words, and I agree. This letter is one of two dozen, the others already dispatched. Armin, forgive me. I could not wait for debate and disarray.*'

Tell's breath caught audibly. Offrian was leaning so far forward he had nearly bent himself in half. The gallery could have been a tapestry for how still each reeve had become.

'*The order has been given. No more half-wars. No more wasting men on battles that cannot be won, and perhaps should never have been fought in the first place. I have declared a general withdrawal from Croí.*'

Uproar. Reeves were on their feet, shouting and clamouring. Even Tell, that monument to precision and control, gripped the sides of his plinth as if he meant to tear it from its moorings. Or as if he were holding onto it for support.

'Is that . . . What else did he say?' He cleared his throat. 'My Queen, what else did he say? Where is he? Is he coming home? What sort of withdrawal? What *else did he say*?'

Kalifsena rifled through the pages again.

'He's written me a poem,' she said, and gave their horrified expressions a cheerful smile. 'Would you like me to read it?'

7

Sister Wake

THE RAT WOKE up.

This came as a surprise. The second last thing it remembered was a scrap of meat on a square of paper, and the *last* thing it remembered was pain; a dry agony tightening its body into a shivering ball. It was still just a pinkling, far from the old, wiry monsters that feared nothing but the ratting dogs. Young as it was, however, it should have known that humans didn't just leave out food.

But it had eaten the food anyway, and then the pain had come and eaten it.

That was before. Now the rat rose to its hind legs, stretching experimentally, wondering where that pain had gone. It had no idea how long it had been curled up under this floorboard, or what was causing that thick, unpleasant smell, but rats were not ones for dwelling on things.

Besides, it was hungry.

Sister Wake was making friends.

Not with the *ríthe*, of course. Council over, they had closed ranks once again, setting up on a hillside overlooking the fortress, leaving Sister Wake and Brother Wight outside the ever-growing crowd of messengers relaying orders to the army below.

It was late morning. The sky was as blue as the reflection on a blade, the air packed with the scent of murdered trees. Even gouged by the oppressors, the land was beautiful. They should have put a window in her wagon, so she could see what she was helping to retake.

Before the Answering, the countryside before them would have been roofed by oak and boxwood, carpeted by ivy and wort. Now a plain stretched to the other side of the valley, pale and pruned as a newly shaved scalp, and at the centre of all that plucked and mangy earth sat Shieldwood Keep, blocky and alien against the land.

It wasn't that the Croí didn't lumber. The old and the angry liked to pretend that the age before invasion was miraculous and without sin, that none of the old clans warred or hated, that the island and the people and the gods lived in blissful harmony.

This was, of course, a lie. But for the Croí, forestry was like fighting – petty, instinctual, pruning away what should be pruned – and for the Answering it was *industry*. They built to last, and tore up by the root, and then when all was bare, they put down a castle, like a brand on a bull.

Such things were not easily removed, and yet the collected might of two *túatha* had taken their places on the plain, just beyond range of arrow or shot from the keep. More people than Sister Wake had ever seen in one place before.

She watched as formations came together in mongrel blocks and rippling, uneasy squares. The *lucht tighe* of each *rí* – the reduced household guard each Croí *rí* was allowed by law to train – had mail and shield and padded gambesons, their axes and spears held parallel across their chests. Professional soldiers, despite their ceremonial status. There were *ceitheirne* too – light skirmishers, armed with swords and bows and slings, or daggers and bundles of fletched darts; long as javelins and deadly at close range.

Professionals were in the minority, however. The rest were shepherds and farmers, bare-headed or in pot helms, their *léinte* stuffed with wadded cloth, holding spears or billhooks or clubs. Many held ladders, and it was those that Sister Wake felt for the most. Her people were new to the idea of siege warfare, and nobody wanted hot oil as a teacher. They would die getting those ladders they held into position, and more would die climbing them.

If those cannons began to fire, they would never reach the walls at all.

And yet, despite herself, she couldn't help but feel the strangest sense of pride. For three hundred years the Answering had managed the Croí like herds of cattle – taking land, culling the troublesome, keeping close track of the numbers of fighting men. They'd stopped just short of clipping ears. The only true and trained warriors left on the island were the ones who had bent the knee, or the ones like Brother Wight who fought in ditches and bogs and back alleys, avoiding fair fights like the plague.

There were no uniforms on the Croí side. No unity in faith or formation. As many reasons to fight as there were swords in the fighting.

No two Croí had the same reason, but that, right now, was what made them mighty. Taking an oath and a factory sword meant fuck all when there were uncountable legions to stand with you. When there were thirty generations of soldiers in the graveyard with the same coat and boots and pressed grey trews. When it was a job.

For the Croí it was survival. Life or death.

Us against them.

Brother Wight's crest of black hair was streaming in the wind. 'We're ready,' he said.

What are you fighting for? Sister Wake asked herself.

There was no good answer, so she closed her eyes and thought of rats.

Hunger was a hook in the heart of the rat.

Young rats didn't become old rats without caution. You had to stick to the shadows you knew. But the pinkling's hunger was a crazed, nauseous thing, pushing it further into the castle than it had ever ranged before.

There were other rats too, bodies low and scampering. A grass snake undulated alongside as well, which added to the confusion, first because snakes were the holy terror of a young rat's life, and also because the snake didn't seem to have a head.

The rat's own head wasn't built for thoughts like this. All it understood was that the hunger was worse than the poison had been. Its comrades peeled away one by one, and the rat's nose twitched as an acrid scent reached it; the kind of scent that a day ago even a pinkling wouldn't go near.

Now, its mouth watered. It was close. It would eat.

'Tell her to hurry!'

The words arrived in a language Sister Wake didn't know, before she remembered whose head she had started out in. A small part of her, the part not currently piloting twenty-nine recently dead animals into position, noted that even now Abacus didn't have the *clocha* to speak to her directly.

'I assure you,' Brother Wight said smoothly, 'she is hurrying.'

'It doesn't *look* like she's hurrying. Does she know what will happen if those things fire?'

Brother Wight's voice was calm. 'You can explain it to her if you like.'

Just what she needed – another voice in the din. The death of grass was a bubbling drone, three thousand men and women churning it to muck even standing still. There must have been plague in the town recently, because Sister Wake could feel the tight, hard knot of mass graves in the shadow of the walls.

There were fresher deaths too, singing out, two already, because some fucking fool had decided to turn around with his sword out and accidentally jabbed it into another man's throat, and now that man's brother had run him through.

And there were fifteen rats, ten mice, three swallows and a garden snake currently clamouring for attention in Sister Wake's head.

It was a good haul of corpses, in fairness. The castle staff must have been very into traps. Lot of broken necks, some sore stomachs. She could work with that. It wasn't that she *couldn't* wake an animal that had been cut in half by a trap, but right now she needed nimble and quick.

There was a race in waking. People assumed Sister Wake simply raised the dead like the saints of the Cailleach in the stories, like a puppet on strings. Responsible for every movement, every twitch.

But you didn't animate a puppet. You manipulated it.

Sister Wake influenced, not controlled. Birds wanted to fly, even after their necks were broken, and so she encouraged them to fly, and looked at the world through their eyes. Rats wanted food, and they wanted dark places, and so Sister Wake put hunger and hope into their heads. Every life had a destination. Everyone was shackled to some kind of stone.

If she was pressed to put it into words, she might have compared it to lying in a foreign language. To be more accurate, it was like lying in twenty-nine separate languages, with the added wrinkle that if the person you were talking to realised you were lying, they would die on the spot.

It happened, even as she thought it. A mouse suddenly stiffened as its body talked itself out of being alive. A swallow blinked and spiralled out of the sky. The more complicated a creature was – and all creatures were complicated, in their own complicated ways – the harder it was to lie to them that they were alive.

Even as Sister Wake cajoled her charges closer to their targets, increasing whatever phantom reward had ruled their waking lives, she felt them fight her. Animals didn't run towards humans and their pointless constructions – the wood, the rope, the oily, smelly steel – they ran away.

That was instinct. That was fact. A fact more real, in fact, than the man striding up to her with his hand on his sword.

'If you don't take out those cannons, you little . . .'

There was a noise. Just a whisper really, barely audible through the jumble of souls in Sister Wake's head, but she caught it all the same.

The Abacus had stormed up to her, and now Brother Wight was between them, and his knife was at his neck. It was a little like dream logic, where you knew things you couldn't see, and saw things you couldn't possibly know. Sister Wake's soul was halfway out of her body, split between twenty-seven living things, and yet she could still see the hairs on Brother Wight's neck dancing in time with her breath.

The return of the gods had upended just about every power structure on the island. It wasn't clear, just in this moment, who outranked who – a *rí* or the *geis*-sworn warrior of a living saint.

And then Brother Wight lowered his knife to point at the earth.

The grass under Sister Wake's bare feet had frozen stiff. Some of it smoked with cold.

'For your protection,' he said gently, 'I would stay back.'

The Bear hadn't even looked over. He was fastening his coat of mail around his shoulders, its battered links reinforced with scavenged panes of steel. The kind of armour you wore when you led from the front, when you were going over the wall to meet someone coming the other way.

'If you're ready,' he said, speaking again directly to her, as if the Abacus and Brother Wight weren't there at all, 'I'll sound the charge.'

Sister Wake had been meant to die on the side of Crom Dubh. And though she still stood here, in the ice-cold gaze of the Cailleach, something *had* died that day. Emotion, for Sister Wake, now came only with effort. It had become largely something she did for effect. For response. For the Rising, when she could force it.

So she reminded herself to find things beautiful, and she made jokes to Brother Wight, and she hoarded little grudges because that was what people did when they were trapped in wagons for weeks on end.

They didn't even trust me with their names.

And this man had thanked her.

'I'm ready,' she said to him, her voice distant and cold. 'They'll never fire a shot.'

He nodded, and she was away again, on the walls and beneath the walls and over the walls, as the shout rang out across Sciáthcrann to charge.

Sister Wake couldn't help herself. She was sweating with the effort of the waking, and yet she found some dram of strength more to find the body of a dead rook and send it spinning into the sky, a dream of freedom in its rotting little head.

This was a moment that deserved to be witnessed. A moment so huge, so grand that the only way to observe it was from as many angles as she could. A crystalline moment. Faceted. Beautiful. Distressingly sharp even through perished eyes.

The Bear took his place in front of his *lucht tighe.* He exchanged words with his men. Clasped hands. Drew the brutal axe at his side and tapped its top-spike against the palm of his hand just once, as if making sure it was real.

The Pious took his place in the front line as well, she was surprised to see, though the only thing he exchanged with his household were muttered prayers and teeth clenched in fervour.

Spears were hefted. Blades were bared.

And then the Croí formations began to run.

Sister Wake saw and heard it all. She heard the Answermen on the walls shout, defiant and fearful, but there was no sound from the Rising side at all.

Three hundred years, she thought. Three hundred years of whispering.

And then in the uncertainty, in the terror, in the exultation, Sister Wake heard her people roar.

It was the signal to go to work. Each bombard was a monster – a man-long tube of iron with a stained, scorched mouth, shielded from rain by a little tent of thatch. They were huge, and grim, and solid as warships, and an army of rats wouldn't have made a dent in their half-ton frames.

And yet by themselves, they were useless. Just statues without . . .

There. Worried men with padded trolleys, the squat little barrels on each strapped tightly in place. Even if Sister Wake hadn't known they were coming, she would have recognised them, because they reeked solidly of death.

As she watched, the first barrel was cracked open, and above, nestled in the thatch, the first rat struck its match.

Yoe was not a soldier. He was from the wet fields of Cilkeld, a good thousand miles from here, and had been promised a farm. Not a large farm, understandably. That hadn't needed to be explained to him by the recruiters. But it would be a farm, and it would be his, and most importantly, it wouldn't be mostly water with a little dirt floating in it.

What he had not been promised was a sword in his hand and thousands of screaming heathens coming towards him.

'Calm yourself, boy,' Captain Barne said, though he was Yoe's age and looked just as scared. 'And get that barrel open.'

Yoe found himself unable to look away from the approaching horde. It was fascinating, in a horrible way. Faces and blades rippling like the scales on a hauberk, one thing made of many things, many and one and many again.

'Boy,' said Captain Barne. 'You ever see one of these things fire?'

Yoe hadn't, and if he were being honest, he didn't want to either. He got sick at the sight of blood, and everything about the huge cannon seemed hungry for it.

'Mince,' the commander said. The thought seemed to calm him. 'It will mince them.'

'Oh,' Yeo said faintly. Something brushed against his foot. He flinched, but there was nothing there. 'Good.'

He ladled the gravedust into the bombard's mouth, his grip sweat-slick on the copper loading scoop. Slow, soft movements. Any bit of friction at all might cause a spark, and if that happened there would be no farm, and probably no Yoe either.

His bag strap was chafing. That was odd. He'd thought he'd left it at his feet. He reached back and grabbed the long, cold length of leather.

It twisted to strike a match off his chest.

The first explosion was like a tree living its whole life in a heartbeat – a branching bloom that soared as flame and slumped as ash.

The detonation shook the wall to its base, even as the second bombard went up, and the third, sending the left-hand gatehouse reeling. The fourth actually lifted the shattered carcass of its bombard into the air, the great cannon making one full revolution before coming back down hard enough to crack the stone beneath it.

Rubble rained down. Fire squirted like blood. The sight nearly halted the Croí charge. Whole sections of *ceitheirne* slowed, before the veterans behind them goaded them back into a staggering charge.

Sister Wake couldn't blame them. Running towards a wall bristling with matchlocks was one thing. Now they were charging towards light and fire and screams. You didn't charge toward fire. You ran from it. People were like rats in that regard.

The noise and light made it easy to convince the next rat to jump. The open mouth of the gravedust barrel was dark and inviting, and the rodent lunged for it like a mother's burrow. The lit match it was holding did the rest.

Five down.

People did not ask Sister Wake about her powers very often. They didn't care how they worked. They didn't know that sometimes people died so violently their last memories banged into her head like the recoil of a bombard, that she'd know the last thoughts of Yoe from Cilkeld for the rest of her life.

They didn't know that violent deaths were the worst deaths, that they flared so hard in her saint's senses that the sounds they made became points of blurring pain.

She had never told anybody that they all sounded the same. Answering and Croí. Oppressors and oppressed. Nobody had ever asked.

And then . . .

Men and women were still dying. Flames scraped at the sky. But all of a sudden, Sister Wake couldn't focus on any of it.

Her *tabharthas* – that saintly sense stretched out as it was – had *caught* on something, like a cloth on a hook. It was painful. Dizzying. She felt it in her stomach and her spine, a vicious pull that yanked her back to stare into Sciáthcrann's burning heart.

With no human recourse, no words to explain it, Sister Wake found herself falling back on that strange medley of other, borrowed lives. Those sinews of want and terror she pulled on all the time.

Instinct. That was what it was. The same way a mouse knew winter or a bird knew south.

It was instinct.

She turned to Brother Wight to say . . . something, anything, and then she realised she had forgotten the sixth bombard.

The cannon firing was so loud it re-killed every little creature she'd woken. Sister Wake tasted blood, and vomit, and soot, as the icy feedback of all those deaths rattled through her. It felt like someone grabbing the base of her spine and cracking it like a whip.

Everything was very loud. Warriors were shouting. The gatehouse walls were thick with ant-like figures. Even as she watched, whole portions of the battlements gave way, and those that remained were a lurid, sweating horror through which soldiers screamed and ran and died.

Only one section of the walls still stood strong. In front of it, Croí warriors lay flattened in a perfect cone of red ruin and scorched earth.

Brother Wight kneeled beside her. His face was completely calm, which told Sister Wake just how angry he was.

'What happened?' he hissed.

It wouldn't do to see a saint and her *geis*-knight fighting, but as Sister Wake pushed herself to her knees, she saw that the Abacus wasn't watching Brother Wight at all.

He was staring at Sister Wake. Not with impatience, or horror, but with the look of someone who had thought they had copper but discovered it was gold.

'We have to get into the fort,' she said, her stomach knotting with the death of rats.

Brother Wight's hand was still on his pistol.

'Why?'

Sister Wake spoke with absolute certainty.

'Because there's someone in there. Someone like me.'

II

People Like Us

8

Sister Wake

THE RISING HAD rules for everything, and being a saint was no different.

Light and sound discipline, protocols of communication, *geiseanna* of loyalty – follow them, or you may as well hang yourself and save the Answering the rope. And while saints in the scripture were cute hoors who could do what they liked, in an occupied land you led by example, or you would not be swinging alone.

Saints were the link between mortals and the divine. They were the bridge to the Evergreen Undercountry from which the gods had come. It had been saints who had stood against the demons of the Bulging Men in ancient days, and saints who had founded the hidden faith before it *was* hidden.

And a saint could be a firebrand, or a lunatic, or glide along with eldritch calm, but the one thing they couldn't do was be seen to panic, because that hurt the story the Rising was trying to write.

Sister Wake knew all that, and yet she ran, and Brother Wight ran after her.

If the plucked earth before Sciáthcrann had been miserable before, now it was a wasteland. Cinders drifted. Worms squirmed in upturned clods. Grass burned like spots of mange. Thicker smoke rose from deeper holes, pillars in some roofless church. Impact wounds – craters where still-sizzling chunks of the bombards had punched right down into the soil, like a wheellock round through flesh.

Ahead, smoke haemorrhaged from broken battlements. Where the first two bombards had once stood, now only flame and ragged stone remained, and the detonations of the third and fourth had tipped both gatehouses down upon the gates they were supposed to defend. Grit drizzled down like rain, trying and failing to bury hundreds of corpses, Croí and Answering both.

Every occupied town and fort had a firing range in a prominent spot – a lesson to all watching how half a spoonful of Answering gravedust, judiciously applied, could zip a lead ball through armour, leather and flesh.

Now, Sister Wake was seeing what five barrels of it did to masonry and men, and in the echoing, polluted silence that followed, the click of Brother Wight's wheellock was very loud.

Sister Wake stopped running, and slowly raised her hands.

'Put that away,' she murmured when he was close enough to hear. 'You're making us look bad.'

The pistol was part of the story too. A prop in a play. *Caged beast and handler* went down well with a certain type of *rí*.

'*I'm* making us—?'

He bit off the rest of the sentence, and she turned to see the black steel mouth of the wheellock aimed right at her skull.

'There's a *saint* in there,' she said, resisting the urge to grab the pistol off him and throw it somewhere. 'We need to go in and get them.'

A cinder landed on Brother Wight's cheek and put itself out. She could smell the gravedust behind the bullet, or maybe that was the barrels she'd ignited. Maybe she'd never smell anything else ever again.

'You don't break character,' he said. Behind him, up the slope, the Abacus and his ragged, homeless little household of warriors. Behind her, thousands of Croí warriors swirling around the burning battlements like dirty water round the mouth of a bottle. 'You don't run off.'

'Shoot me, then,' she snapped carelessly. 'Or listen. Lose a saint or gain one. I'll let you choose, Knight of the Hollow Eye.'

Nothing. That face gave her nothing. Dead sparrows felt more like people to her than he did sometimes.

'They're like me,' she said, and hated how her voice cracked over the words. 'They're a saint like *me*.'

Five saints had so far been found in all the Church's scouring, from the northernmost tip of Bairís Point to Adhbha in the south. Five saints, each one worth their weight in gravedust.

Brother Able for Macha.

Sister Eel for Manannán Mac Lir.

Sister Ore for Smithing Brí.

Brother Alabaster for Luige of the Oath.

And Sister Wake, for the Cailleach.

That remorseless seizing of her senses. That blood-deep *knowing* that even now sat on her soul like an altar . . . The gods had returned, and saints with them, but still so much was a mystery. *Did the Cailleach choose me? Or was I just the last girl to wear that chain, and in the right place at the right time?*

The poisonous mystery of it had provoked so many sleepless nights in the last four months that Sister Wake found herself desperate to see a god's hand in matters.

And to have a new saint simply fall into your lap, found by the one saint uniquely placed to identify them. Finding a *second* saint of death . . .

It was very nearly a miracle.

The pistol went back in its holster, and Brother Wight called out to the *rí* on the hill.

'Your *lucht tighe.* With me. Now.'

'I don't need an honour guard,' Sister Wake said coldly, desperate to be away.

'You've never been in a battle before,' he countered. 'We don't know what it will do to you. I don't want them to see you forget yourself. Any more than you already have.'

Sister Wake rolled her shoulders. Fifty paces away, a shrapnel-shredded horse lurched to its feet and began cantering towards them, drizzling blood.

'I don't need help reminding anybody who I am,' Sister Wake said, as the sound of the Abacus noisily vomiting cut through the smoky morning air. 'Are you coming or not?'

Even before Sister Wake had joined the Rising, it was a wise Croí that treated Answering townships as enemy territory. Where they hadn't taken the land outright, they took its deeds and charged you a tithe, or made you grow what they wanted to feed their conquests elsewhere. Even their names were a theft, replacing the lyrical poetry of Croí with blunt and child-like titles.

Goodkeep. Blackwater. Shieldwood.

It had always taken effort, the couple of times she and Da had visited occupiers' keeps, to tell herself this was still her homeland.

The air smelled different because the Answering used fine sieves to separate the bran to make a white loaf. The clothes abandoned on the washing lines were not *léinte* or leggings but dark dresses and woollen trews.

Bonnets drooped like lilies hanging limp after rain. Cobbles, flat as nail-heads, jostled each other underfoot. As if the Answering, not content with merely stealing the land, wanted to nail it down so it couldn't be taken back.

Sister Wake had barely had the thought before she was suddenly Drebbin Ol. Drebbin Ol, who was twenty-one and engaged to a baker's daughter. Drebbin, who would always be twenty-one, pinned to that age by the blade through his sternum.

Drebbin Ol, dying on his back, flapping his hands uselessly, the pain so big and icy and awful that neither he nor Sister Wake could see past it to the snarling Croí warrior driving in the sword.

And then Drebbin Ol died, and Sister Wake was someone else.

Fiach. That was his name. Fiach, who had fallen into a doorway, hands slippery with blood that was mostly his own. There was a family standing over him – a woman and a girl, screaming at him to get out and get away, and Fiach wanted to, he really did, but his legs wouldn't steady beneath him.

He didn't think the bullet was still in him, though. That was something. The agony was coring right through. His back was soaked. Was that why they were screaming at him? Because he was bleeding out all over their floor?

And then Fiach died, and Sister Wake was in the head of Eochaid Óg, who'd signed up to the Rising because Answering soldiers had beaten his brother half to death for spitting when they passed, and Eochaid Óg didn't know what else to do with his anger but find someone in the same uniform and teach them how it felt.

Eochaid Óg, who'd felt alive, incredibly alive, as he charged shoulder-to-shoulder with his kinsmen. Eochaid Óg, who had killed an Answering trooper in the ferocious scrum for the gate, hit him good and hard on the side of the head with his axe while the bastard was trying to saw his sword over a Croí shield, but then the fucker had turned while falling and a flicker of silver had gouged Eochaid Óg's throat, and now all his strength was gone, and he and the foreigner were lying beside each other in the muck like men exhausted after a hard day's work.

And then she was somewhere else, and someone else, pressed up against death after death after death after death . . .

'You're not them.'

Brother Wight had twisted around in the saddle to shake her, like she was a child who had fallen asleep. 'You're not them,' he repeated. 'Remember why we're here.'

His skin felt hot on hers, but Sister Wake knew that it was she who was cold. She blinked furiously, glaring out at the chaos she could see because one set of eyes was better than the hundreds in her head.

The Cailleach and Crom Dubh had put a distance between Sister Wake and the world. But it had opened her too – made her live in other heads, let them force their way into hers.

Grief was as one-sided a thing as there could be, and there was no better proof of that than her sitting here grieving for dead men who didn't even know she existed.

I wish I'd had this gift when I was on the mountain. A familiar little sting. *To hear the girls who went before.*

'I'm fine,' she said. She jerked her hand away, but the heat remained, like a band of fire around her arm.

She wasn't sure how long she had been . . . out of herself, but Brother Wight had taken them through the gates, following the inside curve of the wall, and down one of the township's eight wide streets.

Sciáthcrann – not Shieldwood, not any more – was built like the spokes of a wheel. The houses were small and sturdy, roofed with thin overlapping slates, and they were houses with love in them, because many of them had flowers and faces and bright yellow stars painted on the wooden window shutters and doors.

Love had deserted some of those houses too, though. A handful on every street had been methodically burned, the ceilings collapsed the way the Answering did when they were burying bodies they did not want to touch. *The Croí aren't the first calamity to come here*, Sister Wake thought, drinking in the slow-smouldering panic of sickness-slain souls. *Just the most recent.*

And yet, it might have been a market day, had the Croí army not arrived. Now, battle had rolled over those eight streets, tearing up everything that could be torn up. Carts had been overturned. Pulley scales and tables were hacked apart and destroyed, turnips and cabbages crushed into the ground. Chickens lay as ragged tufts in the mud.

Falling masonry and shrapnel had torn holes in those slates. Punched down straight and clean, or gouging long cat-scratches that skipped and bounced.

Some Answermen had survived the carnage at the walls, or maybe fled before the bombards went up, and Sister Wake could see them falling back to the keep in droves, baying to be let in.

Some hadn't been fast enough, or had been cut off, or were in shock, and now were fighting for their lives, firing from behind the ruins of wagons, or battling Croí in the middle of the street. It was like the rock pools Sister Wake and her da used to pick at – desperate, squirming pockets of violence and survival, fighting to the death over no ground at all.

Brother Wight abruptly yanked the reins, and there was enough left in the horse's soul to understand what the motion meant. The animal yawed sideways as a tangle of Croí and Answermen staggered past, hacking at each other and roaring. They didn't even register the dead horse standing among them, so intent were they on each other.

A blade bit and tore, skiting blood in a vertical plume so close Sister Wake could taste it, and then a twist of her will put the horse into a lurching gallop, intestines lolloping along the ground.

'This was a mistake,' Brother Wight said, trying to find a clear spot amongst the carnage. 'A stray bullet, an arrow, and we lose a saint instead of finding one.'

'I know.'

'You're too valuable to be risked like this.'

'I *know.*'

'Then do whatever it is you have to do,' he said. 'And do it fast.'

Sister Wake looked around, forcing her gaze to be light – never resting on one thing for too long in case she had to see these deaths from the inside. She made herself pointedly incurious. That bundle of rags just a bundle of rags, that streak of red devoid of meaning, holding no more significance than the colours of a dream.

No sacrifice too great.

'Hurry!'

'Shut up,' she snapped back. 'I'm trying to concentrate.'

Her eyes were streaming from the smoke now, not that it mattered. It wasn't her eyes she was using. Not her hearing either, which was a blessing, because the explosion was still rattling around her skull, and battle was *loud*, louder than she could have believed possible, even on the fringes.

Screaming. Cursing. The bang and cough of gunfire. Everyone wanted to be heard. Killing or dying, nobody wanted to go quiet.

And there was another cacophony, though nobody could hear it but her. Sister Wake thought of her gift in terms of sound, though it was not the kind of sound that entered you through your ears. It was a sound you felt in your bones, something internal and external all at once, like the popping of a knuckle or a thundering slap to your jaw that left your whole head ringing.

Men and women died. She felt their souls as chiming notes, pealing out before vanishing to . . . wherever it was that souls went. The Evergreen Undercountry, according to the sermons. A land of eternal plenty.

She was Olaver with an arrow in his lung, forcing blood and air out of his mouth and the bubbling hole in his chest.

She was Suibne, who'd spent his whole life killing Answermen where he could, who'd been part of the Rising before it had *been* a Rising, sitting in the dirt with a halberd wound too big and too deep to come back from. He knew that, at least. He'd done enough damage in his own life to know it.

'Fuck,' he was saying softly to himself. 'Fuck.'

You can't help them. She could only help the Rising. Somewhere in this burning, dying town was a soul like hers. A soul Sister Wake's *tabharthas* had clanged off like a clapper of a bell.

Someone she had resonated with.

Sister Wake had raised a bat once, and it had been a shock to learn that they painted a picture of the world by singing to it. Out went the song, and back came the echoes, and from that knowledge they made a map of the universe, or at least the parts of it they could eat. It was such an astonishing bit of craftsmanship that you had to see the hand of Anu in it.

And in a similar way – or not, perhaps, but it was fucking hard coming up with a metaphor in a language of one – souls had their own picture of the world. Their own associations. Their own maps of emotion. The shelf where you kept your mother's old rings. The hillside on which you'd had your first kiss. Everywhere you went, you stained the world with meaning, central and personal to you, and like a shout in a small room, the world shaped your soul as well.

What had been the geography of that trapped, wavering soul? What had been its north and south? She tried to recall the shape of it, orient herself by it – turning in the saddle, moving her head back and forth, trying to feel from which direction the echo had come.

It wasn't easy. She must have looked like a maniac, dipping and twisting her head, but Sister Wake had practice navigating spiritual geography, and looking like a maniac didn't bother her that much anymore.

They passed the mouth of another street, all the fighting at the far end, spilling out into the great square before the keep. But there *were* people – Croí warriors, going door to door, kicking them open with blades in hand. *Looking for ambushes*, Sister Wake thought, and tried to believe it.

'The civilians,' she said suddenly, thinking of the wailing Answering family that had stood over poor dead Fiach. It hadn't come up in the councils she'd sat in on. The talk had been of the *land*. Taking the land back, repossessing it, handing it to its rightful owner. There hadn't been a lot of discussion about the foreigners unrightfully trying to live on it. 'What will happen to them?'

'The occupiers?' Brother Wight corrected her. He had his spear loose in his hand, though nobody was paying attention to a lone horse and its two riders. They watched a fist fight break out in a doorway between three men over a cooking pot. 'Our quarrel isn't with them. They can go back to where they came from.'

'Oh,' Sister Wake said. 'And how will that—'

There!

Sister Wake let the horse die again without a thought, and only her twinned understanding of its body guided her free from its collapse without harm. Brother Wight barely escaped too, cursing harshly, but Sister Wake was already running for the second time that day.

You could hardly have called it an alleyway. It was just a space where two houses did not quite sit flush with each other, some miscalculation of architecture or imperfection of the bedrock that necessitated a gap less than two metres wide. A little rebellion of the soil.

Someone had been dragging bodies there.

Bodies of soldiers, in the banded black and greys of Answermen, those neat-pressed coats the ragtag Croí loved to mock, now rumpled and bloody. Bodies of Croí warriors too, unceremoniously stripped of armour so that they no longer looked much like warriors at all, just men and women who might have been on their way to this market on a better day, before inexplicably deciding to lie down in the dirt.

There were other bodies as well.

'It's a war,' Brother Wight said, panting. He hadn't seen what she had. 'There's no such thing as civilians.'

At the opposite end of the alleyway, a Croí was picking his way through the heaped bodies. She didn't know which *túath* he hailed from. That was the strength of the Rising, according to Mother Promise. One nation united to throw off its chains.

He had his back to her, but she could see the sack swinging heavy from his belt. Full of nails and belt buckles, most likely. The Rising was short on everything, but especially weapons. It would take the whole bag to make a sword.

There was a bow and arrow in his hand.

'Stop!'

He turned to look at her in shock. So did the little girl in her Answering bonnet and dress.

You had to be incurious. You had to control where you focused, let your eyes skip over what did not fit the story you were trying to write. Mother Promise did it, in her careful speeches that were always about victory and never about death. The *ríthe* did it when they spoke to their men, because taking on Shieldwood was one thing, and the entire empire of the Answering another.

Brother Wight did it when he casually trimmed a township of distinct, contrasting, conflicting souls into the brutal simplicity of *us* and *them*.

But that wasn't Sister Wake. Even now, she couldn't help but question. Couldn't help but focus on all the wrong things. She saw that the Croí was just a boy, younger than her, his features handsome and delicate and a little confused. She saw the lines of red on his breeches where he had wiped his arrows clean.

She saw the hollow slackness of the little girl's face, and the dead woman lying in her arms.

'Leave her alone,' Sister Wake snarled, and then realised her mistake.

I don't need help reminding anybody who I am.

Except she did, because even if this Croí had seen her before, it had probably been when she was wearing a bag.

The boy grinned at her, a little sheepishly, and brought up his bow, nocking and loosing in one practised move.

'No!'

And the corpse in the girl's arms caught the arrow out of the air.

The boy never even had the chance to be surprised. Brother Wight's spear took him hard in the throat with a pop of cartilage, and then Brother Wight was there with it, as if it had called him to its haft. He twisted and jerked down, and the boy went with the spear point, pumping red over the bodies he had robbed.

'How did you do that?'

Brother Wight couldn't hide his shock. The first thing Mother Promise had asked her to do was wake a man from the dead. And

Sister Wake had tried. She'd tried *hard*, kneeling in front of him in that clearing, searching for strings to pull.

'What was his name?' she had asked.

Kindness in Mother Promise's voice. 'Will that help?'

'I didn't,' Sister Wake whispered, staring at the girl.

It hadn't worked. It never worked, not in all the times she'd tried. Too complicated. Too many competing wants. Mother Promise had been disappointed. 'Imagine,' she had said, 'all the dead of Croí coming back to free it for the living. All the Answering's murders undone.'

Slowly, very slowly, the little girl reached out to touch the arrow vibrating a foot from her face.

Someone like me.

An Answering girl, just like her.

9

Abelard

CROÍ SLUNK INTO view as if ashamed.

The Exemplar Accords described the land in glowing terms, at least. How else were you to lure settlers to a new life in the hinterlands? Lush meadows. Forests thick with lumber. Rivers teeming with fish. Good servants too, if you had a firm hand.

But there were darker stories too. Noble Answering men had died in those meadows. Those forests hid thieves and raiders and rebel kings with long blades and longer memories.

What was agreed was that Croí was a wild place – soaked and stormy, capable of delivering four seasons of weather in a day – and though the Answering had done their level best to civilise it, some trace of that wildness remained, stubborn as roots, elusive as mist.

The *Channel's Cry* swayed as it worked its way through the gnashing waves. Spray bit and blinded him, forcing his first impressions of the island to the corner of his eye – a blur of a coast, bruising the horizon in dark fog and hostile green. A sullen smudge on the coast resolved into a modest skyline of stubby towers, broken up by the occasional spire or campanile. *Cusp.*

It should have been a relief, to know they were that close, but all Abelard could think of was that floating scab of wreckage, and just how exposed they were against the roiling black sea.

What could have destroyed that ship? Croí's eastern coast was a warren of sheltered bays – a breeding ground for pirates and reavers the Answering's warships and privateers had never fully been able to erase. Yet as far as Abelard knew – which wasn't far at all, admittedly – they usually struck at merchant convoys, stealing supplies, munitions and even ships they could use in their futile war.

But there's no profit here, he thought, scanning the horizon for the black scratchy lines of approaching masts. *Not in slaying helpless refugees.* Maybe he was being foolish. Maybe for a Croí pirate, the loss of Answering lives was enough.

'Cailleach's Blessing,' a sailor near Abelard muttered, scratching at an impressive facial scar as he stared out at the fog. The man was Croí, and he straightened as the Terod poet approached.

'I hope not,' Netha said, flashing a grin, and the sailor smiled half-heartedly back.

The *filí* had not been idle. They'd made the ship their own, criss-crossing the deck to study the wreckage, interrogating whichever sailor would give them the time. Few Answermen did, of course, but the Croí seemed happy enough – the shared culture clear to them, if perhaps not everyone else.

'Cailleach?' Abelard asked politely, stumbling a little on the word.

'Fog is the hair of the Hag Queen of Winter,' Netha said casually, as if that were a sentence you had call to say all the time. 'A *tabharthas* – a blessing – from the Goddess of Death.'

'That doesn't sound particularly helpful,' Abelard said, attempting some levity.

'All blessings are curses, depending on how you look at them,' Netha said, and the sailor nodded. 'Croí gods are capricious folk.'

As they spoke, they unwrapped a bundle of thick sackcloth, and from within spun a cloak of three colours around their shoulders. Dusky orange, a fine, unblemished white and – of most interest to Abelard – a fringe of truly astonishing blue feathers that must have belonged to a bird the height of a man.

'Only the Ard-Ollamh in his *cúirt* may wear six colours,' they said, fastening it with a brooch of white stone. 'But some of us only need three to look spectacular.'

'I was looking at the feathers,' Abelard said, and wondered why he was blushing. 'I've read a little about Terod fauna, but not . . .'

'All?' Netha's laugh was the chiming of coins. 'You could read a book a day for a life the length of your empire, and never know the half of it. Terod means "world", my friend. No one will ever know it all.'

Underneath the cloak there was a sword and pistol, the handles of both worn with use.

'The part of *filí* – songsmith, saga-crafter – now traded for that of explorer,' they mused aloud. 'Swashbuckler. Daredevil. Even, dare I say it, warrior, should the need arise.'

'You speak of parts,' Abelard said carefully. 'As if you were always on a stage.'

They nodded. 'We all are. The first lesson a *filí* must learn is that the world will write you if you do not write yourself. Your body, your voice – all these can be turned the way a sailor turns a sail. To underline a point. To intimidate, or charm, or amuse.'

Abelard thought of the battered old gamekeeper's coat he wore for comfort, rather than the pressed suit the servants laid out every morning. He thought of how eyes glazed over at his father's parties when he forgot his manners and spoke as himself rather than as who his family needed him to be.

'I don't think I'm very good at that,' he said.

'Well,' Netha said. 'That's telling too.'

'You're very honest about these things,' Abelard said. 'Surely, announcing such strategies lessens the effect?'

Netha shrugged. 'You're not the intended audience.'

Abelard looked around. 'Then who is?'

Netha pointed. 'Home.'

Cusp's port was a modest affair compared to Dreodyrne. A natural deep-water bay emptied into by the wide River Marrow, with the curved smirk of the harbour deepened and built on – first by the natives, and then reinforced to an Answering standard.

Watchtowers and stone revetments emerged from the mist like stones from low tide. Abelard began to be able to make out the dock, and the makeshift flotilla that crowded it. The *Channel's Cry* edged its way into the harbour, and he could not help but be reassured at trading the open sea for a close press of timber and sail.

'Rowboat's up here, milord,' the scarred sailor said. 'They'll take you to the pier.' He pointed at the grand custom house ahead, standing out against the warehouses like the last clean tooth in a tobacconist's gum.

'Won't that slow the loading of refugees?' Abelard asked, frowning.

The mate looked uneasy. 'We're not doing any more. Captain's orders after seeing the wreck. We . . .'

Abelard didn't wait for the rest of the explanation. He was already running up the deck, darting around surprised crew.

'Captain! Captain?'

The captain was old and haggard, and wisps of white hair jabbed from his scalp like hangnails.

'I'm afraid not, my lord.'

'You don't even know what I'm—'

'I have a crew and a ship to think about,' the man said flatly. 'My lord.'

'I understand that,' Abelard said. And he did. He wasn't even sure why he was arguing. He wasn't the argumentative sort.

'Then you'll understand why you should be getting to that shore. I'm not heading into deep water again until I know what killed the ship that came before us.'

'You were ordered to help with the evacuation.'

'I was,' the captain said. 'But I wasn't asked to fight. I wasn't asked to go into enemy territory. And that's what this is now. I know my privateer accords, my lord. That's a different proposition.'

And then he simply turned away, as if Abelard's protestations were just another piece of paperwork he had to complete.

Maybe that was what did it. A day ago, Abelard would have simply accepted that reaction as his lot. He thought sometimes, in those bleak trudges across the moors after breakfast, where no amount of fresh air or enticing flora could distract him from how perpendicular he felt to the world, that he must somehow encourage it. If you were used to being useless, being dismissed felt like a relief. As if you had both come to the same foregone conclusion.

But now the nearest of the crew had turned to watch, attracted by his desperate flight up the deck. Netha had drifted over too, looking up at him with those warm, measuring eyes.

For what might have been the first time in his life, Abelard felt the treacherous thrill of having an audience.

'What,' he said coolly, three centuries of Caudefoy poured into the word, 'makes you think I am asking?'

The pier the *Cry* approached was crammed with refugees, pressed together like corn awaiting the scythe. And yet they all somehow contracted to make room for Abelard when he stepped from the gangplank.

It wasn't easy – he could see that. The pier was narrow. They'd fought hard for the little space they had. But at the sight of him, parents lifted children and old men shrank further into themselves.

It felt different. It shouldn't have – the servants at home moved out of his path all the time, ever since he was a boy. Good Answering citizens, Father would say, and good Answering citizens knew their place, just as Abelard knew when he should bow and tug his forelock to those who outranked him.

But it did feel different.

'Are you going to be sick again?' Netha said, stepping past him off the pier. 'You've gone waxy.'

Cusp's docks were already a warren, and the evacuation had made them over-clogged and febrile with bodies. Anything resembling the flow of produce had ground to a halt beneath a sea of refugees.

In Anfloga, the tension of the crowd had been leaking away, leaving empty stares and relieved exhaustion in its wake. Here, the water was boiling. Several fights had broken out, miserable scuffles over a couple of metres in snaking queues half a mile long. A baby was wailing – long, high reels of sound. The soldiers did not look much better; sweating in their grey-banded coatees, struggling to keep the lines from becoming an uncontrollable flood.

There were even people sitting on the scaffolds clinging to the newer warehouses, the lack of space on the cobbles forcing them upwards to stare morosely over the crowd. Children clambered over bales of produce, only to be roared at by beleaguered officials in long coats.

Netha returned the gaze of a little boy with a fierce grin that made his eyes go huge.

'I may have made a mistake in coming here,' Abelard said. 'In sending the *Channel's Cry* back over the crossing. I'm not used to—'

'To what?' Netha asked bluntly. 'Why did *you* find yourself on that ship, Abelard Caudefoy?'

'I . . .'

He was on dry land again. The nausea should not have been so fierce. He could have – should have – done what his father expected. Provide a presence. Let competent men like Taber and the dockmaster do what should be done. After that, he could have vanished as he always did, wandering off to observe some natural spectacle or curiosity that fascinated only him.

But this wasn't vanishing. This was being *visible*, and Abelard was going to be in trouble for it.

'One of the refugees spoke of . . . creatures,' he said haltingly, suddenly conscious of how foolish it all sounded. How foolish *he* sounded. 'I wanted to . . . investigate.'

'For the empire?'

'Not specifically,' he said, and was surprised at the answer. 'I wanted to be helpful.'

It wasn't the most rousing battle cry in Caudefoy history, but it was the truth. And it seemed to sit better with Netha than it did with Abelard himself, because the poet gestured back at the queue now shuffling up the gangplank.

'I'd say you have been. To them, at least.'

The settlers were still ragged and exhausted. Dried mud caked boots and legs. Tears tracked clean paths through grime. Some of them looked as if they were about to fall any moment.

And yet there was a straightening of shoulders. Heads had lifted, as if there was something worth seeing ahead.

It was a nice thought.

'Where are you going?' Abelard said, as Netha passed. 'Where do you . . . begin, with all this?'

'I'll visit the old places,' the poet said. 'Search for truth and those willing to speak it. You could come, if you like.'

'With you?' Abelard said, blinking in surprise. 'I . . . I suppose we are both researching.'

'I wouldn't put it like that,' they said, 'but that's why I'm the poet. We're both seeking answers. Might be a good idea to braid our paths. Combine our resources.' They grinned. 'Especially because I don't have any.'

'Oh,' Abelard said. It wasn't him they were courting at all. It was the Caudefoy name, and whatever that might buy them. He was surprised by how much that stung, and not just because he was a poor representative of it. 'I believe I can find my own path, thank you.'

'In enemy territory?' Netha asked. 'With that bearing and that voice? It's my voice that will carry further in these lands, Abelard, and I have been studying Croí since I was a child.'

'Studying,' Abelard snapped. 'Exactly. You're not from here either.'

The poet stepped very close, very suddenly. Abelard's throat went dry.

'Is that for you to decide?'

'Milord!'

He was saved by the call of a couple of soldiers, half walking, half running down the street, uncaring of who they jostled. They were young, younger than Abelard, their grey coats and trews those of a Croí-based regiment, though which one, Abelard didn't know. Croí was not a desired posting; he knew that much. The wet. The mist. The seething disquiet.

They came to attention in front of him, chests heaving with exertion and relief.

'My lord, there seems to have been a mistake,' the older of the two said. 'If I may escort you?'

Father, Abelard thought in horror. *Father has sent soldiers to drag me back.* First Among, but they had found him so quickly you could believe the Marquis had *expected* him to wander so catastrophically off course.

For an absurd moment, he thought about fleeing, but Netha was right. He didn't know where he was supposed to go.

'A mistake,' he said. 'Yes.' *I made a mistake.*

'You have your own path so,' Netha said quietly.

Abelard had become so used to the mellifluousness in the poet's voice that it was disquieting to hear it so flat. His mother would have found some neat way to apologise without surrendering any ground. His father would have not seen a need.

But it was only Abelard here.

'It was lovely to meet you. I wish you all the answers you seek.'

The soldier who had addressed Abelard did not so much as acknowledge the Terod's presence.

'Thank you, milord,' he said, gesturing through the crowd. 'Lord Seneschal has decreed that any remaining Peerage must cast off from . . .'

The words died in his throat.

At first, Abelard thought it was another fight. A wave of thrashing and shoving had broken out in front of the customs house, and like a whirlpool between two rocks, it was stirring the whole current of the crowd to a frenzy. They had been fighting to get *to* the ships. Now, he realised, they were fighting to go back the way they had come.

He turned. Sharp ridges of stone were shredding the clouds to the west.

A mountain, he thought immediately. Certainly not a tower – there was none that high even in Dreodyrne.

And then the ridges *moved*, shaking back and forth like sails, and Abelard realised what they were.

They were horns.

A crown of knotted horns, white as snowbound peaks, cast a great and tangled shadow across the dockyard, and everywhere that shadow touched, the crowd went still. *Like mice*, Abelard thought. *Like mice on a kitchen floor when a lamp has been lit.*

No one screamed. No one moved, as cloud billowed back across red fur, a demented eye, row after row of flat, square teeth.

It was a mare's head, fully the size of the *Channel's Cry*, crowned with that nest of dazzling horns, a collar of bright white stone around its throat. Its neck was thick as a castle tower, its shoulders bristling domes of fur, its body so broad and simian with muscle that whole regiments could have clashed in the trenches of its scars, the valleys between its breasts.

A hand – *a hand* – reached out to sweep aside more cloud, and Abelard saw with surreal clarity that its nails were chewed and split in runnels as long as he was tall.

It was enormous. It was astonishing. It was easily two hundred feet high. Abelard could have stood in its mouth and not been able to bridge the gap with arms outstretched.

Its glare had the unspecific aggression some horses had – an omnidirectional resentment that made its red-rheumed eyes gleam. Breath snorted, tattering the fog, an organic, volcano warmth Abelard could feel on his face.

Something rolled beneath its great square teeth, the way a dockhand might work a toothpick back and forth.

A mast.

'It's Macha,' Netha whispered. 'Queen of War and Sovereignty.' Tears sparkled on their cheeks. 'It's true. The stories are true.'

As if it heard them, the impossible behemoth charged.

10

Talasa

IT WAS ALWAYS either about to rain in Dreodyrne or had just rained in Dreodyrne. Today, it was the latter, and the midday sky was dark and mottled as evening. Gutters and drains laughed and spat at Talasa as the carriage set off with a grinding splash of wheels, followed by a set of kingscarls on their nimble Croí greys.

Only when the door had closed and the two of them were settled did Talasa speak.

'He can't do this.'

She spoke in the dialect she'd been raised in, knowing that the only people who understood it outside this carriage were blood relations half a world away. The Rationale had put Shoresmen on the Queen's carriage in their first year. *A little taste of home*, or so they said.

It hadn't done them any good, of course. The Answering loved its unity, but the Shore was proudly a thousand nations with a thousand loyalties, hatreds and tongues. You didn't make peace with a Salinsman the way you did a Sorbek. You didn't speak to the Shore like it was all the same.

'He's the King,' the Queen said. 'I am just relaying the words I was given.'

Talasa ached to ask where he had gone this time. But if Kalifsena knew, Talasa would too.

'You're tired,' she said quietly.

The Queen nodded. In almost every way that mattered, their lives were easier here, but for the corrosive exposure of Rubeo's absence. When he was here, the Queen could simply be what she professed to be – a companion, a trophy, an observer, a player in careful but ultimately safer games. When his jaunts were short, their exposure was too.

Twelve weeks.

'It isn't enough,' Talasa said. 'Not this time. Not this long. Not for an order so . . .' She hesitated.

'Finish the thought, Talasa.'

Kalifsena didn't say it with anger. She never did. Not when it had been just the two of them out on the steppes tending a dying man, and Talasa couldn't remember whether you applied bluewell raw or crushed. And not now, when they were the ones under the knife.

'So foolish,' Talasa said, and let the seditious statement hang in the air a moment before pointing. 'Look.'

Founders' Plaza was always mobbed. Messengers chased each other up and down the steps of the Bicameral. Clerks fought to keep papers dry under cloaks.

'Where's the panic?'

'I saw plenty of panic in that chamber,' the Queen said mildly.

'Exactly,' Talasa said. 'In the chamber. But the King's words should have sent the whole building into spasm. It's *their* land he's giving away. Their farms. Their holdings. Tell should have marched up there and snatched the letter from your hands.'

'You think they will stop the order leaving the chamber,' Kalifsena said. 'Suppress it.' She closed the window shutter with a snap. 'Impossible. Treasonous. And anticipated. The King has written to the Lord Seneschal of Croí directly, among others. The order is given and gone.'

'A delay is not treason,' Talasa said. 'They can call it a desire for clarification. They can spend a week arguing about a comma. You know they can. All in the name of carrying out the order *correctly*.

'Mother, every man in that chamber knows what Croí is worth. Not just to them, but to the Answering. Has the empire *ever* ceded such ground? It's an enormous undertaking.'

'It's under way already,' Kalifsena said softly.

'It is not that simple,' Talasa pressed, her frustration mounting. 'Maybe it would be if the King were here to reinforce it. But he isn't. He has made it easy for them to see him as just ink on a page. And Prince Offrian—'

'Prince Offrian is a child,' Kalifsena said. 'A child hurt that his father pays no attention to him. A child who hopes his attempts at statecraft will bring him some sort of recognition.'

That surprised Talasa. It was very rare that she saw something her mother did not, and just for a moment, she wasn't sure if what she felt was worry or pride.

'Everything you're saying is true,' she said carefully, as the carriage slowed for that eternal bottleneck at the Halberd Gate, and their escort shouted coarsely for those in the way to move. 'And he made a good showing of petulance today. He complained so loudly about missing his father's letter that it nearly made me forget to wonder how he *didn't* miss it. He has someone watching us. How else would he have come to the chamber so quickly?'

'Watching you,' Kalifsena corrected. 'Your maid. The one with the freckles. I think I am complimented by the fact he did not try and have someone watching me.'

Talasa flushed. She *knew* that maid had been paying closer attention than she should.

'I'm sorry, Mother.'

'Don't apologise,' Kalifsena said. 'Not to me. Continue.'

'What worries me more than him watching us,' Talasa went on, 'is that he stayed when we left.'

'To listen.'

'Or to offer counsel,' Talasa said. 'To act as king.'

'They won't stand for that,' Kalifsena countered. 'They barely stand for Rubeo, and he *is* the King.'

And whose fault is that?

'And if Croí is at stake?' Talasa asked instead. 'If half those nobles lose their farms and their tithes and an easy place for their sons to cut their teeth hanging boys for saying prayers? What king might they prefer then?'

'He is the *King*, Talasa. Preference does not come into it.'

Talasa didn't know which of them the Queen was trying to convince, but she was tired too, and it made her words come out somehow both clumsy and sharp.

'It does if you weigh him against a colony. It does if he sets himself for radical change in an empire that adores staying the same.'

The Queen's hand was white on the window shutter. That was the only sign she had heard Talasa's words at all.

'The next time a letter from the King arrives, it might be prudent to have a private reading for Offrian first.'

'Talasa—'

'And for Tell, if you didn't want to pick sides.'

'*Talasa.*'

Talasa fell silent.

'We've picked a side,' Kalifsena said, and now her voice *was* a little cold. 'You know we have.'

'The King's side,' Talasa confirmed. 'The only side that matters.'

'Because it's the side that's picked us,' the Queen said.

Woman of the Sinew. That was the Answering translation, or as close to it as the blunt, charmless language would allow. People thought translation was like swapping place settings at a table – a mere repositioning of meaning and alignment.

But there was no one word in the Answering that meant *doctor* and *midwife* and *trusted messenger* and *settler of grudges* and *secret-keeper* and *holy woman* and *mortician* and *reader of skies before great decisions* and *tracker of families' fates across generations*. So maybe Woman of the Sinew was a fair enough attempt. The person who kept things together, in a hundred squabbling scraps of land.

That was who the fourteen-year-old Talasa had been destined to be, until for the first morning in her life, she'd woken up alone.

The memory stung, as it always did. That was the child in her, of course. Not the Woman of the Sinew she was becoming. She had been left with water, and patience was a skill that required constant sharpening. What more did she need?

Kalifsena had come back for her a day later, of course, and when she had, it was to collect her for an audience. The rumours they had heard were true – a foreign king had come, delving recklessly into Shore territory. Seeking knowledge from the wise women who wandered *zemlja* to *zemlja,* dispensing wisdom and secrets and little packets of dried herbs.

A small place for the world to revolve around that day. Just a shabby line of wooden cottages protected by a rough earthen wall. The wind sharp. The sun bleached and heatless in the sky. There were children in the *zemlja* Talasa's age, but they had all been taken inside, and steppe-scoured men sat or squatted in the shadows of the buildings with swords and spears across their knees, glaring at the foreigners they had not the numbers or guns to challenge.

'What can you teach me?' the King had asked.

'Everything,' had been the future Queen's reply.

The carriage still hadn't moved. Talasa reopened the shutter, shrinking back in her seat as she saw just how cramped with people the wet streets had become.

Men with dirty faces and hollow cheeks. Women surly beneath soaked bonnets and caps, hair lank with rain. Many were staring openly at the carriage. Some had even hoisted themselves up on street lamps or bollards to take a closer look.

Some of those expressions were considering. Some were angry. Not a focused anger – it could have been any member of the royal household behind those curtains – but a weary sort of contempt.

'The unrest in Croí is already starving people,' Kalifsena said quietly. 'With the forces there freed, perhaps they could make a difference in the Shore. Feed the people from Zdarind instead of Mag Mell.'

'It's a thousand miles from Zdarind to Dreodyrne,' Talasa countered. 'And only five hundred from Cusp. The King's choice—'

'We are a part of those choices,' Kalifsena said. 'And we could be disloyal to that loyalty. Sell off parts of it. Barter the faith he put in us, the influence, the knowledge, in the hope that it enamours us to men like Tell and Offrian. But that is renting a house when one has been bought for us.'

What about his loyalty to us? Talasa wanted to ask, but she knew she had pushed her mother enough.

Something thudded against the side of the carriage. *A stone kicked up by the wheels*, Talasa told herself, knowing she was lying.

'We take the love we're given,' Kalifsena continued. 'We don't risk it by gambling for more. And I think I would like a sugar knot.'

That last was said in Answering, which was all the signal Talasa needed that the conversation was over.

'Daughter, would you . . .'

Talasa was already pulling back the little slotted door in the carriage wall.

'Vekk's Bakery.'

With a rumbling rattle, their direction changed.

Dreodyrne hadn't been much of a city before the great unification. Just a haphazard tangle of cobbled streets, minor palaces frequented by the thegns and aoldermen of the old nobility, and the university and archive known as Secandeur House.

Now, it was a great toad of a thing squatting by the iron-dark waters of the Dreor, never meant for the role and honours under which it found itself. Nowhere was this more evident than in the placement of the Bicameral Seat. Most settlements kept their vulnerable and important institutions on the inside. Even the *gords* and villages in the Shore did the same, from Grand Sambia to the tiny settlement that Talasa used to call home.

But Dreodyrne was an inside-out city. All of its institutions of power had been constructed *after* it had taken precedence as the capital of the Answering. The richest areas of Theobardy and Eastdeld were not cradled close to the city's centre but instead pooled out like wax cratering under a signet ring.

She'd heard Answermen spoke of that as a virtue. They were good at that – changing what things meant, finding loopholes in language. The design was intentional. It symbolised their outward-facing, expansionist nature. How little they feared attack.

Sometimes Talasa dreamed of screaming at them. Trying to make them admit . . . something. Anything. To give a single foot of ground.

And now they were in Bysmor. The inner city – the last remnants of Dreodyrne before a king called it home, a tiny nub of architectural disunity right inside the enemy's heart. The cobbles were worn, jutting out at odd angles. Tenements leaned forward, cinched tight by washing lines and stubborn scaffolds of rich black ivy, making the narrowest streets feel like a damp, dripping forest. Shops had boards in their windows now, not glass, and the crates outside were empty of food.

It was a brave thing, then, for a little bakery to fly the flag of the duchy of Grand Sambia so proudly. Talasa didn't like to think what might happen in the current climate to old Vekk had he not enjoyed the protection of being the Queen's favourite place to purchase a taste of home.

The kingscarls had cleared the street, but Talasa could see faces watching from windows. A crowd of men and women stood fifty feet from the carriage, eyeing it with a mixture of curiosity and hostility.

There was a neat rap at the carriage door and Lieutenant Gabel poked his head in. He was young for his rank, and smitten with the Queen, which made him seem younger.

'Your Majesty, if you tell me what you'd like, I can—'

'I am going in,' Kalifsena said lightly. 'It would do me good to see Master Vekk and hear the accents of the old country again.'

Gabel was too well trained to argue, but his unease was plain, and Talasa could not help but speak out in sympathy. 'I'm not sure if that's entirely safe, Mother.'

'I have absolute faith in Lieutenant Gabel and his men.'

'You are very kind, your Majesty,' Gabel said, the tiniest flush to his cheek.

He barked orders to set their escort in motion. It was a quirk of the Answering military that their various regiments had formal designations but informal nicknames, taken from the queen who had presided over their founding.

Purple Honoras. Red Grettas. Black Mirandas. Only the king-scarls had no such honorific, and they were to normal soldiers what normal soldiers were to the ragged men outside.

Had the crowd's numbers swelled? Talasa wanted to crane her head and look, but somehow that felt provocative, like baring your teeth at a dog that might bite you. The tenements leered down at her, or maybe that was just the figures in the windows, half hidden behind ratty curtains or dirty glass.

'Wait here,' Kalifsena told her, and lightly placed her hand on Lieutenant Gabel's arm as she exited the carriage.

The crowd *was* larger. It fomented and boiled, closer and closer, less a conscious movement and more an oil spill, indirect and belligerent, a mass of eyes and limbs and curiosity and malice.

'Go home, witch!'

'Who said that?' one of the kingscarls snapped, turning expertly on his mount and pulling his sabre half out of its scabbard. 'Which one of you curs said that?'

Silence. Heads turning away, then glancing back, hostility dimmed but not extinguished.

Two years behind the walls listening to slurs had given Talasa the unenviable skill of being able to write her own misoxeny. *The Queen not only rejects good Answering sense with her seances, but good Answering food as well! Perhaps she hungers for her homeland? Perhaps she secretly serves it!*

Yes, that was it. What if this was a clandestine rendezvous, masterminded by old Master Vekk? Vekk, who was nearing ninety and wouldn't know a conspiracy if it fell out of his nose.

Talasa sat, a little bored and a little afraid and deliberately scaring herself by putting words in the mouths of men and women who likely thought far more about their next meal than what a queen did with her time. She even speculated briefly that this might be a lesson from her mother to remind her just how much they needed the King.

We take the love we're given. We don't risk it by gambling for more.

Love *in absentia* was scant protection. Kalifsena should see that.

She is in love too.

Another stone clipped the varnished panelling above the window. Horses snorted. One of the soldiers, Qulm – Talasa liked knowing their names – bobbed by her window as he tried to steady his mount, his twin snaplock pistols unholstered in his hands.

Gabel's voice was flinty.

'Put. Those. Weapons. Up.'

A third stone then, and a fourth, rattling off the carriage door. Talasa risked a look out the window. The volley of stones came from the crowd in a perverse mirroring of kingscarl firing discipline – kneel, aim, fire, retreat. Someone would roll to the edge of the crowd, a rock would be flung and then whoever had thrown it would vanish back into the roil before their face could be seen.

'Hold the line,' Gabel bellowed, and then, in far gentler tones, 'Your Majesty, I think we should—'

The shot, when it came, was dazzlingly loud. So loud, in fact, that for a full ten beats of her hammering heart, Talasa thought it was a soldier who'd fired. Men were shouting. A woman was screaming, high and raw and angry.

There was a stinging wetness on Talasa's cheek.

Suddenly Gabel was there, leaning inside the carriage door, his eyes ferocious. He didn't look young now at all, though his hand was careful on her chin as he turned her head to the side.

His voice came intermittently through the ringing in her ears.

'. . . you . . . all right, my lady?'

The way he'd tilted Talasa's head left her staring dead-on at a hole in the side of the carriage. Sunlight shone through it, brighter than it should have been for this cramped, overgrown slum. The air smelled unpleasantly smoky.

And then Kalifsena was there, briskly dabbing Talasa's cheek, her own eyes so wide and glassy Talasa could see herself in them.

'Love?' Somehow Kalifsena had no trouble being heard through the ringing, or the pain. 'Cover your ears.'

The kingscarls opened fire.

11

Sister Wake

'HELLO,' SISTER WAKE said. 'What's your name?'

The girl didn't say anything. The corpse's fist tightened to snap the arrow in half.

Swallowing, Sister Wake edged closer. The girl was ten years old, or a tall seven. Her hair was dark, her skin a warm gold where it wasn't splattered with drying red. Her nose had a solid dent in the bridge.

An exemplar's daughter. Someone who had come to this island for a new life – no, someone who'd been *brought* here for a new life, transplanted to Croí by a mother and a father who probably hoped their child would be fatter than this girl was now.

Not that whatever they had wanted mattered any more. Outside this alley there might still have been a question of who would win the battle of Sciáthcrann, but here the losers were plain, piled high and face-down.

Carefully, Sister Wake kneeled, twisting her knee to fit between the crook of an elbow and a face. She didn't dare glance over at Brother Wight, in case the girl took the opportunity to bolt. Sister Wake had very little experience with children. They usually ran away from her or hid. She hadn't been this close to one in a very long time.

Say something. Reassure her. Distract her. Say something . . . normal.

Gods, what do normal people talk about?

That was what solved it for Sister Wake. There was nothing normal about this, and pretending would be a lie so great not even an innocent child could believe it.

'When I wake things,' she said, 'it's a race.'

The arrow trembled. There were tears on the little girl's face, or sweat. The day wasn't warm, but violence brought its own kind of heat to a place.

Soon, every corpse in this alleyway would be the site of its own particular war. Sinews would tighten. Blood would drain. Muscles would lose their grip on bone. Some of them still rang with echoes of souls, like the last drop of water in a drying cup. Loudest of them all was the man Brother Wight had just killed – the boy, really – his soul still chiming its horror at the unfairness of it all.

Sister Wake didn't know how the gods decided what pleas they listened to, but as the soul shrieked and pawed at her, it felt very good to shut that particular one out.

She just hoped the girl couldn't hear it too.

'It's a race,' she continued, 'between me encouraging the creature to do what I need it to do, and the creature realising that I'm doing it. I have to find the language they live by.'

She said all this in Answering, obviously. Even in the wild and ignored tracts of Umhaill you learned it, because when Answermen soldiers came round, you could get the butt of a spear in the ribs for fumbling a word.

'Rats need to eat. Cats need to hunt. I find what they're doing anyway, and I get them to do it for me.'

Someone else might have smiled. Sister Wake had lots of smiles. Smiles would be reassuring. She could do haughty grins, or mad grimaces, or eldritch smirks, which had involved some practice. Smiling was selling – that was what Mother Promise said – and for once Sister Wake agreed. She had to sell this little girl on what she was about to say.

Sister Wake didn't smile. Instead, she showed the girl her true face; a neutral, slack mask, devoid of emotion as the dead at her feet.

'What does it feel like for you?'

'My name is Mathilde,' the girl said suddenly. 'And my mama is dead.'

The whole sentence came out at once, like a running leap, and all Sister Wake could do was nod.

It was such a small word. Such a simple word, to describe the place where every living thing was headed. Everyone thought that it was one half of a coin, that life and death were equal, but in truth life was a failed match-strike, a dart of light against an eternity of cold. You would be dead for far longer than you were alive, and it was only the light and colour of life that tricked you into believing it was creation's natural state.

'Your mam is dead,' Sister Wake said gently, 'and you woke her up. Do you remember how you did that?'

'She didn't want me to be hurt,' Mathilde said. 'That's the last thing she said to me.'

It was all catching up to her now. Sister Wake could see it, blooming wild and ugly on the little girl's face.

'But she didn't say it. She *thought* it. It was everything she was thinking since the thunder broke, and she was thinking it so loud I felt the echo in me.'

The thunder. The walls coming down.

'And then they dragged us outside,' Mathilde went on. 'And I wanted to ask why they were angry at us, but Mama was angry too and it was so loud I couldn't think around it. It was so loud I don't . . .'

Her eyes tracked fiercely back and forth behind a film of tears.

'He killed her, and it was so loud in my head I didn't know where to put it, so I gave it back to her. And she woke.'

Sister Wake had spent more of her time inside other bodies than most, and she couldn't *tell* you how it felt to be a rat. These things were inner architecture. You'd have to be inside someone's skin to fully understand them. That's why she needed that last remnant of rat to do the ratting for her.

It was very strange to hear the inner architecture of her life on the enemy's tongue.

'We need to go,' Brother Wight snapped. Sister Wake had very nearly forgotten he was there. 'Now.'

'*You* woke her,' Sister Wake said to Mathilde. 'That's a very special thing you did. And I've never . . .'

She couldn't help herself. This was the very definition of a secret that should not be shared, and the moment the enemy knew of the saints there would be an unimaginable price on all their heads, but here was someone *the same as her*. The same gift. The same curse.

'. . . I've never met anyone else who could do that.'

'She wants to move,' Mathilde said. 'I just helped.'

The sudden hope on her face was awful to see. The corpse's hand abruptly opened, the two halves of the arrow falling free, and then both hands reached up, and the girl dived into them, and before

Sister Wake knew it, she was dragging the child out of her dead mother's clutching arms.

'No! *She's here I can hear her let me go let me go let me go . . .*'

Sister Wake lifted Mathilde high, and somewhere in that desperate heave, the girl ended up clinging to her instead, shaking so hard it rattled both their bones at once.

Brother Wight took Sister Wake's arm every morning to lead her from her wagon. Once he had grabbed her to throw her down on the earth when an Answering bullet had been loosed in her direction. She had been helped onto horses, and guided down dangerous paths to hidden coves, and had ice-stiff hair roughly clipped from her scalp.

Practical touches. That was all, since Da on Crom Dubh twelve weeks ago.

After a moment, she hugged Mathilde back.

'You know that she isn't,' the saint whispered. 'Don't you? You know.'

Mathilde looked up at her, eyes huge and brimming with tears. Maybe a normal child would have screamed, or fought, or bitten, or railed at all the horrible things she had seen. She had seen the person she loved most murdered in front of her.

Sister Wake had no idea what that would do to a normal person.

She just knew what it had done to her.

'I'm like *you*,' she said, and was horrified to hear her voice crack. 'And you're like me—'

'What are you doing?'

There was an old man staring at them from the mouth of the alley.

'An odd tone to take with those blessed by the gods,' Brother Wight said, hand shifting on the haft of his spear.

They were on the stage again. They were working. They were telling a story, and everyone was on the exact same page. Sister Wake silently prayed that the little girl felt the stage under her feet too. Girls usually did, far quicker than boys.

The old man pawed at his mouth with a shaking hand. Since the Cailleach had blessed her, grief made Sister Wake see her father in men of a certain age. There was no way around it. This man didn't even look like him, with his sloped shoulders and his glum jowls, but that didn't matter. The world had changed, was changing, faster and faster, and Sister Wake saw her father in the men it was leaving behind.

The old man took in Sister Wake's clothes, the dark around her eyes. He was a little quicker than the looter boy had been.

'Oh. *Oh.* I'm sorry. I didn't . . .'

It was hard, sometimes, to remember how unfamiliar normal people were with corpses. He dropped his gaze in deference, and saw the looter boy, still bleeding out onto the Answerfolk he had killed.

And fair play to him – the man drew his sword like he knew how to use it. He hadn't ended up fighting for the Rising by accident, no matter how much he resembled a grandfather lost on his way home after a few too many.

Brother Wight's spear stayed by his side. He left it there, because to raise it would be to admit to a crime.

'What did you—'

'There are Answering soldiers everywhere,' Brother Wight said. 'Hiding in houses. Hoping to spill a little more blood before we spill theirs.' His voice was rich with command. 'There may need to be a concerted search through this part of the town.'

There was already a concerted search happening. The looter boy had proven that.

'I need to talk to . . .' The old man gestured absently down the street. 'The others. They'll know . . .' His mouth worked. 'Would you mind staying here? So you can help us understand what happened?'

'Absolutely,' Sister Wake and Brother Wight said together, and all three of them knew they were lying. 'We'll wait.'

'Thank you,' the old man said, heartfelt, and with one last look at the dead boy, he turned and shuffled away.

Brother Wight made to go after him.

'He won't tell anyone,' Sister Wake snapped. 'For fuck's sake. Did you see him?' She was angry enough that she forgot to be kind. 'And you can stop too.'

Mathilde's little fists were clenched. So too were the corpse's.

'We need to *go*,' Brother Wight hissed.

Sister Wake thought faster than she ever had before.

'Do you feel all the last wishes in the air?' she said suddenly. 'All the things the dead wish they'd done, or wanted to do?'

Soldiers thought about the parry they'd missed. Men thought about whether their wives would be cold. Women thought about their children, sometimes more than men, sometimes not.

'Yes,' Mathilde whispered.

'Of all of them, this whole town of missed chances, only your mam . . .'

The girl hitched a sob back into her throat, and *now* Sister Wake held her, not as a mother but as one fighter to another, hands clamped tight on her little shoulders like she was trying to keep her from flying apart.

'. . . only *your* mam got hers. That was because of you. You let her save you. Wouldn't she be so happy with that? Her little girl kept safe?'

'Am I?' the girl whispered. 'Am I safe?'

Faded stains on white stone. A manacle scar that still itched, but only because Sister Wake was alive to feel it. It was the Rising that had named her a Sister, but it was the mountain and Brother Caid who had given her sisters. Sisters she had been too late and too powerless to save.

The blood had not yet dried on Mathilde's cheek.

'Yes,' Sister Wake said firmly. 'You are.'

12

Abelard

MACHA'S FIRST STEP broke one of Abelard's back teeth.

She moved slowly. Or time did – each second drooling into the next so Abelard had a century to track the flexing of the goddess's thigh.

Muscles rippled under skin like whales in water. Man-thick sinews hawsed tight over bone. Up, up, up came the knee – a mountain by itself, a gnarled, scarred peak. But that was where the similarity to a human limb ended. Below it was the cannon, pastern, ergot and heel of a horse, terminating in the glossy and keratinised mass of a hoof.

It hung in the air, fully the size of a Dreodyrne barbican, and then came out and down.

The impact shattered windows. Punched a city's worth of dust into the air. The entire crowd staggered as one, in what for all the world looked like some badly rehearsed dance. The same traumatic event, prismed through a thousand flailing bodies

Abelard's knees compacted. He felt a jarring snap. A salty crumble in the back of his throat.

Just a step, a single step, but suddenly Macha was terribly close. Her head yawed left and right, venting industrial streamers of breath. Abelard couldn't see her eyes anymore. He stared up at a canted, conquered angle – the way he had looked at his old bullies Saymund and Bonon, whenever they had knocked him to the dirt outside the schoolyard at Bremley.

The bottom of the chest. The back of a fist. The tensing edge of a jaw.

She was awful.

She was *fascinating*.

And then the crowd came unstuck from its terror. Abelard was abruptly in the centre of a thousand shrieking, snorting, pawing bodies, flailing to get somewhere. Anywhere. Away.

But there was nowhere to go, and nowhere to stay. There was no order and no mercy. Currents of people smashed and splintered on alleyways too packed to admit them. Hands tore. Bodies fell. There was *climbing*. Trampling. And then the clog would build again.

It felt mechanical more than biological, like a gear hitching, spinning, hitching again.

Stop-start.

One of the soldiers who had come to get him gripped Abelard's shoulders, shouting noiselessly through a mouth of blood, and Abelard saw a pink sliver floating on his lip. He'd bitten through the tip of his tongue.

RUN, came the slurring scream.

Stop-start.

The soldier was gone. A shoulder hit Abelard square in the back. Hands were in his hair, then jerked away so hard he nearly came with them. *Don't fall*, a part of him screamed. *If you fall, you die.*

Stop-start.

Macha's next step put him on his knees. Shook a watchtower right into the street and turned the air to dust and plummeting brick.

Shouts became screams. Abelard couldn't see. His knees were wet. An elbow crunched into his ear. He tried to rise, but a man in docker's grey was standing on his hand . . .

Just a moment, just a moment, if you could all give me a—

. . . and then the pressure on his fingers went away.

Netha took the man off his feet with a shoulder charge. Before he'd even hit the ground they were turning in a flare of feathers and grabbing the halberd of a soldier right out of his hands.

Its blade was wet. He'd been trying to carve his way through.

Netha gave him the end of it in his jaw, and then flung it disgustedly away. Another soldier, eyes black holes in a dust-caked face, came at them then too. Netha let the head of the halberd slip by them, graceful as a rhyming line, and then yanked on the shaft. Their forehead met the soldier's nose with a crunch. Dust turned to red mud.

The voice of the *filí* was half snarl, half song.

'Get *up*.'

Abelard got up. His limbs felt heavy and stupid, and one side of his head was a mass of heat, but he got up.

Macha was moving too.

She veered north, and every step gave Abelard the most piercing sense of vertigo, her body so large it was fooling *his* body into thinking that he was moving, not her. She tramped through a knot of towers, masonry breaking around her knees like surf on a shore, and Abelard was so entranced he half jumped out of his skin when Netha jerked him by an arm.

The chaotic, fleeing throng was parting around them like a stone in a river, but it would take nothing at all for the *filí* to be overwhelmed.

'She has a sword,' Abelard whispered. It was true, though it barely deserved the name. A brutal, half-worked piece of metal the length of a city street hung from her waist on a thong as thick as the Dreor, swinging with every step she took.

'Come on,' the poet said, the blood-mingled tears on their cheeks utterly at odds with the strength of their grip. 'Come on.'

They stumbled across the cobbles, Abelard looking around wildly. He'd thought for a moment it had been the poet's efficient, elegant violence that had shocked some space around them.

Now he could see that something had given way in the crowd instead. The dock was clearing. The ground had become churned muck, wet as a wound. Cobbles had been lifted from their bedding with the sheer force of the feet racing across them. The whitewash of the warehouses had become a frantic, overlapping tidemark of handprints – blood and sweat and glued grit.

There were bodies everywhere. Trampled into the stones. Bobbing in the water. A few – too few – were trying to rise, or crawl, or just hide, burying their faces in the dirt as if it would somehow hide them. The air was full of a dry, knifing keening, like a thousand shrilling rabbits in traps.

Out in the bay, ships had collided and tangled in a desperate attempt to escape. A fishing tug drifted on its side, men and women hanging on its sides, suffocating each other against the hull. Abelard saw pitched battle on two more – soldiers and sailors actually hacking at each other. To steal a ship or defend it, he didn't know. He wondered if they did.

She didn't even touch us. She hadn't even come close. This was just what being near to Macha had done.

'Where is she?'

His voice came out scraped and dusty. Macha had vanished. The fog her arrival had so effortlessly shredded had come down again. There was nothing above them but rooftops and a hanging caul of fog and pulverised stone.

He could have believed he'd never seen her, except that he knew he had, and who would tell themselves a lie so strange?

'Where did she go?'

Abelard had been in an inn precisely once before; the night Berrigan had received his lieutenancy in the Red Grettas. All four Caudefoy brothers had slipped from the estate under the cover of darkness to engage in what Astor had gleefully called 'behaviour unbecoming of our name and rank'.

Abelard's memories were too piecemeal to say whether that night's spit-and-sawdust resembled this inn, though there was a certain symmetry between his ale-vandalised memories and this place's desecration.

It was a dockers' respite – a wide, low room with a hay-strewn floor and rafters varnished black with decades of soot and linden smoke. The bar – just a low shelf and a couple of casks – was about the only thing left intact. Tables had been overturned. A wall had cracked from ceiling to floor. The ever-stew in a pot over the fire had overboiled to steam and sludge, and there was no sign of whoever might have spent their lives keeping it warm.

'It was a horse,' Abelard said. It was the third time he'd said it, and he didn't feel any surer of himself than before.

Netha was still standing in the doorway. There was a miraculously unsmashed bottle of something amber in their hand, though they had not taken a drink.

Every so often, the ground would shake.

'It was a *horse*,' Abelard said again.

'That's blasphemy,' Netha said, and had to stuff a knuckle into their mouth to stop a hacking kind of laugh.

'I'll admit there were some . . .' Abelard lifted the little notebook from his lap, only then noticing the furious cramp in his hand. He hadn't stopped writing since he'd taken his seat. 'Inconsistencies.'

'Oh?' Netha said. 'Do share.'

'Its head was too short,' Abelard said. 'A little too broad. There was a study with . . .' He took in their expression. 'I can explain the study later. But there's more. I counted eight different structural differences in the ears alone from typical Croí breeds, which are mostly the same as what you find in the Answering, because of our similar climates, you see. And then, of course, you have the neck, which . . .'

Netha raised a hand.

'You have a question?'

'Just a small one,' the *filí* said. 'How far down your list is the fact that it had a human body and was two hundred feet tall?'

Abelard looked down. 'At the bottom.'

Netha uncorked their bottle.

'You think it's a god,' Abelard said, and was shocked to find accusation in his tone. 'You called it—'

'Macha. The Red Mare. Queen of Summer, War and Sovereignty. Second of her sisters, but first in conquests, in vengeance and in the hearts of the Croí, because this is a land of invasions, and our sovereignty has always been under threat. On the field she was matchless, and she would take either your surrender, your hand in marriage or your head.'

Sovereignty. Those spikes of jagged white. A bestial attempt at a crown.

'No,' Abelard said, and stood so fast he toppled his stool. 'My apologies. But no. I do not believe it. I do not accept it. It's ridiculous. It's outrageous.'

'She's outside,' Netha said. 'You saw her. Do you want me to fetch her so you can tell her that to her face?'

'I am telling you it cannot be!' Abelard shouted. Dirt cracked off his knees. He had an urge to slap the bottle out of the poet's hand. Grab them by their stupid cloak and *make* them listen to the good Answering science that Macha had so effortlessly wrecked.

'Why?' Netha asked.

Abelard tried to steady himself. 'It's . . . it's too big. Yes? It's too big for meat and bone to support itself. There is a formula, worked out by Yassick and Bond and published by the Ceolmund Academies' naturalistic press. I read it years ago. It's simple physics – the square-cube law dictates that the volume of leg needed to support the volume of that body would . . .'

He talked for quite a long time, and to Netha's credit, they listened. They listened even when Abelard's voice became so wet and agitated that even he did not understand the words he was saying, and eventually he managed to force himself to stop.

'If it is real,' he said, and waved away Netha's offer of the bottle, 'then I do not know anything. I'm not a scholar. I am a young man who has read a great many books, and all of them appear now to be untrue.'

Netha took this under consideration.

'I know what is true.'

Abelard gave them a half-hearted smile. 'Oh?'

'The *Channel's Cry* got out of the harbour.'

It took Abelard a moment to understand what they were talking about. 'The ship?'

'The ship. The one you demanded take on more refugees. That captain must be commended for his speed. If they ever catch up with him to do so.'

There was blood in Abelard's mouth. He kept finding grainy little pieces of his back tooth between gum and lip. 'Netha, I am not an audience to perform for. Just say what it is you wish to say.'

Netha took a long swig from the bottle and set it down, sinking with it to the floor.

'You stand there shaken to the core because what you have studied, what you have *known* until now, might be false. I am shaken because what I have studied might be true. My god is real, and I am terrified.'

You could not have gotten such an admission from a peer of the Answering with pliers and blades, but the Terod said the words without the slightest hint of shame.

'If what we knew before is false, then we must learn anew. If what was true before is true now, then we must hold to it. You are still your father's son, are you not?'

'I am,' Abelard said softly. 'As much as I ever was.'

'And that,' Netha said, 'is what set the *Cry* and its cargo in flight. So ask yourself then, would he now step forward, or step back?'

13

Talasa

THEY KILLED THREE more people in the rush to escape. That was Talasa's count, though she could not be as precise about it as she normally liked to be.

Three kingscarls had held back their fire for a second volley. Talasa hadn't seen what or who they hit. Gabel had been in the carriage with them by that stage. Though he had not done anything as uncouth as lay himself across them, it was clear that at the slightest provocation he would, and so Talasa had thought it best to stay still.

Besides, Kalifsena's arm was hooked around her shoulder, pressing a kerchief down on the cut hard enough to bruise. She couldn't move even if she wanted to.

Kalifsena always advised against assumptions. The gap between knowledge and speculation, she said, was apt to be filled with anything – hope, fear, ambition. Nothing one could safely build on. But in this case, at least, Talasa felt her estimate was warranted. There was no such thing as a bad shot in the kingscarls.

The carriage lurched forward as they left the bakery and the screams of the crowd behind, and Talasa found herself increasingly obsessed with why three additional shots had been needed.

Had the first shots not been enough to dissuade the mob? Had there been a moment after that thunderous impact, a moment amid the wails and the curses and the echoes of snaplock fire spiralling like birds into the tenement-choked sky, when the men and women of Bysmor had stood their ground? Rallied to charge instead of flee?

The thought was fascinating in its horror. What would a counter-charge even have looked like? The mob would have overpowered the soldiers, surely. There were only six of them after all, and even a kingscarl needed time to reload.

What would the commoners have done then, once the carriage and its occupants were in their grasp? Did they even know? It did not, to Talasa at least, seem like a decision they had taken the time to consider fully.

And yet, a treacherous part of her mind reminded her, *someone had.* You could have bought a street in Bysmor for what gravedust cost to import. Weapons that utilised it were the province of the soldiery, or the Peerage.

Not a lone recidivist outside Vekk's Bakery. Not without planning. Not without sponsorship.

They hit something so hard the whole carriage bounced. Gabel swore, quietly and professionally. Kalifsena's hand on Talasa's cheek never wavered.

Four, she thought quietly. The carriage didn't even slow down.

By the time they reached the Palace, another mob was gathering in the ivy-strewn shadow of Kibard's Door. They spilled out to greet the carriage like confections from a jar, brightly wrapped and saccharine sweet. Talasa nearly preferred the commoners who had menaced them earlier. At least you could believe the words coming out of their mouths.

'How *awful*, your Majesty!'

'Something should be done!'

'We'll find the blaggard, if the good kingscarls did not already!'

'Pick her up,' Kalifsena snapped to Gabel, an instant before Talasa's legs gave way.

Her last glimpse of the nobles was their faces through the closing gate, a smeared sea of bobbing faces and clasped hands. Then the doors slammed shut.

It was comforting to be held. Gabel's arms were like iron, and they never wavered, even when they climbed the Grand West Staircase at an unqueenly pace. Cradled like an infant, Talasa tried to ignore the strange lassitude in her limbs and the arrhythmic tap of her heart. Thoughts had become slippery in her head. It was easier to just not think them, as servants gaped and Gabel's heels snapped against the tiles.

She'd always thought the Palace dishevelled in its luxury. Too many kings over too long a time, seeking to improve or to impress their mark upon the place, and now it was more argument than architecture. You'd navigate corridors built on the archaic sensibilities of the first Answering monarchs only to find yourself in a wing of airy gardens and paper screens inspired by an Erratic's trip to the sweltering south.

Wasteful, she thought. The Answering loved waste. It was a mark of honour. You had to be rich and safe to be wasteful, and there was no nation richer, except maybe the Terod.

It made Talasa think of home.

Everything had a purpose the further east you went. Nothing there was wasted. You used things until they broke, wore them until they rotted apart. Every scrap of arable land would be squeezed of its worth.

Aged six, Talasa could make the *gromnica* candles to sit on the chests of the newly dead. Ten, and she knew birthing and foaling and stitching a wound. Twelve, and she had already begun to learn the *zemlja*-craft all Women of the Sinew knew – the art of knowing which communities to help and how much, which chiefs to support and which to undermine, for the betterment of all rather than a few.

Women were ever the secret-keepers and storytellers, the hidden sinews that dictated a society's reach and grasp. Men could kill each other, but the reasons they did so fell from their mothers' mouths.

Even the Answering knew of this, in their own dim, self-centred way. Talasa had seen the sneering illustrations – hunched-over crones in dank huts hung with dried roots and jars of eyes.

Knowledge made women monsters. That was the message. Power made them ugly.

Talasa was so lost in her own reminiscence that it came as a shock to feel blankets beneath her. The plain black rafters of her bedroom ceiling were overhead. Kalifsena was talking. There were multiple voices, in fact, overlapping and arguing, and she clung to them, trying to purge the fuzziness in her head.

Night had arrived to Dreodyrne with its usual finery. Bells were chiming. The lamps of Civilian Curfew were lit, turning the sulphurous yellow mist a deep and throbbing red. In some distant plaza, the kingscarls beat the butts of their halberds against the cobbles in perfect synchronicity, a platoon's heartbeat arriving as one.

'Mother?' She had to concentrate to deliver the word in Answering, rather than the tongue that she still thought in. That was a troubling sign.

'Hush,' came the reply, and a hand pressed her back down on the blankets before she could rise.

She turned her head to the side instead, squinting in the gloom. Her apartments were those of a minor peer – just a bedroom, washroom and receiving room, the wallpaper patterned with flowers in neat criss-crossing strokes. That was the Answering all over, she had thought as soon as she had seen it. Even the flowers grew in straight lines.

One of her mother's long rolls of curatives was open beside her.

'No,' Talasa said, struggling against the hand on her chest.

'Be *still*, daughter,' Kalifsena said. 'You think I would let an Answering sawbones fumble at you?' A small smile played around her features. She had let her hair down, and it made her younger. 'No offence meant, of course.'

'None taken,' said Armin Tell. He was sitting by the room's only lit lamp, handsome features half in shadow. 'Though I see you're running low on bethanywort. I could have riders dispatched to an apothecary.'

'And now the witch has the Reeve Paramount picking poisons for her,' Kalifsena muttered, dragging the music of her accent down into a deep Answering drawl. 'Wouldn't that do wonders for my reputation with the commonfolk?'

Her pale fingers were cool as they spread the skin between Talasa's brow and cheek. Talasa obliged, widening her eye for examination. It gave her an excuse to try to catch her mother's gaze. What was this? She had never heard Kalifsena be so unguarded. Not with Rubeo. Not even with Talasa herself, these last two years.

'Can Women of the Sinew not recognise patients beyond saving?' Tell said wryly. 'Sometimes all that's left is to make them comfortable while you can.'

He spoke to someone Talasa could not see. 'Lieutenant Gabel, who gave the order to fire on the commonfolk of Bysmor?'

Kalifsena's voice was cold. 'If not for Lieutenant Gabel, we would not be here now. Do you want to explain to Rubeo on his return why the man responsible for the lives of his wife and daughter has been punished?'

Indignation, Talasa thought. A wonderful way to make an admission sound like support.

'I suspect I will have to explain a great many things to the King on his return,' Tell said. 'The career of Lieutenant Gabel will struggle to make the list. Lieutenant?'

'Yes, milord?'

There was an admirable neutrality in the lieutenant's voice. Or maybe it wasn't admirable at all. Maybe for a kingscarl, watching his career end before his eyes was no different than placing himself in a position to take a bullet, or firing one at a dockhand or roofer with a stone in their hand.

'You are dismissed. Report to Major-General Bethane's office first thing tomorrow morning.'

'Milord.'

Now Talasa *did* push herself upright, gently repositioning Kalifsena's hand with her own clammy, numb one. The room swam for a second, her mother's and Tell's faces taking on the too-sharp unreality of a woodcut or dream, and then she found Gabel, about to disappear out the door.

'Thank you, Lieutenant,' she said. It came out more of a mumble, but he nodded all the same.

'How are you?' Tell asked her as soon as the door had closed. Kalifsena guided Talasa back down onto the blankets and began rubbing something into her cheek with swift, sure circles. Yarrow oil, she guessed, from the sweet, slightly bitter scent. There wouldn't be a scar.

'I am . . .'

What were young women supposed to say when shot at? How were young women supposed to speak to the Reeve Paramount, a man just one step down from a king?

Fearfully, she supposed.

I do not want to be fearful.

'I am not the person they wanted to kill,' she said.

'No,' he said. 'You are not.' He lifted a roll of bandage and handed it to the Queen. 'Though if there was one man in this city who wanted you dead before tonight, your Majesty, I can assure you that now there are a hundred. I am not a lieutenant of the kingscarls. I do not presume to know what Gabel should have done instead of opening fire. I just know that he did, and I know that people will believe it was on the order of a foreign queen.'

'I am not a foreign queen,' Kalifsena said. 'I am *your* queen. And theirs.'

'Very well,' Tell said. 'I will tell Gabel's men to reload until all are convinced.'

He stood, smoothing his white shirt.

'There are fires in Bysmor tonight. Not just because of Gabel. Because of soaring grain prices. Because the knowledge is filtering back through merchants and spies that three platoons of Red Grettas were outflanked and slaughtered on the banks of the Dziewona by Shoresmen under the banner of the Bloody Bulls. Civil unrest is a chimera, your Majesty, and one not easily tamed.'

'Perhaps if you fed your people rather than your horses,' Kalifsena said. 'Perhaps if you told your people you were losing the two wars you are losing, instead of telling them they are the most powerful nation on earth and losing is something that happens to other people.'

'They're your people too,' Tell said. 'And your husband's.'

'I have asked him to return,' Kalifsena said quietly. 'You know what requests of a king are worth.'

'This one, certainly,' Tell said, not unkindly. 'But that shot changed more than the arrangement of freckles on your daughter's cheek. Make Rubeo understand that. If you can.'

He fetched his coat from the back of his chair and slid it over his broad shoulders.

'I must order soldiers into Bysmor. Perhaps some of the fires set tonight can be put out without further loss of life. And perhaps you and your daughter might enjoy some time to convalesce at the Summer Palace in Feondhall.'

'You're from Feondhall,' Talasa said. 'Aren't you, Reeve Paramount?'

'I am,' Tell said, and his look to her was appraising. 'And I know it well. Lovely at this time of year. Restful.'

'Armin,' said the Queen. 'If you find the assassin . . .'

'I won't,' Tell said. 'But it will not be from lack of trying. Goodnight, my queen. Lady Talasa.'

Talasa didn't correct him on her title. Neither did the Queen. They just sat in silence as the sound of his heavy tread down the corridor faded away.

'I said too much,' Talasa began, eventually. There was currency in admitting fault before it was pointed out to you. 'I revealed too much insight when I should have been a silly, panicked girl.'

'You need rest,' was all Kalifsena said. 'I will return to you in the morning, and we will think about what we shall do next.'

She kissed Talasa then, a faint brush of lips on her temple.

'I will not let them hurt you again.'

An hour passed. Talasa counted flowers marching up the walls, and recited every use of yarrow oil she could think of, as well as the lineage of the Graf of Salins, marking with clinical detachment how her thoughts firmed and steadied as time went on.

Occasionally, shots would crackle out over the city beyond the Palace walls.

Sometime after midnight, there was a faint knock at the door, and her maid slipped in, carrying a tray of water and sugar-dusted figs. Talasa watched her set the tray down on a table and turn to leave.

'When did the Prince recruit you to spy on me?'

There it was. A crinkling of the brow. A little dash of fear.

'Milady?'

Talasa let the silence hang past the point of comfort, and then smiled so widely it tugged the cut on her cheek.

'Pretend you do not know of what I am speaking and the next conversation you have will be with my mother. Do you understand?'

She had never spoken so. Not on this continent. But the pain in her cheek anchored her to this choice – a reminder of what was at stake. Maybe it would scar after all. Maybe that was fitting.

Power makes you ugly.

The girl blanched. 'Milady, please, I don't . . . I didn't—'

'Enough,' Talasa snapped. 'You will take him a message. Tonight. Stop stammering and listen.'

She gave her orders, and every time she inwardly quailed at disobeying Kalifsena, at risking the image they had so carefully cultivated, she reminded herself what her mother had said.

I will not let them hurt you again.

That bullet had not been meant for Talasa. And if Rubeo could not protect Kalifsena from wherever he was, Talasa would find someone who could.

14

Sister Wake

AND THEN IT was all over, except for the keep.

Sister Wake had enough to be at – dragging their dead steed back to its feet, bundling a drowsy girl onto its back – but a part of her was in that ongoing fight, mapping the keep by where and how the bodies fell.

Each door by the backs against it. Each cramped staircase through the blood drooling down its steps.

Out in the streets, however, the fight was done. And yet, as they trotted by smouldering cottages and sizzling dead, as Mathilde swayed sleepily against Brother Wight's stiff back, it struck Sister Wake that nobody looked much like they were celebrating.

This was it. The first victory of the last Rising. The first battle the Croí had won against the Answering in three hundred years, since those first black sails were seen on the horizon. But nobody sang. Nobody laughed or cracked open casks of ale or *metheglin*.

The streets were empty but for the dead and the damaged, or those so drunk with exhaustion they had fallen without a wound. Everyone just looked sweaty, and dirty, and full of that stoppered, stagnant anger you got when an argument had been had and nobody had won.

Brother Wight nudged the horse into a canter through the gates, and Sister Wake kept expecting one of the *ríthe* to send for them, or for one of those depleted clumps of Croí to suddenly rise in challenge.

It never happened. Sister Wake never had to find out what Brother Wight would have done to those men, or what she would have done herself. In a rare mercy that she could not quite call a blessing, they were somehow allowed to simply slink away.

It was only when she was high on the opposite hill to the *ríthe* camp that Sister Wake looked back. Shieldwood. *No.* Sciáthcrann, in all its liberated glory – field, walls and sky all masticated by flame.

It doesn't suit you, she thought. *But maybe it will, yet.*

'What happens now?' She said it quietly, though she knew from the slack slump of Mathilde between them that the girl was fast asleep. *I slept for days after my first time*, she remembered. *And when I woke . . .*

The mountainside. The bright strip of ice marking out the path the Cailleach had strode. The dream of her father singing in her head.

And the hands of the priests peeling her from the frost.

'Later,' was all that Brother Wight said.

Eventually they traded the ruthlessly pillaged forests of Sciáthcrann for healthier woods and loftier foliage. The burning castle behind them shrank, then disappeared, and suddenly they were out upon low, rolling hills studded with beds of topaz gorse.

South and west Brother Wight was taking them – back across the border into Umhaill. Sciáthcrann was one of four castles that for centuries had served the invader as sentry forts protecting the rich plains of Mag Mell. There were still outposts and patrols beyond them, but the wild russet bogs of Umhaill had never held much interest for the Answering. The land wasn't fertile enough. You couldn't use it for grazing for anything more than a meagre herd.

But as a staging point for a Rising . . . it had done the job.

The sky at their heels was still smoke-bruised from the battle, but Sister Wake found herself peering at the blue horizon all around them. Searching for similar stains. Perhaps other saints and other armies were out there, cracking their own fortresses up and down the border.

Or they could all be dead, she thought, watching flies spin away from their mount's flicking tail, drunk on the stickiness of its exposed wounds. They tormented Brother Wight too, though he was too stubborn to show it.

Sister Wake and the Answering girl they bothered not at all.

'She's dead to the world,' Sister Wake whispered, when the silence had gone long enough to drive her insane. 'Can we talk about what we're going to do?'

There was a stream, wending its way through great bulwarks of sphagnum moss. Brother Wight dismounted, filling a waxed leather bag with water. He always kept a couple, along with firestrikers and other odds and ends, in a sling bag under his cloak. Old Rising habits. It was only in honest battle you had the luxury of going back to your camp. As a rebel, you fled whether you had won the fight or not.

My beeswax, Sister Wake thought then, self-consciously raising a hand to her hair. It was still sitting back at the hillside, by that patch of frost-killed ground. *Fuck's sake.*

Brother Wight stoppered the first of the bags, and then began to fill another, face twisted in that empty scowl he wore whenever he was enduring her rather than listening.

'Come on to fuck,' she said, already angrier than she should be for this conversation to go well. 'She's a *saint.* What are we going to do?'

It was evening. The sun was abandoning them. On her horse, Sister Wake was the tallest thing for miles, and when her shadow fell across Brother Wight, it cast him entirely into shadow, but for the flat glimmer of his eyes.

'We don't know what she is,' he said, and just like that there was a knife in his hand.

'No,' Sister Wake said. 'You . . . *No.*'

'Get her down,' he said.

'What did we fucking save her for?' Sister Wake snapped. 'She's a child.'

'*You* saved her. I saved you. And she's a threat, is what she is.' That hero's mask he had worn for the chieftains, that fierce and vital life that animated his features – all that was gone. 'That's what Mother Promise will say. And she's right. The story we're telling—'

'Fuck your story,' Sister Wake said, and dived headlong into the soul of the horse, searching for threads of anger she could twist into reins. It whinnied, wet and cloggy, but that was the extent of the protest she could muster.

Had it been a warhorse, she might have convinced it to round on Brother Wight. To bite or kick out. But the track of servitude was worn deep in the nag's soul, and she may as well have convinced it to fly.

And over the living, Sister Wake had no grasp at all.

Brother Wight looked from her to the horse, knowing that she was half in one body and half in the other, and set one of the waterskins on the ground to free his other hand.

'We're at war,' he said.

And that was it, wasn't it? It wasn't a war the Croí had started. It wasn't a war where they had set the rules. The Answering had decided that all targets were fair targets. It was the Answering who had declared war on a language. On religion. On proper burials. On the names you were allowed to call your child.

In a war like that, there was no quarter. In a war like that, killing a child was not a crime.

It was retribution.

'I'm not at war with her. A child. A fucking child.' She couldn't even bring herself to say it. *We don't kill children.*

Except that wasn't true, was it? That wasn't true at all.

Brother Caid's hand in her hair, dragging her up the slope. The bite of the chain and the cold morning air.

'She's done nothing to me.'

'She's *Answering*.'

'It wasn't the Answering killed my family,' Sister Wake snapped. 'It wasn't them who killed my da.'

'They killed mine.'

And Sister Wake couldn't even be surprised. Only surprised that Brother Wight had told her when he had never told her anything else. He looked out and beyond her into the past, and told the story with the quick, clipped disinterest of reporting a battle that was already lost.

'They hanged my father for passing around a chapbook of stories about St Ardgal, and they hanged my mother for pulling a knife on them the day they came to take him to the rope.

'And they talked about hanging me. Or two of them did, at least, while the third kept his boot on my cheek so I couldn't pick up the knife my mam had dropped. Eventually they decided that it was enough to beat the shit out of me and leave me on the floor of our cottage. By the time I could stand . . .' He looked down at the blade in his hands. 'I couldn't even cut them down. One of the soldiers had stolen the knife.'

'Mother Promise will want her,' Sister Wake blurted out, desperate for some sort of solution. And more desperate still to be away from the thought of Brother Wight as a child with a boot on his cheek. 'You know she will. You know that the story she's telling is still being written. It can accommodate . . . She can *make* it accommodate Mathilde.'

'That's what I'm afraid of,' he said, and flung the knife point-down so hard it lodged itself whirring in the turf. 'Now get her down from there. We have to be long gone before she wakes up.'

Something hot and ugly as burning gravedust broke across Sister Wake's cheeks.

'You want to leave her here?'

Brother Wight kneeled, placing the waterskin carefully beside the knife. A little offering. 'I don't have any food, and we don't have time to hunt something. Bringing her to an Answering settlement will get us killed. And you're right. Mother Promise will want her.'

Sister Wake had the feeling of a child inching out on a branch they knew would not support their weight.

'And you think that's . . . bad.'

'No,' he said. 'But you do. This is your war. It was your war before the Cailleach chose you, even if you weren't fighting it. If it isn't all of our wars, I don't think we will ever win it. But it isn't her war. Not yet.

'I don't know what she is. And I don't want to know.' He got to his feet. 'A waterskin and a knife. It's more than they left me.'

'Wait.'

He scowled. 'You cannot make a single thing easy, can you? There's nothing in Sciáthcrann for her. You know that better than anyone.'

He was right, Sister Wake knew. What was she saying? Why was she wasting the minor miracle of them agreeing for once in their lives?

And yet . . .

'Were you there?' she asked quietly. 'When they found me?'

'No,' Brother Wight said. 'I'd already made my *geis* when I heard the gods had returned. My job was fighting for the goddess, not tracking her.' He looked as mistrustful of this strange new honesty as she was. 'You've never asked me that before.'

'I didn't think you'd answer,' Sister Wake said. 'When I woke up after . . . Da, and the mountainside, all I had were questions. Questions and terror. I won't leave her with that.'

Red was pouring across the sky behind them, cooling to black at the edges like iron in the forge. The first stars were out, winking in the sky like flaws.

'I can't.'

He looked up at her for the longest time. This warrior. This boy who had sworn himself to a god. And to Sister Wake, too, she supposed, before he'd even known she existed. Was that the source of his anger? Had he hoped for someone better? Someone wiser? More devout?

Instead, all he'd gotten was Sister Wake.

Brother Wight looked up at the stars, and then pulled the ring out of his beard.

'We bring her to Mother Promise,' he said. 'We tell her that a saint is a treasure, and that this girl has a place in the war, just as we do.'

He whipped the knife from the turf with a sucking rasp. Another *geis* made.

'What if she disagrees?' Sister Wake said.

'Then convert her,' Brother Wight said, and gave her the hard sigh that was the closest he ever came to a laugh.

III

The Faith of Rats

15

Sister Wake

MATHILDE WOKE ON the morning of the second day.

Dawn had spread across the sky, pale and unlovely, and Brother Wight was leading them south around the Croghan Hills – modest swells just a hundred feet high, spread wide like the knees of a grandfather under their blanket of purple moor grass.

Sister Wake wasn't sure how long the little girl had been awake. She'd been too busy dreading the next time Brother Wight called them to halt. It was far from horse-riding Sister Wake had been reared, and the pain in her arse had reached a dizzying intensity. *They never mention that in the sermons.* If the *ríthe* at Sciáthcrann had seen her staggering around cursing and clutching at herself, they wouldn't have followed her to a cask of mead.

She'd been off in her own little world of pain, and then Mathilde had nuzzled sleepily into her chest and sent a mat of prickling thorns through the older girl's skin.

The urge to pull back was ferocious. The fear that the movement would somehow dislodge the little girl was equal to it. So in the end, Sister Wake just hovered there, vibrating like a fly, as the dozing child muttered and sniffed against her.

It went on, she guessed, for longer than the occupation. And then, with a jerk, Mathilde woke, suddenly stiff, holding her body against the slow rolling of the horse instead of being moved by it.

Sister Wake felt an absurd pang of pity – sandwiched on the nag between the hard crag of Brother Wight's back and Sister Wake, there was nowhere for Mathilde's embarrassment to go.

'I'll find us something to eat,' Brother Wight said then. Sister Wake had never been more relieved to hear him speak. 'You stay here.'

He'd taken them to the edge of the Bog of Modhruadh. The landscape around them was like a dream of a country – a flat nothing foaming with spiky, mean grass, splitting here and there like taut cloth to reveal divots and pools and bog-holes.

Some of those holes were only a foot across, but all were shocking deep. As a girleen, Sister Wake had once stepped in one without looking and vanished instantly to her waist, like she'd been cut in half by an invisible blade, and only Da's hand around her arm had stopped the water closing over her head.

Brother Wight took them as far as a wide, dark geometric scar in the ground a couple of feet deep, where locals must have been lifting turf for fires. Sore as Sister Wake was, at least the earthy, exposed smell distracted from the stinking horse.

He helped her down, and then, with a truly annoying lack of ceremony, lifted Mathilde down as well, as if he'd been doing it all his life. Sister Wake tensed, boots sinking into the spongy soil, but Mathilde didn't run, or kick, or do anything. She just sat on the hairy nock of turf Brother Wight led her to, hands folded in her lap like a little lady-in-waiting.

'Don't tell her anything.'

His face was close enough that Sister Wake could see the dimpling of old scars on his cheek. Was it there the gallows boot had gone in?

Sister Wake could have been reassuring. She should have been, maybe. There was a strange little compact between them now, inked in his surprising kindness and her shitty assumptions.

Instead, she was herself.

'You're worried about Rising secrets? Who the fuck is she going to spill them to? The water? The flies?'

'I'll be back soon,' he said in Answering, and left her alone with the enemy.

Mathilde's eyes were red-rimmed and bleary. There was a skite of blood crusting on one cheek, but Sister Wake wasn't sure if she could bring herself to try to clean it. The little girl had probably never been this far from home before. The bleak bog, the morning mist hanging over marsh-holes like steam from bubbling pots – was this landscape as alien to her as the plotted grid of an Answering town was to Sister Wake?

Or was she like the rest of her people, and viewed anywhere they walked as home?

'Are you going to kill me?'

A finger came up and scratched away a little scab of blood. It was a fair question, and yet Sister Wake found herself irrationally angry all the same.

It was the accent. Clipped and hard and interlocking. The accent of magistrates announcing a new tithe and bailiffs setting the thatch alight. You could imagine it specially designed for the invasion, scientifically shaped to put the conquered in their place.

Sister Wake had never heard it from the mouth of a little girl.

'Of course we're not going to kill you,' the saint of death said brightly. 'Don't mind Brother Wight. He's a . . .' She paused for a moment to find the exact right word. 'A prick. But we're going to protect you. Keep you safe.'

'You kidnapped me,' the little girl said solemnly.

'Yes,' Sister Wake said. 'We did, I suppose.'

'Croí take hostages,' the girl continued, like she was reading from a book. 'That's what Rhetorician Daved told us. They take children who don't do what they're told and feed them to monsters. Are you going to feed me to a monster?'

'No!' Sister Wake said. 'Fucking . . . no. All right?'

More silence, as the girl chewed morosely on her lip. What had Sister Wake liked talking about when she was a child?

'Look,' she said, and pointed. 'A horse.'

Some of the horse had fallen off during the night. It hadn't noticed.

'Yes,' the girl said, warily. 'It is.'

The knot of anger in the back of Sister Wake's head pounded harder. Replacement, Mother Promise preached, was the end state of invasion. It was the fat end of the wedge. It wasn't enough to occupy the land. You brought in factory schools to occupy the space inside children's heads. And if that didn't work, and some trace of independence lingered in the hinterland of the people's souls, well then, you just replaced the people.

You parcelled up the land and packaged it and sold it, and you shipped in buyers from far off to take it, and with every new generation that sale became more and more final, and the Croí more and more a distant memory, or an oddity, pushed away and impoverished, forced into the dark corners of their own land.

Made into stories. Into monsters.

The Croí take children.

'Did you ever wonder where dead birds go?' she asked aloud.

Mathilde stared at her like she'd grown an extra head.

'I did,' Sister Wake said, plucking gently at the scrabby grass beneath her knees. 'I used to go looking for them. But anything I found was always bones already. Once, my da found a bit of a whale – a chunk of its backbone, probably, this big . . .' she waved her hands, 'thing. A great driftwood shape made out of bone, washed up on the beach like a message in a bottle. Just for us. I wanted him to bring it back up to the house, to sit by our door.' She smiled wanly. 'And he told me if I could carry it, that was fine by him.'

Mathilde said nothing.

'The *point*,' Sister Wake said, 'is that death is everywhere. Always has been. You and me . . .' A wild phrase. *You and me.* 'We have eyes now to see it. It's like . . .'

Like feeling the life go out of someone.

Like choking on that change.

'Like music,' Sister Wake said. 'Or a conversation overheard. I don't feel them when they're alive. I feel them when they're dying. It's not reaching out. They come to you. Try it?'

Mathilde gave her a wary look, and then scrunched her eyes shut.

Awkward and awful as the whole thing was, Sister Wake couldn't help but be fascinated at what Mathilde's *tabharthas* might look like from the outside. She had only ever seen her own in the eyes of others, and she had never liked what she'd seen.

After a long silence, she reached out and nudged the girl with the toe of her boot.

'Anything doing?'

'How would I know?' Mathilde opened one eye, suddenly furious. 'What is it supposed to feel like? You say *reach out*, but what does that mean? You say it like it's *easy*.'

Lying frozen to the dirt. Blankets suddenly around her. Fingers trying to pick the frost out of her hair. Someone quietly hissing when they saw her hands.

Sister Wake closed her eyes and pointed. 'A badger, five feet deep in a sett. He's old. Survived a fight with a nasty little terrier two years ago, but his shoulder has been in pain ever since and he's . . .' A soft lodging in her throat. 'He just noticed that it doesn't hurt any more.'

She swung her hand to the right, pointing out over the rolling dense nothing of the bog. 'A fox cub. Mother left him behind. Not on purpose. There was an eagle and four other cubs to take care of, and—'

A noise made her open her eyes. Mathilde had stood up.

'What are you doing?'

'Helping it,' Mathilde snapped. Her eyes were shut again, and she was jerking her head in the direction Sister Wake was pointing as if she could bang it off the sound and invite it in.

'You can't,' Sister Wake said. 'We only see a soul as it's leaving . . .'

Mathilde opened her eyes. Glared down at Sister Wake's outstretched arm as if trying to memorise its angle. Then she turned and ran.

'Fuck!' Sister Wake said, scrambling to her feet. 'Come back!'

It was like a *geis* had been broken. Like the simple act of running had reminded Mathilde that this wasn't some trek to see family or a jaunt across the wilderness, but a kidnapping by Croí barbarians.

It didn't matter that there was nowhere to run. Running was the goal.

Brother Wight is going to kill me.

For the second time in three days, Sister Wake ran too. It didn't come easy – the stiffness in her bones, the pain in her arse, too long sitting in that wagon – but she pushed herself until her footsteps banged all the way up to her scalp and her breath streaked like lightning in and out of her stocky frame.

Mathilde dipped and weaved, stumbled and scrambled, jumping clean over some pits so recklessly it put Sister Wake's heart crossways in her chest.

'You can't change it!' she shouted, huffing the words out between each trembling tread. 'That's not how it works!'

And then the girl disappeared behind a tussock, and Sister Wake flung herself those last few yards to find . . .

It wasn't a pretty sound fox cubs made. A shrill squeak, like a badly oiled hinge. But as far as Sister Wake could tell, it sounded happy. Just happy to be touched.

The other-echo, the sound below sound of a life nearing death . . . went away. Sister Wake could only see it and hear the wriggling creature through her mortal eyes and ears.

'You can't change what's going to happen to it,' she said. Her voice was trembling. 'You save a fox cub; you starve an eagle.

Everything's connected. Death has to happen. It's a chain. Changing a link . . .'

Mathilde was kneeling, holding the little pink thing close.

'I found it,' she said. 'And it's going to be all right.'

Brother Wight pinched the bridge of his nose.

'A fox cub.'

'Yes,' Sister Wake said. Mathilde glared at him from behind her. 'And it's coming with us.'

'Put it between your chest and your dress. Under the cloth. It's going to need your warmth.'

He looked at Sister Wake

'And we're going to have to hurry – it needs milk, and we don't have any here.'

'Oh,' Sister Wake said. 'I . . . Good.'

They rode on, through evening and out into a frigid, moonful night, and it wasn't until they saw a god that Brother Wight pulled the nag to a halt.

It wasn't a very big god, truth be told. Not all of them were. Before the occupation, Croí had been a land crowded with deities. Goddesses of the rivers like Boann and Sionann Fox-Eyed, the Fir Glas with their antlered crowns. You worshipped them, or appeased them, or just bribed them, the way you would any other powerful neighbour.

Most were forgotten now, of course. The Answering had hewed them down like trees, pulling them out by the root until only worship of the most known gods persisted, the ones whose domains reached into every life.

The sea. The summer. The making of things. Winter and death.

Where the Warping Man fitted into all that, Sister Wake did not know. She had never heard stories of him growing up. He had been popular in *túatha* that saw a lot of battle, and all the battles her *túath* might have fought had been lost long ago.

The Warping Man was a hero – a demi-craithur, the unearthly by-blow of a liaison or an experiment or a bet. In the south, the Érainn said he was Macha's son. In the mountains and grey stony beaches of northern Tirconaill, he was a warrior who'd come out of the sea, a madman whose berserker rage was so great that it turned the veins in his neck to standing rods, splitting his jaw like a swallowing snake.

Right now, though, the Warping Man did not look angry. He looked confused. He was fifteen feet tall and lean as a dancer, and he came out of the water of a moonlit pond like he was made of it – pale skin aglow with streaming wet, a trio of braids heavy around his shoulders. Even a hundred yards away, Sister Wake could count his veins and his bruises and his many, many scars.

He did not have his madness upon him. That was something. His face was still handsome, almost boyish, tilted upwards to the sky as if trying to catch rain that wasn't falling. A sword was a flat line of torc-stone down his back.

Mathilde went rigid. 'What . . . what is . . .'

'*Shh* . . .' Sister Wake hissed, because she knew what the Warping Man was supposed to be, but not what, in this moment, in this bog, what he would be to them.

The practice of observing religion was an old one on Croí. The practice of observing *gods* was new.

So they hid, retreating to a copse of downy birch and huddling in it, hiding from a god the way you might an elk or a bear. Brother Wight had his spear close but not raised, because the Warping Man, like Macha, who might have been his mam, loved to rise to a challenge.

Eventually, after more than an hour, he lowered his head and moved on, as if he'd seen all he needed to see. When he left, Sister Wake saw a group of men in dark *bratanna* rise from hiding spots in the bog and follow him.

There could be new commandments tomorrow.

16

Abelard

'MY LORDS AND ladies,' called Symon Aetsomne, High Chieftain of the Cauci and Lord Seneschal of Croí, 'if you could just *listen* . . .'

Nobody listened. Nobody had even taken their seats. More than a hundred nobles of Croí's fractious, half-blooded Peerage had descended upon Aetsomne's private residence outside Cusp, and the wait had only fermented their panic and anger. Men in odd mixtures of Croí and Answering finery outright shouted at each other, pushing this way and that in an effort to make more room for themselves and their voices.

But Abelard could not help but notice that no matter how many new bodies entered the Lord Seneschal's private meeting chamber, nobody would stand by the great arched windows. As if those panes of glass were somehow more vulnerable. As if Macha couldn't simply come through the wall.

The thought put his chest in a vice, and he had to speak to ease it.

'Perhaps we should come back when there's less—'

'It's going to get worse, not better,' Netha said quietly. 'You don't make the powerful listen by speaking after they've had a chance to make up their minds.'

The Lord Seneschal was not a tall man, and it was easy to imagine that it was his responsibilities that had made him so rather than some accident of birth or parentage. He looked *squeezed*, as if the weight of presiding over Croí had squashed his square head into his thick chest, the flesh of his face running downwards like wax retreating from a flame. His hair had migrated almost fully to his chin, leaving a broad swatch of pink, shiny scalp that he rubbed constantly, as if morbidly anticipating the ceiling coming down on it.

A plausible worry, today.

'My friends,' he said.

Four soldiers in grey coatees and trews stood between Aetsomne and his friends. They did not look particularly friendly themselves.

Abelard found his chest getting tight again. He hadn't been able to bring himself to search the grey-coated bodies on the ground for the soldiers who'd come looking for him. He hadn't even learned their names.

'I wish to assure you all,' the Seneschal continued, 'that we are—'

'What *is* it?'

Abelard didn't see who asked the question, but at the words, the whole chamber erupted. More questions were shouted. Half a dozen arguments broke out. And from quieter corners, one word was said over and over again, breathing through the room like a prayer.

Macha.

Netha was tense beside him. It said something to the fear in the room that a Terod had not drawn more attention, though Netha had found a dun-brown cloak in the inn and thrown it over their *filí* garb.

Not the time, they had said. *Not yet.*

But the old ways were in the room all the same. They had appeared above the city, two hundred feet tall, and the Answering's work at dismantling superstition and pagan stories had all come undone.

'It's Macha, isn't it?'

'Where's the Lord Protector?'

'Where were our cannons – I did not hear any cannons.'

'What are you going to *do*—'

In the enclosed space, the shot was very loud. A woman shrieked. Men gasped. And the Lord Seneschal handed the little pistol he had fired to one of the soldiers and flapped away some sweat from his pink and shining scalp.

'An Answering weapon,' he said. 'Made by Abnetts' of Burkeshire for my family, to celebrate a century of alliance. An Answering weapon in a Croí hand.'

'And full of Terod powder,' Netha whispered under their breath, a trace of anger in the words.

'We are of Answering make too,' Aetsomne said, looking around the room. 'All of us here. We were redesigned and reforged. It has not been a perfect process . . .'

Smiles, here and there. Rueful shaking of heads.

'. . . nor an easy one. But like any reforging, it cannot be reversed. Not without destroying what has been made. So when I *hear that name in this hall* . . .'

Soft as he seemed, the Lord Seneschal's voice rang out like iron.

'. . . I know it invites destruction of everything we've built.'

He walked to the window, clasping his hands behind his back.

'I do not know what *it* is, and I will not speculate or guess. All I can tell you is what we are doing to counter it. Cursors have been dispatched to Fort Roe, Promontory, Heronry, Merrymain. Purveyors are assessing both the damage to the city and what grain stores are accessible, considering the tithes we have to meet—'

'Tithe quotas?' an old man in a saffron cloak snapped. 'Is that what concerns you?'

'Yes,' Aetsomne said simply. 'Because it is what concerns our cousins on the mainland. More ships will come. More regiments. They will not abandon us, providing we do not panic and abandon them. Am I understood?'

Murmurs broke out. He stilled them with a raised hand.

'I remind you; you were all invited to take your leave of the city two days ago at Lambent.'

Abelard remembered the soldier's words. *The Lord Seneschal has decreed that any remaining Peerage must cast off from* . . . That was why Abelard had been approached. Peers were fleeing too.

The Lord Seneschal continued. 'You wanted to be sure there was a threat. You wanted more time. Now, time is what we ask of you. We are used to being under siege here, are we not?'

More grins. It bought the Lord Seneschal enough silence to leave the room. The soldiers around him closed ranks as the nobles broke into a dozen babbling groups.

'Come on,' Netha said, pushing through the throng. Abelard didn't hear what the *filí* whispered to the biggest soldier blocking their way, but he jumped aside as if he had been burned.

I don't know what I'm going to do with this fear, he thought. But Netha seemed to. There was a febrile energy to them. Abelard had read accounts of sieges where men fought to get *out* rather than in, because when the army pressed at you on all sides, something mad and wild in you could try to attack that pressure before it could attack you.

Netha had something to *do* now, and that gave them fuel.

Beyond the meeting chamber was a private study raftered with sunlight from high, narrow windows. Servants darted back and forth with arms overladen. There were brighter patches on the walls where tapestries had been removed, and two men were in the process of taking down a tray of what appeared to be pawprints cast in dried mud.

An old Croí claymore, nearly six feet of polished steel, sat beside an armchair. Whether it had been taken down to be removed like the tapestries, or whether Aetsomne had taken it from its hook himself, Abelard didn't know.

'Who are you?' Aetsomne snapped, standing up from his desk. A woman in dark velvet twenty years his junior stood behind him. 'What are you doing here?'

Netha removed their cloak.

'I am Netha Tal-Aneririn, fifth in train to Akinidad, Ard-Ollamh of the Six-Coloured Court. In exile.' Their smile was sharp. 'As well you know.'

In the dusty sunlight and muted wood of the study, the white and fierce blue of the garment was painfully stark. At the sight of it, the Lord Seneschal's face lost what little blood it had.

The woman who must have been Lady Aetsomne stepped into the silence. She was pretty, maybe a couple of years older than Abelard, and dressed, insofar as Abelard understood such things, for travel.

'A long-absent honour. To host a *filí* in this house. May I fetch you some food? Something to drink? You have travelled a long way.'

'Someone who knows the old customs,' Netha said, and inclined their head in a delicate bow. 'We would be most grateful.'

Only when she left did the Lord Seneschal force his voice to work.

'Are you here for judgement, *fili*?' he croaked. 'What other hoary old legends are waiting in the wings to assail me today?'

'I enjoyed your speech,' Netha said. 'Very inspiring. And you've taken a blade off your wall as well, Rí Seiseadh MacGiolla. To fight alongside your goddess? Or against her?'

'That's not my name,' Aetsomne said quietly.

'I know,' Netha spat. 'You *translated* it.'

Aetsomne slumped back in his chair, reaching out for a half-empty jug of cider on the table and slopping some into a cup.

'Is she here for me?' he said, after a long gulp. 'Is that why she's come?'

'She should be,' Netha said. 'The moment you invited invaders into our land, the moment you gave them port and landfall, Macha should have charged out of the Undercountry and plucked you like a blade of grass. I do not have curses long and spiteful enough for you, Rí Seiseadh MacGiolla. The world does not have enough days left for me to relate the crimes that could be laid at your door. The door you owned, and now borrow from the foreigners you sold it to.'

The poet pressed both hands against the small of their back as if their contempt was a physical weight. 'But if Macha did come here to judge you, she took too long, and the damage is done. The wolves are slain and sold, because the Answering could not teach them to kneel.'

Wolves kneel all the time, Abelard thought, suddenly and sickly recognising the pawprints. A trophy of something dead and gone. *But only to other wolves.*

The thought spurred him to speak.

'It is further deaths we wish to prevent, my lord.'

The Lord Seneschal fixed him with a glare.

'And who are you?'

'He's Abelard Caudefoy.' A man in Answering military garb had entered the room, his voice clipped and precise. Lady Aetsomne followed him. She at least had the decency to look embarrassed.

The man regarded Abelard and Netha with a dry, dead sort of interest.

'The question is, why are you here?'

He didn't appear an imposing figure. A little lean, a little vulpine, but to Abelard it seemed the sleek and sinewy narrowness of a fox who had spent its entire life fighting and had every scrap of weakness shaved away.

There was a pocky little scar high up on his neck. A bald spot had opened up along his forehead like an attack of mange.

'And you are?' Netha asked.

The Lord Seneschal stood so fast he splashed cider from his cup. 'Lord Protector Meilyr. I am grateful to see you have joined us, though I wish you could have spoken at the meeting. The nobility are—'

'Your concern,' Meilyr said. 'Which you must have laid to rest, seeing as you have the time to entertain civilians. My concerns are military.'

'And what does that look like?' Netha asked. 'I didn't hear bombards, or matchlocks. Where were the city's defences?'

Again, that bland look of not-quite-interest. It had taken Abelard a moment to place it, which was strange, because he'd been observing it his entire life in his father. It was the look you gave someone who wasn't important.

But Netha had the stage now and would not be ignored. 'You didn't dare fire, did you? Because even your crabbed, foreign little soul recognised that Macha—'

'Worship of profane idols is forbidden in the Answering,' Meilyr said curtly.

'Well, you can tell her that,' Aetsomne said. He was angry too, and it had thickened his accent. Abelard wondered if he'd noticed. The practised Answering edge to his voice was eroding beneath his anger. 'I'm leaving.'

'I have advised against that, Aetsomne,' Meilyr said. 'It sends the wrong message. You are the duly appointed Lord Seneschal of Croí. That is your responsibility. And your reward.'

Aetsomne came out of his slump like a chained dog, rounding on the Answering man with fists clenched. He made it two steps before the invisible fetters of propriety pulled him short.

'*My reward?*'

Meilyr was silent.

'I have done everything I was asked,' the Lord Seneschal said. He spoke the words to Meilyr, but his eyes were on Netha. 'I've taken the Rationale's taxes and quotas and applied them. With all necessary force. To my people. To my own people. I've set laws and I've enforced them. As my father did. As *his* father did. I've stamped out raids, and I've strung up rebels, and I've rebuilt the settlements burned down to settle those scores.'

'Your responsibility,' Meilyr said again. 'And your reward.'

'We are *hated*. You know that,' Aetsomne hissed. 'We are the traitor Cauci who allied with the Answering threat. And we have served that role for centuries. We have done every dram of dirty work, and now *she's* here. And I don't know if it's judgement, or if it's fate, or if the prayers of two thirds of this island have finally been answered, but all I know is we are on the *wrong side.*'

'It's the side you picked,' Meilyr said.

'But the King wrote to you,' Aetsomne said. 'He ordered the evacuation. This is what he wants!'

They seemed to have quite forgotten their observers, and Abelard could not help but listen intently. Macha's attack had driven all thoughts of anything but survival out of his head, and it was suddenly deeply reassuring to think that somewhere there was a king and a bevy of regiments preparing a response.

At least, it had been. Looking at Netha, there was a tiny part of Abelard that was not as sure.

'The King bade us withdraw,' Meilyr countered calmly. 'Not to flee with paintings under our arm and an antique sword that has never seen use. You are not a military man.'

Now there was a strange, stark passion in his tone.

'I will show you what a withdrawal means. It means pulling back in order. With all possible military strength conserved. We are not going anywhere if that retreat exposes us to further bloodshed and embarrassment' – he spoke as if the two were one and the same – 'at the hands of these savages. I will tell you when it is time to go, Lord Seneschal. In the meantime, you' – he pointed at Abelard – 'with me.'

17

Talasa

THREE DAYS CONFINED in her chambers, and as the cut on Talasa's cheek shrank, her dread distended and grew.

The first day she spent entirely in bed, futilely trying to track Tell's peacekeeping efforts by the clamour of deploying kingscarls. The shouts of sergeants and the shrieks of horns told her nothing, however. The Answering thought Women of the Sinew read fortunes in entrails and thrown bones – random patterns generating truth. Just this once, Talasa wished that were true, so that she might divine the future in the crackle of distant guns.

The worst part was that she might have known more had she looked out the window, but to her shame, she found herself quite unable to approach it.

You're being foolish.

There are fifty kingscarls and a stone wall between you and the gates, never mind the gates themselves.

Go *and* look.

But she couldn't. She simply couldn't. It had taken some hours to get as far as drawing back the blanket, glaring down at her white knees poking out from her chemise, but she could not make her legs move.

That was how Kalifsena found her on that first evening, when she arrived alongside Talasa's supper.

'Tell me everything,' Talasa said, trying and failing to keep the hunger out of her voice. She felt like Nadene at the Queen's last seance – desperate for some morsel of knowledge to put a shape on her future.

Was Kalifsena going to curtail their trips into the city from now on? Move with a platoon at her back instead of a measly six king-scarls? Were there theories on who the assassin might have been? Tell had said that finding the attacker was next-to-impossible, but perhaps if they had learned *how* he had gotten his hands on a pistol, they might—

'No,' Kalifsena said. 'Rest and eat.'

Her maid was a waif too small for the tray she was carrying. She set it down and began removing silver cloches from plates.

'Mother, I . . .' *Have been alone with my thoughts for too long. I can feel them crowding me out of reason. If I could just give some of them to you . . .*

There had been no response from Offrian. There were whole hours where Talasa forgot she had sent her message, and then something small would remind her, and she would feel sick with fear. How did the risk of defying her mother outshine the risk of an unknown man with a pistol?

Tell her. Just tell her.

'Are you having bad dreams?' Kalifsena interrupted. 'I can prepare you something.'

'I'm fine,' Talasa said. Dreams would have required sleeping. 'I would just like to know . . .'

The maid sat a legged tray over Talasa's thighs. Bread with butter and sage, a steaming pewter plate of lamb, and a little glass of red hippocras served hot.

'Eat,' Kalifsena said, already at the door to leave. 'And rest.'

That was the first day. The second was worse.

'This is good work, Princess-Undynast,' Master Colby said, pushing the stack of paper back towards her across the desk. 'You have a fine hand.'

It was late afternoon on the second day. There had been no shots at all for a long period the night before, and then a single shot fired around midnight. Talasa had been up since, and it took great effort to see her writing as not belonging to someone else entirely.

They sat in the little stateroom attached to her chambers. The open window was humming with insects and the quiet breathing of their chaperone kingscarl, a gentle counterpoint to Master Colby's creaking wheeze.

Any Answering girl of substance could expect tutoring in music, dancing, languages and sewing. It had also been deemed necessary for Talasa, as a foreigner, to be given passing instruction in the more masculine subjects of history and geography.

Talasa wasn't sure where the Queen had procured Master Colby – a man built to the design of a newborn sparrow, all neck and wattle and querulous bobs of the head. He did not display the proud red-and-whites of the Ceolmund Academies, and so might have been from one of the smaller, poorer colleges they had replaced.

Talasa's rapport with Master Colby was her rapport with the Answering in miniature. Excelling would have garnered the wrong kind of attention, so instead she asked dull questions designed to receive dull answers. She displayed no interest in her history lessons towards matters of war and state, and a modicum of interest towards frivolous details like dresses and what people ate.

Diligent but uninspired. That was how Master Colby described her to her mother. Not that Talasa needed to hear it. She had put so much work into eliciting that response, it felt like she was writing the reports herself.

Previously, it had merely irritated her. It was easier to pretend to be unremarkable out in the world, where nobody was really looking anyway. In here, she had to stare into the eyes of another person and intentionally disappoint them.

But that had been before. Before a night spent trying to work out just how careful the Palace was in hiring its stable hands, and how far one could get into the building before being challenged. Before a night spent pressing her split skin into her cheekbone, and wondering how far it would have to tear before her mother would understand her fear –

'And the content of the essay, Master Colby?'

'Perfectly fine,' he said, skating over the score of mistakes, inaccuracies and misspellings she had deliberately included. 'And of course, you have a fine hand.'

Talasa's fingernail scratched at the pristine white margins of the essay. It was customary to leave space for masters' marks and corrections, but Colby had not written any.

'I did notice one inaccuracy,' she heard herself say.

I know what you're doing, Mother. Kalifsena had been a healer before she had been a queen. If she thought Talasa needed rest, rest was what Talasa was getting.

But there was no blank white space inside Talasa's head. And it was hard to believe that resting was safe, when she had spent two years being invisible and a bullet had still managed to find her cheek.

You did not make me to be idle.

'You should not berate yourself,' Colby was saying, tapping the page. He was missing the top of his index finger, Talasa noticed. Just below the nail. It must have made turning pages irritating. 'Even true scholars make mistakes in their work. Why, I remember—'

'It isn't my inaccuracy,' Talasa said. 'It's yours.'

Master Colby looked like a hatchling that had fallen out of its nest. 'Excuse me?'

'You told me that the Answering formed as a result of an invasion from the Tattered Shore. Led by the Starling King.'

'Uh . . . yes. Four of the easternmost fiefs bonded together to repel the barbarian . . . ahem . . . hordes of the Shore. After the groundless attack had been defeated, their leaders – the First Among – realised that togetherness meant strength, answering hostility with—'

Don't say it. People remembered arguments, and being remembered was not what Talasa was for.

'You say groundless,' she said. 'All the books do too. None of them mention what happened the summer before, when a raiding party from Longreach crossed the border and burned two villages to the ground, or the spring before that, when boats from Feondhall travelled up the coast and butchered . . .'

She stopped when she realised the pages in her grip had crumpled and torn.

'I find myself quite tired, Master Colby. My apologies. Could we take this up in our next lesson?'

He left without a word.

On the third day, Talasa went mad.

It was a quiet kind of madness, characterised more by hiding symptoms than displaying them. She spent the morning washing and combing the sweaty, exhausted tangles out of her hair, before being perfectly amenable to the maid . . .

Not the usual maid; the usual maid had not returned.

. . . and eating a light breakfast of porridge, nutmeg, and apples.

You would be hard pressed to tell, just by looking, that she had gone mad. She had spent an hour staring in the mirror to make sure that it was so. But she must be mad, because her mother had told her to do one thing, and now Talasa was doing another.

I have an appointment to keep, she told herself. *Wouldn't it draw more attention to miss it?*

There were two kingdoms run out of the Palace of Dreodyrne.

The first was the Answering, obviously. A half-million square miles of once-proud fiefdoms, from sun-baked Lodemagan to the frigid upland slopes of Druingill and Cilkeld, now uneasily mortared into an empire by men long-dead.

This kingdom might have been wandering in sluggish circles without the guiding hand of its King, but still it moved, and day in, day out, the neat little men of the Royal Cursors set out with orders regarding everything from the maintenance of the King's roads to the price of his fish in the rivers.

The second kingdom was smaller, but no less vital, and it was run from a single office on the third floor of the Palace's east wing.

Talasa had dressed in a demure black kirtle belted below the bust, a transparent partlet reaching bodice to chin. Her hair was bound beneath a soft pointed cap in a dull rose, which took a little notice from the stark red scab on her cheek.

For all the architectural largesse elsewhere in the Palace, the east wing was far more functional. Corridors were narrower, ceilings lower. The general pace here was faster – it was unbecoming for servants to run where a peer might see, but down here, they ran all the time. The floor tiles were meticulously cleaned but old, chipped but not replaced.

Nowhere were they more worn than outside this door.

Talasa paused before knocking. Her hands were wrapped around her narrow wrists, but even if they had not been, she was sure they would not shake.

That porter's eyes had lingered too long, hadn't they? Ogling the Queen's daughter? Or wondering was now the time to drive a knife into her . . .

Sweat was hot and rashy down the hollow of Talasa's spine.

She had just been raising her hand to knock when the door opened. The man who had opened it bowed to a societally proper degree.

'Princess-Undynast.'

'Master of the Elaborate.'

You might picture a man who kept the appointments of the royal household as being nimble, or delicate. Like a letter opener, or a quill – a dainty tool for dainty work. That was true, to a point.

The Master of the Elaborate was an enormous man, blocky as a guardhouse, his every breath a strain on the buttons of his neat black coat. When he moved, though, it was on a precise and hidden set of hinges – everything contained in its neat, oiled arc.

He bade her enter, and she did. The office was merely an antechamber to a far larger room, one she had never seen, where the true and chaotic nature of the work was done. This room was meant for entertaining those guests of higher status, and so was passingly comfortable – a low settee for waiting, a cushioned chair set up before the Master's enormous, pristine desk.

The great book of his office was already out in front of him, turned to the correct page with a single clean swipe. Inside it, detailed in his neat hand, was every request, invitation and letter the Queen had received in the past week, so that Talasa could relay them to Kalifsena for review.

'I trust you are well?'

No mention of the chaos outside the Palace. It made it easier to lie.

'Very well, thank you. And you?'

'Well and hearty, Princess-Undynast.'

It was the answer he always gave, and it looked to be true. There was something of the Speaker of the Bicameral in the Master of the Elaborate. Someone whose role in the Answering's hierarchy had subsumed their entire identity, or just replaced it completely. Men were groomed from birth to be reeves too, of course, but they still carried their name and family interests into that role. It was a means to an end.

The man before her probably did have a real name. Potentially a family too. Most men his age did. But his position was what mattered, and that, as always, made Talasa feel quite bad in what she was about to do.

'Please let me know if you need any clarifications.'

He said this every time she visited. People liked to think that ladies of the Peerage spent their days fanning themselves and drinking tea, perhaps with some light reading or flirting alongside. Talasa might have thought the same, if she had thought about Answering ladies at all before coming here.

But collecting your mother's appointments was a tradition even in families that did not boast a Master of the Elaborate. It was a neat education on how to manage a schedule, how to write letters, how to accept and reject an invitation gracefully.

In their own way, the young women of the Answering were all of the Sinew too.

Talasa leaned over the leather-bound ledger, withdrawing a small bound table-book in which to make notes.

'Thank you, sir.'

The Master of the Elaborate probably thought her stupid. Most people did. It would have taken anyone a long time to jot down every single request for an audience with the Queen.

For Talasa, it took twice as long. She usually made a little performance of it – frowning to herself, scribbling out and rewriting names, poking the tip of her tongue through her lips as she counted twice or three times over.

'I wonder,' she said casually after some time had passed, 'if I might have a glass of hippocras?'

Last week, it had been water. The week before, she had not asked for anything at all. You didn't want to give the Master of the Elaborate a pattern to learn.

'Of course, Princess-Undynast,' he said, and vanished into the back.

Talasa did not hesitate for a moment, dragging the book to her and skimming as many of the thick, creamy vellum pages as she could.

It wasn't the most exciting act of espionage that had ever been conducted in the Palace. Most of the requests weren't even secret. Those that were undoubtedly went through other channels – clandestine meetings outside the Palace in back-alley taverns where pomades were hidden in fists to block the stink.

And if the Master of the Elaborate sent a servant to fulfil Talasa's request, which he often did, then she couldn't see anything at all.

Oh, it had paid dividends once or twice – given Kalifsena some morsel of knowledge or a connection she could use – but more often than not it was as useful as pretending to laugh for lords at a banquet.

Busywork, Talasa thought, for the first time. *All the things you gave me to do. Was it just busywork?*

Requests for audiences and accepted requests were recorded in different sections of the ledger. Talasa knew that from experience. The former for the King was overflowing, which was no surprise: lords asking for audience on petty matters, a bevy of academies, concerns and trusts, even her own Master Colby, though the reason for that request had not been recorded.

The most recent were, of course, those with the most to gain and the most to lose from a withdrawal of Croí.

'Was it frightening?'

There was a girl standing in the doorway. She might have been sixteen too, maybe a little older. It was hard to tell because she was only a head and a pair of hands, poking out around the door frame like an illustration in a picture book.

Talasa froze, trying not to look guilty about the book on her lap.

'Was what frightening?'

The girl came around to lean against the door frame. Her servant's coat and white kirtle were marked here and there by a strange, personalised insouciance. The sleeves had been rolled up to expose broad, tanned arms that immediately reminded Talasa of girls at home. Her collar was unlaced, and sprigs of dark hair had fallen down around her long, freckled face.

She didn't so much as glance at her father's purloined tome.

'Being shot at.' She said that last with a tiny touch of exasperation, before remembering herself. 'Princess. Princess-Undynast. Your Grace.'

Talasa could not help but smile. 'Just the middle one, I think.'

What was the right answer here? Should she play the uncouth foreigner, unfazed by violence? Or the proper Answering lady, scandalised that the staff were being so forward?

'Yes,' she said plainly. 'Yes, it was frightening.'

The girl nodded thoughtfully.

'You're the Master's daughter.'

They looked alike. The same square frame, the same forthright thrust to the chin, even the same dusting of freckles, as if they'd shared the same summers between them. Which, Talasa supposed, they must have. The only point of difference really might have been the smile, as Talasa had never seen the Master smile, and this girl was smiling even as she talked about fear.

'He'll be a minute. Some of the porters didn't show up today, with the riots and all. And there are quite a lot of gifts.'

'Gifts?' Talasa asked.

'It must have been frightening,' the girl said, as if Talasa hadn't spoken. 'Your poor mother too. The Queen, that is. I wanted to ask her, when she summoned me, but of course that would have been—'

'Wait,' Talasa said sharply. The girl blanched, hands reaching up to shove those errant curls under her cap. 'What do you mean, when my mother summoned you?'

When the Master of the Elaborate entered again, Talasa had not returned his book.

The man was controlled enough in his reactions not to speak, but she could see the tension in every line of him that some part of his miniature kingdom had been annexed.

'My mother has already received her appointments. And apparently denied each and every one of them.'

A prickle in those impassive features.

'At her request, Princess-Undynast. And I must apologise for my daughter. She's a curious girl.'

He didn't sound apologetic. He sounded proud. Normally Talasa would have liked that, but right now she could feel that brittle madness again, drawing tight every muscle in her skull.

'Can you tell me where the Queen is now?'

The Master of the Elaborate looked as uncomfortable as she had ever seen him. 'I'm afraid not, Princess-Undynast. She left the Palace this morning. I do not know where.'

It was a long walk back to her chambers. A long walk during which Talasa's body moved as if it were sleeping but her mind worked harder than the porters carrying an endless parade of letters and gifts.

The Master of the Elaborate had informed her she would soon have her own section in his book for requests and messages, but if that was supposed to be a comfort, she did not feel it.

Well-wishers. The pile on her receiving table grew and grew. Talasa saw the slim black cases in which Tatana's put their chocolates. The air filled with the vibrancy and sweetness of flowers.

Gone. Kalifsena had never left the Palace without her. Even when Rubeo had been so adamant about showing her the estate in Idegeld where he'd grown up, and they hadn't left their bedchamber, and Talasa had spent a peaceful two weeks wandering the grounds by herself.

The last time they had been apart for any more than a few hours had been that day on the steppes. The day the Queen left Talasa to seek a king.

The memory kindled in Talasa, hotter and hotter, until she felt like flinging the window open and standing before it to feel fear again instead of rage.

It was truly bad luck for the freckled maid that she chose that moment to reappear.

'Where were you?' Talasa snapped. 'I sent you to—'

The maid wordlessly handed her a card.

Talasa recognised it as soon as she saw it. She'd helped write enough of them over the years, sealing them in envelopes and carrying them down to the Master of the Elaborate so that he could send them to admirals and ladies and yes, even a prince, though he had not responded.

Until now.

It was the very same invitation Kalifsena had sent Offrian – though by the yellowing, it had spent the last two years on a windowsill or a desk being slowly varnished by the sun.

Talasa recognised her own handwriting, detailing the chamber in which the seance was to be held – *had* been held, by now. The original date and time had been scratched out.

Underneath, in fresh black ink, the prince had written one word.

Tonight.

18

Sister Wake

TODAY, THE BEATING heart of Croí's last Rising was an Answering manse on a hill, overlooking the black and angry waters of Sceir Bay. An eternity of spray and salt had pared the hill it sat on down to a jagged talon of stone, and on either side, cliffs bracketed the setting sun, funnelling the wind right into the back of your skull.

There were many secret ways the Rising signalled its own. There had to be, to find each other if a raid went bad, or ward you away if a meet was too perilous.

Those ways had evolved when Sister Wake had been found. Nobody left two leaves spliced on a rock for her, or a spiral cut into bark. She had been questing out with her senses for days, navigating a path by a dead rook with a broken wing here, a decapitated rat there. She didn't know how other saints communicated with the Rising's leaders. Mother Promise had never offered to tell her.

And Sister Wake had never told Mother Promise that she remembered and resented every sacrifice. Every little life. Why bother? She knew what the old woman would say,

What are a couple of dead mice against the freedom of a people?

'Up there,' Sister Wake rasped. The wind was salty, washing away the resinous stagnancy of the bog. 'I'll let them know we're coming.'

She swayed a little then, and Brother Wight's hand suddenly hovered just a hair above her arm.

Waking wasn't tiring in the way fighting was tiring. It was tiring in the way family could be tiring. Tiring like a day trying to keep little cousins out of the fireplace or arguing with uncles about land or food or who insulted who thirty years before she was born.

Connection had a cost.

'I'm fine,' she said wearily. 'Mathilde, stay with him.'

The little girl did so, the fox cub a sleepy, squirming bulge under her dress. Mathilde was less wary of him now, which Sister Wake wasn't sure she liked, even if she could feel the hungry eyes of the little girl on her back as she led the horse back down the gravel road.

It wasn't privacy for herself Sister Wake was after. It wasn't even really for the horse. Any dignity in life it had possessed had been stripped away long ago, by grapeshot and gods.

But she could do this small thing to give it dignity in death.

'Goodbye,' she said, and pressed her forehead to its damp, flaking muzzle. 'And thank you.'

'I felt it,' Mathilde said excitedly, as soon as Sister Wake returned. 'I felt it go. And there's a mouse in a burrow just under us, and there's a . . .'

Her voice caught in her throat. She looked on the verge of running again, except that there was nowhere to go but into the red sky and the iron waves.

That was the thing about awareness. Once you had it, it was hard not to follow it to the end.

'I feel it too,' Sister Wake said. There wasn't much else she could say.

* * *

The ugly bulk of the manse did nothing to block the wind as they climbed. The gale battered them, insistent as a child, turning Sister Wake's *brat* into a leaden weight she had to push, step by step, up the little gravel path. Mathilde was struggling, plodding. Even the hardy shore grass had given out.

As they approached, shadows stepped out of shadow to receive them, detaching themselves from standing sheds and the house's black gable. None carried torches, despite the sun departing. Light discipline was one of the first lessons the Rising taught you.

Even when the first of the warriors came close enough that Sister Wake could make out their features, it was no real help. Like Brother Wight, any distinguishing details had been smoothed away. Deeds and scars made them the same as each other, and different from everyone else.

Their leader was a rangy woman with dark skin and the hitching gait of an old wolf, her cheeks as scarred and pocked as the spear haft in her hand.

'Knight,' she drawled in the Croí heart-tongue. Most of Mother Promise's inner circle spoke it exclusively, as a point of pride. 'Saint.'

She didn't bow, or kneel, or pray. Why would she? This wasn't the outside world, where deference to a saint was a useful recruitment tool. Here, they were all working the same job.

'She inside?' Brother Wight asked. He didn't say anything about Mathilde, and the woman didn't ask. The grandly carved wooden door opened, spilling light and warmth out into the night. Sister Wake felt Mathilde tense beside her at even that tiny taste of comfort.

'Come in to fuck,' a voice called in Answering. 'Before all the heat gets out.'

*　　*　　*

Beyond the door, there was a foyer you could have put Sister Wake's whole cottage in. The floor was dressed stone. Answering men glowered impotently from portraits. An enormous hearth boiled and roiled with flames, and in front of it, warming her wrinkled hands, was Mother Promise.

'Let me look at you,' the old woman said.

Croí was an island with a lot of cultures and a lot of accents. This was something the Answering, with their ghastly love of unity, had never bothered to learn. The Rising had obtained copies of Answering plays where the Croí characters were consistently shifty and sly – as if bargains with a Tirconaill meant the same as promises to the Airgialla.

But all you needed to do to understand the beautiful fractiousness of the Croí was listen to their voices. Cauci spoke like they were sharpening steel – a nasal lyricality that suited a laugh and a threat all at once. The Érainn sounded like they were about to burst into song with every question they asked.

If you had the gift for it, you could nail a man to his *túath* by the way he rolled his 'r's or dragged the arse out of a vowel. Sister Wake had sometimes wondered whether that was why Brother Wight spoke so little. So she couldn't decipher any more than he cared to share.

But Mother Promise sounded like she was from everywhere.

Nobody would write songs about her beauty. She wasn't tall and pale and sylvan in the way that women in religion were supposed to be, so beautiful they were sexless, high-cheekboned and made of marble. Instead, Mother Promise was squat, and round, and she ran the Rising the way another woman might have run a kitchen, or regiment, or trading shop.

'Were they not feeding you?' she muttered, stepping so close Sister Wake could smell the salt of her breath. 'Did you not make them feed her?'

This was to Brother Wight, who stood with his wrists crossed behind his back. Mother Promise wearied him near as much as his saint.

'You'd expect it from that *rí* Marcan, he'd take the milk out of your tea, but I thought better of Bradán.'

Mother Promise wasn't the only leader of the Rising. They weren't an empire with a king at its head. But anyone who knew anything knew that she was the one that mattered. There were a hundred stories about where Mother Promise was from. Sister Wake had overheard exaggerations and conjecture and outright lies at a dozen different campfires, so many that you'd nearly believe her a saint herself, for all the contradictions.

But what was *known* was that the little old woman in front of her had criss-crossed the island a thousand times, keeping the faith alive through secret meetings and hidden masses and lessons for five or ten children at a time. She'd navigated the ranks of the priesthood – mostly male, mostly old, mostly burdened with the kind of manic ego it took to keep the faith when an entire empire was trading farms for your scalp.

She had to be mad too, Sister Wake thought, as she often thought when the old woman nattered on like an addled aunt and then ordered the assassination of a tax collector without so much as a change in tone. But it was the kind of madness that endured, and it must have been the kind of madness that was catching, because now they were out in the open, and the whole Rising had begun to revolve around her.

'Mother Promise,' she began, squeezing Mathilde's hand in reassurance. 'This is—'

'Food first,' the old woman said. 'Follow.'

Sister Wake opened her mouth to protest, even though it had been a day of hard waking since their last meal and her stomach felt glued to her spine.

Brother Wight caught her eye then. *Let the old woman play the concerned mother*, the look said, *if it buys you some consideration later.*

Grudgingly, Sister Wake relented.

See? She thought. *I can be reasonable.*

Prick.

Mother Promise struck out for a half-hidden door under the stairs, leading them into a long hallway. Rooms split off on either side, and Sister Wake glimpsed more warriors, sprawled out on the floor under blankets or huddled in deep conversation. 'The deeds upstairs call it a *summer* home.'

The hallway led to a kitchen with a table big enough for twenty, and a whole armoury's worth of pots and pans hanging from ceiling hooks. A great sweating stove loomed in a corner, and a saucepan so large you could only call it a cauldron bubbled away on top, along with a smaller pot of water.

'Imagine it,' Mother Promise said, shooing away two of the most murderous-looking warriors Sister Wake had ever seen so she could sit down instead. 'Keeping a whole house stocked with food and servants just on the *off-chance* you might visit when the weather is good.'

'There was fighting?' Sister Wake said as she sat, more for Mathilde's benefit than anyone else's. They could both still feel the wisping soul of the body thrown out the back.

'Silly bastard,' Mother Promise said. 'The other servants were Croí, and happy enough to go home.'

The lean, wolfish woman had followed them in.

'Mother Promise,' she said, almost gently. 'The child.'

Mathilde shrank behind Sister Wake.

'You're right,' Mother Promise said, and plonked a steaming bowl of soup down on the table in front of Mathilde. 'She looks hungrier than all of ye.'

Mathilde looked at Sister Wake, eyes huge.

'Go on, sit,' Sister Wake said. What else could she say? The whole room watched the little girl nervously take a seat, and Sister Wake heard audible intakes of breath as Mother Promise sat next to her and banged a spoon down beside her bowl so hard the whole room jumped.

'And after,' Mother Promise said in heart-tongue, giving Mathilde an encouraging smile, 'you can tell me about the girl.'

'You can get some sleep in here,' Sister Wake said.

The room was large, the carpet bone-white in the moonlight. The night outside had turned bleak and gusty. Clouds couldn't hang onto the sky, and though the stars could not be winkled out of their sockets, the gale was polishing them to a mirror gleam.

Sister Wake dragged the thick curtains closed. There were no servants left to do any lighting of the fires, and the whole house was cold as a tomb.

'You're not staying?'

'I need to talk to Mother Promise. About you, and what you can do.' *And what we're going to do about it.*

'I won't do it again.' The words fell over themselves in an effort to escape. 'Not if they don't want me to. I don't want to make any trouble. I'll . . . I'll stop, and I'll go home, and . . . and you could come too? We could just go.'

We. When had that happened?

Head across the Unbeknownst Sea where there are no priests at all, and I'll wake you every morning with a song.

Wasn't that what Da's great plan had been? Sister Wake could barely remember. She hated him sometimes, though the fire of that feeling lived on the other side of the wall of ice. Hated him for finding her. For giving her hope. For not cutting that chain fast enough.

For lying to her that there was a place of safety in this world.

'I'd like that,' Sister Wake said. 'But I need to speak to Mother Promise first. Don't worry. I'm not going anywhere but downstairs.'

Mathilde looked at Sister Wake's hands for a long time, and then let them go. Sister Wake's last glimpse of the little girl was Mathilde standing in front of a bed that dwarfed her, gently laying the cub down on the quilt.

'People,' Mother Promise said flatly, as soon as Sister Wake re-entered the kitchen. 'She can raise people.'

Sister Wake glared at Brother Wight.

'Don't be giving him the evil eye, girl,' Mother Promise said. 'Did you think I wouldn't have questions as to why you're not at Sciáthcrann?'

It was just the three of them in the kitchen now. The wind rattled the window frames, but the steam above the pot was straight and undisturbed. A square of parchment sat between them on the table.

From somewhere under her cloak, Mother Promise took a stubby bit of lead and began to draw.

The island of Croí emerged from the paper as if from dense, ochre fog – first the headland on which the house stood, then the bitten-in bay of Ceelim, before the grainy sweep north up the Umhaill coast turned into the mountainous headlands of the Tirconaill, where not even the Answering tried to go. From there, the land softened as it drew further south, where the landmass of Attercope, home of the Answering, sheltered even as it strangled.

With quick, delicate movements, Mother Promise sketched lines for the rivers Tuag and Bandea, crosses for the cities of Cusp in the east and Tornflag in the south-west, and squares for forts like Sciáthcrann and Merrymain and bastard Promontory. She turned the lead on its bevelled edge to shade in grey patches for the haunted, holy forests of Dairbhreach Donn in the north and mourned, plundered Craobh Dháithí in the south-east, too close to the Answering to survive.

Then, bisecting the whole thing, she scratched in the mountain range of Anu's Scar, which spread patchily down across the stomach of Croí like a bolt of lightning.

A pause, as if she were savouring the sight of it.

'Three thousand warriors to Sciáthcrann.' She sketched four lines, beginning in the west and spreading north-east, east, south-east and south. 'Another six to Oftenord, with two purloined cannons and Brother Able at their head.'

Sister Wake had met Brother Able. His red eyes. The brutal, slavering head on him, snorting and twitching like a doped horse. Only in battle could he ever be called saintly.

'Sister Ore to Bitanbill. Sister Eel to Fort Domond. Brother Alabaster to . . .' Her finger paused just before drawing a fifth line. 'Well. We all have our *geiseanna*. The things we must do. The way you were supposed to be taking her east alongside those three thousand men, and not coming back here with a little foreign girl in tow.'

Brother Wight looked ashamed.

'Mother Promise, I—'

'Hold your whist, boy,' Mother Promise said, sounding so much like Sister Wake's da that the saint sat straighter on her bench. 'Or are you drunk on victory too? We won a fight. That's all. And maybe we'll be lucky and win the others too. But tell me this . . .'

The old woman ground the heels of her hands into her eye sockets and then blinked angrily at the sheet in front of her, as if disappointed it hadn't changed.

'Was the garrison at Sciáthcrann understrength?'

'It was,' Brother Wight said, frowning. 'How did you know?'

'A year I've spent,' the old woman said, 'courting *túath* after *túath*. Making promises and counting heads and trying to remind broken old *ríthe* what it might feel like to be whole. And I could have done with another year, or two, or five. Do you know that they're digging up the old sites?'

This was how it was with Mother Promise. She had an island in her head, and you needed to be spry in your listening to follow her to every corner of it.

'The old tombs?' Sister Wake asked.

'Aye, at Dornóg and Maigh Slecht and Boilg-on-the-Sea. Men with pulleys and spades and kegs of gravedust, taking our history out of the earth in splinters.'

Sister Wake thought of the walls of Sciáthcrann. Of men pinwheeling in the sky. Coming apart in clouds.

'Why?' Brother Wight asked. 'Why would they do that? What's the point?'

'Same as it's ever been,' Mother Promise said grimly. 'To unmake us. That made me want to go to war, just like I wanted to go war when they hanged Father Lug who came before me and taught me how to make my life a thing of meaning.

'But I didn't. I couldn't. The Answering lose a battle, they raise another regiment. We lose a battle, and a generation passes. A generation where they ransack and ravage us and leave every Rising less than it was before.'

She tapped the page before her.

'Though it kills me to know our land is being parcelled away and our priests are being hunted down, I wanted to wait. Wait until the Answering lose their war in the east, or win it, and are too depleted to win another.'

'What war in the east?' Sister Wake asked.

Mother Promise just shook her head, rising to take Mathilde's empty dish to the wash basin in the corner.

'Instead, girl, we're doing it now, half-arsed and half-prepared, because we know well the enemy's strengths, and those strengths are retreating.'

The word was shocking for how little you heard it.

'From . . . from us?'

Mother Promise snorted. 'I wish. Did you see any gods on the way here?'

'The Warping Man,' Brother Wight said. 'Out on the bog.'

'And how did he look?' She asked the question with the kind of quiet dexterity you might use about a mad uncle in the other room.

'Wandering,' Brother Wight said. 'And . . .'

'Go on.'

Again, that tone, like the demigod victor of a thousand unearthly wars was an ailing grandmother you had to keep away from the sugar.

'Confused,' Sister Wake said.

'Aye,' Mother Promise said, busying herself with filling the basin full of hot water. 'They're like that. Since the turn of summer, we've charted more than a dozen of the People of Anu – her wild and mighty tribe. Ogma the Poet. Manannán Mac Lir and his Nine Waves. Brí of the Smithy. Macha the Red Mare. The Cailleach.'

Something in the stove popped. Sister Wake jerked, and then scowled at it.

'Not just gods either. Smarter priests than me have started calling them *Nemed* – the old word for sacred. Heroes and villains and craithurs from every story and legend we've ever told. The Four Cities have been seen in the clouds. The King of Otters is gathering a court. Swarms of Olliphéisteanna mate in the Unbeknownst Sea. *You.*'

'Me?' Sister Wake said. 'I'm not a—'

'A girl, blessed by the Cailleach, who can raise the dead beasts of our land to defend it. You're as mythic as an oracle crow, and your hair isn't too far off it either, providing the crow was wet.'

Brother Wight coughed suddenly, and Sister Wake fought the urge to tip the boiling pot over him.

'You're a blessing, girl. And doubly so because we know you to be true. We can listen to you. We can talk to you. But the gods . . .'

The full tilt of blasphemy. A line you only crossed when you were desperate, and as Sister Wake looked at the bog-hole-deep furrows on the old woman's face, it occurred to her that Mother Promise had lived her whole long life as scared and desperate as she herself had been on the summit of Crom Dubh.

'And we've tried. We've sent envoys. Followed the old rituals. Made offerings.'

Sister Wake's blood turned to ice. 'What kind of offering are you—'

The old woman didn't turn around, but her shoulders set in a hard line. 'Girl, I've told you. The day we find that monster Caid is the day I show you what happens to men in this Church who hurt children.'

Mother Promise wasn't called that for nothing. There were plenty of true believers in the Rising, but the rest were paid with promises, and that included Sister Wake.

A Brother's scalp would get you a farm.

A foolish hope, to think it could buy Sister Wake some peace, but that was the bargain they had made, once the war was done.

'Yes, Mother Promise.'

'And I've told you that before.'

'Sorry, Mother Promise.'

'Nobody listens,' she grumbled to herself. 'And that's the problem.'

Another bowl went into the suds, and she scrubbed like it had offended her personally.

'The gods are back. That's a blessing. A blessing we've been waiting a long time for. And they're not required to listen to or obey us, certainly. We are but their worshippers. But in the old stories they *did*.

'In the old stories, we prayed, and the gods answered, and we are praying to them now, but they will not listen. Macha stalks from fortress to fortress. Brí of the Smithy has dug herself a nest in the highest peak of Anu's Scar and no offering will draw her out. The Cailleach did not go far past the peak of Crom Dubh, and any priest or messenger I send to her does not return.'

Sister Wake's eyes burned with the memory of ice. For a moment, she couldn't breathe.

'The Cailleach is still there? Doing . . . doing what?'

'I don't know,' Mother Promise said. 'Would that I could have waited to find out, before the island rose.'

Sister Wake couldn't but struggle with that revelation. She wasn't stupid. Of course Croí needed its freedom. The Answering couldn't be allowed complete the long, slow erasure they had begun three centuries ago. That was purpose enough for Brother Wight, and sometimes for Sister Wake too.

And on the nights it wasn't, she told herself the gods had purpose too. That she had to be here. That she'd been chosen for a reason. That it wasn't dumb luck that it had been her on the chain, and not the O'Cuain girl.

The Cailleach chose me. That's why I'm here. That's why I'm fighting, instead of going home and freezing Brother Caid's breath in his throat. That could come after, if there was an after.

The gods had purpose. They *were* purpose, in a way. Avatars of sea. Land. Poetry. Death. They knew what they were at.

Didn't they?

It was harder than you'd think to work out emotion from eye sockets alone. Had the Cailleach looked grimly dignified as she'd stared down at Sister Wake that morning, or . . . had she looked a little lost?

'The gods' arrival has forced our hand. A handful of *túatha* have sworn to rise, but too many seek to watch and wait, or settle old scores amidst the chaos, or worse, turn against us to curry favour with our occupiers.'

'They wouldn't dare,' Brother Wight snarled, more animated than Sister Wake had ever seen him.

'There'll always be those willing to sell wolves.' The old saying was sharp in Mother Promise's mouth. 'Eógan Split-Lip has taken the opportunity to reignite his old feud with the Aidhne. Four full *túatha* have gone to war over the *rumour* that the Spear of Luige, against which no war may be sustained, has been sighted. *We kill each other.*'

In those four words Sister Wake heard the lethal rage at the core of Mother Promise, and she would have rather charged a whole gunline of Answering bombards than the old woman in front of her now.

'Any advantage of surprise we had vanished when the first walls fell. The Answering can respond in weeks. Less, maybe. And when they do . . .'

'A hundred thousand men under arms,' Brother Wight said. 'At a guess. Maybe more.'

For once, Sister Wake didn't have anything clever to say. 'That's a lot of men.'

'We couldn't match it,' Mother Promise said wryly. 'Only a united Croí has a hope against the Answering, and that includes the gods. Everything we've gained. Everything we've risked. Everything we've *preserved* over three centuries of extermination – we win it now or we lose it for ever.'

'How?' Sister Wake breathed.

The four lines. If you drew them out to their conclusion, if you imagined each dusty scrub of lead against paper a marching army, a series of victories, an empire falling back again and again . . .

They met at a single point.

'Promontory,' Brother Wight said.

'That's where we're headed,' Mother Promise said. 'We bleed them as they run. We fight them when they turn. We win, and we win, and we win again, and every victory brings another squabbling *túath* to our cause. And if we hold that bay, it makes their hopes of re-invasion far more dangerous.'

'They'll just land somewhere else,' Brother Wight said. 'Won't they? Promontory is their stronghold on Croí – it's where they like to land, but they're spoilt for choice. That's always been the trouble. They're too close. Reinforcements can be against us in a day. Less, with good weather.'

'That's always *been* the trouble,' Mother Promise said, and drew a curve in the sea that might have been a wave and might have been a crown. 'But our seas are more dangerous now. And Answering generals are creatures of habit. They learn from the previous generation of generals, and them from the generation before that. They'll sail to Promontory because that is where you land when invading Croí.'

'But if we held it . . .' Sister Wake murmured.

Mother Promise gave them both a wicked grin. 'In the first years of the occupation, when Answering influence was spreading out from Cauci in fits and starts and they were chasing our free *ríthe* up and down the countryside and putting prices on our heads, you had a choice. Submit and beg for mercy . . . or go buck wild and hope you caused enough havoc that their only option was to give you a pardon.'

Sister Wake was incredulous.

'That's your plan? *Vex* them into submission?'

Mother Promise shrugged. 'Half their lords think we're a waste of men and coin anyway. If we can convince them a war of retaking is simply too much of a burden between gods and saints and stolen guns . . .'

'Freedom,' Brother Wight said. There was something quivering and starry in his eyes. 'Finally . . . freedom.'

'Which brings me to the girl,' Mother Promise said. 'Where does her *tabharthas* come from? Can she tell you?'

Sister Wake shook her head.

'Shite,' Mother Promise said. They watched her work for a moment, and then she spoke quietly over her shoulder. 'I don't know how any of this works, girl. I wish I did. I'm a priestess. If I don't know, who does?'

Saints, probably, Sister Wake thought.

'But they can't harm the gods,' she said. 'Can they?'

'If they can't now,' Mother Promise said grimly, 'they'll learn. We know how industrious they are in their killing. How imaginative in their oppression.' She chuckled helplessly. 'Haven't they made a study of killing us?'

And there was something about the way she said it.

'Mother Promise,' Sister Wake said softly. 'What has this got to do with Mathilde?'

When Mother Promise turned, white suds clung to her thick arms.

'You don't hate the Answering the way we hate them. And that's good! It's good. I don't want anyone to hate anyone. You're a saint. You're supposed to be better than us. I often wonder is that why the Cailleach chose you, or is it the way she changed you. You hear the dead. You understand the cost of this war better than anyone.'

Her smile was half fond. Sister Wake had seen her forgive men come to kill her with that smile. Had seen her order their execution in turn.

'But I hear the dead too. Three centuries of them. And they cannot have their freedom, but they want us to have ours.'

Sister Wake stood. 'I'm going to see Mathilde,' she said plainly.

Brother Wight stepped around the table to block her way.

'You don't hate them like we do,' Mother Promise said again. 'That means you don't understand them. You don't understand the danger they are.'

'Mother Promise . . .'

'Even I don't,' the old woman said. 'Not really. They took the land, and they made us farm it for them, and pay them what it grew as rent. Even when I was a little girleen like you, I didn't know anyone living who remembered schools. Free schools. Schools that didn't teach Answering history and Answering victories and Answering gratitude for the Answering boot on our neck.'

'Mother Promise, please . . .'

'And then when we still wouldn't behave, they shipped in new versions of us to fill the new versions of the towns they drove us out from. That's why she's here, isn't it? That's why she and her family are on our soil at all. So they can inherit it from us.'

Sister Wake's senses stabbed out, looking for something, *anything* she could raise. Only silence answered her.

'Where is she?'

'I won't have their children inherit my gods as well,' Mother Promise said simply. 'Not when they've taken everything else.'

19

Abelard

'I TRUST YOUR journey was pleasant.'

Lord Protector Meilyr did not sound as if he trusted Abelard at all, even in that small regard. His words were the anaemic pap of propriety the Peerage was duty-bound to offer one another at first meeting, whether that meeting was conducted over brandies at the Peregrine or as shot whizzed overhead.

I think I'm becoming cynical, Abelard thought, and was absurdly delighted. He'd only been here a day.

'Adequately comfortable,' he said. 'And I thank you for the room, and your hospitality.'

One of Meilyr's men had led Abelard to a modest chamber upstairs in the residence to wash and recover himself. In the chaos of Macha's coming and everything that had happened after, Abelard had barely noticed how filthy he'd become. It had taken several basins of warm water to crack and scrub away the coarse patina on his skin and clothes.

Then had come the tray of rye bread, a wedge of butter, slices of ham and a grainy, savoury paste in a thick stone jar. There was even a cup of good Modigmark cider, which Abelard was not ashamed to say he drank in two swallows. The simple acts of eating and drinking had given his mind space to wonder whether he would have been as brave or as foolhardy without the metallic edge of hunger in his head.

He'd barely finished the plate in front of him, hunched over his room's little writing desk, when Meilyr had entered, closing the door behind him.

Lord Protector was not a rank Abelard had been familiar with before today. It certainly came with a handsome uniform. The fog-grey of Meilyr's Croí regimental coat was crowded out by silver brocade, his high-waisted trews cut to the knee to reveal pristine white-stockinged calves. He might have been a picture in monochrome if not for the livid scar on his neck and the precise little flush of his cheeks.

The name Meilyr too was not known to him, though that could have been more Abelard's terrible memory than anything else. It was expected, as a peer, that you were aware of the crucial lineages and kept abreast of crucial postings. The fact that Meilyr had known him was proof of that.

Abelard had been expecting a summons. Certainly, his father would never have deigned to visit a guest in their room. The fact that Meilyr came here personally was not unnerving in the way Macha's existence was unnerving, of course, but it was disconcerting all the same to see simple Answering manners just a fraction out of true.

And now, Abelard wilted under that pale, assessing gaze, feeling an abrupt and unpleasant remorse for all those beetles he had kept in jars as a child.

'The food is hearty here,' Meilyr said. 'At least. I assume your luggage was lost at the docks. Do you need a suit of clothes?'

'That would be very kind,' Abelard said, forcing a polite smile as he brandished a ratty sleeve. 'I fear I would not pass muster in—'

'And then you can explain why your father sent you here.'

Abelard stiffened. 'My father?'

'He is well, I presume?' Meilyr bit off each word precisely. 'I met him once. When he still frequented the capital.'

'He is well, thank you,' Abelard said cautiously. Bad as he had been at learning the Marquis's many lessons, he knew enough to leave it at that. The circumstances of their leaving Dreodyrne were no one's business but his father's, and yet it was everyone else who liked to speak on them.

'Any Answering peer who could leave has left,' Meilyr continued. 'You must be here at his behest.'

Again, that inflectionless, muted passion. Anger?

Or shame?

'I admit to some surprise that he sent his youngest. Then again, your brothers all earned commissions, did they not? And now he has invented one for you.'

It *was* shame. Abelard had lived a life around military men. They often favoured a pre-emptive strike when they felt their honour was at risk.

It made what he said next all the more dangerous.

'My father has many interests here.'

It was the truth. Just as it was the truth that lords and generals had lost their titles and their heads for far less than this unfolding disaster. Just as it was the truth the Lord Protector would have Abelard on the first boat home if he knew he was here unsupported.

And Abelard could not let that happen.

Meilyr's eyes searched his.

Be careful. Be useful.

'But I am not interested in tithes or land,' Abelard said. Another accurate statement. 'My background is in the natural sciences. My interest is the . . . animal. Perhaps if you were to relate recent events to me in your own words, I might be able to . . .'

He trailed off rather than promise anything specific, and Meilyr stepped easily into the gap. He went to the window, hands clasped in the small of his back. There were troops moving outside – clearing the Croí nobles from the courtyard, shouting to each other about deployment and supplies.

'Your brothers have the luxury of serving closer to the heart of the empire, but we are used to barbarism here. You have not served . . .'

It wasn't a question.

'. . . so I will provide some explanatory commentary. As Lord Protector, I am responsible for all Answering military forces across the colony. There are deputies, of course. Some appointed by me. Some not. I can furnish details.'

Abelard wasn't sure why that might be relevant, but it seemed best to show interest.

'I would appreciate that, thank you.'

'Do you know the history of this place?'

'I'm afraid not, Lord Protector.'

Meilyr absorbed this without comment.

'The other men who have occupied this position kept journals. I do too, as a matter of tradition. It helped me, in the beginning, to understand that this is a place of cycles. A map cannot hold the nuance of it. It plainly presents the border as the border. Lands within and lands without.'

He tapped his scar.

'In actuality, a biological metaphor is better suited. After King Ceolmund conquered this island, the position of Lord Protector was only supposed to be a scab. A temporary measure meant to facilitate healing.'

'I understand,' Abelard said. He was quite relieved that Netha was not here.

Meilyr let his arm fall.

'But the people here resist. The scab gets picked at. The growth of healthy pink skin is arrested by probing nails.'

His voice was tight. Angry.

'Animal scratching, arresting any true progress. The scab comes away, and then the wound must be cleaned out so all can begin again. That is my role. That has been the role of my predecessors, to varying degrees of success. Do you require ink?'

Abelard started, then began to organise his writing implements. It was striking, even with Meilyr's stern appraisal, how treacherously comfortable it felt to simply do as he was told. To be useful.

Father will want to know what happened here.

When Abelard was ready, Meilyr began. He spoke for a long time. He spoke in great detail, and Abelard began to understand what this audience had become, despite Meilyr's initial hostility.

A defence of the Lord Protector's character and career.

He spoke about grain production in the fief of Mag Mell, and the quotas that kept Answering men and horses fed. He spoke about missing patrols, and stolen carts of meal, and an increase in the number of hangings, and then he spoke about how the increase in hangings had not led to peace, so the hangings had been increased again.

'Apologies, my Lord Protector, *who* did you hang?'

Meilyr frowned at the interruption.

'There will be a list somewhere. Rebellion here takes a hundred forms. Secret societies, pagan cults, tenants' righters . . . Even in Whiteseal, recidivism thrives like maggots in bread. At first, I believed these stories to be just that.'

'And when did you realise that it wasn't?' Abelard asked. 'Rebellion, I mean. When did you learn that it was something more?'

'When good men started speaking of it,' Meilyr said. 'My men. You have to understand, this colony can very easily turn into a scatter of isolated outposts, with the countryside in between ruled by those who have no right to it.

'Rebels like to bait us. They play at being disorganised. At being unserious. A raid here, a theft there. So you send twenty soldiers, because you are stretched as it is, and those twenty vanish, and no matter what you do to the locals, they will never tell you where the murderers went, even though you can smell their sweat in the rafters.'

Abelard's stylus paused. 'No matter what you—'

'I know which of my men to listen to,' Meilyr continued, as if Abelard had not spoken. 'When *they* spoke of strange animals threatening our good exemplar settlers, I rode out myself. And . . . I saw it.'

'Macha.'

'I did not grant you an audience to hear pagan filth from your mouth.'

Not a muscle of Meilyr's expression had changed. The growl had simply slid out of him like a sword from a sheath, and the raw fury in it folded Abelard's lungs in half.

'I am sorry, Lord Protector. Please continue.'

There was no indication that Meilyr accepted the apology, but he did resume his cold, clinical debrief.

'Seeing the animal for myself was galvanising. I had already expressed my desire for reinforcements to the Rationale in Dreodyrne, but there was no way they would believe a letter stating the true nature of the threat. So I acted in a manner seemingly beyond my predecessors. Decisively.'

The soldiers outside Abelard's window. The nobles crying out for cannons.

I will show you what a withdrawal means.

'In what way, Lord Protector?'

'Cusp is too sprawling and primitive to be truly defensible,' Meilyr said, brushing an invisible speck of dust from a silver-brocaded cuff. 'And there is always the risk of seditious elements within the city as well. I have written to my deputies. Ordered a general recall of all available strength to Promontory, on the east coast. The bay there is far more easily defensible than the one here, and not clogged with so much civilian apparatus.

'Every man that can be spared. Every grain of gravedust. Every artillery piece that can be put on wheels, or sleds. Then we can . . .'

He paused.

'You said you were an expert in the sciences.'

That wasn't quite what Abelard had said, but he did not think it wise to correct.

'Somewhat, my Lord Protector. I—'

Meilyr cut him off. 'Does that mean you have an insight into the animal's behaviour?'

'Understanding anything is a process of discovery,' Abelard said carefully. 'If there is a process here, we are at the beginning of it. Whatever this creature is, whatever its origins, its classifications, physiology, diet, whether it is, and I apologise, a creature of flesh and blood or something else we have yet to understand . . . that is yet to be deciphered.'

Meilyr pursed his lips, but when he did not immediately comment, Abelard decided it was safe to press on.

'The accounts you received of these . . . anomalous animals would be invaluable. I would like to interview those who came to you with stories of sightings. And consult with Netha – the Terod who was accompanying me – as they may have cultural insight I do not.'

'You'll receive whatever you need,' the Lord Protector said. 'I just have one question. Can you lure it?'

'Lure it, my lord?'

'I served in the New Territories as a young man,' Meilyr said, picking once again at that pink little scar. There was a strange urgency to the motion, as if trying to get out something under the skin. 'I've seen it done with man-eating stripers in jungle villages. The natives know their ways and can lure them. Can you figure out a way to draw it somewhere?'

'Potentially,' Abelard said, thinking furiously. 'If its mind works along the same paths and prompts as an animal's, it will stay where there is reason and move on when that reason does.'

'Good,' Meilyr said. 'Yes.'

Abelard was learning that the Lord Protector's indifference was preferable to whatever was happening now. Sweat had beaded on the balding man's pate. His face was flushed.

'Lord Protector, what would I be luring it to?'

Meilyr smiled for the first time since Abelard had met him.

'To Promontory, so that we might kill the damned thing.'

'What?' Abelard breathed. 'Lord Protector, if I may—'

'You may not,' Meilyr said, suddenly and ferociously animated. 'Whatever your father sent you here to do is irrelevant now. We have a chance to burn this crisis out at the root. My orders—'

'Are yours,' Abelard said, his voice shaking. 'I am not a soldier, and grateful of it. Luring Macha from the city . . . it might be possible. And if it is, I will attempt it, because it will save lives. *Answering* lives, as well as Croí. But I will not help you beat her into a trap so that you can perforate her with cannon shot. What if you just . . . make her angry?'

'*It*,' Meilyr hissed. 'Of course, death is a possibility. Do not threaten me with the life I already lead. There is nothing in this world that can face the kind of artillery the muster will provide. And once it is dead . . .'

'My lord, this is madness.'

'. . . then we will devise a solution for the rest of them.'

It was unclear, in that moment, if he were talking about the gods, or the Croí as a whole.

'The King's orders were to withdraw,' Abelard said desperately. 'Not—'

'We are indeed withdrawing, as the King has decreed.' Meilyr sniffed. 'You might be the highest-ranking peer by blood on the island right now. But blood is not everything. Neither you nor the King is a military man. The thought of having to re-establish ourselves is one I will not countenance. This place is not worth another bill of good Answering lives.'

'But you'll spend them on challenging a goddess?'

You are as mad as that soldier at the docks, cutting his way through fleeing civilians, Abelard thought, and was filled with the crawling need to flee back into those flattened streets with their piles of dead, because that felt more comprehensible than the man in front of him now.

He stood stiffly.

'Thank you for your hospitality. But I and my—'

'*Filí*,' Meilyr said, butchering the word. 'That's what he is, isn't he? I recognised the cape.'

Abelard did not dare answer.

'A dangerous thing to be. It was Lord Protectors who organised the first executions.' Meilyr straightened his coat with a practised flick as if preparing for parade. 'Though they are rare prey now.'

'Threats do not become you, my lord,' Abelard said with a bravado he did not feel.

'It isn't a threat. It's the law. My responsibility. As it is my responsibility to not just pacify but civilise the Croí.'

Meilyr sounded like he was reciting something, but the vehemence with which he said it was all his own.

'That is one aspect of them to which I will give credit. No matter what I do. No matter what lengths my predecessors went to. They retain that independence still, and the *filí* most of all.'

He turned smartly on his heel and strode to the door. Abelard flinched out of his way.

'How fortunate to have one available now, so that I may see what happens when I put that creature's head on a pike.'

'I won't help you,' Abelard whispered. 'I won't.'

'Then you'll spend the rest of the crisis in this room,' Meilyr said simply. 'And you can write to your father and tell him you have chosen the enemy's side.'

20

Talasa

YOU SUCCEEDED, TALASA thought, looking down at the dismantled spectre on her bed. *This is what success looks like.*

Under any real kind of illumination, it was a pathetic little thing. Just an oblong of stiff wire teased – with no little effort, she remembered – around a wooden pole with a narrow little cross-bar to serve as a set of shoulders.

The real magic, of course, was the muslin veil. With the right shadows and the right drink in hand, this sad little lozenge of cream cloth and wire became a visitation from the dead. Men had wept before it. Women had left their seats to try to cradle it, only for Kalifsena to call them back.

'I'm always so surprised they listen,' Talasa had once remarked. 'Their husband, returned from his death on the border. Their son, risen from his cholera bed. I keep expecting them to grab at it. To ruin everything.'

'You've answered your own question,' Kalifsena had said, stitching intermittent sections of the veil so that swinging it back and forth created the suggestion of cheekbones, the billow of unearthly wind. 'They don't want to ruin the illusion either. Remember that, my darling. They want this. Own their wants, and you own their soul.'

Talasa had laid out their entire arsenal neatly on her bed. Powders to tint flames, scented candles snug in their straw, a whole succession of wooden planchettes ready to sit under the hand and tap out messages from the gregarious dead.

This preparation was a ritual too. You did not want to discover you had run out of lovage or lemon balm the day before your guests were due to arrive. The speaking trumpets must be clear. Kalifsena had always procured new cheesecloth for every seance, because if you were going to fake the production of teleplasm by producing it with a flourish from your fingers or drooling it out of your mouth – though they'd decided that last was beneath a queen, to Kalifsena's great relief – it should at least be clean.

Talasa's fingers ached from clutching Kalifsena's own planchette – a simple heart-shaped piece of wood on two castors. Would that she could communicate with her mother through it, instead of the *nawia* where spirits were supposed to dwell.

Can you tell me where the Queen is now?

The Master of the Elaborate had not gone so far as to display pity. That was the only thing stopping Talasa from flinging the planchette across the room.

Women of the Sinew had always had apprentices – a way to secure lineage of knowledge, but also because you needed a hand holding the cut closed so you could stitch it. You needed someone to keep watch while you slept. You were not supposed to be alone with the work you needed to do.

It was not the last rule Talasa would break tonight.

'Where are you?' she said quietly, in the language only one other person on this continent understood. 'When the King's grip is slipping, and that grip is the only reason we are permitted to exist?' Herb wraps in waxed paper, slippery in her sweating hands. 'What are you doing?'

And why am I not a part of it?

Anabaster for truth, when you wanted them spilling their guts because they were watching for spirits, and you were watching them. Baleteen for bad sleep and vivid dreams. Metolves for a blurring of the edges, just enough that anything seemed possible. A touch of faewort to make those possibilities pleasant instead of something to fear.

It was one thing to have been left at their little camp in the riverbed. She knew how to protect herself from steppe-adders there.

And then Talasa turned another packet over in her hand.

It was a killer of pain, usually. You didn't use it unless you absolutely had to because it was fiercely addictive. A spoonful in someone's drink and they would experience the most wonderful lassitude for a couple of hours, and then they would kill their own children to have another.

But if I were just to slip a couple of grains into his wine . . .

Own their wants, and you own their soul. That was how Kalifsena had done it with Rubeo, wasn't it? A flirtatious reveal of tradition and lore, the way another woman might reveal a smile or some skin.

Talasa would have to succeed in dosing the wine. Offrian would have to drink it. And he'd have to not realise what she had done, or not even her mother could save her.

She looked at the packet for a long time, and then she threw it down onto her bed. After a moment, she picked it up again and set it back in its clasp, the way Kalifsena would have.

Then she packed up all the equipment neatly and locked it back in its case.

There were a modest eight Gentlemen of the Chamber currently assigned to the royal household. It was a privileged position – assisting the serving monarch with dressing, waiting on him as he ate, providing companionship, guarding access to his bedchamber. The number had been larger in the past. Fought over, sometimes.

Now, however, that august institution had fallen into disrepair, because it was hard to accompany a king who kept disappearing.

Two of the Gentlemen – Lords Baver and Welfin – had disappeared off with Rubeo on his latest adventure. The rest were forced to attend the only royal they were capable of keeping up with, and so it was no wonder that when one did knock on the door of the stateroom, he did so with a barely concealed frustration.

'Sir Adger,' Talasa said, as pleasantly as she was able. 'Are you well?'

Sir Adger Gibb was broad, petulantly handsome and of an age with the King he was supposed to be serving. Waiting on a boy of eighteen years was not, probably, where he had seen this position leading.

'His Highness the Prince will be here in a few moments.'

'Thank you,' Talasa said.

He gave a grudging nod and took up a place by the door. Talasa frowned.

'That will be all, Sir Adger.'

Adger's eyes narrowed. 'If the Prince wishes me to stay . . .'

'He can tell you so,' she said.

A hint of a flush stained his cheeks. Sir Adger Gibb had been on the edge of his seat when the spirits had spoken. Talasa wondered did Offrian know that.

He retreated to the hallway outside, and in the sudden silence she had to fight to keep her heart at a point where it could not be heard outside her skin. The candle fluttered beneath her fingers, a weak point of light against the bright lamps screwed to the walls.

And then the Prince was there, opening the door so hard it nearly blew the candle out.

'Is this it?' Offrian said, by way of greeting.

'Your Highness,' Adger began in tones of saccharine devotion. 'Would you like me to—'

'Fuck off, Adger,' Offrian said, without looking around. Adger closed the door.

'He thinks I don't know he attended one of these,' Offrian said conversationally. 'It was hard enough to take him seriously before.'

The Prince's rich red houppelande swirled around him like autumn leaves as he strode back and forth across the chamber. His hair was longer than was fashionable, and he'd bound it back with a strip of the same material. The lace on the sleeve and collar of his shirt bobbed and rustled as he turned a lamp this way and that on its gimbal arm.

'Good evening, your Highness,' Talasa began. When Kalifsena did this, she sat back straight, shoulders level. She only moved when she wanted to draw your eye to her. Less was more.

'There's a woman in Bysmor,' Offrian said, slapping a lace-fogged hand on the table as he bent to look underneath it. 'I don't know what she did before you two arrived. Probably a fixture of the inn stage and dramatic hall.'

'Did you . . . lose something, your Highness?'

He lifted his head sharply, laying it on the table like a child playing a game. It was unexpectedly charming.

'She has a cabinet,' he said. 'Enormous thing. Though I suppose it would have to be. She invites people into her home, charges them two scruples – *two* – and then gets inside it. When she emerges . . .'

He shoved himself upright and dragged a chair out on which to sit. Talasa had preferred it when he was distracted. Now, the heat of his gaze could have lit a candle by itself.

'. . . she is stripped to the waist. Draped in muslin cloth. The spirits do not have a sense of modesty, it seems. She sways from side to side. Speaks truths about the future. Men can touch her stomach and feel the icy chill from the passage of spirits under her skin.'

He tattooed his fingertips on the table in approximation of applause.

'I was expecting a cabinet, is all.'

'Not behaviour befitting a royal,' Talasa said coolly.

Offrian grinned at her.

'You're not a royal.'

She looked away before he did, and Offrian leaned back in his chair. 'Adger!' he shouted. 'Wine!'

'It's better not to have interruptions when we begin—'

'Have we begun?' Offrian interrupted. 'Where is she? If she's not going to step out of a cabinet, and she's not hiding under the table, where have you hidden her?' He looked at the walls. 'Father used to tell me there were secret rooms. Even promised he'd show me them. Adger!'

The sudden shout made Talasa flinch.

'The Queen didn't send for you,' she said, and despite the exhaustion and the dread and this precarious conversation, there was pride in her words. 'I did.'

The look on his face was almost worth it.

Adger entered, a carafe of wine and two glasses in his hands. For a long moment, the sound of him pouring was the only noise in the room, and to his credit or his training, he knew enough to leave right after.

'Do you know what the first rule of a seance is, your Highness?' Talasa asked once the door had closed.

Offrian's voice was soft.

'Lie?'

She forced herself to smile. 'No, your Highness.' She indicated the bare walls, the bright circles of lamplight. 'The first rule of a seance is that you never conduct one with an unwilling audience.'

'Because the spirits take offence at non-believers. Isn't that right?'

Talasa gave her best approximation of her mother's liquid shrug.

'Because it is a compact. Speaker and listener. You can't talk to someone who does not want to listen, and there is no point speaking if you will not be heard.' She placed her hand around the candle. 'You came. And I'm not here to talk about my deception.'

A long sip of wine. 'No?'

'No,' she said. 'I'm here to talk about yours.'

Talasa was no stranger to discussing the policies of the Answering. She and Kalifsena had spent long evenings dissecting treaties and edicts, learning unfamiliar terms and fief-wide pressures, trying to understand those secret pressures and influences so that they would know danger when they saw it.

But that was in her own language. Saying it in the tongue of the enemy made Talasa feel far more exposed.

She did not wait for his response. 'I was there. I heard the Queen read out King Rubeo's command. And even he knew that the Rationale would drag their heels. That's why he circumnavigated it.'

'It's a complicated situation,' Offrian said lightly. 'I wouldn't expect you to understand.'

'I know you wouldn't,' Talasa said, just as genially. 'And you're right. It is complicated. It's complicated because the Rationale do not want to withdraw from Croí, and neither do you.'

'Why would that matter?' Offrian asked, but she had something, and they both knew it. 'The King has spoken.'

'Written,' Talasa corrected, and the Prince's eyes narrowed. 'Written a couple of lines to instigate what could be a generation's work. I can't imagine what a complicated affair it must be to withdraw from a territory. How ruinously expensive it might prove.'

There was a bead of wine on Offrian's lip. It was a moment before he remembered to lick it away.

'You said no lies, Talasa. I think you've been doing quite a lot of imagining.'

'I have little else to do,' Talasa said. That was honest, at least. 'And I find myself imagining that while withdrawing from Croí is a shocking proposition *now*, it is the kind of proposition that could gain traction. The common folk would like it. Their boys brought home, more support for the larger war to the east—'

'The common folk do not know anything about anything,' Offrian said frostily. 'And they—'

'They know that a king's word is law,' Talasa said, a treacherous little thrill in her heart. She had interrupted a prince. And she was right – she knew she was. She had been right, and Kalifsena had been wrong. 'And it is dangerous for them to learn otherwise.'

'What is this?' Offrian said. 'What are *you*? Kalifsena's mouthpiece? A trained pet parroting her thoughts? Or am I to believe this is you? That you've been sitting there blank-faced for two years thinking about—'

'What else is there to do?' Talasa said. 'What else is there to do when you are the child of someone powerful but watch, and wait, and think, and—'

'Disagree?' he asked, incredulous. 'That's a dangerous sentiment to express to a prince.'

He was right, and Talasa had pushed as far as she could. Her spine was a river of sweat. Her hand ached for being still, her skin cooked by the candle flame.

But it was working. Was it working?

'Do you know why I dislike superstition?'

The change in direction caught her by surprise.

'No, your Highness.'

Offrian leaned forward and poured himself another glass. For the first time since he'd arrived, he seemed to remember his manners, and poured her one too.

Talasa took it and did not drink. She and Kalifsena had spent a series of evenings experimenting with various alcohols so that Talasa would understand their effects. The morning after had been quite something.

'Because Sir Adger went to one of your seances.'

'So you said. I do not attend. What did he tell you?'

'Nothing,' Offrian said. 'That's the thing. I could have embarrassed him. Forced him to tell me everything. But it's sad enough being a man in your forties bound by tradition and ambition to befriend a boy not yet twenty.'

'It is not Sir Adger's fault. My mother swears all attendees to silence.'

Offrian crashed his cup down. He had drunk quite a lot of it.

'Exactly. Exactly! And he listened! He cleaved to that oath, over one to me. I would have had to make him break it. Superstition *clouds*. It is doubt and guesswork. It asks you to forgo allegiance to what you can see in favour of what you can't. It makes a *virtue* of being unseen.'

He steadied himself.

'We excised that weakness a long time ago. The compacts that matter must be clear.'

Talasa allowed herself the tiniest sip of wine.

'And if what the compact asks of you is disastrous?'

'Careful,' Offrian breathed. 'Be careful in what you say next.'

'I promised you a seance, your Highness. Do you wish to have a grand mystery revealed to you? A life-changing truth?' She waggled her fingers over the candle flame and won herself a smirk.

'Go on then,' he said.

'The man who shot at me was Croí.'

Offrian went very still. 'What did you say?'

'I heard his voice,' Talasa lied. 'Distinctly. He shouted something in Croí and then fired. It was not a riot over food. It was not sedition. The people love their king and queen.' She stressed that last word just a little. 'It was an attack on the royal household, by a Croí malefactor.'

Talasa waited for Offrian to correct her as to her position relative to the Crown . . . but he didn't, and that was when she knew she had him.

'It is unfortunate, of course,' she went on. 'Particularly in relation to the King's plans, and the Rationale's hope of executing them. Such aggression from a colony . . . it makes the idea of withdrawal quite unthinkable. An attack on the Crown cannot be allowed to stand. Not even the King could argue with that.'

Talasa gave her best approximation of Kalifsena's coy smile.

'Could he, your Highness?'

'No,' Offrian said. 'I suppose he couldn't.'

Talasa ate dinner in front of her window that evening and found herself asking for a glass of wine as well.

It was a rare clear evening in the capital. The courtyard outside shimmered like lizard scales with the remnants of sunset and rain. Her maid stepped forward and refilled her glass, and Talasa nodded gratefully.

I understand now, Mother.

People craved acceptance from the dead. They craved forgiveness, or insight, or just acknowledgement, and they would believe whatever they needed of the moment in order to get it.

It was potent from the living too, and Talasa could still feel the heat of Offrian's regard on her skin.

When her mother had returned to her, all those years ago, in that dry and yellowed little basin, Talasa had picked wassaline, split some kurvos stems and turned them upwards towards the sun to dry.

Little offerings of hope.

Now, when Kalifsena returned to her, she would find that with one small lie, Talasa had provided an entirely plausible reason to delay the withdrawal from Croí. To scrap it entirely, perhaps. The King could simply reverse his order in light of this new information, without a need to test the loyalty of his Rationale at all.

Or his son's.

A sip, and a welcome burn at the back of her throat.

You'll be angry, Mother. Even though we need this, I know you will be angry.

Parents were always angry when their children achieved something they could not.

I'm angry at you too, Mother. Even this, we do together.

21

Sister Wake

'DON'T DO THIS.' Sister Wake's saintly senses whipped out of her so violently the suds on Mother Promise's arms turned to snow. '*Don't . . .*'

There was nothing. Nothing close by she could use, except the body of that fool Answerman out the back, and there was nothing he could do for her except clog her soul with the fading remnants of his.

'I haven't done anything,' Mother Promise said idly, flicking the snow from her arms with short, deliberate strokes. 'Macha's crown, why do you think the worst of us?'

Sister Wake didn't answer. Surely, *surely*, in a house like this there would be something. A fresh kill in the pantry. A dead fly on a windowsill. *Anything.*

The windows furred and crackled with frost. The soup on the stove began to harden and cling to itself. As Sister Wake's temperature dropped, Brother Wight stood out behind her like an open flame. If he put hands on her, he'd lose a layer of skin.

'Did you clean this place?' the saint snapped. 'When I was upstairs? So I'd have nothing to use?'

'And what would you want to be using?' Mother Promise countered. 'Don't you have a soup bowl and a spoon in front of you? Do you need something else? Are you in an enemy camp? Are we holding knives to your throat?'

Mathilde was still alive. That was something. That was everything, until Sister Wake could get out of this fucking room.

'It's not *my* throat I'm worried about,' Sister Wake snapped. 'Forgive me if I don't sit for another helping of soup while this big lump breathes down the back of my neck –'

'Well, he wouldn't need to if you just did as you were asked!'

For the first time, Sister Wake wondered had Mother Promise children. The exasperation in her voice felt very real.

The old woman grimaced. 'I have never begrudged you your skittishness, girl. Not with what you went through. But don't sit there judging me for mine.'

She whipped the empty bowl out from in front of Sister Wake and dumped it in the basin, where it sat on a layer of ice.

'The younger generation,' she said, tutting. 'Half of ye want to steal a boat and siege Dreodyrne screaming the name of your ancestors, and the other half want to wipe your feet and wait for an invitation.'

She patted her hands dry on a towel and swung her own *brat* around herself.

'I have no intention of harming her. I just need to know which side she's on.'

'Then let me talk to her,' Sister Wake pleaded. 'You know which side *I'm* on, don't you?'

'Oh, I do,' Mother Promise said. 'That was decided for you. I'm just not sure if *you* know yet. Be thankful we all have the patience for you to . . . What is it?'

The holy chill in the kitchen abruptly vanished. Frost sloughed off the window. The soup hissed and began to boil.

'Let me talk to her,' Sister Wake said. 'Right now. Or everyone you sent with her is going to die.'

They had taken Mathilde to the beach.

Midnight had turned the sea below the house murderous. The cove was little more than a pocket of stone rimed with sickly grey sand, and on either side the waves came relentless, filling the air with a constant film of spray.

It salted the back of Sister Wake's throat as they hurried down the narrow little path. Her descent felt like inching around an immense beast in its lair, waiting for the moment it would catch your scent and tear you apart.

'How could you just stand there?' she hissed at Brother Wight beside her. 'How could you let them take her?'

Brother Wight's gaze was fixed on the path in front of them. It was little more than a patch of tramped-down grass that someone, sometime, had littered with a few barrowloads of stones. A little kindness for others. It was the kind of thing her father might have done.

'I didn't know,' he said in a voice so tiny she wasn't sure she heard it at all.

'Hurry up!' Mother Promise snapped. She had pulled ahead with that peculiar turn of speed old people had over people fifty years younger than them. 'All that song and dance and now you're lagging behind?'

Every step Sister Wake took spread ice across the stones, as she strained ahead and back and up into the sky and down into the earth.

A vole, half deaf and bisected in the screaming mouth of a fox.

A patch of silence with blood on its talons, trailing souls from its beak.

A badger, old and groaning, without the size of mind to wonder if it's going to live through the night.

Pointless. *Pointless.* What threat was a vole? What threat a crow or worm or owl?

If you've hurt her, Sister Wake thought, and felt that unfamiliar thrill of blasphemy once again, *you'll find out. I'll have sparrows take your eyes. I'll jam rats down your sleeping throats.*

Beaches were always strewn with death. Even this meagre rind of silvered sand, washed up like a fish against the land. Sister Wake could feel the warbling souls of jellied things, the sparking knots of sandflies.

And she could see the six men, their shadows long and moon-stretched. Mathilde, standing ankle-deep in the crashing surf, didn't seem to cast a shadow at all.

The men were holding bows.

'Leave her alone!' Sister Wake shouted, but the wind took all the heft from her voice and left it thin and high and raging. 'Mathilde!'

As soon as the little girl saw them, she made to run, but the warriors hemmed her in, moving in a loose half-circle, calling instructions to each other, low and calm and somehow unashamed.

'I know this looks cruel,' Mother Promise called out. 'But it is us who are terrified of you, girl, because we don't know what you are.'

Mathilde was small for her age. Surf had painted her hair to her scalp. If they didn't kill her in the next five minutes, she would likely get a hideous dose of the flu.

'Did you meet the Cailleach, little girl?'

'I don't know what that is,' Mathilde said. 'I don't know who that is.'

'Did you see a god?'

'I told *her*,' Mathilde said, pointing at Sister Wake with a hand she could not help but notice was scaled with ice. 'It just happened. I don't remember how I did it. I remember standing there . . .' Her voice hardened. 'I remember standing there, *like this*, with arrows pointed at me . . .'

The warriors were eyeing each other. Three of them lifted their bows, turning this way and that to keep an eye on the sky.

Practised, Sister Wake thought with a chill. The wind had driven all the birds inland. There was nothing in the sand below them but whelks and worms. The sea beyond them was as brimming with death as it was boiling with life, but not a whit of it was useful in a situation like this.

That was why they had brought Mathilde here. Thought had been put into how a saint could be disarmed.

Not enough thought.

She could feel what was coming. Denting her saintly senses like two storms meeting high above the ground.

'Mathilde,' she called, trying to be soothing. 'Can you—'

'Sister Ore came into her sainthood,' Mother Promise called, 'when Brí of the Smithy strode through her home. Sweat came on her like rain, and a quiet, faithful mother of four found herself remade in the goddess's glorious image.'

The old woman approached, hand out before her, as if she were trying to calm a horse or a dog. 'Brother Able, who fights at our front lines with the strength of ten men, he was dying, an Answering spear in his gut, when Macha breathed new life and vigour into his frame. And Sister Wake—'

'Shut *up*,' Sister Wake snarled. She had no desire to hear the polished, propagandic saga that was her life to other people. Worse, she could feel what was coming at them like an arrow, and she had only seconds to stop it. 'Mathilde, don't listen to her. Listen to me. I can feel what you're doing. But if you just come up to the house with me—'

'My worry, child,' Mother Promise said, the wind kicking at her plain brown *brat* so that you could see the thick leather boots beneath, 'is that you are not one of us. You have a coloniser's face and a coloniser's heart. And yet you have been blessed.'

Mathilde's voice was plaintive. 'I didn't want to be.'

'I understand,' Mother Promise said, achingly kind. 'You shouldn't be here. You should never have come to this island at all.'

The temperature dropped so fast the surf turned to anklets of ice around Mathilde's bare shins.

'I was *born here*,' shrieked the girl, in terror and rage. The sea erupted, and the soul behind it impacted Sister Wake so hard it slapped her right out of her own head.

She is enormous.

She is thick and she is writhing. Her hands are strands of jelly the length of a village street. They do not hinge like a human's fingers. They are a seamless, boneless unfurling that starts at the crown of her head and ends in filaments so achingly sensitive the cold air is fire upon them.

Her whole body is a tongue, curling and uncurling, and everywhere the water does not cover wobbles and trembles at the touch of the wind. The wind whistles through the holes in her body. Her eye is the size of an Answering table, and almost completely blind.

She is not meant to see the sun. She is meant for water so cold and pressurised that the only way to travel through it is by brute force or bonelessness. She is the god of a lonely, violent universe, and a century of bloody war has been written across her flesh. Scars in skin that should not scar.

And to leave that lightless, murderous void is torture . . .

The beach. Sister Wake was on a beach, her face against the sand.

It took her far too long to understand why her limbs had rigid sticks in them, and longer to realise she could no longer taste the world with her skin. Sound returned – not as vibrations through ink-black water, but as harsh, directed bursts, rattling like coins around her skull.

Screaming. People were screaming.

Sister Wake lifted a grainy, throbbing cheek, trying to blink half the beach out of her eye. Through streaming tears and sea-wet, she saw . . .

Mathilde. Her back arched to breaking point. Her arms flung out before her. And above and around her, mimicking the girl's straining limbs, were tentacles of flabby, glistening white.

Sister Wake gaped. Seawater fell like rain. Kelp and weed, drawn up from some unimaginable depths, drizzled down from each monstrous, man-thick pseudopod as they swayed. Each pale, tallowy limb could have reached over the walls of Sciáthcrann without effort. Picked up a bombard and crushed it into a useless lump of iron.

Sister Wake remembered that strength. Had been that strength. The soul of the thing was so vast and sucking and alien it was all she could do not to be dragged back in. She wondered whether the other humans on the beach felt what she did. Cowed. Frozen. Like they were in the presence of something so ancient and powerful that they were now the interlopers in its space, and not the other way around.

And then she realised that if Mother Promise and her men were capable of feeling that, they would not live the lives they did.

The bows came up. The men began to fire.

Mathilde spasmed bolt upright. When her hand came down, a tentacle did too, hard as a stone pillar, smashing a man down so hard it rippled the sand in a six-foot circle all around.

Bloscadh. His name had been Bloscadh. His blood squirted through the salt and his soul squirted through Sister Wake.

Another tentacle, whickering through the air at head height. Modwen – beautiful, sarcastic Modwen, who had been kind to Sister Wake right from the beginning – was too slow.

It folded her in two, back to calves, with a snap, and Sister Wake saw that Modwen had thought Sister Wake was beautiful too.

Do something. Warriors were shouting. Running. An arrow kicked up spray on Mathilde's left. The girl's mouth hung open, shrieking without sound. Every wave threw chunks of ice onto the sand.

Sister Wake dragged herself up on resisting limbs, trying to get her legs underneath her, the world a clashing mess of hard angles and hateful solidity.

Behind Mathilde, something was rising out of the water, pulling itself along on pillars of flab. It was eerily white, almost glowing in the moonlight. There were bites, enormous bites, all along its length. Sister Wake would go to her grave happily never knowing what had delivered them.

Even on its side, it was three times taller than Sister Wake would have been standing up. She didn't think it even understood that it was killing. It barely understood that anything else was alive.

And it was that sliver of soul in hers that made her realise exactly what it was she had to do.

Running now. Vaulting over a squirming, shivering tentacle as it arched itself back up into the air. Past the grabbing hands of a man she didn't recognise, who was lifted, roaring, a second later into the air and *squeezed* . . .

And Brother Wight found her just as she found him.

'Are you all right?' His hands were all over her, searching for wounds so roughly she thought she might bruise. 'Sister Wake, are you . . .'

Her hands went low. He stiffened – and she dragged the wheellock pistol from his waist.

'It's her or me!'

Some gap in the wind. A little pause between pounding, crashing surf. They said Cailleach was the Goddess of Storms, after all, so maybe it was a minor miracle that the whole beach heard Sister Wake's cry.

Sure, weren't two of her daughters here and at risk?

A sudden silence fell, punctuated only by the slosh and hassle of the waves and the squeaking whine of meat on meat.

'Hold your fire,' Mother Promise said.

The remaining warriors of the Rising did, scrambling back up the path and out of the tentacles' reach. And so did Sister Wake, backing away from Brother Wight, left hand outstretched for balance, right hand pressing the wheellock to the side of her head.

'You heard me,' Sister Wake said. 'Let her go or you lose us both.'

The tentacles stilled. Each half-ton slab of flesh went as motionless as only a dead thing could.

'Don't tell me you're planning to do the enemy's work for him,' Mother Promise said in heart-tongue.

'No,' Sister Wake replied in Answering. 'I'm offering to do your work for you. Nobody else has to die tonight.' That was as much her hope as a promise. She could still feel every soul wriggling like jellies on the sand. 'But Mathilde belongs to the Rising now. We keep her safe. We teach her. Or we let her go. Whatever she wants.'

One of the oily, reaching limbs simply fell, thundering into the sand and sending up a spume of spray. Mathilde's arm had fallen too. It was as close to agreement as she seemed able to display.

'And what are you going to do?' Mother Promise asked mildly, as if they still sat across the table from each other.

'You said the Cailleach hadn't left Crom Dubh,' Sister Wake said. 'You said none of the messengers you sent to her had returned. Let me go. I'll . . . I'll speak to her. Recruit her to our cause.'

'*What?*' Brother Wight snapped, but Sister Wake ignored him, and plastered on as wild and brave a smile as she could muster, as if she knew exactly what recruiting a god might entail.

I don't care, she realised, looking at the shivering, ice-rimed girl.

A sacrifice.

Fair enough.

'Our cause,' Mother Promise said. 'At last.'

IV

Nothing Sacred

22

Sister Wake

AND AS WAS the Croí way, when the bodies had been buried and the limbs of the great fish had slumped to the sand, there was dancing in the face of death.

Fires had been lit. Thick curtains had been drawn against the dawn and any unwanted eyes. The room had been a dining room once, but now the huge table had been shoved to one side, and sitting upon it were three figures, faces viscera-red in the light of the flames.

Badarn, beefy fingers delicate on the small *cruit* harp.

Laoise, hair a frothing thundercloud, with their *cuislenna* great-pipes, big as a child.

And old Giobhnu, a just-cleaned gash on his old and leathery scalp, tuning his *tiompán* with solid, sure twists.

Everything that could last on the road was packed away, and everything that wouldn't was put out on the edge of the table so it could be et. Bottles too – brandy and whisky for the peers and casks of ale for the servants, and even some peppered wine, a rare thing drunk only through plunder.

The room felt at once enormous in its shadows and cramped with its crowding. Slowly, like a pot cooking, it became warm, then stifling hot. *Bratanna* were doffed and laid down until the hard, sculpted edges of Answering chairs and divans were lost beneath the scratchy softness of Croí cloth.

That was why Sister Wake had come. Or at least that was what she told herself. The saint had made herself a little perch in a windowsill, her father's *brat* set out to dry with the others, her *léine* clammy and clinging. Anyone who had been on the beach was soaked, and this was the warmest room in the house.

She wasn't going to dance. Even in Mother Promise's *lucht tighe*, her houseless household, there were certain things a saint could not be seen to be doing.

But I can watch.

It was Laoise who sang first. Little Laoise, a sprig of a thing. They sang, and neither Badarn nor Giobhnu played, because certain songs needed nothing but that lick of a voice turning the air to gold. It was an old song, but they were all old songs. This one was just a string of names – not names of people but of places, a litany of the lost and conquered, strung together to be preserved for the day they might be washed of their Answering claim.

As they sang, the room filled. A heavy silver cup had been chosen to pass around in the old tradition. Sips were taken – it was the height of bad manners to hand it back empty – or skited over the *bratanna* of those bodies that were even now being buried down on the beach. When Mother Promise's band moved on, weapons would be redistributed, coins shared. Nothing would be wasted. You could still strike a blow for the Rising, even if you were dead.

It was already happening, out there in the dark. Sister Wake twitched aside a curtain, watching warriors slip away on their secret missions – delivering Mother Promise's words out over an island at war.

How many of them would mention Mathilde?

'You're letting the light in.'

Brother Wight was standing over her, a rare plundered bottle of burntwine in his hand. Laoise had finished their song, and the little impromptu band was lost in the skirling, experimental prologue to whatever they would play next.

'They won't thank you for taking that,' she said.

He shrugged. 'Call it an offering.'

'Was that a joke?' Sister Wake asked. 'This really is an age of miracles.'

Brother Wight held out the bottle by way of reply. Grudgingly, Sister Wake lifted it to her mouth, and for the length of that long slug there was nothing in the world but the taste of spiced sweetness and the sound of Giobhnu settling on a reel.

The room was heaving now. There wasn't much art to the dancing. It wasn't as if any of them had ever had time or reason to practise. Men were prancing like goats, not so much dancing as jumping with a kick to it, and women jumped too, or swayed hard, banging their heads side to side with the beat of feet against floor.

Brother Wight sat down across from her and took the bottle back. He had taken off his *brat*, and rolled up the sleeves of his own *léine* so she could see the snaking blue tattoos around his biceps and the dirty-looking scars beneath.

His throat worked as he swallowed, and she looked away again, out to where dawn was smearing the sky.

'Are they still on the beach?' he asked.

'Aye,' Sister Wake said. The old woman had snapped momentum right back off Sister Wake as soon as the saint had lowered the wheellock, as if it had been her own plan all along. 'Mother Promise thought Mathilde would be happier in the presence of a friend.'

She'd sent men running back up the hill for cloaks, and water, and sent Sister Wake to the Answering lady's bedroom to douse a kerchief in perfume against the now mythic stench of the fish – somewhere between ancient piss and bad meat.

And then she'd dismissed her so she could talk to Mathilde in private.

'What you did for her . . .' Brother Wight handed her the bottle.

'It was theatre,' Sister Wake said, taking a swig and passing it back. 'We've done it a hundred times for a hundred audiences. Mother Promise is no different.'

'It was brave,' Brother Wight said simply.

'Oh fuck off,' she said, but she couldn't put a bite to it. There was a warmth from the burntwine spreading through her chest, and for once she didn't feel an immediate rush of cold tamping it down. 'If you're only going to act like a human when I put a pistol to my head, it's not going to be much of a partnership.'

He might have smirked into the bottle, she couldn't tell.

'I didn't know we were partners.'

The silence then was almost companionable.

'So,' he said. 'The Cailleach. Do you have a plan?'

Sister Wake snorted. 'I suppose I should, shouldn't I?'

'You don't think she'll . . .'

'Kill me? She didn't before.' *I just wished she had.* 'I suppose I'll do what Mother Promise does. Work out what she wants. Figure out a trade.'

'I don't know if the gods care about trades.'

The next sip didn't taste half as sweet.

'I think that's all they care about,' Sister Wake said. 'It's the *fair* part they probably take issue with.'

Well used to her blasphemy, Brother Wight said nothing at all.

'They're not even *angry*.'

'The Cailleach?'

Sister Wake took another long slug of burntwine.

'No! The . . . *Them*.'

She waved the bottle at the dancing warriors, wincing as her voice came out too loud and rough at the edges. Nobody looked over, of course.

'There's four of them being buried down in wet sand because of Mathilde and Mother Promise and . . . and me. Four of them killed by some scared little girl.'

She went to take another drink, but somehow Brother Wight had wrapped his fingers around the bottle. When his skin touched hers, she jerked her hand back and he was left holding the burntwine, an unknowable expression on his face.

'I suppose,' he said, 'that maybe they think it was worth it, for another saint to join the cause.'

'Bloscadh had a wife in Ratamhlagh. She thought he was a wastrel, because he spent the whole marriage with one foot out the door for Mother Promise, and then one day an Answering bailiff got a good look at his face and so he ran, hoping his wife would be safe if she had no idea where he went. He died never knowing if he'd killed her too.'

'Sister Wake—'

She tried to snap the bottle off him, but he was too fast, jerking it back so her hand swept uselessly through the air.

'Modwen thought about getting out. She thought about leaving. Walking away. And I only know that because it was the last thing she thought about before—' She punched her thigh, hard enough to bruise. Funny, but it was Brother Wight who winced. ''S too late now. Always too late, by the time I hear about it.'

She made another grab for the burntwine, but Brother Wight caught her hand instead.

'And what do you want?'

Giobhnu was singing now, his voice a low growl. Even the empty bottles seemed full of firelight, but the heat in Brother Wight's gaze was all his own.

'What do you want, Sister Wake?'

Nobody had asked her that since Da, and it shook something loose in her head.

The Cailleach. The mountain. The chain. The girls.

Mathilde.

'I want to go home,' she said softly. 'I just want to go home. I want to go back to where I'm from, and I want to—'

Brother Wight let go of her hand.

'They're coming up the hill,' he said tonelessly, and left her with the dregs of the bottle and the lingering warmth of his fingers on her damp, cool skin.

'Good morning,' Mother Promise said brightly, as Sister Wake made her way out onto the porch. 'Did you sleep well?' She cocked her head. 'Though it doesn't sound like there's much sleeping going on.'

She clapped her fingers against her palm, and Sister Wake handed her the bottle.

'Ferocious,' the old woman said when she had finished it. 'They don't do everything wrong.'

'Are you all right?' Sister Wake asked Mathilde. The little girl was blinking sleepily, but her fear had disappeared. Instead, there was a febrile sort of energy around her. A wideness and wildness of eye, the kind you got in normal children when they ran so fast and so far that they felt slightly sick and slightly invincible.

'She's wonderful,' Mother Promise said. 'I can see why you like her.'

'But what does it mean?' Sister Wake asked. 'Her gift. Who she *is*.'

'Mean?' Mother Promise said, surprised. 'Oh. Nothing. She's Croí.'

'*What?*'

'My grandfather's father,' Mathilde said solemnly. 'He was deported to the New Territories for the crime of stealing bread for his family. Used as 'ndenture.'

She stumbled a little over the word.

'We used to call them the *aduantus*,' Mother Promise said. 'Our children, lost in unfamiliar places. But the gods do not forget us, no matter how we are scattered. Maybe the seeds of sainthood were sown then, out in the sweltering fields. Maybe they were just waiting for your return to bloom.'

'But how do you know all this?' Sister Wake asked. 'Mathilde. How do you know—'

'The Rising remembers,' Mother Promise interjected. 'And is it not a story we've heard before? When we know *filidh* exist in the lands under the setting sun? When all we've had here for centuries is the mercy of the pestle grinding us down and separating us out?'

She grinned then.

'Are you faulting our ability to hold a grudge, Sister?'

'They took him away from his family,' Mathilde said. 'Does that mean that some of them might still be here? Could we find them?'

'Of course,' Mother Promise said, and gave the girl a quick and easy hug across the shoulders. The sight of it made Sister Wake's stomach clench.

'So that's it,' she said, harshly. 'That's the answer. An Answering girl is blessed by a Croí god and—'

'She isn't Answering,' Mother Promise corrected. 'She's one of us. Descended from us. The Cailleach sees it. Who are we to argue?'

The sea heaved in the bay, and yet it was Sister Wake who felt the ground move underneath her feet. Just like that, and the scripture was expanded. Just like that, the rules were changed.

'Mother Promise, I—'

'Don't worry,' Mother Promise said. 'This changes nothing about you, or your status. It just makes you Sisters in truth.'

Sister Wake was horrified. 'That's not what I was—'

'Do I get a new name?' Mathilde asked, looking between them. 'Like Sister Wake. Are you going to give me a new name?'

Mother Promise smiled down at her. 'We'll come up with one together.'

They went back to the kitchen. Music still skirled, raking and impudent, from the dining room, but the room was emptying as the sun rose and the Rising called. Mother Promise sat at the head of the table, and Sister Wake could not help but notice that Mathilde sat beside her without needing to be asked.

Brother Wight had retrieved his cloak. The warmth he had briefly displayed was gone too, escaped out into the harsh dawn. Burntwine still sloshed around Sister Wake's skull, dulling and fuzzing the edges of her thoughts. *Did I say something wrong?*

Don't I always?

Standing beside Brother Wight was the largest woman Sister Wake had ever seen, wrapped in a coat of mail so heavy it could have deflected a cannon shot. Mail like that was rare outside the *lucht tighe* of a well-off *rí*, but what really drew the eye was the buckler at her feet.

Not its outside curve – weathered cowhide fastened by brass – but the inner side. *Ribbons.* A dozen ribbons, red and green and blue, some bright and some grubby with age. Sister Wake immediately knew what they were.

Red Grettas. Blue Adelaides. Grey Preciosas.

It was a mercenary custom. An advertisement. You didn't see it much on these shores, where even being caught with a shield without permission could be a death sentence. Sister Wake didn't know what the Answering would do to you if that shield was covered in trophies from dead soldiers. She just knew they'd probably take their time with it.

The woman caught her gaze with heavy-lidded eyes. Her face was curiously soft for a warrior, lips thin and set, her cheeks freckled with the kind of scarring you got when you'd crossed a castle wall and someone had been pouring boiling oil down to dissuade you.

'This is Creidne,' Mother Promise said. 'She looks after me. Now she's going to look after Mathilde. At least until one of the new Knights of the Hollow Eye can swear their *geis*.'

'There are other Knights?' Brother Wight asked, startled. 'Since when?'

'Since I've been telling people about ye,' Mother Promise said, and then her voice took on a deeper, richer intonation. 'And at Sciáthcrann, did not Sister Wake turn the cannons of the enemy upon the walls themselves, so that stone broke and wood burned, and the ways of the fortress were laid open to the heroic warriors of the new, free Croí.'

She grinned. 'That'll be the next sermon. You're a good lass for stories, Sister Wake, despite your temperament. Boys shiver at the thought of the Cailleach staring from your eyes and wonder whether your lips are cold. Little girls like your hair, when they can see it. There'll be a legion of Knights yet, all hoping to march at the shoulder of the Cailleach's favoured girl. Or one of them, at least.'

She patted Mathilde on the shoulder. Mathilde smiled blearily. Sister Wake did not.

'What?' the old woman said. 'You don't like me using your actions for legend? We're all being used, in one shape or another. Used for the Rising, used by the Answering, used by a husband or a wife or a child. Or alone, using ourselves up for nothing. Wouldn't you rather be used for good?'

Sister Wake had no answer for that.

'The answer was in the scripture all along,' the old woman admitted ruefully. 'And it took you to make me see it. Saints are the go-betweens between mortals and the divine. The messengers. The herders, sometimes, when a god is being too fucking stubborn.'

Creidne unfolded the map. It said something to the paranoia of the Rising that even in a house filled with the faithful, Mother Promise kept it under guard.

'You'll take a curagh north around Donn's Seat, hugging the coast,' the former mercenary drawled in a thick Cauci accent. That told a story about Creidne in itself. Cauci often made the fiercest rebels, precisely because of what their *rí* had seen fit to give away, all those centuries ago. 'But you'll have to come ashore here . . .' She tapped the page with a thick finger. 'A Muirdris has claimed the Bay of Claws.'

'Anu and her children preserve us,' Brother Wight whispered.

Creidne lifted her finger, but not before Sister Wake saw the minute tremble there.

'Aye. Not all Nemed are a blessing.'

'All the more reason why we need gods on our side too,' Mother Promise said brusquely. 'Go on, Creidne.'

'You'll go inland,' Creidne continued, 'giving the coast a wide berth, and then north the last hundred or so miles overland, across Scáthach's Plain to the foot of Crom Dubh.'

'Crom Dubh,' Sister Wake repeated. 'The Cailleach.'

'And the only girl who has survived her gaze,' Mother Promise said with relish. 'I should have seen it. I was too busy thinking of what ye could do for us in battle. Should have listened to you, Brother Wight. You argued for Sister Wake to be away from the fighting from the start.'

You did?

There was the faint patina of colour on Brother Wight's cheek.

'You soft boy,' Mother Promise said, with no little affection. 'Thinking any of us can ever be safe.'

'There may not be much safety there either,' Creidne added. 'Ye'll be away from the main push east, but not all armies retreat cleanly, and you may come across cut-off Answermen. Holding out. Hoping this is a Rising that might blow out or over.'

'I'd send more warriors with you if I could spare them,' Mother Promise said, 'but numbers are not our strength. You are. And what you might bring back with you.'

'Who'll look after the fox?'

Mathilde looked tired, which made sense, and happy, which didn't. Mostly, she looked attentive, bleary as she was, peering down at the map as if she understood half of what was being said.

She ground a little fist into one eye as she blinked up at Sister Wake.

'I don't think we can bring it. Can we?'

Mother Promise didn't do anything so graceless as hesitate or look to Sister Wake to break the little girl's heart instead of herself. Say what you liked about the old woman, she was no coward.

But you could hate her for not having to deliver the hard truth all the same.

'Can we have a moment?'

Only Brother Wight dithered, and then Mother Promise was up and shooing them out of the kitchen until it was just the two saints sitting across from each other.

By then, of course, Mathilde knew.

'Please don't go. Please don't go. Please don't go.'

It all became one breathless word, and the windows fogged and froze as heat and cold chased each other across every surface in the kitchen. Goosebumps danced along Sister Wake's bare arms, made nubby hillocks of her skin.

'You can't come with me,' she said finally, into that desperate, teary fusillade. 'You'll be safer here. Safer with *her*. Until I come back.'

An empty promise. Wasn't it? How could it be anything but, when Sister Wake had no idea whether they would ever make it to the mountain, let alone what would happen after?

No.

That was the curse of a promise. You could mean it all you wanted when it was made, until the world proved it a lie. Only in myth did a promise have power beyond the words in your mouth.

Isn't a creature of myth what I'm supposed to be?

'Stay,' Sister Wake said. 'Learn. Practise your *tabharthas.* Your blessing. And choose whether you want this to be your war, or whether you want something else. And I'll help you find it. I promise.'

'If it's your war,' Mathilde said solemnly, 'it's mine too.'

And just like that, it was done.

Another link in the chain.

'I'll be good,' she said. 'I'll learn like you did. Until you come back.'

'Until I come back,' Sister Wake agreed numbly, and reached out a cold hand for the little girl to squeeze.

23

Abelard

MEILYR HAD TAKEN Netha to a schoolhouse.

There was one outside the Lord Seneschal's estate, tucked away from the road behind an artfully unkempt row of birches. There was a similar enough arrangement at home – somewhere for the local Peerage to send their boys before they were old enough to leave home for boarding colleges.

Meilyr had not sent a soldier to escort Abelard. He clearly hadn't felt the need.

The road sloped down a low, broad hill towards the ungainly sprawl of Cusp a few miles south. Dust still hung like a storm front over the city, and underneath that greying cloud sat Macha, a hundred feet tall even at rest, her head bowed against her chest, sword across her lap. She appeared to be asleep.

But if you didn't look at that – and Abelard was trying very hard – the walk was actually quite pleasant. It was cold, but the sun was shining. Birds were singing. Grass had been allowed to grow untidily over the verge. He spotted pyramidal and bee orchids, as well as wild clary and creeping buttercups.

It had always been a source of comfort for him – the quiet,

industrious work of life in a thousand different forms. A place for everything. A solvable, understandable hierarchy.

It did not last. Turning a hedgerow corner revealed the schoolhouse – a low building in wood and biscuit-coloured brick. The narrow gravel path surrounding it had been made narrower by overreaching rhododendrons in rich and white-tinged pink, and the arched windows had been stained green and blue.

A squad of Answering soldiers in smart coatees and trews lingered outside, their horses churning the neat lawn to rut and muck.

'In there, my lord,' one of them called, though the gesture was entirely unnecessary. Abelard could hear Netha. The poet's cursing could have salted pork.

He followed the soldier who had spoken through high-ceilinged corridors, their steps loud on the floorboards. Abelard had been given new clothes before Meilyr had let him set out; a pair of tight, high-waisted trews, a loose, blousy tunic and a waist-length jack coat. None fitted, and the boots were especially hostile. He tried to distract himself from the squeaking discomfort by examining the walls as they passed – all festooned with drawings, schedules, lists of precepts for children to learn and flaws for them to avoid.

'*One would think, with their brutish and shifting loyalties, their clannish, unsophisticated broil, that common Croí could find the flexibility in themselves to learn manners befitting a civilised society.*'

The voice was coming from the classroom at the back of the building. The soldier outside looked desperately relieved to see them, and nearly forgot his matchlock behind him in his hurry to allow them entry. Beyond the door were serried ranks of tables, little chairs made bright and waxy with paint, and an ever-growing pile of tattered, broken books.

'*There is a stagnant, poisonous pride to even the least of them. A passion for an invented past fed to them with mother's milk. By adulthood it has lodged in their hearts. Granted them a bovine stubbornness that the harshest correction cannot erode. But perhaps . . .*'

'Netha,' Abelard said gently.

'*. . . perhaps we can fix their children.*'

Netha flung the book so hard at the wall it broke along the spine, spilling pages of closely printed script out onto the floor.

'A teaching manual,' they said, voice light and humming with rage. 'Expensively and lavishly printed. I had a look at some of the others.'

Abelard could see that. There was an intestinal spill of pages across several of the floorboards.

'It's a robust syllabus. Reading the Answering tongue. Writing the Answering tongue. A comprehensive breakdown of each fief and its history, along with major turning points in the reign of the Medalwyn family and the Rationale, that acts out the best interests of the empire.'

'Give us the room, please,' Abelard said quietly. The soldiers were only too happy to comply.

'You're going to tell me it's practicality. Gods know Croí children need this to be useful, if they wish to work as servants or stevedores or – if they are ambitious enough – move to the *fucking mainland*.'

They threw another book. It exploded like the others.

'The *mainland*. Not a clod of dirt moved, and yet suddenly we are not our own land but a vestigial limb of theirs.'

'Netha,' Abelard said. 'I need to speak to you about Meilyr. He—'

'Sent me here to mock me,' Netha said. To Abelard's great discomfort, there were unabashed tears in their eyes. 'Of course. I made a request to MacGiolla. A request in good faith, as a member of a Croí profession in good standing.'

'A request for what?' Abelard asked.

'Texts,' Netha said simply. 'Our tradition was always on our tongues, carried from *túath* to *túath* by wit and memory, but tongues diverge in isolation from each other. We in the Terod Union know some of Croí under occupation, but only through the coloniser's laws and the coloniser's boasts.

'I wanted to know how we've *changed*, Abelard. I pictured . . . a library. An archive. Some edifice of the enemy where they've recorded their treatment of us and how our language and stories have changed. Maybe then I would know why Macha—'

'Why Macha has what?' Abelard asked, desperate to distract the poet from three centuries of inherited hurt.

But the *filí* simply slumped back against the teacher's desk, shoulders limp and dejected.

'I knew. I knew this. I told myself I would not rail against it but learn from it, so it could be undone. But to read it. To see it. It's . . . *procedural.* Industrial. They are sanding us down. Starting with the children.'

'The danger is more immediate than that,' Abelard said, lowering his voice with a glance back at the open door. 'Meilyr has charged me to lure Macha to Promontory. He is conducting a great muster, and hopes the combined force of arms and artillery will be enough to . . .'

'To kill her,' Netha finished, smiling grimly at Abelard's hesitation. 'There is no need to be careful with me. Not in describing the intentions of your countrymen, at least.' They crossed to the window, where dust still crowned the city. 'I had hoped to be leaving Whiteseal. Hoped to have my songs heard by those who understand what it took to keep them and were grateful to me for bringing them home. But perhaps this is my role to play instead.'

An attempt at straightening those bent and broken feathers, a smart little clearing of the throat, and then they drew their pistol and held it high.

Abelard took a step backwards.

'What . . . what are you doing?'

'I'll need your help, of course,' the poet said. 'It's you Meilyr wants to see, after all. Agree to his plan. Tell him you have something important to say about Macha and her intentions.'

'And then you'll assassinate him?' Abelard said incredulously. 'That won't . . . They'll kill you, even if you do succeed!'

Netha shrugged. 'Die for a goddess? My ancestors should have been so lucky.' They peered past the raised barrel at Abelard. 'Unless, of course, that offends your own loyalty?'

It should have. Berrigan Caudefoy would have taken Netha's hand off at the wrist with one stunning stroke. Astor, less physical but no less keenly martial, would have made a good attempt at manfully wrestling them to the ground.

And you, Father? What would you do?

'Contrary to what you might think,' Abelard said stonily, trying not to look at the pistol studiously not pointed at him, 'a peer does not simply do as they are bid without any regard to the sense in it.

Hierarchy for hierarchy's sake is madness – it is about the right person in the right place, finding your level, doing as . . .'

Netha's eyes had narrowed. Abelard had the sudden sense he was losing his audience.

'What I mean to say is . . . Meilyr's approach is not one to which I could cleave. He has an unwisdom about this that is most concerning.'

'Oh, such harsh words!' Netha said. 'Are you sure you're not a *filí*, to lay a curse so?'

'Netha, *please*,' Abelard said. 'If you kill Meilyr, I cannot promise you another man will not simply follow his example. There are those who will. You are right in that at least. But perhaps *we* can work together to bring reason to him. Give me time. Time to map out some alternate, less ruinous path.'

Netha shook their head, but Abelard pressed on.

'And I can offer you something. Something Meilyr offered me. Look.'

He joined Netha at the window, where the courtyard of the Lord Seneschal's residence could just be made out behind drooping trees and bartizans of hedge. Soldiers were amassing, but these ones were manhandling boxes instead of matchlocks.

'All Meilyr's . . . research,' Abelard said. 'Eyewitness reports. Testimonials. Knowledge of Macha. You wanted texts. Meilyr is providing them. Promise me you'll stay your hand. Promise me you'll follow my lead, and perhaps we can find a way through this where nobody has to die.'

'An unfulfillable *geis*,' Netha said, and slid the pistol back under their cloak. 'But I'll let it stand for today.'

*   *   *

It took a couple of hours. Meilyr's reports arrived in neat stacks tied in string, a military order that did little to soften the brutality contained within. Painfully conscious of the fragility of their truce, Abelard had entertained a flimsy hope of keeping secret the nature in which some of the testimonials had been obtained.

It did not last past the undoing of the first bundle. He had come across an academic master at Lofgeorn when making his first application, who had spent a lifetime proselytising on the insights one could glean from the examination of handwriting. It took very little of that expertise to read fear in every shaky line and blot of ink.

Some of the pages had other stains too.

They read, and read, and read. Macha had lingered on a lone border tower for almost an hour – flaking the structure to powder between her fingers – but stalked right by the market town of Mereweather without so much as a glance. She'd crushed Fort Domond, striding through clouds of matchlock fire, bellowing at the men below as she annihilated firing posts one by one with stamps of her feet.

The sun traced its slow progress over the classroom's greying wood floor, and while Abelard sat in the schoolmaster's chair and read as he always did – hunched, intent, any and all movement pushed to the extremities of himself, a tapping finger, a trembling eyelid – Netha was the opposite.

The *filidh* did not make quiet readers. This was not a complaint, as it turned out. Abelard found himself welcoming any and every indication that he was not alone with the words he was reading. The poet conversed and cursed each page they consumed, speaking aloud to nobody from their position cross-legged on the floor.

'No! No . . .'

'Hillmarket would that have been? No, too far east . . .'

'This is pointless!'

Abelard had become so used to the one-sided conversation it took a moment for him to realise that Netha was speaking to him.

'I'm sorry?'

It was evening now, and the poet drew themselves up off the floor with exaggerated care. With a marked delicacy, they began to pick up each page and set them back in their bundles.

Abelard rose creakily as well.

'I don't even know what I'm looking for,' Netha said. 'She tramps around. Destroying some. Sparing others. It's . . .' They pinched their brow with long fingers. 'It's very godly, I'll give her that. But as for some clue or insight as to her motives or purpose . . . No. As it should be, I suppose.'

'What do you mean?' Abelard asked, laying down his own pile of notes, fighting the urge to scrub his hand down his coat. Meilyr had been very precise with his scribes' instructions. Every detail had been recorded. Every plea.

Macha still sat in the ruins of Cusp, head bowed like a snoozing old woman. They watched her together for a long moment, and then the poet turned away.

'It was never a thing of laws and scripture, Abelard. Your love for the gods was your own, kept under your breath or in the deep of the woods or on a shore where the vastness of the sea stood for Manannán Mac Lir. Yes, we came together at times, to burn offerings and roar out our faith, but those were holy for the rareness of them.'

They spread out a sheaf of pages.

'Every *túath* would have fifty stories of Macha. A hundred. You weren't meant to reconcile them. They're gods – they're unreconcilable! Even with themselves. Sitting here and trying to . . . track her across the hills like a lion is not—'

'Oh,' Abelard said. '*Oh.*'

'What is it?' Netha asked.

'I'm not sure,' Abelard said. 'And I don't want to speculate until we can—'

Netha was suddenly before him, their eyes wild. 'Before what? Before you tell Meilyr? Abelard, tell me right now, or—'

Their next words were lost to a subterranean shaking. Charts and paintings heaved themselves off the wall. Little tables thrummed themselves across the floor.

Macha was rising.

Abelard didn't think he had ever paid so much attention to someone stand up before. It was not a fast manoeuvre, nor a graceful one. After a certain size, even the movement of an organism began to take on the shuddering ponderosity of the mechanical.

First, the head – long as a battleship, draped with kelpy strands of coarse hair hanging down to form a matted point. Wattles slapped against each other, loud as sails.

Her gauntleted left hand swung out like the arm of a crane, casually obliterating in a hemisphere every building over a storey tall, before coming down with such force that it collapsed the remains.

Then a heave so strong that Abelard felt it in his knees and back, a heave that set the trees above them rustling and the soldiers on the street outside leaning on their spears. Birds swirled up, startled, from hedges.

'She's limping.'

Abelard hadn't noticed it during the goddess's first wild charge. He had been too busy keeping alive. But there had been a distinct clumsiness to the motion of one leg compared to the other – a placing more careful on left than right. It had a little of a beast, that tentative compensating, and a little of an old soldier, expecting pain before it arrived.

'An old war wound, dealt to her by Cichol the Wizened – a demon of the oldest days,' Netha said quietly. 'In the days of the Second Invading, under a torcstone sky. Macha and the other gods met the hateful forces of Cichol and the Bulging Men he led, and in the red dawn her hair shone redder, and blood turned the sands of the Airgialla forever crimson in the north.'

Macha launched herself upright into the last surging light of sunset, limb and horn whipping up dust devils in their wake.

The next hour of Abelard's life was chaos, but it was a chaos as neatly segmented as a portion of fish on a monger's block, chopped out and apportioned by the footsteps of a god.

First, the flight in disarray from the schoolhouse. Meilyr's men invading the room without so much as a word of explanation, harrying and shoving them out and down to the horses.

And then distant Macha took another step, and it was like the turning of a page, whipping Abelard's attention away from something as insignificant as another human. It even sounded like a page turning, or at least the motion of the step itself did – a waterfall hiss, the roar of some deluge just out of sight – before the punctuation of the hoof coming down, so hard horses screamed and staggered, so hard it bisected the world.

Not just noise, but pressure – a hard, hot slap of air and shaking earth that even at this distance hurt Abelard's chest and made his head spin.

The soldiers led them in a line up the tree-shaded avenue from the schoolhouse, Abelard on his own horse and Netha and a soldier sharing, until they came out on a low grassy hill overlooking the road to Cusp.

The countryside to the west of the city was neat as graph paper, or stained glass – each field a piece in a puzzle, drawn in by the dark stroke of a hedge or road, or bisected clean by the wide path of the Marrow as it flowed to the sea.

But Abelard saw now that in the hours he'd been in the schoolhouse, a great exodus had begun. Even the soldiers paused to watch it, heaving back on their reins. Cusp was emptying itself out onto the wide western and northern roads. Two rivers, black with bodies, both miles long already.

'Where are they going?' he asked, more to himself than anyone else.

'Away,' Netha said simply.

It might have been Meilyr's doing, though Abelard could not have pictured the man spending the least bit of thought on civilian concerns. But if it was, any order the retreating masses might have had vanished as soon as Macha began to move.

Every step the goddess took drove paroxysms through the streaming crowds, the heaving impact of each step rippling through bodies as if it was water.

The crowds who had chosen to flee north simply ran. The western exodus was not so lucky. Macha strode *through* hundreds of people as if they weren't there – kicking before her a crust of tangled limbs, so bullied and broken they looked like mud spreading before a boot. Abelard had to turn away to vomit a creasing, spattering line of heat down his horse's side.

'I'm sorry,' he mumbled. 'Sorry, I . . .'

Someone took the reins then, and led him, as the world retreated to nothing but a patch of ground in front of him and screams from somewhere far away.

Meilyr's forward camp was a group of hastily pitched tents, set up outside some renting stables a few hundred yards from Cusp's eastern gate. It was only when the horses stopped that Abelard judged it safe to lift his head and look around. The low line of barns was full of nervous, kicking horses that still screamed and reared every time one of the god's steps resounded over the world.

Tents swayed and fell. A command tent, red and billowing, stood only because an embarrassed-looking soldier was stationed at each of its four points, one hand on a spear and the other on a guide pole.

Abelard slid off the horse, staggering backwards a little. He wanted nothing more than to ask for a pail of water and a sponge to make right the mess he had made of the horse's flank, to lose himself for just a little while in the quiet strokes and familiar smell.

But Meilyr was waiting in the centre of the red tent, his arms folded, staring out through the canvas at exactly the point where Macha was traversing and traumatising the landscape. There was nothing else in the tent. Abelard presumed Meilyr had no plans to sleep, and the little man did not look like he ever ate.

He was just standing there, the red space erected around him. It should have been ridiculous. In fact, to Abelard, it was riotously sinister.

'Explain,' was all Meilyr said.

Abelard opened his mouth, but suddenly Netha was stalking by him.

'We will tell you nothing,' the poet said flatly. 'You'd see her caged, or dead, the way you have her caged in your textbooks. *The Croí faith in higher powers is no doubt a method of culturally processing their proximity to a superior neighbour.* I'm surprised you didn't write a history where your kings simply killed our gods, but then I suppose you'd have to acknowledge they existed.'

A slow and awful smile crept across Netha's face.

'She will rewrite them now, Lord Protector. She will rewrite all of it.'

Meilyr spoke slowly, as if addressing a child. 'I'll hang you.'

'Then I'll be in fine company,' Netha said. 'I'll meet my heroes on that rope. There is nothing in your bag of coloniser's tricks that will sway me. My bones and flesh belong to the greatest empire on this earth, and my soul and tongue belong to a land you have spent three hundred years failing to tame.'

The poet's voice had risen. Answermen, busy in their packing and stowing and loading of guns, were stopping to listen. And Croí were too, because there were always Croí – stevedores or horse handlers or those men who would not be trusted with firearms or gravedust but with carrying sacks and laying tents.

Another footfall. Each one seemed to split the world into binary. Before and after. Those who flinched away from the sound and those who strained into it. Those who could think and those who could not.

Us and them.

'And you, Caudefoy?' Meilyr asked. 'I set you a task.'

Abelard said nothing.

'Out with it, man! The animal is heading west. I need you to lure it north, so we may meet it at Promontory.'

'You're going to go yourself?' Abelard asked.

'If I don't, how will I know it's been done?' Meilyr snapped. 'I am not sitting here waiting. There has been enough waiting. Tell me what is driving it. Tell me how to slow it down.'

Abelard said nothing.

'Come on, man,' Meilyr said, his voice rough and hungry. 'Where do you stand?'

'I . . .'

Netha's eyes were boring into him fiercely.

'I . . .'

'Have it your way,' Meilyr said, turning to one of the waiting soldiers. 'Fetch a rope.'

When Abelard was a child, he had enjoyed drawing pictures in the corner of his notebooks. If you thumbed them at a consistent speed, you could jerkily animate the pictures. Astor had been better at it than him, both the drawing and the flicking of the page. There was a trick to it – the smoothness, the pace. When you did it wrong, the image simply jumped from pose to pose, with no movement implied.

That was how it looked when the *filí* drew their sword and nicked it cleanly through the throat of the soldier coming towards them.

The man's wary advance became a bow-legged stumble, blood squirting, and he simply folded down around himself into a dismal little slump.

The filidh *of the Six-Coloured Court do not resort to crass physicality*, Netha had said loftily. *Except when we do, of course. Then we try and be very good at it.*

It was the first time Abelard had seen them err on the side of understatement.

In the poet's other hand, the pistol gleamed. Meilyr examined its black mouth impassively, and then into the silence came a chorus of clicks, like grasshoppers in the weeds.

Twenty matchlocks had taken aim.

'We'll go together then, shall we?' Meilyr said.

Netha tensed.

'It's about challenge.'

They both turned to look at Abelard.

'Macha's a god of war,' he continued, trying not to meet Netha's eye. 'But more than that, she's a god of *sovereignty*. Or she's an animal – as you say. An apex beast. And apex beasts are territorial. She's roamed across half the east, only fighting those who fought her. Who offered her challenge. She's re-staking her claim.'

'Damn you,' Netha said quietly. 'An Answering peer after all.'

'There is no such thing as damnation,' Meilyr said. 'Speak.'

'If you wish to lure her,' Abelard said, 'you offer her a challenge. Tempt her to Promontory. Seeing the muster there should do the rest.'

'How?' Meilyr asked shortly. 'How does it recognise a challenge and something that is not?'

'How do salmon know where they were born?' Abelard asked. 'How do birds build nests? Knowledge is not always a product of teaching and books. Sometimes it is . . . bound into a thing. We don't know how.'

'Then what use is this art you practise?' Meilyr asked. 'How is it better than magic and fae tales?'

Abelard had nothing to say to that.

'I can help you with that,' Netha said. There was a vicious sort of resignation in their voice. 'Take your sword and go. Stand before her. See if you're worthy of the goddess they called the Proving Ground.'

Their voice rose, and Abelard realised with a chill they were timing their curse to the hammering tread of the distant god.

'Are you a coward, Meilyr? *GO!*'

The guns didn't waver, but Netha's challenge, pitched loud enough for everyone to hear, sent a ripple through the men. The wind plucked at the tent, breathing the sides in and out, as Meilyr considered.

'Speak to Colonel Droit,' he said eventually. 'Have him gather a hundred men, split into five groups. Give them guns. Give them horses. Tell them to harry the monster and turn it north.'

He paused.

'But gather them from Aetsomne's household. Promise them a half-scruple for every round they discharge and tell them any coward will hang. And put them in Answering dress with Answering flags.'

He didn't look at the poet, but his voice was for Netha alone.

'Let's see if a god can tell the difference.'

The men nodded. Abelard saw smiles, even. *Smiles.*

'Now,' Meilyr continued, as if he had just finished ordering breakfast and the proper day's work could begin. 'Bind their hands. Find them horses. Shoot the poet if Caudefoy resists. Bury that private. We ride north. For Promontory.'

He favoured his men with an acidic smile.

'Let's bring the bitch down.'

Abelard had his wrists tied to the sound of cheers.

24

Talasa

'THIS BUILDING,' THE rhetorician said, running a hand lovingly over the rosewood pulpit, 'is not a church.'

The rhetorician was short, and he was stout, and in front of the sombre black suits and dark giornea of the congregation, his red cheeks were the only colour in the hall.

'And I, you will be relieved to know, am no priest.'

Talasa had never been so relieved to hear an Answerman speak. She'd seen rhetoricians before, of course. The Ceolmund Academies did not just record the thoughts and doings of empire, they *proselytised* them, up and down the Answering, at state events and fiefdom festivals and union day parades.

Each had their own practised, curated style – the pacers, the ravers, the quiet, intense starers – and each was as adept as Armin Tell in knowing the strategic value of a long, expectant pause.

There had been exactly that kind of pause as Talasa entered the barbican, and she was deeply grateful to him for breaking it.

It had been a long and lonely morning, after a longer and lonelier night. The third glass of wine had soured in Talasa's stomach, as had her sense of victory. It wasn't the lie she had told. Part of her wished she'd devised it sooner, so that she could share it with her mother and get her blessing to deploy it.

That was the problem with loyalty. Defiance in service of what was right . . . was still defiance.

What about your loyalty to me?

And then the little note had come, written in Offrian's expansive hand. An invitation. What else could she do but accept?

The barbicans were not chapels. Talasa knew this because they were not called so. Oh, there were *similarities*, of course. So many similarities that an uncouth foreigner like herself might have thought them the same, considering both were a building everyone was culturally mandated to attend silently and listen to men talk about virtue.

But they were not *called* churches, so they weren't churches. Churches were barbaric places, where uncivilised people threw themselves down before profane altars. The barbicans were community hubs where good citizens of the empire gathered to be thankful for their own moral fortitude.

It was Talasa's first time in one, and not even a prince's invitation could stop the stares, the mutters, the clearing of throats.

The barbican still retained some of its old features from when it had been a pre-unification guardhouse – the thick walls, the narrow windows, the massive metal doors. The insides had been gutted since, of course, and it was hard to imagine that men had once slouched and smoked here while they guarded now-redrawn fiefdom borders.

Now, the refurbished barbicans hosted reeves and lords and generals each week, the buildings' bloody history a flourish for the storytellers of the state.

Precepts from the Ceolmund Academies had been delicately carved into the walls.

Keep Loyalty to High Principles

Bad Company Perverts the Dutiful

Be Prudent in Pleasure and Sorrow

Rename a thing, Talasa thought, *and you can wash it of the meanings you didn't like.* That was the Answering religion. That was how they worshipped themselves.

She made her way up the aisle between the narrow barricades of sunlight, eyes suitably downcast. She knew them all, of course. Not just from seances or awkward social gatherings – these were the reeves and ladies of court that everyone knew, because it was their Answering you were living in.

There was Eorl Henmaw, a man comprised mostly of moustache, whose twinkling eyes and rough laugh belied a cruel streak deep as the Dreor. Desdemona Culzean, of course, even more fabulously beautiful in the daylight. Talasa saw admirals and merchant generals and duchesses ranked like pikemen, and far more distressingly, they saw her.

You belong here.

Her shoes whispered on the bright-polished tiles.

You were invited here.

A cough. A loud, trumpeting sniff. She didn't dare look around to see who.

And you're late.

Silently she cursed the press of carts and commoners that had delayed her. *You spent too long dressing, too.* That was foolish. She'd dithered between dressing fit to stand beside a prince at what was in essence a social gathering, and dressing as demurely and self-effacingly as the Answering liked to be.

She still remembered the prickling of the maid's breath on her cheek as she'd laced up the narrow grey gown.

'It's exciting.'

'Excuse me?' Talasa had said, perhaps a little sharply. She had not meant her actions and last night's good mood to encourage any sort of familiarity between them.

'Sorry, my lady. Sorry. Just . . . the invitation. It's exciting.'

Talasa had not replied.

'We are architects,' the rhetorician said, as if he still commanded everyone's attention, and not the sixteen-year-old girl awkwardly trying to find a free seat. 'You and I together. We did not raise this building. That was done in the bad old times when fortification was needed so close to our doors.'

Find Offrian. That was her fortification. Her reason for besieging this bulwark of Answering superiority. Talasa knew low-ranking reeves sat at the back, and higher ranks at the front, so surely that was where he was.

She tried to peer through the crowd without looking like she was peering.

Nothing.

Just keep walking then. Keep walking to the front. Keep setting yourself ahead of each silent, judging row.

'But then came the First Among, and under their guidance guard houses and fortresses across the Answering were converted to places of introspection. Note that, dear friends. To accept unity is to turn yesterday's fear into today's peace. Father to son, mother to daughter, *that* is what we build, with every choice we make.'

Pity then, sudden as summer, and a rueful shake of his head.

'Let those outside our borders cluster together in their churches like frightened tribesmen around a fire. Our church is unity. Our church is everywhere.'

Talasa found the first bench like a soldier setting a hand on the top of a besieged wall, and fought the urge to press her sweating face to it in relief.

It was empty.

The whole row was, and she could have reached out her hand and touched the rhetorician's blankly beaming face.

Offrian. Where are you?

And then the rhetorician took her hand.

'And what better example of what happens when unity fails than our own Princess-Undynast?'

Talasa had been so lost in herself that she hadn't noticed the little man descend from his stage. He was standing too close to her, beaming, his hand soft and warm and powder-dry.

'Just a few short days ago, disunity was on our doorstep. A disturbance of the peace unlike any we've seen in decades. Of course, before it could spread, it was smothered. Our stalwart kingscarls saw to that. Now you could walk the streets of Bysmor and never know that it happened at all.'

That might have been true. Nobody here would ever visit Bysmor to check.

'A brief spark. Easily quenched. Fading like the mark on a young girl's cheek.'

Talasa's cheeks were burning so hard it felt like her cut might reopen.

'But with carelessness, sparks can spread. And when one of those sparks can rise far enough to score the cheek of one of our own – the

Queen's daughter, no less – we must be vigilant. We failed you, Princess-Undynast.'

To her horror, she saw lords and dukes nodding along. Eorl Henmaw looked livid on her behalf. Katharin Dayle was shaking her head in outrage. It would have been gratifying, if Talasa were not able to see the manner in which the sympathy spread.

Once Lord Madzen nodded, the baronets, knights and marquises most loyal to him did too. Anyone who did not show support – and there were a few, Talasa noted – kept their bondsmen's hearts in line as well.

And she saw Armin Tell at the back of the barbican, and his shock was her own.

The rhetorician gave her a dazzlingly patronising smile. 'How frightened you must have been. Yes?' He did not wait for an answer. 'After coming here for a better life,' he went on sadly, patting her hand, 'you found to your dismay yet more barbarism. A canker that has festered for too long in our midst. On our doorstep.'

An ugly light in those soft eyes.

'Unity is a choice. So too is disunity. For three centuries, we have worked to uplift our neighbours. To put them to good use. But what do you do when a child strikes their father? What do you do when those who seek civilisation are threatened by those who reject it? How far should our paternal kindness stretch?'

'Hear, hear!' someone cried, and then another. The rhetorician's thumb crossed Talasa's palm, light and quick as a tongue. She fought the urge to jerk it away.

And tried to match his smile with her own.

* * *

'What did you think would happen?'

She found him in Leopold's Garden.

It was one of the oldest parts of the castle – a stepped amphitheatre dating to before the construction of the Bicameral Seat, where reeves would have gathered under the watchful eye of the King to debate policy or hear Peerage testimony.

But then Leopold the Second had proposed to his first wife here and been so entranced by her acquiescence that he had declared the moment be immortalised for ever.

So the seating had been removed, and soil laboriously carried up twelve flights of stairs. Great wooden trays had been assembled to mimic seed beds and hide the dull grey flagstones. *It must have looked barren and strange for years*, Talasa thought. Apparently it took load upon load of manure to keep things growing in the thin, cold air.

But at least that made following Offrian easy as he darted between trellis after trellis of clematis and rose.

'I thought you would *be* there,' she snapped. 'And I did not ask to be a show.'

'Not in so many words, I'll admit,' Offrian said. He was on his knees, wearing what passed for labouring clothes – a tight-fitting jacket over shirt and hose. 'But did you think I would share the details of that pernicious attack with just the Rationale? You said it yourself – the King wishes to secure his withdrawal by circumnavigating the Rationale. He cannot do that to everyone.'

Be bright. Be grateful. Be a young woman who thinks about nothing more than dresses and fine meals and how to address people correctly. Be uncomplicated.

'It's blunt,' she told him flatly. 'It's authorial. You don't rule the space inside people's heads regarding . . .'

Two years' worth of careful hiding. A decade of following her mother's directives to the letter. Kalifsena had only been gone four days. Rubeo twelve weeks.

She let out a ragged breath.

'I do not *like* being abandoned.'

'I don't rule anything,' Offrian said. 'But the Ceolmund Academies and their Order of Rhetoricians have always been a gracious ear.' He yanked out a piece of bindweed that was threatening a rose stem and tossed it down by his feet, his conspiratorial grin made patchwork by petals. 'But I thought you would make the point better alone. And you were brave. And we did fail you. So.'

'What is this? Why are you . . .'

The words slipped out before Talasa could stifle them. She wasn't even sure what the end of the sentence was.

'Being kind?' he said, rocking back on his heels. 'Sit. I'm nearly finished.'

Grudgingly, she did so, gathering her skirts around her.

'It's nice to see you angry,' Offrian said, smirking. 'That muted little ember. I knew there was something. It was quite a boring two years watching you trail after your mother and pretend to be so-so at weaving.'

'I am actually so-so at weaving,' Talasa admitted, and felt a surprising spike of gratification when he laughed. 'The pretending was—'

'Clever,' Offrian said. 'It was clever. Tell's fond of saying that every class is a merchant class. Only the goods change.'

Do not let him distract you.

'Is that how you think my mother ensnared your father?'

He shrugged ruefully. 'It's always a trade. Ever since the first days of the Answering. It used to be children, of course. An appropriately barbaric practice we adopted from the Croí. You take my child and I take your child, and if you betray me, I'll kill yours. And if you don't, we might get married. Fertile soil for love, I'm sure you'd agree.'

'Worse than marrying a witch for love?'

'You're not witches,' Offrian said. 'Because witches are fiction. But there was real hope here in the capital that Father might grow out of his hobbies. I know I did. And then he met *her*.'

He grew quiet then. *Is he managing his anger out of guardedness?* Talasa wondered. *Or . . . for me?*

'His trips have grown more frequent. His letters rarer. I don't know how Armin Tell feels about you, because nobody knows how Tell feels about anything, but it's clear he thinks running a kingdom through letters is no way to run a kingdom.'

'And what do you think?' Talasa asked boldly.

Offrian's amber cheeks flushed. *He wouldn't be handsome until his portrait*, Talasa thought. Seeing him and knowing Rubeo just made you aware of the missed opportunity between sire and heir. But when Offrian spoke like this, it was like the fervent light of his hunger dimmed, and she was able to make out more of the young man beneath.

'Until now, my father being distracted hasn't stopped him from ruling. It's made things more difficult, yes, but those letters prove he is thinking of his duty. If not . . .'

'If not what?'

'If not his family.'

He worked in silence for a few moments, dead-heading roses, leaving a scattered trail of foliage across the cold grey flagstones. Despite herself, Talasa thought about moving closer. Flanking around the lattice between them.

She thought about taking his hand.

'You miss him.'

'Don't you?' Offrian asked. 'Three months, he spent with you and your mother in the Shore. I don't remember the last time he spent three months in the capital, and when I ask to accompany him . . .'

The little cutting knife trembled rather than bit, peeling off a long curl of stem.

'What was the word you used? Ah yes. *An unwilling audience.*'

'We did not speak much either,' Talasa said. 'He mostly spent time with Mother. But he did tell me about you.'

Offrian's head came up. 'Really?'

The steppes had been so vast that wind and the crowning blue sky ate your words as soon as they were out of your mouth, so Rubeo had to lean down and practically yell at her each time he wanted to speak.

He was the kind of person who shouted anyway – shouted instead of talking because he was so excited, moment to moment. Rubeo delighted in things. He demanded to know the names of all the flowers and what their uses were, whether they were medicinal or poisonous, how best to store ragweed or claimwort, whether the word for spirit differed from *zemlja* to *zemlja*, what happened when a priest who followed Oauk of the Ending met a priest who followed Oautho the Sunset Blade.

And Talasa had first found out about Offrian the day she'd arrived in Dreodyrne.

'He told me that you were clever, and dedicated, and that you hated sword-fighting but worked at it to the point where even your tutors thought you needed to slow down. He told me that he'd loved your mother, and when she'd died giving birth to you, it broke his heart.'

'He told you this.'

'It's easier sometimes to tell a stranger of your pain than tell the only other person who might share it,' Talasa said.

Offrian nodded slowly. 'And your father? How did he die?'

Talasa blinked in surprise. 'My father isn't dead.' She thought for a moment. 'At least, I don't think he is. My mother would have said, if she'd known.'

Offrian was incredulous. 'You don't know?'

Birds rooted in the thin soil, looking fruitlessly for worms. Talasa watched them for a long moment, unsure what exactly to reveal. How to explain to a culture so obsessed with lineage of father to son that other lineages could exist? That Talasa's father – a *zemlja*-lord somewhere past the Screaming Hills – had been honoured simply to intersect with a tradition that pre-dated his own modest line?

'My mother was a wise woman,' she said eventually. 'I was to be one too. We have our own heritage to propagate and protect.'

'Purpose,' Offrian said, consideringly. 'You're a child of purpose. Like me. All princes are children of purpose. That's what my tutors say. We are keys in a lock. Croí is just the beginning.'

'It is?'

'Father has left this place untended for a very long time.' Offrian was uneasy with what he was saying, still. Talasa could see it. There was a palsied frenzy in the way he attacked the weeds, and when one strand of bindweed did not unwind, he tore at it. 'I tell myself none of this would be possible without that neglect. That it shouldn't be so easy to step around him and begin to organise what must be done. But the ground was prepared already. We are not as above our superstitions as we would like to believe, and foremost among the old beliefs was that for a king to *be* king, the work of the office must be done. If not . . .'

He made a fist, and slowly released it.

'Rot has set in. It may be the work of a lifetime to reverse it.'

'Your lifetime,' Talasa said softly.

'And yours,' Offrian said. 'You were discussed today, on the floor of the Bicameral Seat. I thought about inviting you. There was genuine distress.'

'I was discussed?'

What was that, tied up with her anger at being used?

Was it . . . satisfaction?

'Assassination attempts on the Peerage are not uncommon,' Offrian said, as dead leaves fell between them. 'Or so I'm told. But on the whole, they are confined to Croí. There hasn't been an attack in the capital in fifty years, let alone on a member of the royal household. It was . . . galvanising.'

'Galvanising towards what?'

He gave her a look of mocking reproach. 'Don't tell me you think you can play at being a callow country girl again. You know exactly what will happen next.'

'The order to withdraw will be delayed,' Talasa said. 'The King will have to return if he wants to see it through, and by then . . . and after your rhetoricians have had their way . . . there will be no support for it. It will be forgotten.'

'Oh,' Offrian said. 'Oh, you are naïve. That's almost a relief.'

Talasa's cheeks burned. 'What do you mean?'

'Withdrawal is impossible now,' Offrian said, picking a morsel of plant flesh out of his cutters. 'But that is not enough. Not with the reports of unrest. Not with the Lord Protector's call for aid.'

And not with a prince looking to prove himself the equal of his father.

Realisation was a sickness in Talasa's stomach. She only appeared to be a poor student of history, and even a poor student knew that Croí had oft been a place where Answering princes proved themselves.

With rope, and sword, and gravedust kegs.

'That's not what I—' she began, but Offrian was already rising, their audience over.

'An example will have to be made, Talasa. The people will want nothing less.'

'I thought you said the people don't know anything?'

Offrian placed down his little knife and put his head on his knee, the picture of imploring earnestness.

'You convinced me,' he said.

25

Sister Wake

'I WANT TO stay with you.'

It had been a morning like this. Bitter cold. One whole side of the world bright as lye until you had to stand with your back to it, or at an angle like an old man.

'I know you do, girl. I wish you could too.'

This morning it was Sceir Bay. Back then, it had been a riverbank, in the shadow of the old portal tombs the gods were said to have left behind them. A grand origin for such a meagre thing – just a half-hump of white torcstone turned green by a thousand summers of moss.

Mother Promise had given the tomb a nod as she passed, one old soldier to another, and then walked the girl who would be Sister Wake down to a little curagh boat.

Sister Wake had never had many friends, even before sainthood. She'd had people she knew everything about, because that was how a *túath* worked, and she had people you said hello to on the road because you said hello to everyone.

And she'd had people she feared, of course.

And then had come the mountain, and the god. When she'd awoken, they'd told her she'd been asleep for a week, fussed over by muttering priests and nervy warriors who did not speak aloud for days.

They'd carried her, scurrying like prey animals – moving, sleeping, moving, sleeping – through open fields and down the narrow gullet of rivers, always with one eye behind them and a blade in the hand. They'd run and hidden and even killed once or twice, when hiding hadn't been enough.

And when they'd put her in front of Mother Promise, the old woman began to talk. Explaining what had been. What was. And what could be, if the girl who would be Sister Wake *became* Sister Wake.

'Did you come up with the name?'

Even then, she'd been a little cheeky.

'Names are a promise, girl. All names, not just mine. They're a hope. They're a threat.'

Sister Wake had met more people in those first weeks than she had in the nineteen years previous. She'd been drilled day in and day out in skills that might keep her alive while the one skill nobody could teach her had grown bigger and louder in her head.

Convulsing as she tried to move wings she didn't have.

Waking up every morning covered in the bodies of dead creatures, because she'd dreamed them into thinking they were asleep.

And then, just as she was beginning to thaw, they had brought her to a riverbank, where a boy waited by a boat.

Now, that same boy rowed stroke by stroke out into Sceir Bay, the curagh rocking with the passage of every wave. Sister Wake was familiar with the little skin-and-wicker rowboats. Sturdy enough to manage the unpredictability of the Unbeknownst Sea, and light enough that a man could carry one on his back. Many were the stories of saints and outlaws who had done so, with enemies hot in pursuit.

Mother Promise hadn't come down to see them off. *Too cold for these old bones*, she'd said, as if they hadn't spent half the fucking night out getting frozen. But she'd hovered like a mam as Brother Wight had packed in the kitchen, dodging around his lanky frame to point out spaces he could pack a fire-cooked spud or another jar of *menedach* into his leather bag.

Don't be starving her! She has a god to meet!

Like it was nothing.

They'd left the bay behind by morning, the towering spurs of craggy rock reluctantly releasing them to the wildness of the sea. Brother Wight turned the boat expertly to follow the northern cliff, balancing their little craft between a dangerous proximity to the shore and the sucking, impersonal pull of open water.

For his part, that tease of warmth that had come with burntwine and music was gone. Brother Wight was the same surly siege he always was – his face turned to the horizon, bound up in pretending she wasn't there, as if she wasn't his whole reason for being present.

Sister Wake had said something. Or done something. Or maybe he was just missing Mathilde, the little girl they both barely knew. The saint had no idea, and as always around him, any words she could string together felt spiky and hooked.

'Five days,' he said finally, when he'd stopped for a break and a couple of strips of flatbread.

There was no shelter from the wind out here, and he said every word through gritted teeth. The cold didn't have much of a hold on

Sister Wake, but the breeze was trying to make up for it, flicking spray at her or pushing the corner of her *léine* into her mouth.

Finally, he looked at her.

'You'll need to scout along in case any of the old lookout posts are still manned.'

In the first century of the occupation, the Answering had erected lookout forts all along Croí's coast. Some were squat towers garrisoned by single squads, with flags and horns to signal to one another and inland. A couple were proper castles – Balepoint, Geslike – with their own Answering commander and a standing force ready to deploy in case of raiders. Most, however, were little more than huts big enough for one soldier with sharp eyes and another to watch the door.

'Fine,' she said, and it was a relief, even to herself, to rise out of her body and leave that enduring pettiness behind.

The coastline was jagged, chewed to flinders and islets by the Unbeknownst Sea. As the saint drifted out through limestone cliffs as pocked and flawed and beautiful as Creidne's cheeks, she saw that each of those coves and inlets was its own little empire with its own little wars, with no knowledge or interest in the one raging all around them.

There. A red-banded cormorant curled up and lifeless on an outcrop of stone. Sister Wake didn't know what kind of disease had killed it, and neither did the bird – all it knew was that the base of each of its feathers had begun to feel like burrowing knives, and then a miserable night had turned to a peaceful kind of cold.

This didn't bother Sister Wake. Poison and traps were one thing, but you didn't get angry at animals falling sick. You'd never have time for anything else.

The disease had stopped the bird hunting, but it didn't stop Sister Wake. She ignored the beginnings of an itch at the base of her scalp, and with a waddling jump and a clench, she and it were airborne. The bird knew exactly where the forts were – it lived in a world defined by movement and freedom, and what put shape on that world was fear.

The soldiers took potshots at them, Sister Wake thought. Or remembered. Or was told by the mind she floated in. *Not for eating. For boredom and for fun.*

And now, she found, those soldiers were gone. There was roughly one fort every fifteen miles, and as the morning dragged on, Sister Wake kept the cormorant ranging out in ever-expanding circles, taking in first one, then another, then a third.

'Anything?'

Brother Wight's voice was tinny and distant, and hard to focus on through the buffeting of the wind and the feeling of seasickness and airsickness all at once.

'No. They're empty.'

They were wrecks was what they were. Burned out. Torn down. Even the smallest of the forts had been built to last, using Croí workers from a local village, most likely – four solid walls and a tar-sealed wooden roof. She kept the cormorant a mile out – no great distance for a bird used to catching shapes in water – but as the day progressed, she found that every fort they encountered had been systematically pulled apart and torched.

Did you even know the country was rising? she thought to herself. At least two men to each – one to sleep, one to guard. *Were you focusing out on your little patch of sea, and didn't notice the Croí coming up the ridge until their billhooks and axes were hammering on the doors?*

Lookouts with their own little patch of sea. She didn't mourn them. They shouldn't have been here. But it was impossible not to pity them, just a little.

'She's better off,' Sister Wake said suddenly.

Brother Wight didn't answer her. He'd been like this the first morning on that riverbank too – disappeared somewhere within himself, just a body with a scrap of a soul inside. His mane of dark hair was plastered down around his scalp from the lick of the spray. Beads of it stood out like jewels on his cheeks.

Who was to say it was a lie? Nothing Mother Promise had told her about the Answering was untrue. Sister Wake knew they had to be stopped. Driven out, before they ground down the Croí entirely and scattered them like ash.

'Even the children of the Answering support us,' she continued, hunting for a reaction, spitting each word into the wind. 'Even their children betray the empire and flock to our cause.'

A good line for the next speech. In old stories, some saints had the god-given ability to shift shape into hares or seals to escape capture or trick a foe or, in a disturbing number of cases, to impress some young one they wanted to ride, which to Sister Wake had always raised questions about the young one's taste.

Mother Promise was no saint, but her gift was to make people shapeshift into whatever the Rising demanded.

And by the gods, with Sister Wake, she'd tried. So had Sister Wake, at first. There was nearly a kind of fun in it. Learning how to play the freakish wain, or the solemn virgin, or the cackling *geis*-drunk witch.

Saviour. Leader. Monster.

It was just a different kind of *tabharthas*. That was what she had told herself. She wasn't making people do things they didn't want to do, just like she couldn't make animals act against their nature. She was helping them. The Answering had killed the Croí's hunger for freedom, and Sister Wake was there to wake it up.

She had just never managed to wake it in herself.

You did the right thing. You saved Mathilde. You recruited her, even. You helped the Rising, and Mother Promise, and even the girl, because if there is a reason for all this, if there is a chain, then Mathilde is a link in it too.

And maybe I'm to follow it back the way it came.

They made camp in a narrow cove with a lick of sand and no access from the cliffs above, as defensive a place to sleep as they could want. You'd have to be leaning far over the edge or approaching from the sea to see their fire, and if their luck was that bad, they might as well just give up.

Brother Wight was poking the meagre fire to life, trying to get the driftwood to do more than charring itself to ash. It wasn't warm, but at least there was shelter from the wind.

'Another day north in the boat,' he said. 'Then inland to Scáthach's Plain.'

Sister Wake licked salt from her lips, and dug herself closer to the fire, trying to inch more of herself into the warm. Brother Wight must have been properly freezing – he'd jumped out of the boat into knee-high waters to pull her and the curagh up onto the beach, and the legs of his trews were dark with wet.

'Right,' she said. He hadn't acknowledged her earlier outburst, but it sat between them like treacherous ground, making every step and motion precarious and foolhardy. 'Good.' *And then home.*

'Do you remember the first *rí* we worked over?' she asked suddenly.

'Fursa. Of the *túath* of Tír Ollíol. What about him?'

'He had a dog,' she said, a little uselessly. 'Do you remember? Mother Promise made this great speech about our time finally arriving, and about new strategies and that shipment of swords, and you were standing there . . .'

Glowering, she was about to say, but managed to stuff the word back in because she was trying to talk like a person and not a mad, angry bitch.

'. . . and then I came out, two dead ravens on my shoulders, the *image* of the Phantom Queen from the stories, and he took one look at me—'

'And,' Brother Wight said, a half-smile lurking around his features, 'spent the rest of the night telling you about his favourite hound that had died when he was a boy, and asking whether you could bring it back to life for him.'

'I did offer.'

'You did.'

What was wrong with her? Sister Wake's whole *tabharthas* was about finding the secret wants of things. That was what Mother Promise was doing as well, except for *ríthe* and their men.

Why did the thought of getting what she wanted make her feel like Brother Caid with a girleen's hair in his hand?

'When will you turn back?' she asked.

The stick stopped in the fire.

'What?'

'Well you're not going to come all the way with me, are you? Not when I'm going to see a god who can kill with a look. She'll spare me. Probably. You're just . . . *you*.'

'Yes,' he said eventually. 'I suppose I am.'

'And you can look after Mathilde then,' Sister Wake said, a little frantically. 'Help her speak for herself. Make sure Mother Promise keeps her safe.'

'None of us are safe,' Brother Wight reminded her. 'Who's going to look after you?'

'I'll look after myself,' Sister Wake said. 'Sure who else would?'

He was silent for the rest of the night.

26

The Onchú

THEY WERE CALLED the Onchú – the Hounds of Many Mothers – and by morning they would all be dead.

Onchú was the name chosen by themselves, not one given to them. The Answering sergeants who went in among the Lord Seneschal's *lucht tighe*, dragging out the best riders and the fastest shots, did not think to give the hotchpotch force a name at all.

There was simply First Platoon, Second Platoon, Third, Fourth, Fifth, and that was only so Meilyr's quartermaster could keep track of which Croí had been trusted with a matchlock, so it could be retrieved later.

Or collected from their corpse.

Individually, the names of the one hundred and twenty warriors assembled at Meilyr's now-abandoned forward camp were recorded. They were not men used to queuing, and so a thin-necked scribe named Hafely came to them as they shuffled and smoked, clerk's robes swishing shallow patterns in the dirt as he went from group to group.

He explained the conditions of their conscription. He recorded the names of their next of kin. For every shot fired, a half-scruple to the family. It had the potential, he said with awkward cheer, to be a life-changing amount of coin.

Each of the men had signed, or scratched a symbol if they could not write. None of them believed for a moment they were being offered a choice, but it was a welcome novelty to be offered a reward. This was not the first time Meilyr had used the Lord Seneschal's *lucht tighe* as an expendable resource for impossible demands.

Many of the men here had survived more than a couple, and those were the ones who joked with each other, with the scribe, even with the Answering soldiers shepherding them. Were the Answermen not jealous that the Croí were the ones leaving with pockets of coin?

And then the sergeants explained what this particular mission would entail.

The mirth was quieter after that. Some of the men stood alone, staring out at where a mare-headed titan lumbered towards a retreating sun. Others just shrugged and went back to their dice, or the games of *fidchell* they had set up on the ground.

Uniforms were unpacked. Matchlocks arrived in splintering wooden crates, though the ammunition would not be delivered until just before the Croí were to take the field. Just in case.

They were left then to dress. To prepare. To pray quietly, in ways and places the sergeants would not hear.

In the end, it was the shirtless Domnall Ua Briain, Answering trews half pulled up around his knees, who named them. The *onchú* was a battlefield spirit. A chimeric thing – fox-headed, eagle-chested, small and fast but with a bite so poisonous it could kill a creature a hundred times its size.

The men were all Cauci, of course. If the people of Umhaill and Érainn hid their shrines and their stories and the people of Tirconaill put them in the hollows of glens and hills where no sane Answerman would trespass, the Cauci under MacGiolla had forsaken and broken and betrayed them.

But you never forgot. Not completely.

The name spread from platoon to platoon, and though even in this small fraternity there was disagreement over what exactly an *onchú* looked like or was, it seemed to fit them all as one.

Macha was ten miles outside Cusp when the Onchú set out. Guns were loaded, horses were brought up and saddled, and there would have been no delay at all except that the leader of Fifth Platoon, a grizzled old stump of a man named Lugha, noticed that their Answering scribe seemed not to be saddling up with them.

'How are you going to count,' he said, in genuine confusion, 'from all the way back there?'

Hafely had an answer. He had several answers, in fact, because he'd thought the exact same thing and wanted to have some kind of protestation prepared. However, looking up at the Croí warrior bursting out of his unfastened coatee, he found he couldn't argue at all.

That slowed Fifth Platoon a touch. By the time Hafely had been helped up onto a horse and set out down what the Croí called the Slighe Mhór – the Great Road – and what the Answering simply called Highway West, First and Second Platoon were already engaged.

In a way, the tactics utilised on that misty morning were not dissimilar to the tactics of the old Croí outriders, the hobelars. Light skirmishers suited to the terrain who darted and nipped at larger forces like marsh midges. Sometimes hobelars were so confident in their speed they would actually dismount to fight with javelin and sword after a charge and only take to the saddle when the shock of their attack began to wear off.

Other times, they would stay on horseback, quick as swallows on the turn, and let volleys of arrows pepper and prick before fleeing to a safe distance and letting the whole dance begin again.

That was the tactic they deployed that morning, against the shins of a striding god.

Macha was ahead of them, a swaying mountain on pistoning, pillaring legs. She was in no hurry, it seemed, though the sound and violence of even her slow prowl made it hard to imagine what she would be like at a run. She moved with the kind of rolling, forward-leaning gait you saw in warriors who killed off the battlefield as well as atop it.

First and Third Platoons went left. Second and Fourth Platoons went right. Fifth Platoon fell into rearguard, dodging occasional crumbs of masonry that fell from her fingers, each digit as long as a young oak.

The Slighe Mhór wasn't the equal of even a regional road in the Answering. It wasn't something clearly defined, because the old Croí didn't have the means of shaping the landscape but instead shaped themselves around it. So instead it was a winding, gracious piece of track that Answering kings had covered with stone as far as the western border of the Cuspwood. It was said that the hoofprints of the first Croí *ríthe* still survived underneath the coloniser's shale.

Now Macha drove new hoofprints down atop it, each one man-deep and paces wide.

In those few short miles the god did more earth-moving and excavation than any king in the Medalwyn line. Trees were flattened into splinters or knocked drunkenly forward like fangs. Mud drizzled down even on the stones that were not skewed or broken, tarnishing the whole road to a cattle trail.

There were bodies everywhere Macha had trod. A sea of them, turning the ground into a lumpen quagmire of burst flesh and jagged bone. The horses had to dance over or swing wide, and even the simplest manoeuvre was made a feat of strength and dexterity by those hammering hooves coming down.

And yet by the tenth mile, the Onchú knew to belly themselves low in the saddle on impact, rise up in time with her foot, what words to use to soothe their mounts. The first tenets in a new discipline.

Hunting the divine.

They arrayed themselves back and diagonal so as not to catch each other in the crossfire, using the border of the road as a sighting line. Not because there was any chance of missing the bulbous shin, but because extreme range after that first shot was their best chance of potentially firing a second. One scruple was better than a half, after all.

The leaders of each platoon raised their fists and pointed. There was no point in shouting. Not over the tidal wheeze of horse breath, the liquid swish of muscles under skin.

The Onchú unlimbered their guns.

Took aim.

Muttered prayers and apologies under their breath.

Fired.

Hafely, a half-mile back on a scrubby little hillock – there was no way he was coming any further – made a note.

Every man. Every round.

Macha turned. Slow at first, but with the slowness of autumn – a slowness that crested into a frightening kind of speed. She did not draw her sword. It was ludicrous to think she might have needed to. She simply brought a hand down in an irresistible arc and tore a chunk of soil the size of a city street away with the tips of her nails.

The sacrifice of the Onchú would not be recorded anywhere in Answering military history, nor even in the muddled, earnest military saga-writings of the Croí.

It would have taken a saint of death to hear the prayers they whispered as they fired, as they fled, as they died, as hands like warships plucked them from the earth and flung them angrily into the sky.

But there were no saints on the field that day.

27

Talasa

IT ALL MOVED quickly after that. Suspiciously quickly, one might have said, though this was a sentiment Talasa expressed to no one but herself, and nobody asked.

She had said quite enough already.

The dress was Bearm silk, charcoal grey cut a little low over a snow-white kirtle, with a hood in the traditional boxed style. There had been a debate over whether to trim her cloak with ermine, and what kind of statement it made, but in the end, Offrian had decided against it as being too disrespectful to sumptuary law.

They'd breakfasted together that morning – a pinched, quiet meal where he was swarmed with Cursors delivering messages or finessing final details. Talasa had picked at bread and salted butter, and wondered what would happen if she picked up one of the fat grapefruit halves between them and squeezed it over her dress. Probably they had spares.

'It's nearly healed,' Offrian said, not looking up from whatever report he was reading. He had been in the Bicameral from sunup to sundown the last three days. Debating. Cajoling. *Listening*, which had deeply confused them.

He confused Talasa too.

She reached up and touched her cheek. 'It is.'

'Shame,' he said. 'It makes a statement.'

They set out from the Palace in a procession six carriages long – flanked on all sides by kingscarls, both mounted and on foot. For once, their passage through the winding streets went smoothly, instead of the usual jolting, fitful mess. Work had been done to clear their path, Talasa supposed. Another great effort Offrian had overseen. And this morning at least, everyone in the city was moving in the same direction.

In the Shore, my entire life was walking. Mile after mile after exhausted mile, eyes set determinedly on the narrow shoulders in front of her because Kalifsena knew where she was going and Talasa did not. Hours upon hours of making meaning out of wilderness. Of learning that featureless dune and track and steppe was in fact a library, a museum and a storehouse – a place where anything could be turned to usefulness.

Even Talasa. Especially Talasa.

This morning, however, it was Offrian making that meaning, and she was not the only one who had followed him. Dreodyrne sat on a miles-wide flood plain – a strange, semi-artificial sprawl of reclaimed marsh, winding riverlets, embankments and farms. Villages here were as singular and well defined in their purpose as the Master of the Elaborate – Tikney for your wool, Hanton for your salt.

Codlethaf for executions.

Talasa had never been to the little hamlet before, and she did not truly feel as if she was there now. When she exited the carriage into the wet, midgy air, she found freshly cut boards of birch placed down as a path, because Codlethaf had no cobbles to speak of.

Rows of kingscarls, neat and straight as the planks under her feet, stood as an honour guard on each side so she could not see the houses either. Just the faces of the crowd through the soldiers, pale and slick in the rain, shucked like whelks out of their city by the chance of spectacle and the invitation of a prince.

A viewing platform had been constructed, ten feet high and twenty long, crowded by a sombre clutch of specifically invited peers. That had been a late night for Offrian too. Deciding who would benefit most from an invitation, and who would benefit most from having to make their way here amongst the peasant stock. Talasa had offered counsel on that, but the Prince had declined.

An invitation had been prepared for the Queen as well, but neither Talasa nor Offrian had known where to send it. Talasa had entertained a mad, wild hope that when she arrived at this platform, Kalifsena would be there, that word had reached her somehow of what was happening in her absence.

Children always believed their parents knew everything.

But it was just Offrian, smiling down at her from the top of the stairs, extending a gloved hand. He was in red, and he had worn ermine, at neck and cuff. It made him look younger.

Talasa took his hand, and they paused together, her a step below.

'They're quiet,' she said under her breath. It was true. The turnout was impressive, an undulating carpet of commoners, stretching almost to Kilpick to the west, but the miserable morning seemed to have leached the sound from the air.

'They're waiting,' he said.

No one had ever tried to assassinate a Princess-Undynast before. There had only ever been a handful of them to begin with, and each of them had lived quite unremarkable, quietly miserable lives. Talasa had looked them up, of course, very early on, and been mutely enraged on their behalf at how little she'd found.

To be Undynast at all was to be unorthodox. There had been a mistake, or passion, or rules broken to create someone so outside the norm. Surely that warranted more? More than a paragraph in a book it had taken Master Colby a week to find?

Another question Talasa would never ask.

But Princess-Undynasts were royals, of a kind at least, and those who tried to assassinate members of the royal household were by custom executed outside the gates of the city. Locating a suitable village, the construction of the platform, the dress . . . It had taken days.

Strange then, perhaps, that finding the actual culprits had seemed to take no time at all.

'Come on,' Offrian said, and she stepped up beside him. Another platform had been constructed in Codlethaf's minuscule village square. At some unknown signal, six men and a woman were brought out to stand on it.

The Speaker of the Bicameral had an equivalent for these matters too, though they were rarely called upon, and it seemed as if the role had much diminished, or never been a position of high office to begin with. Just a thick-jawed man in shapeless black, standing next to the shivering Croí in their chains.

Talasa didn't listen as he read the charges, but she did listen to the names. They were musical, fanciful almost, and it occurred to her that this was the first and only time she had ever really heard any Croí. She did not have an especially good ear for languages. It had been hard work to learn Answering as quickly as she did. She worked hard at these names too, but the shape of them did not quite fit in her head.

The man in black stumbled to a halt over the last of the ornate phrases, and then the first of the men was pushed hard to a little block. The boxy hood that Talasa wore made a frame for it, forcing her to see every detail in sharp relief.

He looked like a labourer. He had a scar on his pate and thinning hair and a belly. He looked as if he was no stranger to the back of a soldier's hand.

They stretched him out. Bared his wrist. The man in baggy black hefted the axe a couple of times. Rolled his shoulders.

'You're just taking his hand?'

Talasa didn't realise she had spoken aloud until Offrian answered.

'The hand that did the deed goes first. That's tradition. Then you do the rest.'

The axe came down, and then, at last, the crowd began to cheer.

Afterwards, there was a reception at the Palace.

Nothing too ostentatious. Just a hundred or so of the Peerage in the Ivy Room, with a sit-down six-course meal and the Wlanc choir performing a selection of compositions from the Age of Decency. Most of the invitees came straight from the execution and were met at the Ealdfaeder Gate with glasses of hot port and delicate parcels of sturgeon and blackbird.

Talasa liked the Ivy Room. She wandered it sometimes when it was between uses, when the tables and candelabras had been cleared to reveal a space large enough to fit the *gord* in which Rubeo and

Kalifsena had fallen in love. The floor was in white pile, and the walls were patterned with the same black ivy that choked half the buildings in Dreodyrne, so when it rained you felt like you were in a version of the city made just for you.

Now, however, the rain could not be heard, and the lonely, welcoming grandiosity of the place was choked out by colourful dresses and braying, satisfied laughter.

'You'll sleep better.' It sounded like a command, but then again, so did everything out of Rhetorician-General Hlaew's mouth. 'Knowing those bounders have been slain.'

'Not just me,' Talasa had agreed. 'All the Answering, I think.'

He'd chortled. Told her he might use that line himself. And at least he'd spoken to her directly. Most of that cramped, overheated afternoon was spent drifting ignored through spaces as narrow as the wall passages she'd used to hide behind, though here they were made of elbow and gut and gesture.

'What did that last one shout?'

'Which one?'

'The woman.'

'Something in Croí.'

'I know that, Terrel, I know it was in Croí. Does anyone know what she *said*?'

Terrel, Eorl of Hofermod, who owned a third of the new exemplar settlements they were trying to fill in Cauci, snorted into his burntwine.

'How would we?'

She endured three more congratulations, four more well-wishes and what she was almost certain was an invitation to courtship before she stumbled out onto where the balcony overlooked the West Gardens.

Rhetorician-General Hlaew had been correct. That lone woman, rain-smeared, chained at the ankle and stretched tight as a bow at the wrist by two men trying to prepare her for the axe. Her head thrown back, roaring something in that fluid tongue that not a single person in the crowd could understand.

That would feature in Talasa's sleep for a long time to come.

The natural dusk was infinitely preferable to the hot, perfumed twilight she had left behind, and though the hemisphere curve of the balcony was clotted with little groups, they all seemed far more interested in each other than her.

Talasa closed her eyes. Let the cool air leach the flush from her skin.

'Enjoying your night?'

It was Tell. He wore a black robe against the chill, and a single mussed curl stood out proud from his beard like a claw against his throat. Talasa could not help but stare at it. That little detail out of place.

'Reeve Paramount,' she began. 'I hope you are—'

He cut her off. 'Tired,' he said. 'Mostly I find myself tired. As you must be. Such a shock. Such a tumultuous few days.'

'I am . . . improving,' Talasa said.

'I thought so,' Tell murmured. 'Considering how much more you now seem to remember.'

She stiffened. 'Reeve Paramount?'

He turned away from her then, folding his arms and leaning on the carved railing. Laughter drifted up from the gardens. Lanterns had been set out, but the majority of the lawn was in shadow.

'You were in shock, of course,' he said. There was no sympathy in his voice. 'Perhaps it was only after some convalescence that the memory returned to you. Some . . . ministration from your mother. Or a kind word from the Prince perhaps.'

'The *Queen* did not minister to me overmuch,' Talasa snapped, loud enough that heads turned in their direction. 'And Prince Offrian was not there. I remembered the nature of the attack on my person by myself.'

What did she expect from that revelation? What did she want? Understanding? Respect? A moment where someone, *anyone*, understood that she was not a wire puppet bound up in cloth but the hands that stitched that cloth in place?

Whatever she had hoped for, she had not expected scorn.

'I wish you hadn't,' Tell said. 'I fear we all will, before this is done.'

The Queen's apartments were in the eastern wing of the Palace, looking out over the Dreor in a view that might have been beautiful had the weather ever cooperated. Talasa moved silently over rich-piled rugs from northern Terod – favoured by Queen Preciosa – and traditional Shore kilim, so familiar she had the urge to slip off her shoes and feel the flat weave under her toes. Plunder from some centuries-old raid – Rubeo had ordered them taken from storage and cleaned so as to better welcome his new Queen, completely unaware that it did exactly the opposite.

How is it so easy to get it wrong? How can we be such strangers to those we love?

Talasa had no idea what she was looking for. If the Queen did not want to be found, for whatever reason, she would not have left an indication of where she was going. All Talasa was hoping to find was a clue to her mother's actions that she could use to find her. Some little insight that the Queen had not anticipated or guarded against.

I deserve some kind of truth.

Two years of being a ghost. Of preserving her mother's secrets. Of acting the dullard. Of living in the walls. *Deserve* was a word she had never been allowed to play with before. *Deserve* was a refuge of kings and people with power.

When you had nothing, *deserve* was a threat.

There was a kingscarl outside the Queen's apartments. Talasa positively revelled in his shock when the meek little girl, the shadow to the Queen's brilliance, snapped that the doors be opened.

He hopped to as if she were a prince.

Why was that never discussed? Why was there never a world where I was allowed not just to speak but to shout – a world in which I moved instead of being moved?

The disappointment in Tell's eyes.

Worse, the fear.

The pathetic little pile of hands lying on that stage.

If you'd trusted me to be more than a shadow, would I have known enough not to lie?

The Queen's apartments were as sprawling as Talasa's were cramped. Even here, in this private sanctum, you could see the careful push and pull of culture and camouflage. The receiving chamber was decorated in as classically an Answering style as one could wish, with a painted floor depicting the wives of the First Among, the walls plastered in white-slashed black where they were not hung with tapestries depicting Answering undertakings and triumphs.

Only Talasa could spot little hidden rebellions – the wild flowers collected every day from the Heroes' Glade, a ceremonial tea set that once belonged to the Duchess of Salins, donated in a rare show of friendship between two nations.

She slipped like a spirit from room to room, skim-reading correspondence and fumbling through desks, earning a coat of sweat that was more nerves than exhaustion.

There had to be something. Some clue. Some explanation. Something that would solve her tangled heart and allow her to confront Kalifsena. Or better yet, allow her to go back to her room and wait patiently like a little doll, content as she always had been that her mother knew better than her.

It was true night by the time she gave up. She stared at it out the window as scraps of plans ran through her head – beg Offrian to reconsider taking action against Croí, tell the Rationale she had lied – but none of it would do anything.

They didn't want the truth to be true. They preferred the lie instead.

She had just resigned herself to leaving when she caught the sound of an argument outside. The kingscarl, voice flat and plodding.

And someone else. Female. Agitated. Young.

'You have to let me see her. Please!'

'She's not *here*. Now get out before I send someone for your father!'

'What is going on?' Talasa asked, slipping from her mother's quarters. The kingscarl flushed. Beyond him, her servant's kirtle and coat as rumpled as ever, stood the girl Talasa could not help but think of as the Daughter of the Elaborate.

'Princess-Undynast,' the kingscarl said gruffly. 'Do not concern yourself. This girl was looking for the Queen and—'

Her hair was loose around her shoulders. She'd done up her coat wrong, and it had made one side of her collar lopsidedly high.

'And I will have to do,' Talasa said. 'Come inside.'

They sat in the receiving room. Talasa lit a handful of candles, briefly worried that her frantic search of the place would be detectable, but the Daughter just looked around, eyes enormous. Even to someone who'd grown up in the Palace, this was an order of finery she'd never seen.

'You wished to speak to my mother,' Talasa said gently.

The Daughter scrubbed at her nose. Looked everywhere but at Talasa.

'I have a brother in the Red Grettas. He says it'll be war. War with Croí. New regiments founded and sent out. Is that true?'

Talasa said nothing. Offrian had spent days at the Rationale. She was no longer qualified to say what was true or not.

'Is that . . . why you came?'

The Daughter swallowed hard. When she did meet Talasa's eyes, she looked nothing like her father and everything like a scared little girl. 'The Queen has to make the King come home. To stop all this.'

Well, they wouldn't take her hand at least, Talasa thought numbly. *But the Master of the Elaborate will have to find himself a new title.*

She was about to warn the Daughter just how reckless she was being when the girl reached out and grabbed her hands. The Daughter's were sweaty and ferociously hot, or maybe that was Talasa's, but either way the sudden intimacy of it made Talasa want to recoil.

'If you write to her, she'll listen,' the girl babbled. 'Won't she? I can bring it to her if you . . . *You have to tell her.* She'll listen to you. Won't she? Just write to her and tell her . . .'

'Write to her,' Talasa repeated. 'Are you telling me the Queen is still receiving her correspondence?'

'I'm sorry,' the girl babbled. 'She was so kind to us. Wrote a letter of support to my brother to apply for his regiment. She wanted to . . . to stay across everything, but not have anyone use it to track down the King . . .'

The King.

'Look at me,' Talasa said. '*Look at me.*'

Eyes brimming, the Daughter obeyed.

'Do you know where they are?'

28

Sister Wake

SISTER WAKE JERKED out of sleep to the sound of Brother Wight's laugh.

They'd made landfall the night before, at a narrow beach cupped by grass-thatched dunes, seals watching sleepily from the surf, barking and rolling as if drunk. Sister Wake sat upright, feeling the beach's clamminess through her blanket, and looked around to find the Knight of the Hollow Eye on the very edge of the tide.

He was feeding an elk made of moonlight.

'What the fuck—'

'Shh!' he said, without turning around. The elk angled its huge wedge of a head to look at her. That was what shut her up more than anything else. The beast was enormous – fully seven feet tall at the shoulder, bearded like a grandfather. You could have put three of Sister Wake toe to crown in the spread of its antlers.

And it stood, daintily, on the top of the waves.

When Sister Wake said nothing more, the elk lowered its silver muzzle down to Brother Wight's hand and resumed its snuffling, searching licks.

'It likes the salt,' he said. 'I tried some rushes, but it didn't seem as interested.'

There were more of them. Ten, fifteen – it was harder to tell the further away they were. Breakers sloshed up and *through* their legs, though flecks and drops of the water seemed to hang inside their gleaming white haunches before dropping down as rain.

Only this one had come close enough. When it rubbed Brother Wight's fingers with its tongue, the young man laughed again, low and gentle.

'A great thing. Look at you, you beauty.'

It snorted into his hand, as if it could understand him.

'What are they?' Sister Wake asked. The hammering in her heart had subsided, replaced by a surprising hunger. She came down the beach slowly, sweeping up her *brat* from where she'd used it as another layer, and shook out sand.

The elk watched her warily.

'I don't know,' Brother Wight said. 'There haven't been elk like this since long before the Answering. I don't know who these . . .' he circled a hand uselessly through the air, 'belong to.'

'Do you know,' Sister Wake said, and for once the smile she gave him was not tinged with anything but joy, 'I don't know if I care.'

They should have gotten on the move. There was a Goddess of Death on the northern side of Umhaill, and they were on the south, and every extra day it took Sister Wake to reach her might cost lives or the island entire. She mightn't have trusted Mother Promise, but she didn't disagree with her on that at least.

It was desperately selfish. Somehow Sister Wake's personal want and that of the Rising had aligned to lure her home. Worse, Mathilde was waiting and hoping for them to come back. Sister Wake knew what it was like to wait, as the dawn rose.

But this morning, they fed a spectral elk that kicked sprats of water at them until Sister Wake squealed and Brother Wight led her laughing back. Two more of the beasts came over now – moon-haunched and horned fit to crown a king – and these ones seemed to like Sister Wake more, yawing their massive heads side to side so they could look at her first with one eye, and then the other.

'What are ye thinking?' she asked them quietly. 'What are we to you? Are we intruders in your land or are you intruders in ours?'

She wasn't sure if she'd been expecting it to actually respond or not. Stranger things had happened. But the elk's only reaction to her gentle blasphemy was to look at her with its bright, soulful eyes.

And then the sky rang with the distant sound of matchlock fire. Suddenly the beasts were in full flight, jerking away to wheel out over the waves, and Brother Wight was between her and the rest of the beach, his spear in his hand.

'Follow me,' he hissed, all humour gone. 'And stay low.'

They left the beach behind, weaving between hairy dunes and outcrops of rock before eventually cresting the hill. To the south was the ragged swell of mountain they called Donn's Seat. North, Scáthach's Plain was a rumpled coverlet of barley fields and stubbly, stubborn grass, river-scored and mist-threaded, sprinkled with clusters of whitewashed cottages like seagulls nesting too far inland.

'No,' Sister Wake whispered, and Brother Wight cursed too, shifting his grip on his spear.

It was all burning. The houses. The fields. The destruction was clear and methodical – a spreading, gnawing line of light like fire eating a page. *The Answering.* You knew their work by the neatness of the carnage.

Sister Wake caught herself, buffeted suddenly by the distant chime of dying wheat. The demented panic of plovers, their ground nests swept up by crackling heat. Field mice running and running and finding the flames far faster than they could ever be—

She stopped rigid, pulled back by Brother Wight's hand on her arm. She'd been walking forward without realising it. He pulled her down onto the slope, the grass scratchy under her elbows, prickling her chest through her shirt.

'But Mother Promise said the Answering were retreating . . .'

'They are,' Brother Wight said. 'But not all at once, and not at the same speed. And when the Answering go, they burn what's behind them. Especially if it could be more than a season until they take it back.'

'Don't,' Sister Wake said, seeing his calculating expression. 'Don't tell me you think this is a *good sign*.'

She shouldn't have been surprised. As if the occupiers would just go home like a child with a slapped hand. Winning would be as bloody as losing, until all was torn up, root and stem.

'Cut-off forces,' Brother Wight said grimly, as if she hadn't spoken. 'That's what Creidne said. I thought we could avoid them. That they'd lie low, afeared of retaliation. Hoping for rescue. But Answermen fear nothing unless they're taught. Maybe . . . What are you doing?'

The wind was picking up, tidying strands of mist before it. The closest of the villages was dwarfed by the smoke cloud above it, fat and violent against the sky. It was at the absolute terminus of her saintly senses, but it was close enough for her to hear the wavering song of souls at the brink.

Like the shriek of a fox cub, pleading for help.

'I'm just going to see,' she said, and the casual lilt in her voice tried and failed to hide the anger. 'Won't be a minute.'

'No,' Brother Wight said instantly, and then reached for her hand as she began to walk. '*No.* This isn't our fight.'

'It is our fight,' she said. 'That's what people keep telling me.' She looked back at him, the ragged cleft on his cheek, his shadow stark against the hillside. 'That's what you keep telling me. Isn't this, right now, what we're for?'

She could see the fire reflected in his dark eyes, until he closed them, and raised his spear.

'Lead the way,' was all he said, and then together they began to run.

There were ten Answermen in that first village. By the end of it, Sister Wake knew all their names.

It was an ugly, stupid little battle, and it was all the worse for being fought piecemeal through the smouldering carcass of innocent lives. The soldiers of Thirteenth Squad, Seventeenth Regiment – known colloquially as the Grey Preciosas – had been left behind in the wake of the general withdrawal east.

Nobody was calling it a retreat. Men had been whipped for that. Serving in a colony meant serving at the whims of paranoid, fragile leaders who saw enemies in every shadow. Sometimes those enemies wore the same uniforms, and if you disagreed, you could become the enemy too.

That was the reality of serving on Croí. The problem was that you could threaten whipping all you wanted, but whispers spread like plague through regiments, and the whispers were that reality was not cooperating on the island any more.

That was *outside the levy*, as the Answering parlance went, for the soldiers of Thirteenth Squad, even before Brother Wight killed them. Every regiment had a squad like the Thirteenth, if not several – a drain around which all the malcontents, idiots and cowards gathered like scum.

Withdrawal procedure if you were going to burn a Croí village was that you always left at least a squad behind. To make sure the job was done. To make sure you caught any rebels the fire beat from the undergrowth. And to kill anyone who tried to put it out, of course.

Croí were only capable of half learning the lessons you taught them. Sometimes it took a second go. And the Thirteenth were good at teaching. That, at least, was an area in which they excelled.

Private Ansel was the first to die. He'd also been the first to set a fire here, because Private Ansel enjoyed fire the way other soldiers might enjoy ale. He did not count the days to off-rotation as other soldiers did, but the days when the order was given to set flame stood out in his dreary life like . . . well, fire.

He'd wandered away for a piss, away from the village's measly main square and through a knot of cottages to a little patch of wildflowers – pink and saffron against the green. He hadn't needed to go so far. The village was not large, but it was a messy, overlapping tangle of cottage and laneway, and the smoke had added new hazy architecture, so there was plenty of cover.

Hell, he could have pissed wherever he wanted. Henroch would have. Certainly Daui. There were no Croí men left in the village to do anything about it, even if they dared.

But Ansel was not brave, except when it came to fire. He, like most of the Thirteenth, and many of the Grey Preciosas, had never been in a standing battle. The time when a Croí might fight you was long gone, aside from a panicked, brawling kind of fight, like an animal in a trap.

It had been gone before Ansel had been born.

Still, the way the women looked at you as you dragged the men out and made them kneel in the dirt. The way the children watched, uncrying, from behind them, each one less a person than a seed, an ember yet to catch.

Fire was easier. Fire, Ansel knew, was grateful you set it.

He was tucked pissing into a porch when Brother Wight drove his spear directly into the space between his shoulder blades. Ansel went from standing to kneeling in an instant, hooked down like a sleeve on a nail, and his last moments were spent frantically trying to stuff himself back into his uniform trews with hands that no longer worked.

Sister Wake read all that off the smoking heat of Ansel's lifeblood and felt nothing. Villages, after all, did not have souls to mourn.

The next to die was Happy Paud.

He was named this because he was always happy, or never happy – Sister Wake wasn't sure. A stupid nickname, something stupid men came up with when they were forced into comradeship and cohabitation by the stroke of a clerk's pen.

Sister Wake would never know, because it wasn't what Happy Paud was thinking when Brother Wight came around a corner with knife held at chest height, point out. With Brother Wight's other hand on Happy Paud's mouth to stifle his gasp, you couldn't see if he was smiling or not.

Smoke churned like brambles as the two Croí moved through the village, hunting. It was a strange, procedural arrangement – Brother Wight darting from cover to cover the way you might climb a cliff, every nook and cranny like a handhold. From woodpile to shadow to old standing stone miraculously undestroyed after three centuries of foreign hate.

And then Sister Wake, coming like winter, frost stiffening the skin over her hands like brass knuckles or scabs. She didn't feel the cold, though she knew it was there, smoking around her in particles of white.

Her eyes weren't closed. She just wasn't seeing out of them.

Instead, she saw out of the eyes of a pony, glassy and ruined in their beauty as a mirror knocked from a shelf. She did not consider waking it. It had been through enough. But its murderer still stood over it, leaning on the spear driven into its side like the handle of a shovel after a long day's work, and just for that, Sister Wake sent her Knight about his work.

Four in the square then, loitering around what had been the village hall. Sister Wake mapped them through a hundred dead eyes. Peered through a curtain of dissipating souls like an oul one spying on the neighbours.

Garbled details of the village swam through her. She knew that the hall wasn't a hall, but the house of Old Maci, who had known how to build houses but not really known how to stop, and so it had a large room in the front that doubled as a drinking house and an infirmary and whatever else was needed for the day that was in it.

Something about the way the Answermen stood itched at Sister Wake, but she had no time to look deeper because . . .

Two other fuckers, west of the square and north of Brother Wight. They walked side-by-side, one complaining about the smoke stinging the spot inside his nostril, and the other half listening and half wondering should they have robbed some of the houses before they put them to the torch.

Theobard. Jon.

Sister Wake plucked their names from the dead. She would have loved nothing more than to drag those bodies upright, to wake the men who had lived and loved in this modest little place and let them take vengeance on the Answermen who had slain them.

That surprised her, because until now she had always been poisonously relieved that her talents only stretched as far as they did.

What had changed? Was it Mathilde? Was it jealousy that a child could do what she could not? Or was she only now understanding what it meant that the Croí were an occupied people? That occupation wasn't just a theft of land or wealth or crops or resources or religion or language, it was a theft of *lives* – thirty years of fatherhood from this corpse, twenty years of housework and planting from that.

Or maybe we'll just leave, hah? Go down the coast to Érainn. Or maybe we'll become sailors. How about that?

'What gives you the right?' she said aloud, as Brother Wight shoulder-charged Theobard forward onto the dirt, whipping his knife around to pin Jon's hand to his screaming face. 'What makes you think you deserve this?'

The saint of death looked into the Answerman soul and found nothing there that made it superior. They didn't love anything any more than rats did. They weren't capable of the fear of birds.

Answermen were just *men*, men with bad backs and night terrors, who hated that being in a foreign land scared them and enjoyed the power of harming it back.

Brother Wight tore his knife out of Jon in a welter of blood, and then turned to Theobard, who was trying to run. Sister Wake had no insight into Brother Wight. She didn't need it. She just gritted her teeth and tried not to hear the name of Theobard's mother, or about the callus on his hand, or any of the stupid shit that went through the soldier's head a split second before the spear did.

Just men. Which meant they were no different than—

An entirely different cold went through Sister Wake. She spun to Brother Wight in a flurry of ice crystals.

'The square,' she shouted. 'Now!'

For once, he listened, leaving the bloody boy at a sprint. Sister Wake was sure the remaining Answermen heard her too, but that didn't matter. She'd been distracted. Piecemeal. In too many heads to assemble the thought they were all half having.

But by the time Sister Wake and Brother Wight reached the square, the Answermen had already set the hall ablaze.

Flames climbed the log walls like ivy, opening runnels of gold in dark, dry wood. Sparks and smoke hazed the air. The thatched roof miraculously had not yet caught, and Sister Wake saw with languorous horror an Answerman, reed-slender in a too-big uniform, like a child dressing up as a soldier, draw back and fling a torch end-over-end up onto the dried, mud-plaited reeds.

It took with a gleeful purr.

There were four Answermen left. Two were by the hall's wide wooden doors, examining how they'd barred it with contemplative satisfaction. Another, the sergeant by his pips, was kneeling on the grass, sorting through the meagre shit they'd managed to steal. What could it even amount to – a week's wage for one of them? Two?

Sister Wake had killed herself by coming here. Brother Wight too. Only in stories did you take on more than four men at once and live.

But she didn't care. The door of the hall shuddered and shook. Hammered on from within.

The grass died beneath Sister Wake's feet. The air cracked with cold. Her clothes were mortis-stiff with frost. Somewhere distant, the world was hot and brutal with spilling blood. Somewhere distant, steam boiled from Brother Wight's cheeks as his hands sought an Answerman's neck, a knife already in the occupier's belly, but not deep, not deep enough to kill.

For Sister Wake, it was cold and quiet as the mountainside of Crom Dubh, and footsteps were echoing through her whole being, shaking the world.

Her footsteps.

The roof was properly ablaze now – a roaring sunset of orange and white. But Sister Wake was at the doors, and frost gauntleted her fingers, so that the sparks swirling around her turned to steam as they met.

A wrench, and they split apart. What strength was that? Not hers.

The doors opened, and she saw frightened faces. Streaked with tears. Sweat. Blood. They stared at her – and the fear became horror.

Horror at her.

'Goddess,' one of them swore, and then the roof fell in.

* * *

She didn't lose consciousness. Sister Wake was awake and aware when Brother Wight found her, heaving aside rafter and board in a frenzy, sick worry on his swollen face.

The thought of calling out had occurred to her, but then it had just drifted away. Her thoughts were leaves in a frozen pond, secure and separate in their own little sheaths of ice.

It was only when he cracked away the caul of frost covering her face that she found herself moving, hissing with pain at the heat in his hands.

'Anu above us,' he swore. 'Are you all right?'

Sensation returned piecemeal. Sister Wake was on her knees. Fastened to the ground by a skin of blue-glazed white, as if she'd kneeled down in a hundred-year blizzard and the world had packed her in snow.

Her skin felt like stone.

'Sister Wake,' he repeated. 'Are you—'

She heaved herself upright without responding. A whole section of roof fell from her shoulders. Plates of ice sloughed off like armour with its straps cut.

Brother Wight stumbled back, suddenly looking up at her, rather than down.

'I feel good,' she whispered, her tongue gritty with snow. *I feel strong.*

The ruin of the hall still stood, despite the fire. It might have collapsed entirely, except it was now supported by a scaffolding of frost, twinkling palely in the evening gloom. Ice covered the stamped-earth floor, thick as paving. It hung between the exposed ribs of rafters like monochrome gore, a ghostly reminder of what might have happened had she not intervened.

'What about you?' she asked.

He looked like shit. One whole side of his face was swollen. His left arm was a hacked mass from a flailing set of slashes, and he was standing as if he'd had a rib or two bruised.

Without thinking, she placed a hand on his injured cheek. He hissed, but she kept her freezing fingers clamped against him and she could see his eyelids flutter with relief.

'I'm . . . all right,' he said into her palm. 'They didn't put up much of a fight. Too busy . . . looking at you.'

'And the women?'

It was a stupid question. She knew their lives had been saved, yes. Saved to starve. Saved to eke out some sort of survival in a ruined village with their crops burned and their men slaughtered.

'They're grateful,' he said. 'But we should go. We've lost near a whole day as it is. And they said they'd do the burying. I think they'd like to . . .'

'They'd like me gone,' Sister Wake said. 'That's what you mean. I scared them.'

'You saved them.'

She shook away a cloak of frost. 'But I scared them.'

'You don't know, do you?'

'Know what?'

'Your eyes,' he said. 'Your skin. When you broke the door. Just for a moment . . .'

Her throat was raw. 'Say it.'

'You looked like her.'

Mother Promise liked to talk about the Croí that might have been. What progress the island might have made without a boot on its neck. What allies it might have, what poetry might have been written, what buildings raised.

The Rising grieved for the might-have-been.

And Sister Wake threw back her head and began to laugh, trying to wrap her head around how she'd begin to grieve for herself.

V

We Will Be a Land of Ghosts

29

Sister Wake

IN THE END, it was the crying that drove Sister Wake away up into the fields behind the village, the way a stick might drive a dog.

She must have slept after she and Brother Wight had spoken, because she woke in the dark with her fingers pressed to her eyelids, feeling the round and gelid orbs cradled beneath. They felt real. They felt like they always had, or at least as they had since Crom Dubh.

Dry.

The roof hung down across the doorway, but embers still stubbornly smoked in the remains of the houses across the square. Sister Wake pushed herself to her feet, wincing as she did so. She felt old. Her joints popped like shards of ice in water, like the cubes she had heard Answering peers liked to put in their gin.

A part of her wanted to stay in the burned-out home for ever. It said something to how shook Brother Wight had been by her antics that he didn't force their leaving, but simply stated his advice. He hadn't stayed, and she hadn't blamed him. How could he have endured the cold?

There was a wail building in a throat, somewhere out of sight.

Sister Wake ducked beneath a fallen rafter of ice-slicked wood and stepped out into the damp grass of the square. It was deserted.

Even the bodies were gone. Even the smoke, gathered away by the star-filled sky. The place could have been just a village again, a little knot of living souls at the centre of four laneways of packed earth, each one bisected by a stubborn tuft of grass like the fuller of a sword. It was hard to see any blood on the earth at all. *Failures to the end*, she told the souls of Thirteenth Squad, as they decayed in her like slush in mud.

She moved urgently now, darting between the houses, as hungry not to be seen as when the place had been full of Answermen. Was there a graveyard? Would they have buried the men all together, somewhere out in the fields?

She didn't know, or care. All that mattered was escaping the hitching, holy whine.

The Answering called it *keening*. Sister Wake knew this because the Answering was crammed with men who wrote about Croí women the way you might write about interesting dogs, and because the Rising had a *keen* recollection of every institutional insult levelled against them.

So keen, Mother Promise liked to say, it would sharpen your knife.

A second voice joined, flat and chisel-like against the sawing trill of the first, and the saint of death found herself running – flinging herself over low walls and trampling patches of hawthorn and dock.

Keening. That was what they called it, because the Answering butchered pronunciation the way they butchered men. They drew cartoons of ugly round women falling over themselves in tears like inn-stage clowns, cheeks and eyes swollen. The practice of women weeping so publicly and unashamedly, they wrote, was at best a sign of the raw childishness of the uncivilised soul. At worst, it was a base scrambling for posture by the deceased. A monetisation of tears. A status symbol. The more they wept, the more you were loved.

Of course they would see it as such. No Answering could picture weeping for Croí dead to be anything other than performance.

It was incredible, Sister Wake thought, how a people could know so much and understand so little. Incredible that you could hear the wail of the *caoineadh* and call it *crying*, when it bore as much resemblance to simple grief as a teardrop did to the sea.

Were there women who showed up to every funeral, black-veiled and grey-braided, ready to cry, whether they knew the dead or not? Yes. Death was death. The *mnáthan-tuirim* – the women who shared their *caoineadh* with the world – did not need to love someone to feel loss. Besides, these women *did* know everyone, because everyone knew everyone, and that meant every loss was felt.

Was it public, and unadorned, and hiccupingly, retchingly honest in a way that few people would ever show another? Yes, of course! Why was sorrow a secret? Why were tears a source of shame?

Maybe because sorrow so public was an act of rebellion. Maybe because this was a land of flattened people who saw their own killed out of contempt every day, and if you were allowed to mourn, you might start to resist.

Caoineadh wasn't crying. It was a song. It was a snarling, shrieking, spontaneous choir that harried Sister Wake out across the village wall and into thick grass that plucked and slit her legs. It was a song, bitter and magnificent and entirely unique to the soul in the ground. There was no match to it in this living world, and the saint of death ran from it in terror, because it was far too like the music she heard when a soul was beaten from its sheath.

'I thought I'd find you here.'

The shape in the darkness unfolded itself, lifting its spear from its knee.

'Don't worry,' she snapped, scrubbing a sleeve across her face. 'I wasn't planning on sneaking off.'

'I didn't think you were,' Brother Wight said, and rearranged himself on the long, flat rock he had taken as a seat. After a moment, glaring at him suspiciously, Sister Wake sat too.

'Who moved the bodies?'

'I did.'

'Sweet of you.'

He sniffed. 'You were sleeping.'

The hill was broad and flat, tipping towards the village like the hat brim of an Answering dandy. Boulders littered it like beads, some sunken into the earth, others sitting proud as if they had been dropped just yesterday, though all were green with moss.

Sister Wake picked at it with a finger.

'What were they like in your *túath*?'

Brother Wight thought for a moment. 'There were three of them that I knew. Gormlaith, Márgrég and Sabha. They might have been sisters. They certainly looked alike.'

The *mnáthan-tuirim* were in the full glory of their grief now, sharpening their voices against the sky with swift, short strokes of sound. A sob to a scream to words to a sob again, following no metre or plan. Like grief, the women did not know the shape of the noises they would make before they made them.

'I used to hate them,' Brother Wight said.

'Because they wept for your parents?' she said.

'Aye,' he said. 'And I was terrified that the sound of crying would bring the soldiers back. They used to put a couple of Answermen at every funeral.'

'In case a Brother showed up,' Sister Wake said.

'Or the family were a little too rebellious in their grief. But they didn't know what to do about the *mnáthan-tuirim*. Too old to club with a spear. For most, at least. But you could tell they wanted to. That sound . . .'

Sister Wake knew what he meant. To stand there, party to murder – as the soldiers were, to a man – and to hear that wail, day after day, funeral after funeral . . .

'My mam was one,' she said softly. She scowled. 'I say that like it was a job. Like it was all she was. It wasn't. She was funny. She was devout. She could argue an oyster out of its shell. But I used to be so . . .'

The song was like a fist now, battering the sky.

'. . . I used to be so frightened of funerals, because when she left the cottage barefoot in her shawl, I could see it welling up in her. Changing her. On those days, it *was* all she was.'

She picked at the moss again. Gentle, because if she killed it, she'd know.

'It could take a day for her to recover. She'd be snappy. Confused. Sad. Just . . . just deeply fucking sad. And at first, I wouldn't listen to Da. He'd tell me not to try and warm her up – that it was just her, that she'd be back to us soon, but . . . I was only a wain. I wanted my mam to laugh with me. And when *she* died, the *mnáthan-tuirim* came from all around. Women I'd never seen before. You could have heard her lament all the way up on Crom Dubh.'

'You didn't find it a comfort?'

'I couldn't find *her* in it at all,' Sister Wake said. 'I wanted to scream at them. *You didn't even know her. Why can you find your voice when I . . .*'

She stood up suddenly. 'Shouldn't we get going? Don't want them down there to finish their lament and start asking why we couldn't save them sooner.'

'You did save them.'

'Not all of them. We . . . cavorted on the beach like idiots for half a morning while they were losing their husbands. Their sons. Their brothers.'

Brother Wight raised a hand to his mouth, and Sister Wake realised he was hiding a smile.

'Cavorting,' he repeated. 'Is that what we were doing?'

She flushed. 'What? I . . . No! I just . . . What's so funny?'

He shook his head. 'You. This is why you're so reluctant? Not because you don't think fighting will change anything, but because you don't think it will change *everything*?'

'I know it won't,' she said. 'I can see that it won't. And saying it like that makes me sound petty and stupid. So thank you.'

'Actually, I was going to say that it's very sweet.'

She tensed. 'You were?'

'Yes,' he said. She could barely make him out. Just an eye and the very apex of his lip. 'It's not like you.'

'Oh fuck off,' she said, and then her heart became a part of her tongue as he took her shoulders and turned her towards him.

'What are you—'

'Look,' he breathed. For a brief, mad moment she wanted to wrap that plume of warmth around her like a cloak. Wrap *him* around her, until you couldn't have separated him from her with a blade.

And then he lifted his hands away, and she was staring away from the village, into the burned scabs of the fields.

The *caoineadh* had died away, and there were lights now – globes of gold texturing the black. Torch poles, illuminating the eastern approach to the village – a road you could almost call wide, the earth bare of grass and rutted by carts and horses.

Now, though, it was full of people. Nearly fifty women and old men, most in *léine* and trews, or *brat* and shawls against the night-time chill. All were soot-streaked, slumped with the particular kind of exhaustion that came with short periods of focused trauma rather than long periods of effort.

And yet they were laughing, and calling to each other, and smiles gleamed like daises in the golden dark.

'The children,' Brother Wight said quietly, as little forms moved through the crowd, seeking, shouting, laughing. 'Someone saw the Answermen coming and got them out and up into the hills before they could arrive. You know what—'

'What Answermen do,' Sister Wake said. 'I know.'

One of his hands was still on her shoulder.

'They're lighting the torches to guide them home, but it's a good walk back from the hills, and they're already halfway there, so I think the *caoineadh* guided them.' His voice was soft. 'There was someone left to sing. That's the point of it, I think. Otherwise, they might have come back to find . . .'

His hand shivered on her shoulder.

'You were there,' he said. 'It isn't everything. But today, it was enough.'

They stood there in silence for a long time, until part of the ceiling of the hall subsided and collapsed with a clatter of weakened timber. The ice was thawing.

'I saw into their heads,' Sister Wake said quietly. 'As we killed them. They didn't know much. Not the kind of men you trusted with any great wider plan. But there are more men like them out there. Burning. Killing. We could—'

'We have our mission. There are people relying on us.'

'I know,' Sister Wake said. 'I know what we have to do. But maybe on our *way* . . .'

'Is that what you want?' he asked. 'Right now? Is that what you want to do?'

Sister Wake had never been as afraid as when the single word left her lips.

'Yes.'

'Then we do as much as we can do,' her Knight of the Hollow Eye said, easing himself to stand with a hiss of pain. 'Aye.'

30

Abelard

AN HOUR BEFORE the Onchú left to die, Meilyr ran his men north to Promontory, eager as a dog for a fox.

The coast north of Cusp was all greening mudflats, thick with intestine weed and the belligerent calls of geese. Tidal channels and inlets met and meandered, textured as human skin. The evening air was made of midges, heavy with the pungency of decaying ectocarpus and the threat of oncoming rain.

The trunk road – that wide and raised esker that the Answering called Highway North – stood like a proud vein from the flats. A fast horse could make the run to Promontory in a day, if you didn't care what it did the day after. Meilyr had plenty of fast horses, and Abelard doubted he cared if they died beneath him.

But there was no traversing the trunk road now. Abelard did not know whether there was any direction or strategy behind the desire to escape the ruin Cusp had become. Certainly, Meilyr had not displayed any concern for those civilians under his care. But whether the decision to flee had been made by family, or by street, or by district or alone, Cusp was disgorging its inhabitants out along the roads that spread from it, and now an unconscionable number were fleeing north.

It was not a tidy migration, and the road could not contain it – bursting its borders like a river at flood time, bodies spilling out into the neat and ordered fields to the west and the soft marshes to the east that led down to the sea.

Bodies burdened with crates and bundles. Carts dragged along by horse or by hand, until the swell of flesh became too great, forcing them out of the main flow like splinters from a palm. Some tumbled down the esker's slope. Some stopped, to help or to watch or to loot.

Most just trudged on.

'There must be twenty thousand,' a soldier breathed. 'Thirty.'

'Quiet!' his sergeant snapped, with a look to Meilyr.

The party had stopped after just a couple of hours of riding, dismounting to lead their horses up a low hill thick with cordgrass and wildflowers. Black and white oystercatchers, smart as soldiers, darted around them, hunting for worms in the dirt.

Abelard watched them, or the fleeing crowds, because Netha would still not meet his eye.

The Lord Protector looked even more unhealthy in the sunlight. You didn't get a lot of pure colours in nature. Blacks were blue, or dark brown, or green. White was grey, or a little blue, or yellowed. Grey could be anything. Meilyr's monochrome neatness made him unnatural against the purple dusk.

'We can outpace them when they sleep,' he said with a papery sniff. 'Retake the road. Make up time.'

He was wrong. They struck on, plashing through narrow river crossings and past the black mouths of estuaries. Twenty riders hammering hell out of their mounts, the soldiers more liberal with their spurs than any rider Abelard had ever met.

But what was one more cruelty in service of the Answering?

Night came, and maybe those at the fringes of the exodus slept or made camp, but the body of the column did not, because to stop would have been to be trampled by those behind.

Macha was no longer visible on the horizon, but she loomed large all the same.

It was during one of those crossings, when a man had dismounted to assess the depth between a pair of stained old marking pillars, that the sergeant called out. 'My Lord Protector.' Abelard had not caught his name – a stout, hirsute man with a scabby upper lip. 'I wonder if we might stop until first light. We risk the horses on such uneasy ground.'

'Risk?' The word came out flat as iron, and the sergeant bobbed his head away from it, scrubbing his hand across his mouth. Abelard began to understand where that raw, abused skin might have come from.

'If we lose a horse, my lord—'

'Then we lose the man,' Meilyr rasped. 'Do you all hear that? Fall and walk, or hand back your matchlock and join that column of wretches instead. I'm sure they will take you gladly.'

He glared around him. 'You have until the moon rises.'

It was with a great deal of gratitude that Abelard slid off his horse. He was not used to riding such rough paths, and at such speed. He could not keep the stagger from his step as he crossed the little clearing, navigating the curious gazes of the men.

What did they think was going on here? They had witnessed Abelard help Meilyr. Seen the rage of the *filí*, and the death of one of their own. Netha had not been allowed to dismount, and three soldiers stood around them looking like they very much hoped the poet would try to fight.

One of them had Netha's sword belted to his waist.

'My lord?'

It took Abelard a moment to realise the soldier was speaking to him.

'Back to your horse, Caudefoy,' Meilyr called.

'You heard him.' The poet sat ramrod straight, the picture of nobility in their mud-stained cloak and blood-skited clothes. '*My lord*.'

They rode under a half-hearted moon, and then into an equally half-hearted dawn, and only then, a mile up the road, could Abelard see the column's head.

By that stage, of course, the column had made good notice of them too. People had shouted. Waved for help, or guidance, or direction. At one point, a group of men tried foolishly to run out and intercept Meilyr, desperate for aid, or maybe just their horses. It was only when twenty guns took aim that they faltered, cursing and afraid.

Abelard hated how quickly he began to yearn to be past them. He had endured the dubious pleasure of two great exoduses in the past days but at least the one to Anfloga Dock had been trammelled and dampened by the sea and the promise of safety. This was a flight from insanity into uncertainty, and that fear came out of every mouth in a furious tide of sound he wasn't even sure people knew they were making.

All he knew was that it was driving him mad too. He could feel it on his skin. Rattling around his head. Not just the noise, but the panic – breathless and instinctual, like some pumping animal migration from one Terod savannah to another.

And like any migration, it was not long before the predators came.

Abelard didn't notice at first. They were perhaps twenty miles from Promontory, and the great esker had begun to wind and wriggle as though trying to shake off its cargo. To the east, the ground had risen, trading the low shores and flats for craggy hills and attempted cliffs. To the west was the mist of morning, jealously occluding Croí from the settlers who had tried to conquer it.

Abelard was mostly concerned with keeping his seat, and riding with your hands bound did not make anything easier, especially when keeping up with Meilyr and his men, who rode like their narrow Croí greys were part of their anatomy.

And it was easy, damnably easy, to not look at the teeming, screaming masses as they stumbled, or trotted, or flat-out ran.

But then something in the timbre of the crowding masses changed key. The disorganised, throaty melee of thirty thousand souls in distress lifted in pitch. Found a horrid unity. The tapering tip of the column – a mere dozen souls wide instead of hundreds – swung as if struck by a single meaty hand, drizzling people like rain as they tumbled off the road into the road's low, long ditch.

'Stop!' Netha was bellowing, voice carrying hard and high over the shrieks. 'Now!'

Something had *impacted* the other side of the crowd. Slammed into it with terrible force.

Unable to see anything past the heaving masses and the morning fog, Abelard thought for a moment it was cannon fire. It had to be. What else would make bodies cartwheel through the air? What else would come with such a bass roar, send people shrieking and careening into each other?

And then, as the crowd parted and shredded, he saw.

It was a young woman with long red hair.

It was the story of Abelard's life that only the most useless details caught his eye. He was doing it now. It was such a foolish feature to latch onto, as he watched her pick up a fleeing man by leg and wrist and kick him in half with a bare and dainty foot.

She stepped into the red rain with her mouth open, and all Abelard could focus on was that hair – twelve feet long and curling like the tail of a thresher shark.

And there was another. Identical. Beautiful. Running so fast her feet slapped up great craters of shale, that banner of red hair a streak of blood in his eye.

And then there were a dozen of them.

And then there were a hundred.

Slowly, very slowly, that punch-drunk veer of the crowd spread back its length. Like a tray of beads lifted at one edge, the staggering, shambling cacophony began to run. Away from the ravaging women.

Towards Abelard and Meilyr's party, and the waiting, hostile sea.

'*Go!*' Meilyr screamed, and the world became a blur.

Had they been still picking their way across the mudflats, they would have been overrun. As it was, the terrain was hard and hilly but fundamentally solid, and terror glued Abelard to his saddle as his mount *flew*.

The world was a streaking blur. One entire side of it was faces, numberless and screaming, and Meilyr's party beat a path along its edge like a child running along a beach, trying to outstrip the tide.

Abelard caught a glimpse of two of the red women burrowing into piles of the fallen like maggots into a wound. One staggered around as if drunk, slick from head to toe with blood.

No. That wasn't right either. Her skin had flushed the way a leech flushed, and what she was drunk on was blood.

Netha was screaming something too. It sounded like *Shoot them.*

Abelard couldn't look. He couldn't look away. He couldn't look at the horde, because the sucking gravity of their faces would slow him and the horse down, he was sure of it; they would just falter and fall and maybe that would be better than another instant of seeing this thing, this awful thing . . .

He closed his eyes and clung, and hoped that when he opened them again order might have returned to the world.

31

Talasa

A TRUE MONSTER OF a storm was coming in from the west, clouds bulging like the flanks of a bull, overstuffed with muscle. Lightning marbled it like fat. Warm in her carriage, Talasa stared out at empty streets, the rain thrashing down on kingscarl checkpoints and soaked, huddling patrols.

Offrian had expected unrest, after the executions. Nothing could be allowed to undermine the story of justice being done. What he hadn't anticipated was the weather itself. Every roof had become a waterfall, and only when the streets narrowed sharply did the carriage lanterns pick single gables or doorways out of the murk.

It was only at the Halberd Gate out of the city that the carriage slowed to a halt. Talasa spun in her seat, a hideous flash of fear gripping her – another crowd, another attack – but it was the driver who stuck his head in the door, his rain cape heavy and shining with wet.

'Bit of a delay, Princess-Undynast,' he said through a thicket of drenched whiskers. 'The Dreor is already groaning. Sent the other driver ahead to see if the road's all right.'

He didn't wait for her to say anything before disappearing back out into the roaring deluge.

Talasa folded her shawl around herself and sat back to wait. She understood his worry. People died on nights like this. Bridges were washed away – not the proper stone constructions in the city, but the rough shanty crossings commoners constructed upriver because they couldn't afford the tithe.

In here, she had the space a family in Bysmor would have been grateful for, and some enterprising servant had even placed fat terry-cloth towels and cloth bags swollen with hot water. Talasa was warmer than she'd been in the Palace.

They'll notice you're gone. She dismissed the thought as soon as it arrived. They hadn't even noticed the Queen's absence. Or if they had, it no longer mattered. That was the Answering for you. It was *here* that was essential. Here was the world. If you removed yourself from it – as Talasa had for so long, as the King had, as the Queen had – you ceased to be relevant. How could you be, when you had walked away from where power lay?

It was the mistake the Queen had made.

Or . . . the mistake Talasa had *thought* she'd made.

Why leave the Palace? Why leave the capital, where all things were decided?

Unless power resided somewhere else.

Boxed in by the drumming rain, Talasa's world was the carriage. She couldn't hear anything outside, or maybe there was simply nothing to hear. She couldn't decide which was more unnerving.

And yet . . .

It had taken a bit of finding, but Women of the Sinew never threw anything away. Maybe the Queen still had hers. Talasa hadn't seen it in her chambers. But after that rushed, panicked conversation with the Daughter of the Elaborate, she had gone back to her own chambers, taking care to skirt the Ivy Room and its still-carousing guests.

It had been a great pleasure to strip off the fine Bearm silk and toss it in a corner. To crush the clean lines of the boxy hood. To reach into the depths of her closet and pull free the linen underdress, slip it over her head and knot the long linen ties. Then the *panova* wool apron and belt, and finally the bracelets that held the long sleeves back.

Despite everything, it felt good to be a Woman of the Sinew once again.

She lost track of how long it had been. More than an hour, certainly, as she stewed in her fears and her anger and the clatter of the rain. Long enough that they could have reached her destination by now, and that just made her angrier.

Is that where you've been, as everything began to crumble? Just ten miles north? Both of you?

She could have shouted with relief when the door to the carriage swung open. At least until she saw who it was.

'You can't be here.'

Offrian shook rain off himself like a dog as he climbed in through the doorway, his dark hair smeared to his scalp.

'I'm a prince. I can do anything I want.'

It wasn't regicide when you killed a prince. Talasa didn't know what it was called. Maybe they'd tell her before the execution.

Offrian grinned as if he knew exactly what was going through her head.

'Besides, you ran out on our reception first.'

He rapped his knuckles against the carriage wall, and to Talasa's horror, it began to move.

'Which begs the question . . . where are you going so late at night?'

'If the driver is in your pocket,' Talasa said stonily, 'then you already know.'

'Everyone's in my pocket,' Offrian said. 'It's my city. The question is – why go there at all? Why run out so hurriedly? Unless . . . you'd been summoned. Now – get up!'

He slid across the wooden seat opposite her, scattering cushions as he did so, and flapped his hands at her to rise. Talasa stood awkwardly, bent-backed and bracing her hand against the ceiling, and then yelped as the carriage bucked and she landed across the bench and on top of him.

Gently, very gently, Offrian sat her right. Then, before she could arrange her addled thoughts, he leaned forward and opened the lid of the bench she had been sitting on.

Inside, gleaming in the single lamp above their heads, were bottles and glasses, set into carved, cushioned gaps.

'Offrian,' Talasa began. 'Please listen to me. Turn back to the Palace. They'll be wondering . . .'

Maybe it was not too late to lie. Offrian knew only her destination. Maybe Talasa was simply on an errand. Maybe she was . . .

No. No lie she could tell would hold him for a second. There was a world, a world just a few days ago, where neither of them had much power to expose lies. To challenge the order of things. But they did not live in that world anymore.

I didn't destroy that world, Talasa thought. *I just have to live in it.*

'Let them,' Offrian said jauntily, but there was a vein of anger in it too. 'Is an hour or two too much to ask?'

A bottle was hoisted; its label turned towards her.

'A Bealusip white! This is the first wine I ever tasted. I felt like such a man drinking it, though I know there must have been less than a finger in my glass.'

He tutted and placed it back.

'Wait . . .' He rummaged further, withdrawing a squat little bottle that strobed gold and black in the light of the swaying lantern. 'Look at this. Croí whisky. From Whiteseal, obviously. It's outlawed everywhere else. Though I'd love to get my hands on a bottle of the stuff they brew out in the wilds. Heathens love their spirits.' He grinned at his own joke and plucked two glasses out with his fingers.

The sight of it made Talasa think of that morning. Of those musical, impenetrable words.

'This isn't a game, Offrian. You're using me to start a war.'

'A game?' Offrian said, suddenly serious. Rain was still beaded in his eyelashes. 'Talasa, I am the only person taking this seriously. The only person doing what they are supposed to do. All I want is for him to be doing the same.'

He offered the glasses. 'Hold.'

She did so.

'Answer me honestly. Is she out there?'

'I don't know,' Talasa said. 'That's the truth.'

He sloshed a generous measure into the first of the glasses and took it from her. His hand was shaking.

'Is he?'

'I don't know that either.'

He didn't look like Rubeo, Talasa was realising. Oh, there were similarities, of course, but the more she examined him, the more superficial she realised they were. The same dark hair, the same coppery skin, the same handsome features you could find on any portrait in any corridor of the Palace.

But Rubeo had an air of constant distraction to him, like you were catching him one step out of any conversation. It made him a perfect subject for portraits, actually, on the rare occasions he was in the capital long enough for one to be painted. That half-alert gaze, lingering on a point just outside the frame.

Offrian, however, was all attention and focus and energy, poured into whatever was in front of him. Good or ill.

The whisky smelled like embers, and pepper, and smoke without smoke, and Talasa suddenly found there was a treacherous part of her that did not want to turn around. That *wanted* everything revealed, no matter the cost.

How did I not think he was beautiful?

She took the bottle from him and poured herself a large glass too, so intent on not letting the liquor slop out that she only half saw him finish his own glass.

He raised it to her.

'Let's find out together.'

Secandeur House was very large, and very old, and it protruded from Secandeur Hill like a skull unearthed by a spade.

It was not the oldest building in the city. That honour officially went to the Palace, though as with much in the Answering, it was hard to know if that were true, or whether it simply *fitted*, and therefore became the truth after the fact.

But the university did pre-date the founding of the Answering, and that had contributed to the institution's decline. The Ceolmund

Academies were more fashionable. More aligned with the principles of the Answering. Places like the House were relics, like things found mouldering on the riverbed when the Dreor ran low.

It was still grand, beneath the tumorous moss and clinging vines. Talasa had seen it in daylight, during those dizzying first months in the capital. Rubeo had taken them there to point out the huge horseshoe concourse of the main address, and the long, straight terraces that had once housed faculties for economics, and military history, and commerce, and diplomacy, before diminishing numbers had shuttered them for good.

Now, of course, Talasa saw nothing but rain, until sulphurous lights opened like eyes in the dark. There was something feverish in those lamps. It was easy to imagine shapes hunched over in their light, scribbling furiously or arguing over some desiccated point of semantics.

The luxury of it, she thought. So much of the heritage of the Sinew was about memory because memory was easily carried from one place to the next.

The sound of the carriage changed from the claggy drum of wheels on mud to the hoarse drone of gravel. They'd stopped along the narrow, tree-lined avenue so Offrian could commandeer the driver's shirt and cap, Talasa and the man sharing a mortified moment on the road as the Prince insisted the driver struggle into Offrian's coat under his rain cape.

Then Offrian had changed in the carriage as it took off again, and Talasa had stared out the window quite determinedly until he was done.

'I look ridiculous,' he said when he was finished, tipping the cap up and down his still-wet scalp. It was true – the carriage driver was far broader, and Offrian looked like he was wearing a small woollen tent. One foot was braced against the seat beside her. His other knee swayed back and forth with the motion of the carriage, tapping warmth against her leg. 'Could we not just knock? It's not like they can turn me away.'

'That's true, your Highness. But they can take you on a long walk to precisely nowhere, show you everything but who you came to find and then politely show you the door. We cannot search the entire university. You'd need an army.'

Offrian's smile didn't waver. 'That's not out of the realm of possibility.'

'Wonderful,' she said. 'So now we've graduated from you wanting to pass unseen among your subjects to formally invading one of your own universities.'

He opened his mouth to argue, and then slowly closed it.

'You don't look ridiculous,' Talasa said soothingly. 'You look invisible.'

She was working harder than she had ever worked under Kalifsena's eye. It was like the seance again. Talasa had no control over Offrian bar what she could invent. Everything had to be channelled through what Offrian wanted and how he could get it.

But if they were about to expose Rubeo and Kalifsena's hideaway, she wanted to speak to her mother first.

The sheer face of the House loomed up out of the night – a wet grey mass barnacled with gargoyles in the old architectural style, when the Answering had let themselves believe in icons of protection and good faith. Now, their weeping heads drooped with age and erosion, their muzzles bearded with plumes of rain.

Offrian took another swig of whisky. When the carriage stopped, the glass clinked against his teeth, and he coughed.

'And ease up on the whisky,' she said. 'Coachmen don't attend upon ladies drunk. Maybe we should wait until the morning.'

'No!' Offrian said, and knocked back the rest of his glass before rolling it anxiously between his palms. 'No. You're right. You have to understand . . . this is new to me. Nobody talks to me like you do.'

Talasa took a sip of her own drink. Only her long experience with spice and heat allowed her to handle it without coughing. The heat didn't stay in her mouth either. It left, creasing her scalp and blurring outwards like lightning across a summer sky.

'Like I know better than you?'

He chuckled. 'No. Everyone talks to me like they know better than me. You're the only person who seems like they actually do.' He set his glass down and tucked two cushions around it for purchase. 'I'll be a coachman. I'll be quiet. I'll let you do the talking.'

Talasa let the moment hang, his face open and pleading, and then sighed. The carriage door opened, the rain coming down like iron nails, and they ran past the driver to the domed and pillared porch of Secandeur House.

The front door was a colossal, moss-bearded thing, and centuries of fingertips had reduced the knocker to a formless, snarling knob. Set into the wall beside it was a narrow porter's door, and it was this that Offrian and Talasa approached. The Prince rapped on it twice sharply, and Talasa offered him a smile.

'That was good. Very official.'

Make it a game. Make it an adventure. Maybe she could distract him. Send him on some folly-chase through the university while *she* found her mother and extracted some answers. Maybe there was a path here that did not ruin everything.

'I so rarely get to knock on doors myself,' he said. 'I've always wanted to try it.'

With a squeal of ancient hinges, the door opened a foot's width, and a slice of face filled the gap, all bleary eyes and ratty beard. The porter's voice was pure Modigmark – thick as bread and drawling.

'You best have a good reason for being out after curfew, my lad—'

Offrian's voice was crisp. 'Announcing the Princess-Undynast Talasa.'

The door could not have opened more quickly. 'Beg pardon, my lady. Come in.'

Beyond was an office smaller than one of Kalifsena's closets. One wall was hung with rain leathers so stiff with use Talasa could taste them; the other almost entirely keys, like a host of static raindrops, whispering softly on their hooks in the wind.

The porter scratched at his beard, clearly uncomfortable at his proximity to a young woman of high standing. He did not so much as look at the keys before choosing one in total confidence, and then led them both to a waiting room where wooden chairs sat mouldering under a film of dust.

'There's a kettle and a stove in there,' he said gruffly, pointing Offrian towards an antechamber before plodding out the door. It took Offrian an almost amusing amount of time to understand what it was the porter was saying.

'Do you need help?' Talasa asked, teasing.

'Yes, actually,' he said, dipping into the antechamber and then retreating again. He sounded so earnestly disappointed in himself that she had to smile.

'I can show you, if you like.'

She did so, and by the time the porter reappeared, they had warmed themselves somewhat on large cups of tea. Offrian had even found two thick blankets and wrapped one around her thin shoulders and one around his, though as soon as the porter arrived, he stood up sharply and shrugged it off.

With him was Master Colby.

'A great pleasure to receive you, Princess-Undynast,' the old man said. He wore a burgundy mantle of an archaic design over his scholar's robes, and there was a stiffness that spoke to just being awoken. 'And, I confess, a little surprising.'

Talasa could feel Offrian vibrating with tension beside her.

'I apologise for the late intrusion, Master Colby. I did not realise you were attached to Secandeur House.'

Is this where Mother found you? The connection, however minor, gave Talasa hope.

Pride turned the scholar's face into a maze of wrinkles. 'Why, it has been my life's work. This little haven. And you've come. I had related to Her Grace many times that you should be included. No child should be without their mother, if such a thing can be avoided. Especially when I heard about your training. The knowledge she was imparting to you.'

Talasa stiffened. 'She . . . told you about that?'

'I confess,' he said, a little admonishingly, 'I did not see it in your work for me. But there are many types of knowledge. Even I find the Answering's scholasticism dull and unambitious at times. The influence of the Ceolmundites has done much damage.'

Anger looked strange on his scrawny, bird-like frame.

'But without ambition, how can any choices be made? How can enlightenment be found if we do not step outside what we already know?'

'I agree,' Talasa said hastily, not sure she did, still stunned that the great secret of her training had been so casually shared.

'I thought you might,' Master Colby said. 'I thought your mother did too. The King certainly did. That was why he chose us. Come. Come and see.'

He beckoned her forward, but as Offrian made to follow, the porter held up his hand warily.

'Where do you think you're going, lad?'

Talasa neatly placed herself between the man and Offrian's outrage. 'It would be improper for me to wander the halls of this august institution without an escort, would it not? You do hear stories of wild student antics.'

'Don't know anything about it,' the porter said stiffly, but when he looked at Master Colby, the old man nodded.

'As you say, my lady. Just make sure he keeps his hands to himself.'

Talasa felt her cheeks pink.

'I mean, there are valuables, my lady,' the porter added quickly, Colby blinking owlishly between them both. 'It'll be my head and his if any go missing.'

'Nothing will go missing,' Talasa said. 'I'll make sure of it. Now – may we?'

Rubeo's tour two years ago had not extended inside the House. From the outside, Talasa had been expecting high-vaulted ceilings, wide arcades and gloomy, overgrown courtyards. Faded grandeur, but grandeur nonetheless.

What she found instead was a rat's nest. The porter retreated into his office and Colby led them out of the waiting room and into what might have been an imposing foyer, except that every square metre of it had been crowded by shelves.

Glass-cowled lanterns tried and failed to pierce the gloom, interrupted as they were at every step by stack upon stack of shelving. Each was at least twice as high as Talasa was tall, chopping the enormous space into narrow, dusty paths.

Some were finely made, as befitting an ancient place of learning, a stylish match to the carving-dimpled flagstones. Most, though, were hasty constructions of board and brick and strut, and all were clumsily jammed with rough crates and sheaves of paper that stuck out at all angles, seemingly with little regard for safety or organisation.

Colby led them out along a wide cloister made narrow and claustrophobic, through shelves where sheaves of loose and flaking pages had been shoved between a host of massive leather-bounds, with stitching loose as spiders' legs. Talasa had to step over where a box of journals had split and spilled, only to be roughly stacked back against each other.

'This is his collection,' she said softly, and heard Offrian's intake of breath.

Colby's expansive gesture disturbed particles that might have been dandruff and might have been dust. 'It is our honour here to house his Majesty's Great Archive, yes. An enormous task. Unsuited to those fledgling academies of Ceolmund.'

The Ceolmund Academies had been established three hundred years ago. Maybe that was young if you were of the House.

'If the King did not take such interest, we would struggle without his patronage. It was he who ordered the great collecting. An assessment of all the Answering might have forgotten, in its long supremacy.'

Offrian was tense at her shoulder. Talasa spoke simply to remind him she was there.

'Surely he does not plan to read them all?'

'That's what we are here for,' Colby said. 'We who remain.'

He had not lit a lantern and seemed to be navigating through memory alone. Talasa wasn't sure how he managed it. In the first ten steps, she caught herself painfully on corners and edges of document cases. Offrian cursed quietly as his broad shoulder took a box half from its perch, and he had to stop to right it.

'Careful, boy,' Master Colby said with surprising sharpness. 'Some of these items are older than the Answering.'

If that were true, it hadn't earned them any kind of reverence. Talasa had expected something . . . grander. Not mouldering crates covered in sackcloth, or yellowed pages half-forgotten in a stairwell, curling like moths' wings in the dark.

The place was silent but for the creaking susurration of a manor settling in its damp, and the vast cacophonous unnoise of waiting paper. Maybe the rain had gotten in somewhere, because there was a little kernel of rot in there too – something strangely sweet.

Talasa began to feel a little light-headed. All that knowledge. All that *concentration* – thousands of hours by hundreds of people scratching their thoughts into paper. How did you get anything done with all those pages around demanding to be read?

The 'fledgling academies' were probably grateful to do it. It was very Answering – shipping out all your unwanted ideas to where they could safely rot away and make room for newer thought.

They climbed a staircase and the shelving climbed with them, racked up at angles on the steps, tied with twine so that they didn't separate. Talasa could feel Offrian's frustration behind her the way she'd felt him change his clothes – a tense, trembling heat. She wasn't sure he had ever been so silent for so long.

And yet even though the place was perishingly quiet, there were noises. Footsteps echoing through the choked-out hallways, hurried and loud. Talasa jerked as she heard a man shout something, and a chorus of high laughter in return, though the man had sounded angry, not as though he was making a joke. A slam, distant yet loud enough that it plucked a sheet or two from a shelf as they passed.

It was only after another three staircases that the strata of knowledge began to change. There were still scrolls and books, hundreds of them, but now there were more crates and chests. Most were closed, but some sat open. Stacked in them Talasa could see dozens of packages wrapped in paper. Some were so large they would not fit in crates, and instead stood free, man-height and man-shaped.

'They say that the love between the King and the Queen was born out on the steppes – a wild thing, for a wild place.' Master Colby stroked a pile of tomes as he passed. 'That may be true. I cannot speak to it. But I like to think I was able to observe that love flourish and mature in our modest little House, as his collection grew and grew.'

They stopped outside a door of wood and glass, with a set of faded names stencilled on a card.

'If you give me a moment, I will send one of the porters to fetch her.'

She is here.

'Yes,' Talasa said, trying to keep her voice neutral. 'Thank you. I would be very grateful.'

He opened the door and slipped inside.

When Talasa was sure he was out of earshot, she turned to Offrian, only for him to bob away from her, face flushed, rolling a little on the balls of his feet. She slid her hand beneath his cloak before he could react.

Inside was the carafe of whisky – far lighter than before.

'What is *wrong* with you?' she snapped.

Offrian snatched it back from her so hard her palm stung. 'What? How dare you?' His voice was angry, but his eyes were red.

'This is where he has been,' the prince whispered. 'This . . . fucking grave. Fawning over old scrolls and statues while—'

His mouth clacked shut as the door opened and the tousled head of a young man poked through.

'Princess-Undynast. Come through, please.'

It was a very gentle face, permanently flushed, soft-cheeked. Talasa made out a stocky build, a short beard, a peculiar notch in his left ear. He gave her space to enter, but before Offrian could follow her, the scholar stepped into his path.

'Just you, Princess-Undynast.'

An ugly anger flickered across Offrian's face.

'A moment,' Talasa said to the scholar. 'Please.'

The young man retreated.

'Get out of my way,' Offrian hissed. 'Get out of my way so that I can—'

Talasa kissed him. It was not a very enjoyable kiss, though she did not have any to compare it to. They couldn't all be like this, she reasoned, otherwise people just wouldn't do it.

But it served a purpose. They broke apart, Talasa's lips whisky-seared and sore from being mashed against his teeth, and Offrian could not have looked more confused than if she'd hit him with a hammer.

'You're not the only one doing what has to be done,' she whispered. 'Trust me. I will call for you when it's time.'

He gave a hard jerk of his head that might have been a bow, and Talasa sagged with relief, turning to open the door.

The young scholar was waiting on the other side at a respectful distance.

'Assistant Archivist Stord,' he said, with that same soft smile. 'Your man is very dutiful.'

Talasa could still see the shadow of Offrian through the dusty glass. 'Yes. He is.'

After the cramped labyrinth she'd just traversed, the open space here was a relief. Stord led her through a set of interconnected classrooms and teaching laboratories, stocked with a fortune of distilling equipment – tubes and glass rounds and spindly, insectile pouring apparatus. None of it appeared to have been used in a long time.

They stepped through a set of double doors into a space nearly as large as the foyer. A teaching auditorium, perhaps – a great hemisphere, with two balconies above the one on which she stood, the distant ceiling criss-crossed by what might have been gantries and walkways. There were more shelves here, pushed up against the walls, but other boxes and packages stood in precarious piles, like the rock pillars you sometimes found on the steppes that not even the Women of the Sinew could explain.

The centre of the room was a sunken pit. Light pealed from inside it – candlelight, streaked with something paler that left a smearing sheen on Talasa's eyes.

She could not see any further because Master Colby stood in her way.

'Where is my mother?' she asked.

'Your mother is resting,' he said. 'The work tires her. It tires all of us, but her especially. I do not blame her. Women make poor academics.'

He reached up to scrub at an ear with his missing finger. The light made parchment of his skin. She felt like she could see through it to the bones beneath.

'This is not an easy calling. It demands sacrifice.'

32

Sister Wake

THERE WAS NO joy in Sister Wake's heart as the saint and the Knight took the fight to the Answermen on Scáthach's Plain. How could there be?

They travelled north, skirting burning fields where nothing could be done but mourn the hunger that would come. They navigated damp woods ripe with wild garlic and the toxic smell of cuckoo pint. Groups of hiding women ran from them in those woods, scampering like deer, dragging their pale, wide-eyed children along with them.

For once, that didn't faze Sister Wake at all. She wasn't here for them.

The first village they came across was already dead. Twenty-eight men hacked down, some as they ran, but most lined up in neat rows like the winter barley they should have been tending. A couple had tried to fight and were being strung up when Sister Wake and Brother Wight came across them.

It wasn't a battle anyone would sing about. Brother Wight was one man, and Sister Wake could not be risked. They'd already passed one small settlement that had nearly fifty men camped inside, and that was simply beyond their reach.

And when they did fight, there was no such thing as heroics, or fairness, or rules of engagement. That was not the kind of war the Answering had trained the Croí to fight.

Orman Birley was first. He chased a wounded hare into the shadows of a barn, hoping to add a bit more meat to the squad's stew that night. His last thoughts were of how dispassionately the animal watched him as he bled out on the ground.

Parr Axton was sent to find Birley when his absence was noted. He managed a strangled yelp before the hand went over his mouth, but nobody heard. They were too busy watching in horror as the pig they had spitted for dinner tried to pull itself out of the fire and attack.

Not joy, Sister Wake thought, shaking their souls off afterwards in a flurry of frost. But a certain amount of satisfaction.

That night, she and Brother Wight fell asleep like puppies, curled up under a poky little tent Brother Wight had made out of some purloined blankets. Nothing really had been said about it, though it was a departure from the way they normally slept, in that he didn't, and she slept angrily turned away.

This time, though, they lay face-to-face, Sister Wake's knees touching Brother Wight's, her nose just inches from his.

And she *talked*. She talked for hours, as if the thawing of the burned-out hall had taken some of her own ice with it.

'We don't have a *rí* – the place is too small for that. There isn't even really a *cúirt*. There's just people you listen to and people you don't.'

Brother Wight was breathing into his hands to warm them. Sister Wake had been worried it had been her making him cold, but the *tabharthas* of the Cailleach slumbered in her after its grand showing all day, and she was as close to warm as she ever got.

'I don't know what they'll think of you. We had heard stories of the Rising, of course, but you got a good clip across the ear if you were caught talking about it too loudly.'

He didn't say it. Neither did she. But they both knew that her old home would have far more to say about one of their own becoming a living saint than the presence of a Rising warrior in their midst.

That was all right. She had things to say too.

'The closest Answering garrison is twenty miles away, but they send riders out every month. Just to stare and shout at us mostly. We only really got to see more than five Answermen together when we went to Uthredton, and that was only when one of Da's tools broke and he couldn't fix it himself.'

'Uthredton is sacked,' Brother Wight said softly. 'I heard some of Mother Promise's men talking about it before we left.'

'Uthredton is gone?' Sister Wake barely remembered the place, so what she saw in her head was Sciáthcrann aflame.

'It's free,' Brother Wight corrected, but the usual salt was gone out of his voice. 'But you were telling me about your home. The village. The *cúirt* you didn't have.'

Sister Wake talked well into the night. She told him about stupid rivalries and love affairs and arguments over fences, and after a while she wasn't sure whether she was telling him or reminding herself.

There was nothing to the place that would be new or unique to him. There was nothing there at all that made the place where she had been born feel like it was the place where *she* had been born.

It was just a place. There were a thousand thousand like it.

But Sister Wake prepared her Knight the way he had prepared her for the meeting of seven *ríthe* who hated each other, and whose feuding could kill the Rising before it began. She guided him through its laneways as if they were as dangerous and essential to their survival as that of the villages they were liberating.

She had just worked up the courage to tell him why when he fell asleep midway through one of her sentences. She wasn't even annoyed.

There was nobody to save in the next village, so Sister Wake saved their names instead. Imag and Oilbhe and Tómnat and Duibheasa and Catirfina and thirty-eight others.

She would lay those names at the feet of the Cailleach and see if it made her move.

'Are you frightened?' Brother Wight asked her that evening, as they huddled beneath their *bratanna* by the shore of the Tur – a stubborn little crease of a river with water so cold even Sister Wake felt it.

They could have had whole houses to themselves, of course. Anything that was going to burn in that village had already burned, and there hadn't even been any Answermen to kill. But nothing could have made Sister Wake stay in that place, and so they camped half a mile downriver, under a parasol of gentry thorn, its red berries musking the air.

'Of going home?' she asked, distracted. They hadn't much in the way of medicine, and so she had fallen into a custom of placing her cold hands on his bruises to ease the swelling.

'Of . . . *Ah*. Of speaking to the Cailleach.'

'No,' she said, trying to find comfort against the headland of his chest and keep her fingers where they could do some good. 'I thought I would be. But I'm coming for *her* now, and that makes it different. I want her to speak. I want to question her.'

Why me? Why did you do this? What are you for?

What am I *for? Did you choose me, or was I just the girl on the end of the chain?*

'To ask her to help us,' Brother Wight finished, and Sister Wake could not bring herself to correct him. It was no luxury, the life he'd had. Except for the luxury of being certain. You always thought of gods as being certain, but that did not seem to be the type of god that walked Croí now.

In some stories, all the Cailleach wanted was death. Death for everyone. Death for trees and birds and fish and people, a great gathering of all the souls that ever were into the endless blackness of her eyes. In others, she was a kindly grandmother who stood with you so you did not have to face the cold and the dark alone.

Maybe that was why Sister Wake found solace in the minds of rats. Why it was more comforting to convince birds on the wing than to inspire the Croí. Maybe the real blessing was a want simple enough to comfortably fit in one head.

I want to go home.

I want to free our people.

I want souls not to go unheard.

I never want to hear a soul again.

One way or another, not all of those wants would survive.

*   *   *

It was in the village of Tintreach that the two of them nearly died.

It was boldness, or exhaustion, or comfortability that had done it. They ranged further and further from each other now as they fought. Trusting Sister Wake's *tabharthas* to see everything and Brother Wight's spear to see the killing done.

Tintreach was a hair too small to be a town, and Sister Wake's arrival had sparked something of a miniature revolution. The twenty or so Answermen had been content to scare the locals rather than methodically massacre them, and so had holed up in an inn drinking and threatening and using their matchlock stocks to get what they wanted.

Sister Wake had sent a half-butchered ox through the window. The smart soldiers had run. The stupid ones had opened fire, and it was when they were frantically trying to reload that Brother Wight and some locals had come through the door.

Sister Wake was watching it all – the air a clinging mist around her as the bite of her presence spun air into crystal – when something took her off her feet.

For a moment, she thought she'd been stabbed. Or shot. A bombard of terror went off in her skull, and her hands flew convulsing across her body. Looking for holes, protruding shafts, *something* to explain the sudden shrieking sense of her own impending death.

Nothing. Just the sounds of fighting from the inn. The spatter and pop of matchlock fire. The rising clamour as more and more cowering Croí dared leave their homes to find the Answermen in disarray.

But the *fear*. The terror. She had never felt anything like it. She'd never felt so afraid, not even when staring down death itself . . .

And then she ran towards the inn's kicked-down door.

The inside of the place was in chaos, and most of that was the fault of Sister Wake. Oxen did not make for neat creatures, even when alive, and before it had gone down to a point-blank fusillade, the ton-weight beast had broken everything it could break.

Chairs, tables and men were a ruin on the floor. Most of them were Answering. Some were Croí. Some moaned, or kicked, or tried to rise. The air was a heaving mass of half-shucked souls.

But there was only one soul Sister Wake had eyes to see.

The lone remaining Answerman was a monster. You would have needed an empire to feed and clothe him, and even then every ounce of him was coming out of his creased coat. His trousers were hanging down around his arse. The back of his neck was ribbed as an earthworm with roll after roll of pink, sunburned flesh.

That was all of him Sister Wake could see, because he had Brother Wight up against a wall and both hands around his neck.

Brother Wight struggled and kicked or tried for the wheellock at his hip, but the Answerman knew how to pin. He knew how to strangle too, and the Rising warrior was running out of air.

And then he saw her over the soldier's shoulder, and the screaming fear in Sister Wake's head doubled in strength.

Not fear for himself. Fear for her if she had to go it alone. The Knight's mouth worked.

Run.

She picked up a sword instead.

*　*　*

'You're cold.'

She tried to push back his matted crest of hair, but her fingers only made it halfway. He hissed at the gentle tug of it, half demolishing their little tent, and she shushed him. *Blood.* Old and new. It was becoming hard to tell them apart.

'We'll wash it tomorrow,' she said absently. They both looked like horrors, if she were being honest, but during the day, that just didn't seem as important. Sometimes it even helped, with the work they were trying to do.

'What would we be washing it for?'

'We're *washing* it. Shut up. Now – you're cold. I should—'

'No,' he growled, as his fingers found hers, and fit. 'I'm not.'

That might have been all they did for half the night, or for a minute. Sister Wake couldn't tell. Just his fingers rolling over hers, the rough brush of knuckle over palm, finding and losing and finding again.

And then she hooked her calf around his leg.

'Good,' she said. 'Me neither.'

It wasn't very saintly behaviour, what followed. But then again, Sister Wake had never been much of a saint.

'Wait.'

Brother Wight glanced at her curiously. The man he was about to stab, lying on his back in the dirt, was too afraid to look away.

It had been a fishing village, before all the boats had been dragged out and burnt, the nets thrown up over the fires in tangled clumps. They still smouldered sullenly. Not consumed, just ruined. The houses had burned easier, as easy as the people.

'Witch,' the man breathed. 'You're a witch.'

It wasn't a word Sister Wake knew in the Answering tongue. Probably it meant something bad. The village came right up on the shore, and the mucky foam of the ground looked like it never dried, even in summer.

Now, though, every rut and footprint was hard as rock, pinched into shape by the frost leaking from Sister Wake's *tabharthas*. Her hands were curled into claws by her sides, the scars on her fingers red against the dead whiteness of her skin.

She didn't know if she still had eyes. It seemed irrelevant when she already knew what they would see.

Brother Wight firmed up his grip on the spear and began to push, and the man – Demond, Sister Wake knew, reading it off his lifting soul – screeched.

'Wait! She said wait, didn't she? Please . . . please . . .'

Sister Wake pointed. The village was just two rows of cottages facing out onto Lough Maol – a forty-mile stretch of water that she knew from its other side. Cross it, and they were nearly home.

'What were you supposed to be doing with that?'

The soldier's gaze followed her finger, goggle-eyed with fear. 'What?'

'The portal tomb,' Sister Wake said patiently. Demond was the first living person in days she'd spoken to that wasn't Brother Wight, and she was in relatively no hurry for it to end. 'You were uncovering it. Digging it out. Why?'

It sat on a rise overlooking the fishing village, as if to watch over the first settlers who had come here. Four great white stones standing upright like coffin lids, bearing a flat and jutting stone above as a roof. The back piece that might have formed a third wall was gone or had fallen. You could walk through it like a door – not that anyone would, except giggling children when no Brother could see.

'We weren't! I swear, we weren't!'

Brother Wight shot her a look. 'Can't you just read it off him after he's dead?'

Demond's face lost what little colour it had possessed.

'Not always,' Sister Wake said. She kneeled. Beads of sweat on the man's face became little pearls of white. 'And he hasn't killed anyone.'

She'd learned that last from two dozen souls – some of the people killed in the village, though many had taken to the lake to avoid the Answermen, and then the Answermen squad themselves, as Brother Wight had made his way through them one by one.

Demond stared up at her with a mixture of horror and relief. 'How do you know . . .'

'Because some of your squad knew it,' Sister Wake said. 'There was *talk*. You were a bad shot. You scrambled for the tasks that wouldn't involve hurting people, and it was only the fact you'd literally do anything to make up for it that kept you from being punished. Private Demond, the Answerman who's dug more latrines than half the Seventeenth. Have you ever killed *anybody*?'

'No,' Demond whispered. 'I haven't.'

'Right,' Sister Wake said. Some of the cold was draining away. 'Get up then and tell us what exactly ye were at.'

Brother Wight took the spear away, but Private Demond did not rise.

'I'm telling you again, miss, we weren't.'

Sister Wake's footsteps crunched over the hard mud. One whole half of the world was a blank bank of fog, eating what lay ahead.

She had so many scraps and slivers of soul in her after the last couple of days that she felt like that water – brimming with a hundred thousand rolling waves, forming and rising and breaking apart.

Compared to that, the tomb should have been reassuringly solid. A construction so old Croí had risen and fallen around it – free nation to chained, and maybe, just maybe, to free again.

But that wasn't what had had captured her gaze. She might not have noticed it at all if not for the chopped and distressed remains of worms that surrounded it, and what Mother Promise had said.

Taking our history out of the earth in splinters.

'Look,' she said. Brother Wight was dragging the hapless private up to his feet, pushing him along with the haft of his spear. *Tell him to stop. Tell him not to* . . . The thoughts came from nowhere, skating across the top of her mind. Were they hers? Or some vestige of affection from one of the soldiers they had murdered?

Not murdered. You didn't murder people in war. You defeated them.

It just looked the same.

Sister Wake climbed the low rise, scrambling a little on the loose shale, and kneeled by the bottom of the tomb. The spades of white rock were covered with moss, a furry plaque of the type the women in her own *túath* collected and boiled in milk and honey for a sore throat.

It should have extended all the way to the ground. Instead, there was a foot of clean stone where there was no moss at all.

'Here,' she said impatiently. 'You were digging at it. Weren't you?'

'Digging?' Demond said in a bewildered tone, and Sister Wake had to parse out her frustration from that of the late Sergeant Tacim, currently stiffening behind a shed a few hundred feet away. 'Digging with what?'

'He has a point,' Brother Wight said. 'I've seen what they use to break down tombs. Teams of horses. Janny-cranes. Sleds, sometimes, to take the stones away. There's none of that here.'

Sister Wake ran a finger down the edge of the exposed stone. It looked scraped clean. Not as if it had been worried at with shovels.

As if it had pushed up from beneath, like the growth of a tooth.

'The mist is beginning to clear,' Brother Wight said. He was right, too. Some eddy of wind or the strengthening sun had started to burn away the grey sheath over the horizon, and Sister Wake saw it for the first time.

The mountain. The mountain where it had all started, distending the horizon with its weight. It stood exactly as it had in every memory from her childhood, that brutal black spike with its gleaming white pinprick, glinting like a reflection in the black pupil of a god.

Something about that tugged at her, but there was so much strangeness to this new Croí that it was getting harder and harder to narrow down exactly what to fear and what to accept.

'There's a boat hidden a mile west,' she told Brother Wight. 'The man hoping to use it didn't get to it in time.'

Brother Wight nodded, and then the spear came up, blade winking like a sliver of ice.

'Stop!'

It was Sister Wake who had shouted. Demond couldn't speak around the spear point at his throat. Another heartbeat, and his soul would have been all over her as well.

'I told you,' she said, some of the old harshness returning unbidden to her voice. Brother Wight's lips twisted, and remembering the taste of those lips should have quelled her anger, but it didn't. 'He didn't kill anyone.'

'That's what they all say,' Brother Wight snapped. '*I was a cook. I was a horse-hand. I never liked it. I never wanted it.*'

His hands were trembling. Private Demond was moaning. The point of the spear was carving little red lines in the pink skin of his neck.

'It's the truth,' Sister Wake said. 'Leave him. Or I walk on alone.'

There was a long moment, a moment that was probably far longer for Private Demond, where Sister Wake thought Brother Wight would simply ignore her and drive the spear home.

But maybe the Knight of the Hollow Eye had thawed as well.

He jerked the blade back and pushed Demond hard away to sprawl on the ground. He and Sister Wake began walking down the slope, leaving the portal tomb with its skirt of clean, unnerving stone behind. They had only gone ten paces before a shout rang out.

'Wait!' Private Demond said. 'What am . . . what am I supposed to do?'

'Fuck away off home,' Sister Wake said without turning around. 'You should never have been here in the first place.'

33

Abelard

THE SOUND OF the refugee column took a long time to fade, but Meilyr rode the horses to exhaustion. It was late morning when they slowed to a walk, and that was only because the men had to dismount and find their way through fields that had become silent and hostile with growth.

The grass was high and wild, dotted with wildflowers and vivid yellow weeds. Hedges had slipped their bounds, bulging like veins in distress, so tall the once wide fields felt like the rooms of a mansion. Vision was limited. The air had a thick, not entirely pleasant smell.

After what they had seen on the road, the silence should have been a respite, but it was not. Soldiers slipped like old men from their horses, blinking stupidly, reason fled. Netha had lost their cloak, or shed it, and stood in the saddle gasping in great heaves of breath like a diver submerged to the neck.

Only Meilyr seemed unaffected.

'Into them,' was all he said.

The soldiers took to the hedges with brush axe and loppers, and for the first hour seemed almost grateful for the work. But the blackthorn and birch were stubborn, and the day was hot. Sometimes they would spend an hour hacking through the hedge because it was quicker than going around, only to find just twenty clear feet of grass before another hedge blocked the way.

Where that left Abelard was a pastime he had once considered his only source of true happiness – sitting in the midst of a meadow with nothing to do but look around.

It was all poisoned, though. There was no peaceful hum of nature, only the cursing grunts of men taking nature apart. And every time a branch snapped or a bush rustled, the men froze like dormice, waiting for a leeching woman to come take them away.

But it did not transpire, and slowly, very slowly, the bright and blatant horror of the morning began to fade into a sweating kind of unease.

And for Abelard, anger.

He found Netha by a stream, barely a hand's-breadth wide. The bright yellow flower was everywhere – gleaming from the hedges like veins of gold in the wall of a mine. It had even grown up through the water, yellow petals floating on the water as if jealously keeping it for themselves.

'What song are you going to sing about that?' Abelard's throat itched. He fought a cough, knowing that if he started, he would not be able to stop.

The poet did not acknowledge him. Pollen had settled upon the shoulders of the *filí*. Their eyes were streaming, leaving two stark trails of black down their yellow-dusted cheeks.

'Well?' Abelard said, voice shaking. 'Or those people Macha trampled. How will you cast them in your story to justify what was done?'

The flowers eddied in the water, bright as the yellow warning labels they used in academies for compounds that could burn or sear.

'What do you want me to say, Abelard?' Netha asked finally. 'That I condemn what I just saw? That I denounce it? I do. It revolted me. You heard me, did you not? Calling for Meilyr's men to fire on the Daughters Dearg? Do you think I would not? Did you think the purpose of my stories is to make heroes out of demons?'

He had heard Netha's shout, as a matter of fact, but right now Abelard's hand was curled into a fist, and he could not get it to open.

'You were content to die for Macha,' he said quietly. 'Why would lying for her be any different?'

'We never lied!'

The poet's voice was nearly a shout, and even they seemed uncomfortable with the volume of it.

'The virtues of a god are half its story. Less than half. We told it all, and our people were free to make their own choice as to who to follow and who to condemn.'

They drove the heel of their hand into their eye with unnecessary force, trying and failing to rub away some of the yellow dust.

'Do you know what a *geis* is?'

'No,' Abelard said. 'And I don't care. I don't care what clever scrap of native wisdom or old atrocity justifies allegiance to such things. I can accept they're real. I am forced to. But I cannot accept the cost of that to us.'

'Exactly!' Netha snapped, and was suddenly on their feet in a drifting curtain of gold. 'Exactly. Our gods were accountable to us. A promise held them hard as it held us. If they are real, then the old compacts, the old *geiseanna*, the old . . . *promises* should be as well. They could be. That might be our only hope.'

'I do not,' Abelard said stiffly, 'have any idea what you are talking about.' He cleared his aching throat. 'My father had a . . . a veterinarian when I was growing up. It was the fashion for peers to find themselves a veterinarian from the academies – someone young and erudite, as much at home sharing witty anecdotes over a glass of wine as elbow-deep in birth fluids.'

'Disgusting,' Netha said, with a half-hearted grin. 'Do continue.'

Abelard would not give them the satisfaction of smiling back. Instead, he looked around him, at the toxic yellow tangles, at Meilyr shouting at the men through puffy, irritated eyes.

'My father, however, preferred his old stablemaster Jonas. Jonas with his diabolical tobacco and his dirt-encrusted trousers and his constant, constant swearing. He said . . . he said it was easier to doctor men than animals. *Men can speak. They can point. Tell you where it hurts. With animals, you have to truly listen.*'

'He sounds wise,' Netha remarked.

'He would have hated this,' Abelard said. 'The growth. The weeds. If you introduce a cat to a new locale, the birds will not know to flee it. A handful of seeds can destabilise a fiefdom if the conditions are perfectly right or perfectly wrong.'

He rubbed the pollen between his fingers to a smear.

'Nature owes us nothing, Netha. You cannot bargain with it or ask it to show restraint. This is an invasive species, and it would be better if we pulled it up by the root.'

'You're one to talk,' Netha said simply.

Abelard sat with that in silence for a moment. He had not really expected any other answer. 'Tell me this, then. You left home eleven months ago.'

'I did.'

'Long before this . . . calamity descended.'

'Yes,' Netha said.

'To see your homeland. An arrow loosed long ago. That's what you said.'

What was that? A wariness? A hunted look, swiftly hidden?

'It is.'

'And that's all?' Abelard asked. 'You crossed half the world. For what? Because you were wistful for a place you've never been? No other reason.'

'No,' Netha said.

Abelard nodded. 'That's the least believable thing I've heard all day.'

A few minutes later, the next palisade of weed fell, and an hour later another. They led the horses through more corridors of toxic overgrowth, tracking and backtracking, walking fifty feet sideways for every ten feet ahead.

Even the sky, the only thing to Abelard's aching eyes not polluted with acidic yellow, began to turn gold at the edges.

'We'd be faster on the road,' Meilyr complained bitterly, but one look at the faces of the men and even he did not suggest a return.

One of the men had said you heard Promontory before you saw it. Abelard had been straining for the blare of regimental horns or the clanging of the great iron bell in its tower, but for the longest time there had been no sound but the rustling of the weeds and the oppressive hum of insects.

He found himself passing the time by trying to parse the sound. It was too high to be bumblebees and had the sharper edge one might associate with hornets or wasps. But they weren't pollen collectors, and there was nothing sweet to attract them.

Eventually, the Lord Protector had had enough. He gestured, and the soldier standing guard by Netha grabbed the poet by the elbow and dragged them to stand before the military man.

'This growth. These . . . impediments. What are they?'

'Summer,' Netha said simply. 'Are you not enjoying it?'

The settling pollen seemed to have brought with it a drunkenness, or a belligerence at least, because Netha glared at Meilyr with bleary eyes and a canted angle to their shoulders.

'It isn't summer,' Meilyr said simply, deep frustration on his features that he was even having to entertain this.

'It is where he's from,' Netha said. 'And it looks like he's brought it here.'

'Who?' Abelard asked. He'd been right. The countryside was sick. And as foolish as it seemed to conflate the massacre he had just witnessed with the fevered growth around him – like comparing a severed leg with a head cold – the two instances were symptoms of the same disease.

Something had . . . tracked this weed in here, the way a burr might hang from an animal's pelt.

'I won't say his name,' Netha said simply. 'Not out in his fields, where he might hear. Of all the stories, I wanted him to be true the least.'

They smiled crookedly.

'If we spend a night out here, you'll be praying to Macha too.'

Abelard never got to find out what that meant. He was nodding off in the saddle when shouts went up, and his first conscious breath tasted of salt.

The coast. Promontory.

They chopped through another weed-choked field, the smell of the butchered yellow flowers raw and hot in the air, and then the men at the cutting line stumbled out onto a track of low gravel.

Beyond, a tolling bell rang like summer thunder over a pitted, rocky beach. Further north, a headland of stone rose, and from that, standing proud like the flung mallet of a stonemason, was Promontory. Watch keep and bastion of the First Colony.

Abelard attended barbican with his father and mother every week, and rhetoricians loved taking the eager parishioners on a narrative tour of the wild and exciting frontier. It cut a dramatic portrait too – surrounded on three sides by the black waters of the King's Channel, warding the sheltered inlet of Marne's Bay from the rocky promontory that had given the Answering fort its blunt and forthright moniker.

Approaching Promontory from inland was no easy feat. You either crossed the open, spongy sand, leaping across pools and dragging your feet out of muck with every step, or you fought along the narrow arm of the headland, where it was a fifteen-foot drop on either side and you were an easy target for shot.

Not even the yellow wort had managed to conquer it, though a living scab of yellow flowers had spread as far as Abelard could see to the north-west. There was a new and acrid stink in the air, replacing its cloying scent. Black smoke hung in low, sludgy clouds, picked at and tattered by the sea wind.

There were shapes in that smoke. Enormous and ruined.

As a child, Abelard could have named the sieges that had broken against Promontory, though that was mostly because the stories stuck in his head far more than dry precepts and worrisome flaws.

Each time, of course, the Croí had broken before the Answering did. The Brothers Athnach. The Bastard Cudder, so named for his birth and for what he did to Answering soldiers he took alive. And a woman – a queen, no less, one of those wild half-mythic female Croí chieftains who so often found their way into silly and salacious plays in the capital.

They had broken on Promontory. They had fallen. The rhetoricians had made that very clear. And now it seemed the pantheon of the Croí had broken as well.

Netha had dismounted, and there was no one there to hold them when their legs gave way. Not in weakness, but in grief.

A serpent as long as the *Channel's Cry* had slithered in great undulating patterns across the beach, before brutal fire had raked it, tearing away scales as black as the inside of a cave. Two of its heads were missing. A third stared hopelessly at the sky.

A bloated, shapeless thing of hands and eyes and the enormous staring eyes of a lemur or tarsier lay in a rock pool, and what Abelard had thought were spurs and knots of rock were actually three more. A pack of the things; buffeted and broken and excavated by volley upon volley of shot.

To his horror, he saw one of the red women, pale and lifeless. The sand around her was black and crusted with blood, but somehow her hair still lived, licking back and forth along the ground.

Netha's lips moved, fast and quiet. Fluid syllables like well-worn gravestones, and despite a soldier's hard and angry shout, the poet staggered to their feet and stepped out onto the field.

Names, Abelard realised.

A list of the dead.

Meilyr turned and snarled at his men.

'The signal flag! Quick!'

One of the men unslung it from his bag and unfurled it so the clean sea wind snapped it back and forth. It remained black and white for only a moment before drifting pollen began to stain it and drag it down.

Across the field, the gates of Promontory began to creak open, dislodging a pile of dead things higher than Abelard was tall.

'Now it begins,' Meilyr said with satisfaction. 'Now order can be restored.'

34

Talasa

'I WOULD LIKE to see my mother now,' Talasa said.

'This pre-dates your mother,' Master Colby said. 'I think she may have forgotten that.'

The light from the lecture pit was doing strange things to the shadows. Talasa could not tell whether there were other academics there, scurrying between the teetering crates, or whether it was simply the dancing illumination painting and repainting darkness on the walls.

'I've known the King for years,' he continued, placing a hand gently on the railing of the pit. 'There was a standing stone on the Tamwither estate where he spent his summers as a boy. He had taken these tracings from it and wanted to know what they meant.'

A quick little polish, and the mark of his fingers vanished from the brass.

'This was thirty years ago. I was staffing for Master Eduin at the time. By rights, the letter should have gone to him. But Eduin was a drinker, and when that white-sealed envelope crossed my desk, I did not feel like waiting through the man's shouting hangover to answer. I like to think a friendship began that day, and it has been a pleasure to be useful to the King ever since.'

There *were* other people here. Not just the softly smiling Stord. Talasa could hear the shush of cloth on floorboard. The scrape of fingers on parchment.

She was surrounded.

'Master Colby,' she pressed. She did not understand what was happening here. She did not understand it, and she needed to, and she did not have a lot of time. 'Useful doing what? Organising the King's collection of artefacts?'

'*Studying*,' Master Colby said, his tone strangely hurt. 'Not *organising*. We are not valets. These halls hold relics and totems and writings from all over the known world. The majority are Croí, purely for ease of access, but there are etchings from the Starling Kingdoms, records and paraphernalia from New Territory indigens, your own Tattered Shore, even from several of the principalities and satraps of the Terod Union, though how he claimed those I do not know.' Again, that fond little smile. 'It is rather piling up.

'All of them, in some way, pertain to the religious. The ephemeral. The mysteries, in the purest sense of the word. Each is an expression of faith. An attempt to reach beyond what one can see. I like to think of it as hope, I suppose.'

'And what does the King think?'

Maybe it was enough to keep him talking. Maybe he was just a harmless old man who wanted someone to appreciate everything he was doing here. Maybe this was just the unmindful captivity of a boring man starved of an audience.

Was there anything wrong with wanting to be heard?

'The King's attention wanders,' Colby said sadly. 'You know that. One moment he would ask us to trace the lineage of one of the

Erratics. Another day it was all about celestial navigation. He commissioned an entire observatory; did you know that? It's half built, out the back. You could have raised a regiment on what was spent, I understand. We were on track to complete it, but then he became curious about tides and their relation to the moon, and nothing would do but an expedition to . . .'

Talasa did her best to look attentive, but something in her expression made Master Colby offer a thin smile.

'A lens. That's what your mother was to the King. She took that bright, shining hunger and she focused it.'

The lecture pit pulsed with light, as if it agreed.

'Focused it on what?'

Furtive pride in the old man's voice. 'On whether all these mysteries have any workable truths.'

It was lucky, Talasa thought, that the rain was hammering on the roof, and the candles were flickering, and the shadows were drawing Colby's narrow features into something not a hundred miles away from sinister, because if such a thought had been spoken in daylight, she might have laughed.

Faith was one thing. You could never have convinced Talasa that faith wasn't real. It had been her childhood. The word for *faith* in her tongue was remarkably close to the word for *sinew* – the secret connectors between your bones, the rope that kept you from flying apart.

That was what faith was for. All the secrets. All the lies. All the inspiration and the fear and the manipulation – the unreal was there to *move* the real to where you wanted it to go.

'I didn't think faith allowed for questions,' she said carefully.

Master Colby crossed the room to a shelf, the boxes on it marked with red ink, and plucked free a sheet from the top of one of the piles.

'The Oracles at Dharqesh. Have you heard of them?'

He didn't wait for an answer.

'Dharqesh was the old name for the New Territory of Abelsfeld. The Oracles were famous. Even to be in their presence was to be inspired, and even the most sceptical of visitors confessed to feelings of religious ecstasy and enlightenment. What they didn't know was that—'

'The Oracles were drugging them,' Talasa said.

Colby raised an eyebrow. 'Yes. When a slighted satrap eventually stormed their temple with a battalion of men, he found a library of poisons and tinctures. Those sages had been manipulating the fortunes of the Territories for centuries. Impressive, to be sure, but not preternatural. And there are a thousand of these. Misidentified animals. Moral panics. Bad crops.'

He indicated the vast working space around them. 'For years we have investigated these occultic items. Chemistry, metallurgy, responses to heat and light. We've replicated their construction, we've played out rituals and then tested the objects and ourselves afterwards to detect any change. And . . .'

'What?' Talasa said.

'Nothing,' Colby said. 'It's all false. There is no detectable difference between a block of granite and a Sacred Tablet of Lurim. Nothing separates Bealtaine ashes from ash collected at any other time of the year. Nothing transmutative about a goblet that held the lifeblood of a hundred sacrificed men compared to one that did not.' His smile was shadowed, grotesque. 'Except for the stains.'

Talasa was revolted. He said it like it was some great scientific truth, and not a thief proud of thieving. 'You destroyed them?'

'We *tested* them. Isn't that what you do with faith?' He spun to gaze down into the lecture pit, horribly light on his feet. 'We were careful at first. Of course we were. But the King became disappointed, and then angry. We were asked to move at a speed that precipitated . . . damage. And then damage became the goal.'

'What do you mean?' Talasa whispered.

'It's all there in the texts,' Colby said. 'They're rife with lurid punishments. I spent three weeks taking a hammer to the burial urns of kings. I walked backwards in a circle cursing the name of Anu, Mother of Mysteries. I drank more sacred wine than I could stomach and flicked no drops to the cardinal points at which the gods are supposed to rest. Every commandment we could find, we broke, in ways that are supposed to invite disaster. And . . . nothing.'

He clucked his tongue in affront. 'I think that upset the King more than the lack of blessings had done. He *raged*, you know. All those temples raised in antiquity, all those many desperate wars of belief, all that effort and grime . . . and nothing. Nobody was right. Everybody was wrong. Fabrication and insanity.'

'They *belonged* to people.'

Even as Talasa said it, she knew that wasn't true. People had belonged to them. They had revered them. Made choices by them, sworn oaths on them, fought and killed for them. Even if the gods behind them were not real, *those things were.*

And these men had stripped them for parts.

'It's barbaric.' The words came out of her like a whip.

'Barbarism is the seedbed of civilisation,' Colby said coolly. 'A plot of earth from which society can grow. It just has to be tilled first. All the dead weight and weeds plucked away to see what is truly of use.'

'Fine words,' Talasa spat. Caution had been thrown to the wind a long time ago, but still, she was taken aback at just how angry she was.

And how guilty.

Is this what Kalifsena did to entice Rubeo? Play the savage so that he might educate her? Offer up our culture and our secrets as fuel for his obsession?

'My mother. Does she know that you're—'

'Does she *know*?' Master Colby laughed angrily. Laughter from the shadows echoed him, and Talasa felt like she was the one on their butcher's block, a fragile, barbarous thing turned this way and that by uncaring fingers. 'Come and see.'

He bade her follow him to the edge of the lecture pit. Like all of Secandeur House, the pit's best days were long gone by. A circular depression panelled by walnut and pine, it had once been grand, but now every corner and edge was chipped and chamfered by age and by dry, sweet rot. The varnish had receded like an old man's gums, leaving white patches of wear across the floorboards.

And in its centre, where a lecturer might have stood, the academics had erected a fane.

'We might have continued our experiments for a century, had the Queen not intervened,' Colby said, with a grudging respect. 'So concerned were we with finding the *right* religion. The correct set of beliefs. But academia too often works in isolation, even from itself. The Queen showed us that the path was not in one church but many. Sifting fragments. Seeking commonalities.'

He smiled.

'Unity. That was our church.'

It had been a furnace once. A black iron sphere turned onto its back so that the lidded slot of a mouth gaped upwards, big enough to swallow Talasa whole. But that industrial functionality had only been the start of the thing, and like any fane, years of offerings and adjustments had swelled its bulk to something unique to the hands that shaped it.

Something obscene.

The fane filled the teaching pit as if it had been built for it. Built inside it, Talasa realised, for there was no other way it could have been brought in here. No, it had been pieced together in this spherical chamber the way a spider might piece itself together inside an egg – joint by joint, bristle by bristle.

Bulbs of glass studded its skin – so blackened with fire they could have been lamps where the soot itself had become part of the light. Coals gleamed, fed on a diet of scripture. Exposed tubing chugged and heaved with a liquid that did not reflect the light. Segmented slats of brass and copper hooked upwards, each one bristling with long needles, and on each needle a fetish or totem had been nailed.

Pinioned sheets of scripture. Tablets, brutally bored through. Bags dripping black.

'There have always been strategies to court the gods,' Colby explained. 'Devices engineered and philosophical. Materials believed to carry with them a holy resonance. Ideomotive writing. The Seripharq of the Middle Kingdoms with its electrum spines. The torcstone of the Croí. A magnificent alloy of techniques from a hundred faiths with no real comprehension of what they had inferred.'

The holy treasures of a hundred cultures hung like hunters' trophies from the thing, like organs stolen by a shrike bird so that it could feast at its leisure.

'It wasn't enough to simply, unthinkingly blaspheme. That was the insight the Queen delivered to us. We had to make sure they *saw* it. We had to alloy the greatest designs of reverence with the gravest insults. Show them we were unafraid to meet them as equals.'

He stroked the railing lovingly, the light deepening his wrinkles to hard black strokes of a pen.

'We built it. We fed it blasphemy after blasphemy. And after a while, it felt as if it were building itself.'

Something gleamed in the depths of the thing, curdling the flames until they came out white and greasy. A stone. Fat and pale and shining, its gleaming white surface stained dark as if by wine or rust.

Talasa looked down at the dreadful thing, and then began to laugh.

She could not have had more of an effect on Master Colby had she hit him with a halberd. He spluttered. Straightened his robes. In the depths of the shadows there were mutterings and mumblings. Even Stord looked offended, the expression lost and out of place on that broad sheep-herder's face.

But Talasa couldn't help it. Her chest ached. Her shoulders shook. Two years of calculated demureness. Two years of whispering when she wanted to shout. Two years of cutting away parts of herself like trimming a bandage, all for ill-defined goals and a life of luxury she was only really allowed to observe.

This is what you were doing?

This is where you were instead of with me?

'It's . . . it's a trick,' she wheezed. The honesty felt more intoxicating than the whisky.

She waved a hand at the fane, half doubled over, aware she sounded like a madwoman but truly unable to stop.

'It's a ghosting cabinet.'

'A *what*?' Colby snapped.

Kalifsena had really outdone herself. There was something *starving* about its design – the way the mass of it hung forward on chains and cantilevers, the grasping, brooding span of its finger-limbs, reaching out like the cardinal points of a compass, or the rafters of a church, beckoning her in.

The academics had been burning things in its innards and raking through the soot, leaving long black stains up its sides. The whole thing smelled like incense and ash.

'It is a *trick*,' Talasa said firmly. 'Has it spoken to you? Does she get you to light candles around it and map the shadows so she can tell you what they mean? It's prop and theatre. It's . . .'

Disappointing.

Colby endured her ranting with a curiously deadened expression. Maybe he'd had his own suspicions too, that this was just one more step in the Queen's courtship, to hold the attention of a King who was famously bad at staying in place.

But now, in the flickering shadows, there was just the slightest trace of fear.

'It's not a trick,' was all he said, scratching at the stump of his finger. 'It's real.'

And the limbs of the fane began to move.

It wasn't a spider. Talasa had been distracted, she supposed, by the plundered gewgaws and talismans hanging from it, its glass-and-iron innards, where liquid purred and ticked from one mechanism to another. It was a wonder there was a recognisable shape in there at all.

But as the fane stirred and clattered, as the hooks set around its iron maw quivered as if straining against the glass that held them, as the sharp points of its legs scribed idiot scripture in tiny circles on the air, she realised what it was.

It was a tick. Swollen and gleaming. Chitinous plates flexing as unseen parts whirred and revolved, somewhere in that thirsty, ovoid bulk.

She had always hated them. You weren't supposed to. Hating war did you no good on a field of battle, comforting the dying and blessing the dead. You didn't hate gangrene, because amputations were often long and complicated, and hate put undue sweat in your eyes and frustration in your hands. You didn't even hate the mad, drunk, violent or stupid *zemlja*-lords who didn't take your advice, because capricious as they were, all fools possessed a keen knowledge of when someone thought them so.

But ticks hung from their back legs on the underside of leaves and waited for horses or dogs or people to brush by. They carried typhus, and fever, and some were simply venomous all by themselves, and often as not removing them squirted all that poison and more into their host.

They were of spiteful design.

'It taught us how to worship it,' Colby said, as the whirring of the thing became a thrumming, and then a rattling fit to drown out the rain outside. His nail was digging into the stump now. His words were a gasp of pain. 'We showed it we had rejected the old faiths. We showed it we were ready to listen.'

There was fervent movement in the shadows now. The whole chamber had taken on the aspect of a church – not some vaulted, austere barbican, but the pagan, monstrous tableau the Answering loved to imagine the world outside their borders to be.

Firelit. Clotted with darkness. A congregation in robes abasing themselves before a rattling, wheezing idol.

'Make it stop,' Talasa snapped. She wanted to take her eyes off the thing, but another, irrational part of her wanted to keep it in her field of vision, because she had the horrible thought that if she let it away then it would follow her up and over the lip of the pit. 'Make it *stop*.'

'There's no stopping it,' Colby said. 'We've been feeding it day and night. On his orders. And it's—'

'His?'

Talasa turned. Offrian stood in the doorway, the bottle of whisky empty in his hand. His eyes were red. His jacket was half off his shoulders. It made him look younger.

'Get that boy out of here!' Colby snarled, voice sharp with anger and fear.

'Was my father here?' The Prince was slurring. He stood at an angle, head lolling to the side as if twice the weight it had been before. 'Is this what he has you do?'

His fingers moved, convulsive and slippery, on the neck of the bottle, as if he constantly forgot and remembered its weight.

Stord tried to grab him, and Offrian hit him with the bottle. The blow was surprisingly graceful, until you remembered that Stord was an academic and Offrian had been taking fencing lessons since he was six years old.

The corner of the bottle impacted Stord above the cheek and turned his whole body around and onto the floor. It didn't even break.

'This is one of your tricks,' Offrian growled, and Talasa realised with a start that he was speaking to her. 'Isn't it? You're throwing your voice, or you have an accomplice, or your mother—'

'This isn't me,' Talasa said. 'This isn't—'

There was a pressure in the air. A questing vibration. Talasa's hair felt matted to her. Her eyes teared, then prickled dry. Her heart throbbed like a tooth in her chest.

'Your Highness,' she said gently, very gently. Soothing an animal, or a child. 'Offrian, we should leave. Come back to this place tomorrow with clearer heads and—'

'I want to *know*.'

'Then go to it and ask,' Master Colby whispered. The fane was vibrating so hard that all the myriad rasps and clatters had become one long drawl, drooling out of the thing like wax from beneath a signet – thick and soft and unctuous. 'As your father did.'

'My father would not . . .' Offrian's voice trailed away. Even now, even here, with an empty bottle of whisky in his hand and a bucking, heaving abomination spilling greasy light out onto the walls, the prince could not quite bring himself to lie.

'If there is a kingdom above us we must treat with it,' Colby said, all in a single breath. 'Isn't that right? That was what your father wanted. And we *found* it. We did. And it, like any other kingdom, any other state, made requests.'

Offrian's eyes were torches.

'He treated with it?'

'He did,' Colby crooned. 'To the benefit of all. Like a king should.'

Proof. That was the hunger on Offrian's face. Proof his father had not denigrated the Crown. Proof that he had been right to dedicate his life to the pursuit of another realm.

If another kingdom existed, it must be known.

And to the Answering, to know meant to conquer.

'You could treat with it too,' Colby said, as the figures in the shadows drew close, and Stord groaned on the ground, and Offrian edged nearer and nearer to the lip of the pit. 'It asks much. I will not deny that. But when your father returns with its bounty—'

'Returns from where?' Talasa asked desperately. She was right in the Prince's face now, but he did not for a moment acknowledge her.

He lingered on the very edge of the pit. There was an awful look of hope on his face.

'Go,' Colby said. 'Make your own compact. Carve out your own space in the new age it will bring.'

Offrian stepped forward –

And Talasa tackled him around the waist.

The two of them hit the ground in a tangle of limbs. Talasa didn't waste any time. She couldn't. Her elbow pressed down on his neck, her right hand scrabbling for the bottle where it had rolled, chipped and empty, out of his hand.

'Get *off*,' Offrian snarled. He was stronger than her. Much stronger. The only advantage she had was that he was unused to having a young woman try to fight him. 'Get *off*, you—'

She was spared whatever insult or epithet was about to come from his lips. Her hand found the bottle, and she drove the heel of it into his forehead. Two cracks, one from it meeting his skull, and one from his skull meeting the floorboards.

His eyes went glassy. He tried to speak, but the words arrived in a cascade of clumsy syllables and white flecks of drool.

'I'm sorry,' Talasa said, and hit him again.

She didn't know how long she sat there. Long enough for the full understanding of what had happened here to unfurl in her head, to grow roots and plumb the depths of her, reach up and scrape the inside of her skull.

Her mother *had* been dabbling in arcane blasphemies. Everything the populace said about Kalifsena was true. It had always been true. A foreign, heathen witch.

Talasa lurched to her feet, levering herself upwards awkwardly with the bottle. Whisky had glued a curl of hair to Offrian's forehead, tracing the perfect swell of a rising bump. Talasa wanted to fling the bottle away. Add it to the ruined relics crowding the floorboards.

Instead, she brought it up before her like a sword.

Archivist Stord stopped in his tracks. For such a big man, he had made no sound at all as he approached. Now, he stood just a few metres away, that same blankly pleasant look sitting on his face like it had been discarded there, rather than moved by the muscles beneath.

'There's no need for any kind of violence,' Master Colby said from behind him. In the rain-muttering dark, he could have just been another teetering stack of crates.

Lamps had been shuttered. The bite of dark around the lecture pit had widened. Talasa caught the merest glimpse of someone shuttering another – just a streak of black on black.

'I will be taking him with me back to the Palace,' she said, calmly as she was able. 'Do you understand me? One of you can go fetch my mother, and the rest of you can carry him to the carriage.'

'Princess-Undynast,' Colby said, almost sweetly. 'It does look like a nasty wound. Perhaps we should take care of him here. We could make you comfortable too, while you wait for your mother to be finished?'

Stord had taken another step. Talasa's arm was starting to ache. The last dribbles of whisky were winding a ribbon around her wrist.

'Finished doing what?' she asked.

'Communing,' Colby said. 'Did you think this was the only one we built?'

Stord grabbed the bottle out of Talasa's hand and flung it hard away. By the time he reached to grab her, she was already running, under his outstretched arm and into the torch-carved dark.

35

Sister Wake

WHEN THEY STEPPED from the little boat on the far side of Lough Maol, the tracks and trails of Sister Wake's former life rose up before her as if she was the one being resurrected.

There were the beginnings of Aileran's holdings, and there were Aileran's sheep – hardy, half-mad things that did not look up as Sister Wake and Brother Wight passed. There was the end of the old gut road – the causeway sitting up out of the boggy flat like a seam of fabric – and there was the hillside where she'd had her first kiss with Trian MacTyre, a messy, confusing affair that neither he nor she had really enjoyed.

Sister Wake didn't find herself pointing that out to Brother Wight, for some reason.

'Along the road,' she said. 'And then on to the village maybe? They'll share what they have with us.'

Neither one of them had eaten more than scavenged scraps of Answering tack the last couple of days. Sister Wake had a permanent hollow soreness in the base of her stomach, and Brother Wight was an accumulated mass of angry wounds – fight upon fight upon fight, winning each one but leaving a little of himself behind.

'We should go straight for the mountain,' he said, *brat* pulled around himself, face pale beneath his shock of hair. Something was brewing within him. She'd seen it as they'd crossed the lake, growing darker with every hissing sweep of the oars.

She could see it, and she didn't want to intrude or speak because she was concerned – yes, concerned – that what would come out would make things worse, or put him back where he had been, on one side of a crabby divide and her on the other.

Send him away. Send him back to Mathilde.

But she couldn't.

'What's the rush?' she asked, trying to joke. 'Sure when we get the Cailleach on side she'll gather us up through the Evergreen Undercountry and we'll be at Promontory before the Rising.'

They climbed the little seam of earth and stepped onto the road, just a pitted line of stones pocked with mud and water. Used to be there'd be men out here whenever the harvest would allow, repairing and maintaining.

Now, it was deserted. Sister Wake had been hoping they'd see someone, anyone, who wasn't frightened and hiding.

But there was no one in sight at all.

Brother Wight squinted up at the black loom of the mountain. 'We should go straight there, I think. If she's moved on, our path might be longer than—'

'If she's moved on,' Sister Wake said, 'we'll need to speak to the villagers and find out if any of them know in which direction.' *Fuck*, she thought. *I hope they were smart enough to stay away.* 'And if it is a longer search, we'll need supplies.'

'Which they'll provide?' he asked sceptically.

'I'm a saint,' she responded carelessly. 'And you're a sworn spear of the Rising. They'll listen to us. They'll give us whatever we need. You just . . . let me talk, all right? I know them. I'll display my gifts. You stand there and look like a frightening, murderous warrior of the Cailleach – there you go, exactly like that – and they'll answer our questions.'

He frowned at her. 'Questions? What questions would we have?'

She started walking rather than reply.

By the tail end of the afternoon, they had put miles of the rolling landscape behind them, following the road as it curled up and around the beginnings of Crom Dubh's skirt of hills to where its shadow lay across the last stretch to the coast.

Storms came hard and bad in west Umhaill with only one peak to break them up, and Sister Wake's village had been built close to the mountain it feared for what protection it could give.

Before Sister Wake knew gods were real, she would have called that a god – a huge shape that did not know you were there but offered something all the same.

Live here. Think about me. Let me guide how your society works. And I'll shield you from the storm.

For a while she distracted herself by thinking about the idea of staying. She'd make her case to the Cailleach – fuck if she knew how that was going to go – and whether it worked or not, the first thing she was going to do was go home and find a way to fix the door.

Da wouldn't have fixed it. He'd have found it kicked in by Brother Caid and gone looking for her immediately, and then after that had been . . . everything. Everything else.

He was the last person to stand in our home, and he was afraid, she thought, and then she refused to think about it anymore.

Think of the house. She could picture it now – their little garden all overgrown, the path up to the door green with weeds. Maybe she'd pick them. Maybe she wouldn't. It might be good to live somewhere packed with life. They had as much right to the place as she did, really, and it would be nice to have the company.

And maybe when Mother Promise has the Cailleach, she'll have no need for us.

Brother Wight was quiet as they walked. He was bundling up, but she'd already thrown back her *brat.* She'd shrugged open the neck of her *léine* as well, letting the cold air breathe down her sweat-slicked back.

She was walking fast. Of course she was. This was the last road. That first road, really, depending on the way you looked at it. Ahead, maybe a mile or two, was the village, houses clustered like dandelion seeds around the road on which she now stood.

But there was something. Something not quite right. It had been itching in the corner of her eye all morning, ever since she'd seen Crom Dubh. She had been glazing over it with stupid, inane thoughts and talk, the way she did when she was trying to convince a headless snake that nothing was wrong.

But now, running her hand over a cold-stunted bush, Sister Wake could no longer ignore it. She'd walked this road too often, and in all seasons. She recognised when a field was balding to bare earth and the trees were shedding leaves.

'It's winter here.'

Brother Wight let out a long plume of breath.

'It's winter everywhere.'

'No,' she snapped. 'It's the end of autumn. This is *winter.* It's winter *here.*'

He looked at her a little blearily. She'd thought he was just wounded, but he wasn't. He was freezing.

'I was wondering when you'd notice,' he said, pointing at her bare arms, beaded with sweat. 'It's been getting colder and colder the further west we've come.'

She hadn't noticed. Of course she hadn't. Cold was not a thing that meant anything to Sister Wake any more, unless she concentrated on it. And now that she was, she could feel that subtle tension. Trees shrinking into themselves. The ruts and runnels in the road becoming hard as scar tissue, the way the arm of a strong woman might narrow and wizen with age.

'We should go to the mountain,' Brother Wight said. 'Talk to the Cailleach. Do what we came here to do.'

But Sister Wake had already gone, up and out of her head, so fast and so frantic that she did not even feel her human body hit the earth.

She reached out. Listened. But there was nothing there but the bright, popping clarity of an icy winter morning.

That was why she hadn't noticed. Sister Wake heard death, like rain on a pipe, like fingers on a harp. But all around her was eerie silence. An empty house. All the deaths here had happened long ago.

There.

A crow that had been mangy its whole life and mangier in death, a thing that did not have the breadth of heart to be glad of death but had been relieved at the end of the fight all the same.

What did it say about such a thing that it still had a little touch of hope at the idea of finding warmth and comfort? What did it say about Sister Wake that she used that hope as strings to drag it up and into the air?

No time. Doesn't matter.

She flew.

'Sister Wake – wait!'

The words happened to someone else. Sister Wake was flying over low and cold countryside, banking around shrivelled, unhappy hedges and the scrubby disappointments of trees. Crows had an eye for death in the stories. Plenty of animals ate the dead, but only crows laughed while they did it.

But that was the stories, and real crows saw no more meaning in the splayed bodies than a human might in a flowerbed. Colour, texture, sustenance, arranged and open to the air. It was Sister Wake who recognised the meaning in the meat.

Amber Bressal, so called because his family had the strangest yellow cast to their pale brown eyes, slumped in the road, rainwater freezing to crystals in his open mouth.

Elan and her twin girls, lying like stars in the main street, arms and legs pointing in all directions but at each other.

Laisrén, the girl Sister Wake had once counted a friend and giggled with and made fun of and secretly hated sometimes. Her open mouth was full of rainwater, frozen to a pale blue plug of ice.

The crow landed, turning its head this way and that, taking in the forty or so bodies all held in their patina of frost. And in the centre of the village, in a crater of rucked earth like an eye in a head, lay a flung altar stone.

For the first time since she could remember, Sister Wake did not gently untangle herself from the soul of a thing. She just left, and the crow's sudden horror was an exact echo of what was happening in Sister Wake's heart.

When she came back to herself, Brother Wight was standing over her.

'You *knew,*' she hissed.

He looked at her for the longest time. Savouring something he knew he was about to lose.

'Yes.'

She got to her feet slowly, as if putting on mail. Something red and hot was pushing its way through the chill in her brain. 'The Cailleach.'

The Cailleach, who could kill with a look.

'She walked through the village,' Sister Wake said. 'She killed them all.'

'Everything with eyes to meet hers,' Brother Wight agreed. 'Even the trees suffered. That was what Mother Promise heard, from the one man who did return.'

Sister Wake could hear them too, now that she knew what to look for. The souls of faithful men, scattered between here and the mountain. You could tell a faithful soul from one that was not. They were the loudest because they felt death was the most unfair.

'Which means she may still be here,' Brother Wight said gently. 'And that means we can still complete our mission.'

'*Fuck your mission,*' Sister Wake snarled, hands balling to fists 'Fuck it *dead.* You all knew. Even after I told you I wanted to come back here. Even after I talked for *hours* about them. You knew they were all long dead.'

Cold had preserved the bodies almost perfectly. The terror. The confusion. The faces frozen in mild bemusement, as if they had simply caught a glimpse of the striding god out of the corner of their eye, and then winter had bloomed in those eyes for ever.

Another set of people Sister Wake had been too late to help. The chain on the mountain might have made her a saint, but it had wrung this village's neck.

'I'm sorry. There was no good time to tell you. And you were already so . . . conflicted about your place with us. Taking that hope away from you would have . . .' Brother Wight's voice was hatefully even. He was still trying to preserve the little thing that had been built between them, and that made her hate him more.

Even as a part of her lifted away and began to seek and seek.

'Made it harder for you to get me to do what you want,' Sister Wake said. 'That's the truth, isn't it? That's the truth all over. They're not even people to you. None of us are. There are *dead children* in that village. You're probably just upset you didn't get to put a knife in their hand and send them into an Answering gun line yourself.'

'That's *enough*,' he snapped, and she knew she'd riled him, even as she delved and searched and scurried. None of that frantic action showed upon her face. He knew her better than anyone. He knew what to look for.

But if she made him angry enough, he wouldn't see what she was trying to do.

'Tell me I'm wrong. Tell me you're not all liars. I left *Mathilde* with her. I trusted her. And I trusted you.' She dragged nails down her chest. 'And you made me a liar too. These clothes. These speeches. This *hair*. It's all a lie. We're *filidh*, but instead of telling stories about ossuary wolves and the right way to please Anu, we're just walking people into an unwinnable war so we don't have to face up to the fact we *fucking lost three hundred years ago and won't just accept it*!'

'Stop,' Brother Wight said, and jammed his spear into the ground so that it stood freely. Was he going to grab her? Hit her? Sister Wake was *fascinated* to find out. 'You don't have a clue what you're talking about.'

'Don't I?' she asked. 'How much easier would our lives be if we just did as we were told? If we just accepted the yoke and kept our heads down and let Answering prattle replace whatever fucking prattle we were listening to before? Would life be that different? Would there be so many bodies swaying on ropes?'

'Our lives would be ours,' he said.

She rolled her eyes theatrically. 'And what a difference that would be.'

The old boot scar on his cheek stood out white as the gut road.

'It would be a difference to some.'

'Well,' she said, 'maybe those people should have done what they were fucking *told*.'

And it was exactly right. The words rang out over the icy afternoon, and after that, the Answering King himself could have walked by and Brother Wight wouldn't have noticed.

This was the revoking of the *geis* she had attempted over and over again, and all it took was the worst thing she had ever said.

'And what about them, hah?' he said softly. 'What's so important about this place, against everything else? You'd walk away from the real war, let the island languish under another three centuries of murder and oppression just because – what? We didn't let you know a handful of farmers died? A god *chooses* you, and that's the dead you care about?'

'I don't give a *shit* about what the Cailleach wants,' Sister Wake snapped. *Just a little longer* . . . 'What about what *I* wanted?'

Genuine confusion on his face.

'Tell me,' he said, and in the part of her that was still in her, Sister Wake managed to feel bad.

'Everyone said the O'Cuain girl just ran away,' she said. 'That was ten years ago. I was nine. But there was probably another girl before that, and another, and maybe even another, because before Brother Caid was Brother Amedan, and by all accounts he was even worse.'

A ragged punch of breath.

'I've been *doing* what everyone wanted. Never letting what I wanted come into my head, because how could it matter compared to the war? I would come back after. That was her promise. We'd find Brother Caid together. I'd find out the truth. I'd find out their names. I never wanted to come home for me. I was coming home for them.'

She had played and replayed the moment a hundred times in her head. Sister Wake, a saint of the Rising. An unassailable figure of authority and judgement.

Or maybe there'd be Brother Wight with his big thick head, or maybe Mother Promise, who could spin even Sister Wake's thread-bare charisma into gold. She'd line up the villagers, one by one. And Brother Caid too, if she could bear not just having him killed on the spot.

And she would ask them one simple question.

'Who knew?' Sister Wake said. 'That's what I want to know. Who knew that fucking bastard was hurting girls in the name of a god that nobody could see or hear? Who were they? And where are their bodies?'

The words caught in her throat.

'That's the dead I care about.'

Brother Wight pressed his forehead against the haft of his spear. He looked deeply, deeply tired, his strength and anger suddenly leached away by the cold.

'You have your war,' Sister Wake said softly. 'I had mine. And now I'll never know.'

'I'm sorry,' Brother Wight said.

'So am I,' she said, and sent the crow at his throat.

Had he seen through her at the last moment? Did some lax hang of a hand or a cheek make him realise she wasn't all there? Or had he simply seen it coming out of the corner of his eye? She would never know that either. But before beak and claw could bury themselves in the hard cables of his neck, he reached up with both hands and plucked it from the air.

She fought. The crow fought, harder than it had ever fought for anything in life – there was no indignity greater for this smart little scion of air and branch than to be *handled* so roughly – but Brother Wight's strength was irresistible.

His hands gripped and separated, pulling one wing fully away like he was deboning a chicken. Not just killing it again. Making sure it would be no good to Sister Wake if she tried to raise it.

'Don't do this,' he said, and took a step towards her.

He knows me. He knows how I do what I do.

But Sister Wake wasn't done. Spite was a mill wheel in her chest, driving her to greater depths of strength.

A sheep, then, barrelling through the undergrowth with a speed it never possessed in life. She'd had to be rough with it, because there was nothing violent in the creature's head, but fear was an ever-present companion to sheep, and so she put something terrifying *behind* it and sent it towards Brother Wight like an arrow.

It didn't even know he was there until it slammed shoulder-first into his side, and then it died irretrievably a moment after, unable to process striking another living thing.

Brother Wight staggered. Kept coming.

'Let's find the Cailleach. Do what we came for. Perhaps she can—'

'She wanted to hurt Mathilde!' Sister Wake shrieked, and her anger gathered up two voles, a mouse and even the broken, ragged body of the crow, which lifted its head and trilled in sympathetic rage. 'You think Mother Promise wouldn't put us all on her altar if she could?'

Brother Wight kicked a scurrying vole into oblivion, then flinched back as another ran up his leg. Sister Wake's vision blurred, somewhere between staring at his hard face and feeling the flex of his thigh under her claws, and then a plucking, obliterating hand came down and suddenly she was snapped back into her own body like a punch.

Just for an instant, then out again. Her *tabharthas* raked the land, dragging up whatever she could find, and for the first time she did not ask but *demanded*. She took the anger of little souls and sharpened it like knives. She browbeat the slow and the cautious. She riled up the wild and the vicious. She turned her *túath* upside down like a jar of *menedach* and shook out whatever corpses she could.

She did not take no for an answer. She did not wake. She recruited.

And Brother Wight strode through it all, unfeeling. It was not a battle that any *filí* would sing of, as the Knight of the Hollow Eye stamped and kicked and snapped and tore. It was brute force and butchery.

His eyes never left hers.

'If this is what you want, we can find a way to do it. We can ask neighbouring villages. We can find other Brothers who might have known Caid. This doesn't have to be a war between us. We can—'

The stag hit him from the right.

Brother Wight's gasp was a single orphaned plume of breath, before a bracket of antlers scooped him up like a mother's hands and flung him ten feet down the road.

Sister Wake watched the breath shred itself apart.

'I know you still live,' she said. 'But if I ever see you or any warrior of the Rising again, you will learn what a saint of death truly is.'

Kneeling was against every fibre of the stag's soul, but Sister Wake made the creature do so anyway, so she could climb up on its back.

'Goodbye,' she said, and rode away.

VI

Real and Unreal

36

Sister Wake

THE STAG FOUGHT Sister Wake all the way to the village. It felt like penance.

The marshes on either side of the gut road were eerily silent, the unseasonable cold forcing everything into death or flight or unwilling hibernation. Bog water had become black mirrors. The air sparkled, on the cusp of snow.

The village – it had a name, but she only ever thought of it as *the village*, the way you never thought of parents' names – nestled between Crom Dubh like a child hiding behind their father.

Sister Wake traded the gut road for a cow-wide track that circumnavigated the foot of the great mountain, watching ahead as the measly scrap of land between peak and coast revealed itself – just a few miles of sheep fields, scratchy little lakes and then, finally, a long and morose beach too featureless to be pretty, even in summer.

They thought I wanted to come home to this.

She had enough anger to go around right now, but there was a petty little sting in that she could not overcome. The *arrogance*. Had they thought she simply didn't *get it*? That she didn't understand how important the war for the freedom of Croí was? Of course they had. Typical fanatics. She had seen it on all those late nights Mother Promise had railed against the short-sightedness of chieftains who sought to hold men back for the harvest, or weapons for their own *lucht tighe*.

There was never any way but their way. Never any wars but the one they fought. You saw it like they did, and if you didn't then you were selfish, or stupid, or unenlightened. No – worse. It was not enough to see it. You had to match their outlook exactly, heartbeat for heartbeat, blow for blow, rage for rage.

No wonder Mother Promise had wanted the gods brought in line. She was probably resentful of the competition.

Everything the Answering did to us, Sister Wake thought, *you did to your own soul to fight them. Isn't that just as bad?*

Brother Wight would have had something to say to that, but she had left him behind.

She had to leave the stag there too, just a few hundred yards from where the village sat, clustered around the banks of the Dunadhach just before it plunged into the Unbeknownst Sea. The beast had been bucking and stamping since they'd gotten out of sight of Brother Wight – unable to dislodge her from its mind but resolute in its resistance.

Each step was a battle, each bit of progress marred by some backstep or compromise. It seemed to take a great and spiteful delight in shaking her every time she tried to adjust or find some way of sitting comfortably, until she simply had to give up or turn the air blue with curses.

There was other discomfort too. The fight had filled Sister Wake's head with a scratchy red pain, hot and wiry exhaustion behind her eyes. She'd never used her *tabharthas* so loose and so viciously, and now it seemed that the cost and the ceiling to what she could accomplish had truly been found.

She had just enough presence of mind to hold the stag in place until she got clear, and then gave it a full minute of prancing, charging freedom to live before letting its soul drift out of her grip.

I'm sorry, she thought. Not just for the stag, but for all the little creatures she had used so poorly. She had depopulated the *túath* nearly as badly as the Cailleach had done.

And I'm sorry, Mathilde. She took a moment then, standing there on the side of the road, the soft breath of the Dunadhach just on the edge of her hearing. *I promised you I'd come back.*

She was going to break that promise. She had to. She could never look Mother Promise in the eye again, not without trying to put a crow beak through it. She had known, of course. She'd known Mother Promise would do anything for the Rising. Tell any lie. Break any oath. She'd even admired that about her, after a fashion. Certainty was attractive when you had none of it yourself.

But she couldn't be around it.

I'm done.

Done being at the mercy of things bigger than me.

So I'm leaving you to be at the mercy of them instead.

In the stories of saints, breaking a promise was a curse. That seemed to be the only part of the scripture that had not manifested so far.

I curse myself, Sister Wake thought, picturing those sloe-dark eyes, Mother Promise's hand on that thin shoulder. *That'll have to be enough.*

She trudged onwards towards the houses. Passed simple cottages, thatch hardened to a stone consistency by time and cold. The bodies in the streets were all skin and bone, shrivelled into tight grey dolls pulled back along their seams. She didn't see any of the faces she had known in them, and there were no souls in the air to remind her.

Which of you knew? Which of you helped? Which girls did you sacrifice to get what you wanted?

She stepped around and over them. No reverence. No disgust. No guilt.

Just empty houses.

The first three cottages she checked had nothing she could use, not even a blanket. The door of the fourth had so swollen with frost that she could not open it.

Another house. In this one she found a few little pots of herbs that seemed to have some scent to them at least. She came back out on the street just as the afternoon sun was turning the ice in the puddles into shards of light, and immediately knew that she was not alone.

It wasn't a saintly sense. There was nothing newly dead. Not a single finger of a single corpse had moved. There were no new foot-prints, no sights or smells.

But there was something. A passing warmth that had not been there before.

'I warned you,' Sister Wake said loudly. 'Don't make me hurt you again.'

Her head was still alive with pain – she wasn't sure she could raise a fly, let alone a thing that would fight her, and there was nothing for miles that might fight *him*.

Fuck the Answering for killing all the wolves, she thought. She could have done with wolves right now.

Nothing but silence answered her.

That was in itself unnerving. She turned in a slow circle, trying to let herself untense, her eyes drift. An old Rising trick – sometimes you were too busy searching to properly see. Brother Wight would have answered. Which was funny, for a man of the Rising who spent his whole adult life hiding in hedges and forests. He wouldn't come at her without saying something. He would try.

'I release you from your promise!' she shouted, but nothing answered her back.

When she had stood long enough that she had started to feel stupid, she picked another house to go into. Just paranoia and foolishness. She would get what she needed and leave, and begin putting her own house back together. Maybe she would go and speak to the Cailleach. Maybe that was the way to keep the Rising from her door – deliver on her promise, at least.

And maybe Mathilde will come and find me.

The house was Murgadh the cobbler's. The earth floor was packed tight by a century of feet. A curtain had been hung to separate the single room into two, and one side of it smelled of leather and oil. Utensils hung from hooks in the ceiling, over a little fireplace.

The fireplace had new ash in it.

Sister Wake froze. One corner of the room was a knot of tangled blankets – at least six or seven, gathered from other houses – and whatever had slept in them had polluted them with rank, hot sweat. The smell of it after the pure, clean morning got in her mouth with a revolting warmth.

Who . . .

She turned away from the animal reek of the place and walked straight into Brother Caid.

The priest filled the doorway, a half-eaten apple in his hand, its skin dark and ruckled with age. He was ruckled too – gone was the strange paunch and sinewy frame, the body you got from living on the road with meals few and far between, but generous when they came.

Now he was like a shed skin of himself – flesh loose and dried tight in equal measure, pulling back from eye and tooth and fingernail until all you could see were the hard points of cartilage and bone and optical socket.

And what do I look like to him?

Did he even recognise the girl in front of him? The black *léine*, the inked eyes, her once-long red hair now an array of hostile spikes and her skin two shades too pale to be truly alive?

Only his lips remained full as they had been, floating strangely in that desiccated face.

'Síle,' he said.

Sister Wake's stomach turned. She hadn't heard her own name in months.

'You're . . . you're alive.'

And then he burst into tears.

The tears came out of him like she'd yanked the stopper from a keg, his face suddenly flushed and red. He held up his hands as if he'd forgotten what they were for, before turning away from her and striding to his bed.

'I'm sorry. I'm sorry. I haven't . . . spoken to anyone since . . .'

He started plucking at the blankets, lifting them up and turning them around, trying to put them into some kind of order before letting out a half-animal sound of frustration and balling the whole lot up into his arms and flinging them down.

The stag.

No use. Its soul was almost purposely shredded, determined for oblivion rather than being drawn on again.

Rats.

There were always rats, but there were always rats because rats were smart, and as soon as this village had become a graveyard, they had fled to better climes.

Birds.

Nothing close, and when Sister Wake reached out, really reached out, the inside of her head became a red maelstrom of pain.

When it cleared, he was standing in front of her.

'You're weak from hunger,' he said. 'Of course you are. I am too – this is all I've been able to find in days. Here – take it.'

His bitemark in the apple glistened with juice and spit.

She didn't have her knife. She should have taken Brother Wight's wheellock. She would have taken it and jammed it into his—

When Brother Caid smiled at her, cracks opened up along his lips.

'You came back,' he said. 'I thought all was lost. When the Cailleach came, I heard the screaming. I heard the *dying*. Such *caoine-adh* as to reach the Evergreen Undercountry itself. I thought . . . I *doubted* myself. I thought I had made a mistake.'

Sister Wake was moving before the last word left his mouth, but she wasn't fast enough.

'But now you're here—'

The priest's hand caught the back of her father's *brat* and yanked with the strength of the mad. She stumbled right into his other fist, and the blow knocked her, dazzled, to her knees.

Brother Caid was already turning away, confident he had put her down. *Of course he was.* He had practice.

Sister Wake punched him in the back of the knee. Caid stumbled, snarled, and she threw her whole weight into that momentary stagger, trying to drag him down with her.

'Get . . . get *off*!' he screeched, as she split one of those fat lips with her knuckle and his hands mussed and plucked at her hair. Then grabbed. Then *pulled*.

Sister Wake reared back, trying to jab, trying to kick . . .

And he hit her again and again and again.

Somewhere in those impacts, she stopped fighting. Sometime after that, he stopped too. The last thing Sister Wake saw was Brother Caid standing over her with a look of beatific reverence on his face.

'You're here,' he said, 'and now we can do it right.'

37

Abelard

'YOU'RE LUCKY, MY lords,' Colonel Quarles said, saluting so violently his helmet rang like a struck bell. 'You arrived in between assaults.'

Their progress through the packed and angular courtyard of Promontory had not been easy, even though paths had been marked with rope for speedy resupply of men and ammunition. The diamond between outer and inner ward was positively overstuffed with soldiers – hundreds of bedraggled men sleeping in shifts, shuffling to and from commissary tents, even packed like sitting crows on the wooden allure along the walls, their legs dangling like schoolboys.

Quarles led the way. Meilyr's gaze swept back and forth across the forlorn congregation. Where he looked, backs straightened and heads rose. Now that a higher authority had arrived, hope had arrived with him.

Behind him, Abelard and Netha followed, the poet striding a path as far away from Abelard as their escort would allow. It was such a childish gesture that it almost gave Abelard hope.

'How many?' Meilyr asked, as soon as they had passed under the inner curtain wall and into a chemise too narrow for men to have been billeted.

'Seven thousand men, camped here and outside the walls. We've done everything short of stacking them on each other,' Quarles said. He was old, the kind of old that compressed you, made you knotty and strong as dried-out wood. His uniform was as dirty and worn as everyone else's they had passed, and Abelard found himself staring at the man's hands, every wrinkled inch of them black-lined with mud and dried blood. 'Seven thousand out of eleven, when first the muster was attacked.'

Meilyr shook his head. 'And the guns? You were advised to give them priority.'

'We did so,' Quarles said. Flakes of blood cracked off as he fidgeted. 'As much as we were able. Many of the bombards require specialist cranes to lift them off walls, milord, and there isn't a single outpost that did not come under some kind of attack by men or beasts. A number were lost or had to be abandoned.'

Abelard had seen them in the courtyard, almost invisible behind the tattered regiments of men. Mortars, beasts of things on their own little carts, painted with red lead against the rust. Larger bombards too – long as a man was tall and fat with menace.

He didn't have names for half the others. It wasn't a precise science, despite what one might have thought. He knew that much from Astor. You built guns as big as you could build them, or you built them for specific jobs, or you built them for the arena in which they might be used. If it *was* a science, it was a science in the way naturalism was science – not a standard but a bestiary.

Watching men curled up around and even on such devastating weapons seemed deeply strange. As if the carnage you knew could be comforting, and not simply carnage.

'How many?' Meilyr asked.

'Eighteen,' said Quarles.

They entered the keep, passing into a hall that seemingly had been reserved for officers and command staff, sitting in quiet groups on long benches. There was wine here, and cider, and ale – barrels and casks tapped and left for any to help themselves. Some heads were drooping. That and the smoky fires burning in the two great fireplaces might almost have made it cosy, were it not for the twitchy, nervy alertness that pressed through even the drink.

When those that could see saw Meilyr, there were suddenly a hundred tasks to be about. The hall began to empty. To where, Abelard did not know.

'Eighteen?' Meilyr snapped. 'We should have three times that. What about the garrison at—'

'We have the amount we have, *milord*,' Quarles said, and in those seven words Abelard heard miles, and sleeplessness, and horrors that made their journey here look like stories from *Tales of the Hinterlands*. 'There might have been more, but we were pressed for time. Men had to be left behind to secure the majority retreat.'

He scrubbed one wrinkled, callused hand over his mouth, but not before Abelard saw it tremble.

'We lost good men. And bad men too, as it happened, but I'd rather have them here than out there. This might be all that is left of an Answering military presence on this island. Or maybe it's not, and there are fractured regiments and half-companies and squads of men out in the nowhere beyond these walls, but wherever they are, they're not here, and no good to us.'

'How often do they attack?' Netha asked. Quarles blinked, looking at Meilyr for approval. Meilyr waved a hand irritably and the old man cleared his throat.

'It has been once or twice a day, er . . . sir. Sometimes in dribs and drabs – a single creature, or a pack. Other times, it is a horde. We have weathered two of those in the last four days, and each time they stretched our capabilities desperately.'

'But you drove them off,' Meilyr said. 'The field outside . . .'

'Took half our gravedust stocks,' Quarles said. 'And still they nearly reached the walls. The smallest of them take five or ten shots to put down. They do not flee, or break, not until they are studded with iron. It's as if a master drives them. Or a fire, driving beasts.'

Netha let out a quiet breath. Quarles continued.

'We are not . . . used to such warfare, my lord.'

Quarles didn't ask what they were. That struck Abelard too. Quarles had a job to do. He was doing it. Metaphysical conundrums could wait.

'You will have to learn it,' Meilyr said. 'We will have to master it, as we have mastered all else.'

Quarles absorbed this morosely.

'Do you bring good news, milord? When can we cast off?'

'Cast off?' Abelard asked suddenly. Meilyr had kept him and the Terod behind his own soldiers, and only now was Quarles noticing that there was a young lordling there, and that his hands were bound. 'You're going to leave?'

Meilyr rounded on him, one hand raised. Abelard had never been struck before. He was oddly curious as to what it might feel like.

Netha stepped between them with a brash cackle. 'Is that what you promised them, Meilyr? Of course you did. Home and hearth, was it? A chance to be rid of this cursed island?'

'Promise the men under your command nothing but service,' Meilyr said, 'and you will never disappoint.'

He presented the colonel with an awful attempt at a smile.

'Array the cannons to face the southern approach. Find sight lines across the battlefield or build platforms so that our rounds will have clearance. There is one last battle here to fight, Colonel. Against a single foe. Defeat them, and we can leave with our heads held high. Or stay and retake the colony for King and Answering.'

'What kind of foe, milord?' Quarles asked bluntly.

'Did I invite questions? Or did I give orders?'

Quarles saluted again. This one did not ring quite so loudly. 'Milord. And your . . . guests?'

'Put them somewhere with a view.'

They were unceremoniously marched from the hall and up flights of stairs draped with wounded men. Promontory was not a castle designed for comfort, even before a wounded army had descended upon it. The room the guards sequestered them in was little more than a cell fit for a soldier of some small rank. There was a low bed, a bucket and a narrow window. It did not have bars across it, but the effect was the same.

Netha crossed to the window, gaze determinedly fixed on the thrashing sea outside.

'What do you want me to say?' Abelard asked. 'I'm sorry for your loss? I'm sorry I saved your life? Then I am sorry. I did not want him to kill you.'

Netha snorted. 'You think I would have come here if I was afraid of being killed by an Answerman? Do you think I need an Answerman to save me?'

Abelard tried to adopt Netha's lightness – their deft, careless truths – but everything came out plodding and stupid. 'You said you would tell Macha's story true. Who will do that, if you die? Who would be able to, when you are the one who has seen it?'

The *filí* shook their head. 'My calling is not your academies, where you race to etch your signature on every aspect of the natural world. *Me me me! I was there first!* The world existed before you. It does not *need* you. *I* do not need you.'

Abelard's cheeks flushed. 'I never said you did. I simply did not wish to stand by. Your knowledge is the only thing that might—'

'Might *what*, Abelard? Might arm your people against my gods?'

Abelard might have preferred the poet to round on him angrily, to show more than the rigid, static rage they were displaying, but there was nothing of the sort. They never took their eyes from the window.

'What are you *doing* here, Abelard Caudefoy? You say you wish to understand, but what kind of understanding is it that you desire? You say you wish to *help*, but who are you planning on helping? Your people? The people of Croí? Do you even know? Or are you simply planning to dither and watch as an island tears itself apart, and make notes about it in your little book? Perhaps if you bow and scrape nicely to Meilyr, you'll even be allowed to dissect the bodies.'

'I do not wish to help Meilyr,' Abelard snapped. 'The man is a thug.'

'No he isn't,' Netha snarled. 'He's not an aberration. Not a criminal. You just want him to be. What have those creatures done out there that your kings have not done? Is the difference only the law?

Everything Meilyr does is lawful, but only because the laws are written by men like him, *for* men like him. This is what an empire *does*, Abelard. This is what they have always done. Predators, striding through bodies like muck.'

They ran their hands along their shoulders, trying to gouge mud from their cloak.

'You asked me to denounce what I saw. I do. Can you do the same for your people? Or will you just express distaste quietly at parties or write letters in the strongest terms to members of your Rationale?'

'I could do just that,' Abelard said suddenly. 'If my father knew of Meilyr's excesses, perhaps he could—'

'*If he knew*,' Netha said scornfully, and though they had only known each other a handful of days, Abelard could already sense when the *filí* was rising to the role they had set themselves. The deepening voice, the expanding chest. 'As if three centuries of slaughter happened while he was in his study looking for his glasses. How much killing was done under a Caudefoy banner, Abelard? How much of Croí does your father own?'

'I don't . . .' Abelard stammered. 'I don't know.'

And he didn't. That part was true.

He just knew it was a lot.

They shook their head. 'At least Meilyr is honest. Why aren't you?'

Because I wanted you to like me.

Because I want to like myself.

'Because it's done,' Abelard said tiredly. 'It's been done a hundred times over, over hundreds of years. You think the Croí are better, just because you are one.'

Netha opened their mouth, but for once, Abelard took the stage.

'The raiders. The murderers. The hostage-takers, hiding in the mountains making demands no Answering king could ever grant. Farms burned. Knives held to hostages' necks. And your god and those . . . things, tearing innocent fleeing people apart. You're asking me to side with them. You're asking me—'

'To understand that things should change,' Netha countered. 'I am a creature of *law*, Abelard. The gods were too, those that were worthy of worship. That was the *geiseanna*. The compact. A rule that constrained the powerful and the powerless alike. And those who broke it were held to account.'

Quarles's words. *Or a fire, driving beasts.*

Those dry, cracked footprints preserved in the Lord Seneschal's offices.

Wolves only kneel to each other.

A goddess of war, and sovereignty.

'Do you really believe that?' Abelard asked, speaking as carefully as he could in case the thought he was building in his head came apart.

'Yes,' the *filí* said. 'I do.'

Abelard joined them at the window. On three sides, water ate at the bay, and yellow clumps of weed had gathered even there, bobbing like little islands, crashing against each other with every wave. Boats bobbed too, their decks empty until Meilyr gave the order he would rather die than give.

To the west, the narrow blade of Promontory Keep's courtyard pointed out at the low, rolling countryside. From here, Abelard could see the walls, a section of them at least, and every useable inch of them was packed with men and guns.

And beyond a sea of mouldering bodies, something was coming

into view. Massive as sunset, crowned with white and shining stone that did strange things to the light.

'Then I'll trust it,' he said. 'Because I've just had a particularly stupid idea.'

There wasn't enough time to truly prepare. If there had been, Abelard might not have been able to go through with it.

'Are you ready?' Netha asked.

'I think so,' he said. It had been a distressingly intimate experience, their rushed and whispered discussion. He had only stopped twice to make notes. 'But it's a military kitchen. I don't know if they'll have the half of this.'

'Whatever you can find,' Netha said. 'That's how it's always worked. It's about giving what you have. About the sharing, and the sacrifice.' They smiled ruefully. 'It's the symbol, and the symbol will have to do. A reminder.'

The symbol. That was what lords were, really. They were the link to the King, the avatars of royal will. Through them, it filtered down, and some kind of order was achieved. Some kind of unity.

Abelard had been quite bad at carrying that torch, it turned out, but luckily it seemed as if that part of his life would soon be over.

There was a knock at the door. It was that small detail that told him it wasn't Meilyr, even before the door opened and Quarles stepped in, flanked by three soldiers.

'The Lord Protector is sending a boat back to the mainland,' the colonel said. 'With a few men to explain what is happening here. With . . . samples. And he wants the Terod gone too.'

'No!' Netha said, standing. Their sword had been taken long ago, but they still looked ready to take the soldiers on. 'I will not be sent away again. Not from my home. You'll have to—'

'Netha,' Abelard said firmly. 'Wait.'

He crossed the room to the poet, and to the surprise and deep embarrassment of the watching soldiers, pulled them close to whisper in their ear.

It was not a lot of time to say quite a lot of things, but when he drew back, Netha was nodding. *To be as able as you to change roles,* Abelard thought enviously. *To have that shape-changing grace.*

'I would go instead of you if I could.'

'I know you would,' Abelard said. 'Thank you. But it has to be me.'

It was instinct then, in that moment – that machine that defied and defined understanding. Abelard took Netha's hand and squeezed it. After a moment, Netha squeezed back.

'Tell a story about me,' Abelard said.

'A hundred,' Netha said. There were bright and unashamed tears in their eyes.

'Keep them alive,' Abelard said to Quarles. The colonel gave him a curt nod.

And then it was just Abelard. There was a question there as to why Meilyr had not sent him back to the mainland as well, but he knew it was because the Lord Protector still wanted to make use of him.

That in itself was a reason to proceed.

He waited a few moments, and then knocked on the door himself. It opened a crack, revealing a soldier a few years younger than

Abelard who looked immensely grateful that he was in here guarding a peer instead of out on the walls. That was deeply naïve, and hopefully very helpful.

'I am going to speak to the Lord Protector,' Abelard said. He didn't try to be stern. There was no point. Either the guard would let him or not.

'Milord,' the guard said, 'I was told to—'

'You were told to keep me here and safe,' Abelard said, with as much Caudefoy as he could muster. 'Yes? I have knowledge that is critical to the siege. You will not be thanked if you keep it from him. First I need to go to the kitchens.'

It worked. Somehow it worked. The soldier escorted Abelard down the stairs and through the great hall of the castle. The place was emptier than before. Only the very wounded remained, untended and lingering in their pain. Every soldier worth calling such had gone to the wall.

The kitchens were completely deserted, but that was where Abelard's luck ended. The three cavernous pantries he found would have taken a day to search fully, and in the bowels of the castle he had no idea how much time he actually had.

Ropes of onions trembled at Macha's distant footsteps. Jars of preserve and powder juddered in their crates.

After a sweaty, frantic few minutes, all he could trust himself with, he ended up with precisely three things – a little scoop that might have been used for shovelling wheat, a bottle of grain whisky and a sack to hold them in.

It'll do, he told himself, sweat running down his back as he bolted up the stairs, the confused soldier following closely behind. *It will have to.*

Had you asked him three days ago, Abelard would have cheerfully and willingly given up his old life and title for a glimpse at something as majestic and terrifying as Macha.

But now it came to it, he was deeply, deathly afraid.

Out in the courtyard, it was turning towards dusk. The sky was blackening like paper aflame, the red giving way at the edges to sullen night. Torches had been lit, but the light was blocked by the sheer number of bodies crowding the space, a horizon of heads and shoulders squirming and pushing and straining to see out beyond the walls.

Abelard had to bodily shove his way through. There wasn't enough room for soldiers to get out of his way.

What did you call them here for? he asked Meilyr in his head, the only place he felt safe to do so. *Why form them up now in ranks, when all you want is the guns?* Macha could bring down a hand here and by sheer density kill a hundred men.

If they did not bring her down first.

He stepped out onto the walls. The bay was a thrashing violet void, scribbled over again and again by the white tops of wavelets. The lights in the sprawling camp to the north had been doused, but he could pick out scurrying movement in the shadows, silent blocks of bodies ranked to fire in a broad front. Meilyr did not want Macha distracted, he realised. He wanted her coming straight at the castle, where she could be anticipated, if such a thing were possible.

To the south, the men had been put to work. Some of the bloated god-things remained, a riot of colour and textures and shapes, lying in packs or by themselves as single, towering corpses.

But there had been clearing done, to accommodate the no less monstrous forms of eighteen huge cannons, each one lit by torches and manned by their own crew of shouting, fussing men. How much force did it take to break a kneecap? To punch through a thigh? How did you even calculate it?

From there, Abelard could draw a line to the very edge of the killing field, where the bodies gave way to clear grass. It was perhaps a kilometre of ground. Astor would know.

I wish my brothers were here.

He liked to think they might have understood.

And beyond that terminator line of dead bodies, above the field of viciously yellow weeds, was Macha. She did not obscure the sunset. She *was* the sunset – a living eclipse of flesh that took the sun away with every swaying tramp of her feet. Her enormous hands clasped and unclasped at her sides. The evening was so cold that she strode through a constant smog of her own furnace breath.

Abelard had always been behind her, or below her, or miles away. Now, she was powering right at him. That prehensile lip smacked and slapped. Her whiskers danced. Even her forehead was muscled.

Her gaze never left the fortress. It no longer felt possible to argue with his own summation – that Macha viewed what was in front of her as a challenge, and like some antediluvian battlefield, she was limping towards them to declare a duel.

Silence had descended upon the wall, the kind of silence where you wished you knew how to pray. Men stared, their guns drooping, or didn't, couldn't look at all. A man dropped his reloading pouch and cursed, his voice cracking, because there was not enough room to kneel and pick it up.

That was how it was for the next few minutes. Abelard placed his hands on the battlement to stop them shaking. To try to believe the grainy permanence of the walls. They'd stood for three hundred years.

How long had Macha stood?

That was the thought that reminded him he had come here to do something. He pushed himself away from the battlement, straining over to see the state of the ground beneath. He was the only man looking down instead of watching Macha, and he only stopped when a parade-ground snarl delivered his name to the entire wall at once.

'Caudefoy. What do you think you're doing?'

Now men moved, squeezing themselves breathless to get out of the Lord Protector's path. He had washed the pollen off himself. Found clean coat and trews, though they did not fit him as precisely as his own. He hadn't been able to scrub away that mad little flush, though, the punch-drunk bagginess of his cheeks.

'I wanted to ask you one last time to see reason,' Abelard said. 'For the sake of these men, do not do this.'

He had raised his voice as loud as he could, thinking of Netha's instructions – picking a point beyond everyone's heads, speaking *through* rather than *to*.

It was not an easy audience. Not with Macha bearing down on them.

But he had to try.

'Lord Protector, I know the instinct is to do as you have always done. To treat this as a rebellion that can be easily scattered with a good Answering volley. But *look*.'

He didn't need to point.

'This is a new war, and you will kill these men if you insist on fighting the last one—'

It was all he managed before Meilyr was on him. The Lord Protector did not do anything as gauche as punch him. He grabbed Abelard by the back of the neck like a child and spun him into the battlement. Air left Abelard with a crunch. The stone edge sawed into him through his shirt.

Murmurs around them. Sergeants shouting for *Eyes front. Guns up.*

'Tell *me* to look,' Meilyr hissed into Abelard's ear. His breath was sweet and somehow cold. 'You have been here *three days*, Caudefoy.'

'You think you can finish this with a single shot,' Abelard said. 'But you don't finish wars with violence. You begin them.'

'A philosopher too now, is it? Marvellous. The least son of a family with a coward at its head. A conscientious objector – too concerned with his own sensibilities for the halls of power.'

Abelard tried to get his hands under him to push back, but Meilyr held him down with insulting ease.

'Even if you slay Macha, what about the others? There's a whole *pantheon* out there waiting. This is an irretrievable act of—'

'They're all irretrievable acts to someone,' Meilyr said coldly. 'You'd ask them politely, would you? Do you even know how we took this land? Everything we've had to do to keep it? If she is a god, she has no forgiveness for us, and I do not care to seek it.'

Abelard had already braced himself for Macha's next world-trembling step when he realised it hadn't come.

The god had stopped.

The gunnery crews were roaring at each other to hold. Tapers winked in the shadows.

She was just three long strides outside range. With visible effort, she straightened from the aggressive stoop of her walk to her full height. Two hundred feet of slabby, scarred muscle. Pits and craters in the riven battlefield of her chest. Other shots. Other attempts.

He saw her shift weight uneasily, the way his father did when his joints were playing up.

Meilyr saw it too.

'Load!' he roared, so loud in Abelard's ear it felt like an intentional slight. The sound of frantic industry echoed up from the gun line. Casks of gravedust were cracked open. Pitted iron cannonballs were loaded. Quiet discussion of angle and heft.

Macha watched impassively. *Was that honour?* Abelard wondered, scraping his chin bloody on the battlement trying to watch. *Did she understand what was happening in front of her at all?*

He took one last look down at the shot-scarred field. There was a particularly nasty tangle of ragwort beneath them – stinking towers of yellow spores perhaps ten feet tall. Beneath them, a group of eel-like creatures had been shot at point-blank range, curled up almost peacefully but for their shredded hides.

Twelve feet, then. Maybe fourteen?

'I recognised your name,' he wheezed.

Meilyr's grip loosened, just a fraction.

'What did you say?'

'It took me a long time,' Abelard continued. 'I was never the greatest student. And the Meilyrs, it must be said, do not feature large in the histories.'

The Lord Protector ground Abelard's cheek into the stone.

'You dare—'

'It isn't easy, being the fourth son,' Abelard gasped. 'I know. You've worked far harder than I have. Of course, you had far further to climb—'

Now Meilyr *did* punch him, a dirty little snap to the kidneys that really should have been beneath them both.

'You will not distract me,' the Lord Protector snarled. 'Not now. Not at the point where we turn this around.'

The sounds of preparation from below died away. A wind had kicked up, rifling through the bodies between them, setting a forest of fronds and spines and feathers shifting and whispering.

'What is she waiting for?' Meilyr hissed.

Macha drew her sword.

The motion took a long time, a slurping rasp that made Abelard's gums itch and his head spin. The blade was as crudely anachronistic as the rest of the goddess, a brutal thing of iron and leather the length of a Dreodyrne boulevard. She lifted it with one hand, unwavering, pointing it directly, it seemed, at Meilyr, though Abelard supposed it was so enormous it could have included him in that as well.

The message was clear. Across cultures. Across the line of divinity.

A challenge.

A slow, ugly smile spread across Meilyr's face.

'I owe you an apology. She *does* understand.'

Abelard drove his elbow hard into Meilyr's stomach. Unprepared, the other man gagged and folded. A spitty pop of exhalation spattered Abelard's cheek.

'I'm counting on it,' Abelard wheezed, and then flung himself over the wall.

38

Talasa

THE RAIN THRUMMED a mockery of Talasa's footsteps as she ran.

The scholars came out of the dark after her like spiders, grabbing and clambering and throwing themselves at her. The lecture pit strobed and fumed with light as she skirted it half on hands and knees, a shriek banging against the back of her teeth. Only the width of it saved her – the width, and their fear, because they gave that splintered edge just as wide a berth as she did.

She had no idea where she was going. Whether there was an escape here at all. The other side of the chamber was a forest of precarious, teetering stacks that the pit-glow turned to swaying shadows. Talasa turned one to shrapnel, feet skidding on a book cover as another tower reached out to grab her.

She saw wild eyes. A cheek cut in a geometric wound too broad to scab, the teeth inside flashing white . . .

Colby's finger.

Stord's ear.

It asks much.

'Get her!' Colby screamed, somewhere behind her, and Talasa jammed her fingers in that wound and *tore*. The man bellowed, and she was free.

A door. A *door*. She could have wept. She flung it open, threw herself into the corridor beyond, tripped and slipped and banged her way through aisles of shelves, sending protruding scroll cases spinning to the ground in sprays of dust.

She could not see more than a few feet ahead of her. Every looming statue or rolled-up tapestry was Stord about to grab her, a body lying in wait. She turned left, then right, then left again, through hallways made anonymous by centuries of purloined treasures, and for all she knew she was running past a staircase down, or parallel to a window she could use to escape.

She might have been running deeper and deeper into the House and removing any hope she had of surviving the night.

Because they would kill her. She knew they would. You could mock Master Colby with his knobby knuckles, each one like a withered knee. His stammering, sweat-flicked lip. You could laugh at their belief in a higher power. In their hideous dissatisfaction with what they already had, in their need to cram their gullets with *more* truth, *more* power, *more* control. So much so that they had plundered the hopes and holiness of other civilisations and lashed them into service the way they did servants to make their bread.

But you could not, for one second, forget that the Answering would kill to protect the stupid things they believed, and that meant they would kill her.

So Talasa ran. To where, she didn't know. She just couldn't stay here.

Only silence seemed to pursue her now. She had found an atrium – just a disassociated little bud of architecture growing where two wings of the university met – and stopped for a moment, forcing down lungfuls of breath to quell her panic.

There had been nine *zemlje* under Kalifsena's watch. Some small, others larger, one nearly the size of an Answering fief. She travelled. Advised. She guarded. Told fortunes – not the petty fortunes of men, but the grandiose futures of entire dynasties. She was hosted at feasts where she told stories balanced on curlicues of smoke, shaped shames into victories, delivered arch barbs to dismantle egos and stoke feuds.

That was her calling, and she was good at it. And yet there had been a night when something had gone wrong. Talasa did not know what it was, and Kalifsena had never said. Afterwards, of course, things had been too easy to ever really think of it again.

But Talasa thought about it now, because that evening she had gotten up and left the feast Kalifsena was attending. It was their way. Sometimes her mother needed space to do what she needed to do to close that gap. Or Talasa went outside because it weakened her mother's position to have her child standing looking morosely from the corner, because Talasa *was* a morose child, and it was hard to promise a future when your past stood there looking bleak.

She had peered inside at the light and the laughter, at the harsh words and the rattled blades, and then heard a screaming cry from a sheltered little barn. It wasn't human. She hadn't been afraid. Just curious. Nobody would think to harm her – nobody would dare.

She had known very little then.

The inside of the barn had been wet and hot and steaming in the chill. A body had been opened, there in the dark, and a woman had stood over it, a saw and a little knife in her hands. She was old.

Hunched. The memory of handsomeness to her face, now hidden behind a bitter smirk and a single gobbet of gore that stood out bright in the shaft of moonlight.

Another Woman of the Sinew. One who laboured in a different way than Kalifsena. One who had also not been invited, or had been banished, or did not have the favour to sit at high tables and talk high matters.

She had not explained a thing about what she was doing. It was a calf. It was dead. Whatever saving might have been attempted had leaked away into the cold air.

And there had been something in the woman's hand. A knot of tissue, red and white and gleaming. The kind of thing that should have never been outside a body. The kind of thing you were not meant to see.

Without a word, without an explanation, or any change in her expression, the woman had taken her tiny knife and flicked it across the knot, like someone cutting a slice from an apple for someone else to share.

She'd proffered it to Talasa, who had looked down at the opened little thing.

Inside was a perfectly formed tooth.

That was what this place was, Talasa thought, as she looked around the atrium with its dusty cabinets filled with books nobody had read, and tall, thin urns that looked like demure women never allowed to speak. All the Answering's progress, all their haughty pride in having no gods but themselves, and inside, this little knot had been growing, wrapping itself in tissue in a dark space at the heart of an empire.

And you left him there.

Talasa had only had to endure a few days of being unaligned to her mother's wishes. Offrian had suffered that his entire life. No wonder there had been such hope on his face when Rubeo had at last shown an interest he could understand.

Talasa went to the shuttered windows of the atrium and pulled at the heavy bolt until her fingers burned, but it would not slot back. She might have screamed then, or punched her hands bloody on the boards, but the instinct to be quiet was too ingrained, and she had too much training in not giving herself away.

They'll kill him.

They'll keep *him.* Convert him. Recruit him for their monstrous little church.

The only relics of the past the Answering cared about were their kings and princes, and Colby would not squander one or let them burn.

It was just Talasa that was in danger. Talasa and her mother, and the Queen was in this up to her neck.

There was a narrow gap between shutter and window, and suddenly it gleamed with yellow light. Talasa kneeled, pressing her cheek and brow painfully into the boards, and saw that the window looked down on a little courtyard garden.

Men. Men holding lanterns, skirting around hedges and peering underneath them.

Searching for her.

Give in. It would be easy. She could just shout. Let them find her. They'd take her hostage – these men were good at seeing value even in things they did not respect – and perhaps even bring her to her mother, though there seemed to be some tension there that Talasa did not understand.

You were helping them. And then you stopped. Why?

Where was your line, Mother, when you had crossed so many others?

She should give herself up. At least then she would be once again told what to do.

Stand here. Say this. Keep quiet. A simple religion to follow.

She realised then that her hands had clenched into fists.

Stop this, she thought. *Stop being a child. You haven't been one for years. Stop wanting to be led if you are not content with it.*

Stop craving guidance and decide something *for yourself.*

She pressed her hand against one of the urns, and it rocked a little. Something sloshed thickly within.

Quickly, carefully, with one eye on the dark doorway in case she saw light, she reached up and found the stopper. The red wax was black in the gloom. It was probably some sort of blasphemy to lever it off with an old stylus she found in a box nearby, but there were enough blasphemies happening under this roof that she felt she might get away with it.

It was too dark to see much of the liquid inside, but it smelled fresh and clean as grass, with a hint of some warm spice. She reached a hand in and rubbed it with her fingers, feeling the oily slickness of it.

The noise of her tipping the urn over was loud enough that she was sure she was going to be heard, but its thin ceramic skin cracked when it fell, so she didn't waste time levering the tops off the others.

And then she ran as fast as she could.

It was the deciding that was the hard part. Everything after that was easy. They knew this place better than her. Perhaps they'd gone straight to the exits, assuming she'd come to them. They weren't expecting her to criss-cross corridors and hallways, tipping out pages and shaking out journals. They weren't soldiers who knew to hunt in grids, to hide even as they were searching, to not call out to each other as they wandered from room to room, sometimes right by Talasa as she lay under shelves and behind statues.

They had made Secandeur House a place where going unseen was easy, taking wide corridors and making them narrow tunnels, creating a maze that a man could not squirm through but a sixteen-year-old girl could.

More than that, they had made it a place where a single match would be the death of them all.

And Talasa had five, hidden in the pocket of her dress.

She said quick prayers as she lit each one, dropping them deep into the bottom of paperboard boxes and lodging them underneath rolled-up scrolls. Not to the gods to which each relic she passed had belonged, but to the people who had written and cared about them.

She hoped they would see it as being set free. As the men of this place being denied their plunder.

We fed it.

'Now starve,' Talasa whispered.

And everywhere she went, yellow light began to gleam.

Sweat had soaked her through by the time she lit the fifth match. Not from heat, but from the long-drawn-out tension of scurrying and sneaking.

She had hoped lighting the fire would make things easier – distract the academics maybe, draw them outside or send them rushing to the river to put it out.

She was wrong about that, or there were more of them than she thought, but suddenly everywhere she turned – each new corridor, every dusty classroom or courtyard – had a pair of panicked, angry men with torches tearing the place apart looking for her.

Twice she had found a staircase down to a ground floor, only to have to scamper back into the shadows when she heard advancing footsteps. Once, the only thing that had saved her from being cornered in a dusty old classroom was crawling into a crate stacked with fat little fertility idols, trying to press her skinny body into them so she would not stand out.

Huddling there. Bruising herself against old stone. Trying not to flinch as the light of a lantern played over her back.

She listened. What else could she do?

'We should be with the others. If the fire spreads . . .'

Footsteps creaking on the floorboards. Their breath, fast and heavy and frustrated.

'Colby wants her.'

A hitch. A swallow.

'*It* wants her.'

There wasn't enough paper in the university you could have burned to warm Talasa's bones after that.

No more matches. She had to get out.

She retraced her steps through a set of smaller lecture halls and balconies, keeping low, freezing every time she heard a noise. The crabbed, convoluted architecture of Secandeur House looked down and back upon itself constantly, and she risked everything to climb the single narrow ladder up into a little belvedere – an ornamental tower, just a room stacked on a room.

For once, it was nearly bare. Perhaps carrying plunder up here was too much effort. She hefted herself off the ladder and went to the window looking out over the House's flank.

Golden light spread and seeped like blood under a scab, bubbling up through skylights and casements, as if the darkness that marked the House was flaking away.

She had tried to spread out her use of matches as much as she'd dared. If they didn't get the fire under control now, they'd never control it.

Good, she thought, easing herself back down onto the ladder. *Good.*

A hand grabbed her leg.

There was no chance whatsoever of resisting. Of holding on. The hand pulled, and Talasa went with it, yanked straight down like a dress from a washing line. The floor of the room below rushed up to meet her . . .

. . . but she never reached it. She simply hung there, kicking, from a red, soft fist.

'You've really ruined things.'

It was Stord.

39

Sister Wake

THERE WERE NO good mornings to be a human sacrifice, it turned out.

Grainy clouds of dream-fear became mud against Sister Wake's cheek, frozen into swirls like the marbling on meat. Her body came back to her in stages, forced into awareness by hard ground and cold, stiff rope, binding her wrists behind her back painfully tight.

The sun stabbed into her eyes when she opened them – bright and cold and invasive. It set her vision churning, and only a rush of sore blinking made the looming sun resolve into white and gleaming stone.

The altar of Crom Dubh was an altar no longer. Sister Wake had to roll onto her back to take it in properly, gasping as her head protested. The altar stone, that flat coffin of torcstone the Cailleach had forcibly flung from this mountainside, had . . .

Returned.

No. Not returned. It had *grown back.*

She wriggled away from the base of the thing like a worm. Nobody had dragged it back up here, that was for certain. There were no track marks on the ground, and anyone who might have wanted to do it was dead.

No, she could see where the grainy muck had split and bulged like a gum around the base of the stone, the vertical caking on its sides. Like the portal tomb they had seen on the shores of Lough Maol.

'I know,' Brother Caid said softly from behind her. 'Miracles are frightening when they happen so close.'

The first altar could have been innocuous if you ignored the chain. It had been low and smooth. Rounded like a baby tooth. Why it was holy had seemed obvious, even to the young girl Sister Wake had been. A white stone against a black mountain. A beautiful and barren landscape that drew the mind upwards. Away from whatever blood your hands might have spilled.

Now the adult teeth were pushing through. This new altar stone was a bevelled, chiselling tower taller than Brother Wight. Beyond it and the lance of shadow it cast in the early-morning sun, three more were breaching the black earth.

One was the height of the first, another pale and mud-streaked fang. The other two were far less graceful. One was on its side, flat as a shoulder-bone, and had lurched out of the earth like an old man getting out of bed, coming up not vertically along a sharp edge but in a flat and ripping lift that had torn a whole scab of the earth along with it.

Underneath its shovel-like breadth, you could see another stone lifting it, opening a wound into the black ground.

A tomb. A tomb had pushed itself from the earth.

That gap scared Sister Wake more than Brother Caid did.

'What is this?' she breathed.

'I asked myself that.' The priest kneeled beside her, and when she tried to recoil, he did not grab her but instead the ropes around her wrists. *Practice.* 'It was hard, in those first few days, to have anything but questions.'

That voice. It was the only thing that let him be who he was. It drooled like honey, like the only sweet thing for miles, and as soon as Sister Wake heard it, the shrieking terror came.

'*Help!*'

She hadn't even screamed for help the first time she'd been dragged up here. Back then, of course, there had been someone who might have come. This time, the scream came out of her in two worlds at once – a great saintly howl that echoed over the winter-bleached plain of Umhaill in the hopes of finding anyone, living or dead, who was not *him*.

Nothing.

Sister Wake was alone. She was back on the mountain with a shackle around her leg, but this time there was nobody to come and save her. Panic burbled up through her, and she reached out to the cold knot of the Cailleach in her heart to tamp it down, but the fear was a heat that would not be denied.

'You know,' Brother Caid said gently, picking a nub of apple out of his teeth, 'for a little while, for that first, horrible little while, I thought this was because I had done something wrong.'

'You fucking *prick*, you don't understand—'

He hit her, almost casually.

'You've always been like this, Síle. Ever since you were a little girl. Convinced you had a right to question. Convinced you had figured out some angle, some point of attack on the way of things.' He raised a hand, made a dismissive little circle in the air. 'Some clever little argument nobody had thought of before. I remember . . .'

He smiled at her then, actually smiled, and then gathered his tatty grey robe around him so he could sit opposite her as if they were gossiping children.

'It was the first time I ever met you. You were six, I think. Maybe seven. We were making the *subhais* for Bealtaine. And you asked why the gods needed to eat our food, and couldn't they get their own. Do you remember?'

It was like those first few weeks of having her *tabharthas*. Trying to find a language for a head shaped nothing like hers.

'I don't,' she said honestly. 'I don't remember that.'

'I spoke to your da, even then. *Watch that girl*, I said. And he didn't listen. He nurtured that spirit, and he was liked, and when I came back this way along the Dunadhach, I could feel that ten years of rot had set in. Rot spreads from people like him. And people like you.'

He sat back, tutting his exasperation up into the darkening sky. 'Why did you have to be difficult?'

'Is that why you brought me up here before? Because I was difficult?'

There were surely better questions to ask, but Sister Wake could not help herself. Brother Caid shook his head.

'There you go again. Seeking understanding. *It is not your place to understand*. It is not the key's place to understand the lock. Not the link's place to understand the chain.'

'And what does that make you?'

He looked down at the soil, and then smirked as he found something and picked it up. A chisel, mostly rust now, the wooden handle pocked and shrivelled as the finger of a dead man.

'A tool, same as you. Just made for different work.'

'You don't know the work I was made for.'

The words came out of her before she could stop them.

'They found me frozen to the ground. Days had passed. I was starving. Sleeping. Alive. They had to . . .' Her voice hitched. 'They'd already buried my da. I never even got to say goodbye.'

She shrugged herself up onto her knees.

'The Cailleach came through here. She killed Da, she changed me, she flung the altar and went on to the village, but you never saw her, did you? Or maybe you did – she just didn't see you. That's right, isn't it?'

'Be quiet,' Brother Caid said, blood welling from his splitting lips. 'You don't know—'

'I do know,' she said. 'I know because I saw her. I know because I felt my da die in my arms. He looked at her so she would not take me. As for the village, I don't fucking know. Maybe they heard her coming. Maybe they came out to see. Maybe there was screaming, and people ran to . . .'

A laugh wormed out of her throat. 'She claimed everyone but you. Did you even catch a glimpse of her? Were you brave enough? Or did you hide in that little burrow I found you in, hoping she hadn't come for you?'

'Of course I hid!' There was a hint of a wail to the priest's words. 'She found them all wanting. Killed them where they stood. I would have followed her. Went down to the beach, but by then there was the ship, and—'

The ship?

Sister Wake spat, and it was ice before it hit the ground. Brother Caid saw it and scrambled backwards.

'How are you . . .' he whispered. 'What . . .'

'You said it wasn't my place to understand,' Sister Wake said, and there was the strangest twinning to her voice, like even her words had an icy reflection. The air popped. Sweat broke out on her forehead. Drizzled down as frost. 'But I do now. The Cailleach didn't choose me. Of course she didn't. She chooses everyone. *You* chose me. You dragged me up here because you didn't like the way I spoke.'

She smiled so wide she felt the frost on her cheeks crack.

'It wasn't my fault. It could have been anyone. *You* made it me.'

There had always been a part of her resenting the goddess. Hating her. The Cailleach had come and taken Da. She had cursed Sister Wake with ice in her veins. Sister Wake had been chosen, and being chosen had ruined everything, and letting that ice fill her further was a door she could never close.

But now . . .

'Just you. That was all. It could have been anyone, and you made it me, and *she killed my da*.'

'And what of it?' Caid snarled. 'What loss? You were supposed to buy us a better year, and look what you've done instead. Ruined everything. The only thing you were good for, and he ruined it.'

Caid's choice. Not hers.

He'd *chosen*.

And then, just as easy, it felt like Sister Wake could choose too.

What if it wasn't the Cailleach's power. What if it wasn't the Rising's?

What if it was *hers*?

The knife Brother Caid drew was just a rusted, pathetic little thing, but it would do the job. 'When you see him,' he hissed, 'tell him he didn't save you. He just bought you time.'

Sister Wake spat frosty spittle in his face.

'Tell him yourself.'

And a hand burst through the earth behind her.

The men of the Rising had done the best they could with the uncompromising earth. That had been good of them. It had kept away the birds, and the soil here was too dry and cold for worms.

But still, the months had not been kind. His hands were ragged, skinned from scrabbling. His chest had sunk and collapsed as the skin tightened and the muscles withered away. He stood, and some of that great, safe tallness was gone, stolen away by shrinking sinews and a bending spine.

But Sister Wake didn't care. Da was here, and he was overjoyed to see her too.

Brother Caid tried to run, but Da got there first, grabbing with an arm like an old tree bough – hard and grey and wrinkled as bark. The priest howled, swinging the knife. It clattered against Da's skull, rattling around between cheekbone and jaw.

Da gripped Brother Caid's face with the rotting palm of his other hand and slammed his head against the altar once. Twice. And then let him fall.

Silence fell with him.

For a moment it was just them and the mountainside. The hard and searching wind. The great non-sound of empty air.

'Let me look at you,' she said quietly.

He turned away from Brother Caid's limp body. His hair had grown long and shaggy, grey as rain, hanging over the side of his face that still had skin and flesh. The knife had done real work on the other side, and skin hung down in ribbons and tatters.

It didn't matter. It was Da. She saw it, shining from the spaces where his eyes should be.

Tentatively he reached out a skeletal hand and traced her cheek, dislodging a scurf of frost.

'I thought I'd killed you,' she said. 'I thought it was my fault. I didn't understand. Too wrapped up in my grief to see what you wanted.'

Mathilde had said it, all the way back in that bog. She'd known what her mam wanted, that simple, powerful drive – as pure as a bird's need to fly.

He smiled weakly. Not all the facial tendons were there anymore.

'You were trying to save me,' she said.

He held out his arms, and she stepped into them without hesitation, feeling the scratchiness of her *brat* against her skin and his skin all at once. She fitted right back in there, like a body into a grave, or a mind into a memory, and the only difference was the whistling passage of wind through the parts of him that were missing.

'I know it isn't really you,' she said eventually. 'I know you stopped. You stopped a long time ago.'

It was the first rule of waking, but it was a rule she had invented herself, when she was looking at the world through a caul of guilt. You didn't let a creature know they were dead. You manipulated. You tricked, instead of trusted.

But that was when she had thought she was a puppet too. When she had believed that this power belonged to a god, or to the Rising, but never to her.

'The dead are just a conversation the living have with themselves,' she said. 'We're not beholden to them, and they are not beholden to us.'

A new commandment.

She couldn't help herself, though. She had to ask it. The question she'd never let herself voice. The thorn at the heart of her grieving.

'Did you know? What Brother Caid had been doing? The other girls? Did you stand by and say nothing, until they came for me?'

He looked at her with those sad and empty eyes, and she knew that the only answer she'd ever have would be the one she decided on herself.

It was a beautiful morning to know who you were, the girl thought, looking at the tomb opening tilted up towards the sky like a mouth of soil and stone. The dawn was streaky indigo, and despite all the evidence, Sister Wake had the strangest feeling that it might be a warmer day after all.

'You could come with me,' she said. 'It would be good to have . . .' *A protector. A friend. My da.*

'No,' she said into his silence. 'I have to go on without you.' She looked around. 'Will you be all right here?'

He shrugged, and she flushed.

'You're right. It doesn't matter. You'll have left.'

His blank features searched hers.

'I'll be fine,' she said. 'I know what I'm about now. I think.'

They shared a little smile then, as much as either of them was able, and then Da reached down and dragged Brother Caid to his feet. The motion made the priest stir. That was good. She had been worried Da had hit him too hard.

'What . . . what's going on?'

Sister Wake reached up to kiss her father's gravelly grey cheek before stepping back to regard them both.

'I'd love to chain you,' she said. 'But time and Da's chisel put that notion to rest. So instead . . .'

Da slipped his arms in under the priest's and laced his fingers behind Brother Caid's head. The priest yowled at the scraping touch of dead skin against his, but he had not the strength to pull away, and when Da kneeled, Caid was forced down too.

'It wasn't the gods who forged that chain,' Sister Wake said. 'It was men like you. So now he'll be your chain, and you can know how it feels.'

She cocked her head.

'Clíodhna Ni Anluain. Neman O'h-Uisgin. Fann O'Cuain. And Síle too, I suppose.'

The terror in Brother Caid's face was almost reverent. 'Those names. How . . .'

She smiled beatifically. 'I can't hear them up here. I can't hear any of them. They're gone. They're free. I'm hearing those names from you.'

Brother Caid began to struggle, but Da held him firm, tightening his grip until the smaller man shrieked.

'You can't,' Brother Caid pleaded. 'You can't do this. To sacrifice a priest on a holy site . . . the gods will be *enraged*!'

'The gods don't know you fucking exist,' Sister Wake said. 'And this isn't a sacrifice. I'm doing this for them. And for me.'

She turned away from the altar. It was on the eastern side of the summit, looking down upon Umhaill. You had to walk a little to see the western side that led down to the beach. She hadn't had that luxury before, what with the chain on her leg.

'What are you *doing*?' the priest yowled.

'To see if you're telling the truth for once in your fucking life,' Sister Wake said, looking at the enormous footsteps that still clung as ice to the mountaintop. 'To go see if my god is on that beach.'

40

Abelard

IT TURNED OUT to be closer to fifteen feet, actually, and Abelard felt that mistake in his ankles, then his hips, and then his face.

A rush of air, a turn of the stomach, then pain. He landed where he had aimed, to a point, but when his heels connected with the coiled heap of eel-like creatures, he discovered they had set hard as soapstone in death, and the jarring impact turned his fall into a clumsy, painful roll.

The world spun. Abelard bit the inside of his cheek. A fleshy spine whipped across his face like a tree branch. Falling through a thicket of stinking ragwort face-first slowed him a fraction, even as it blinded his eyes and gummed his lungs.

The touch of cold mud was both stunning pain and deep relief. He would have liked nothing more than to lie there for ever, or at the very least until the line of agony creasing his face went away.

'Get him up!'

Meilyr.

'Fetch the stupid bastard!'

That's me, Abelard thought, with bleary pride. Then, gritting his teeth, he struggled to his feet, pushing his body into a limping run.

He had chosen – as much as he had chosen any of this – to make his escape over the headland rather than the beach. The logic was sound. It was solid ground. Less than a mile of scrubby grass and black, slick rock, curling like a talon from the keep to the shore.

Less than a mile of downed demigods and swaying stalks belligerently thriving despite the flimsy soil.

And ahead stood Macha.

Legs spread. Feet planted. It was not hard to imagine her turning that stance into a charge. Rotating at the waist. Sending that blade in a blurring arc that would cut Promontory in two. Flicking a thousand men into the air with a single stroke like drops of blood from a slashed throat.

And yet . . . so far, she hadn't. She just stood there, the shadow of her sword a line showing Abelard where he needed to go.

Abelard ran. It would have been uneven footing at the best of times. Now, the ground was ravaged with claw-prints and shot-scars, or distressingly smooth where blood and other fluids had leaked out and hardened in the cold evening air.

The stink was like a hand in his mouth. Opened bodies. Spent gravedust. The ever-present ragwort. He tried to control his breathing, to limit his exposure, but he had to run, because he knew they were chasing him.

How long would it take for men to follow? Would Meilyr just make them leap off the wall after him? Would they do it if he did? He wouldn't sacrifice the gunnery crews from their posts, that was for certain, and the fiery yellow undergrowth and piles of corpses made sight lines difficult for anyone at the same elevation as him.

Abelard had minutes.

It would have to be enough.

He navigated around the slumped corpse of an enormous otter. Slunk under the toppled form of what might have been a man but for the eddying swirl where its mouth should have been, a hole the size of a grapefruit through its chest. He had to cut and zigzag, backtrack and squeeze gaspingly through spaces not sized for him.

It was almost a blessing. How was anyone supposed to find him in this?

And then, as if in challenge to his foolish hope, Macha began to move.

Abelard was maybe halfway across the curve of the headland – a wheezing, desperate five hundred feet – when the minutest shift in the goddess's weight turned the grey beach white under a scum of displaced water. Even the rock beneath Abelard's feet began to quiver.

Move.

The animal urge then to just bury himself in the dirt and hide was overpowering. You didn't run *towards* something like Macha. A mouse did not challenge a lion. It ran. It hid. Or it died of fright.

Somewhere nearby, a shriek was building. For a moment, Abelard thought it was him – a desperate little whine surely no Caudefoy had ever uttered before. But then the stalks around him began to bend and flutter, and he looked up to see Macha's sword coming down on top of him.

He rolled onto his back against the charnel pile. It was like watching a building collapse. He had no time and all the time in the world to get out of the way. The god's arm came down, straight and unyielding as a windmill blade, turning the air to a numbing, freezing scream.

Every petal of every bloom left its stem in the wake of the swing, and then the bow wave hit Abelard and he was airborne.

The world was spinning shadow. A tide of bodies and pollen. He skipped like a stone across a pond before he finally hit something hard enough to stop.

Black scales. He was lying on black scales. His legs were half covered by something immensely heavy. A face stared into his from inches away – thick-lipped, tusked, its single eye a drooling pit. Petals crowded it like coins in a beggar's bowl.

Now Abelard did scream. Just a depleted little yip – he was owed, this was awful and now he was about to die . . .

Dead.

Dead, thank the First Among.

And then it moved. Jerked. Once. Then again. A petal went into Abelard's mouth and he coughed the horrid thing out. His next breath tasted of gravedust, sharp and welcomingly inorganic.

A black scale on the thing's forehead shattered into a crazed mirror and a wisp of smoke.

They're shooting at you.

Abelard got up. Spat blood and petals. Carmine fluid soaked him. It was in his hair. His eyes. He tried listing the symptoms of a concussion and couldn't remember any, which seemed like a poor enough sign. But it didn't matter. He had a duty.

And something put out the sun above.

The next shot splattered the downed creature's lip. Another passed close enough to Abelard's ear that he felt the creasing heat of it. One side of his face was wet. His left knee was a grinding wart of pain.

And it all seemed quite far away, because Abelard Caudefoy was staring up at Macha of Summer, and she was staring back.

The proper approach to a large animal is critical to safety, he thought.

It was a quote from *Mastering a Farm* – the first book that had ever been his, a book his mother had given him, a book he knew by heart. *Most large animals can see at wide angles around them, but there is a blind spot directly behind their hindquarters beyond which they cannot see. They know this, and it unnerves them. Be seen. Be acknowledged.*

That had certainly been accomplished. Maybe his own side shooting at him had actually helped.

Macha saw him, and even her gaze was heavy. When she blinked, Abelard could hear it, a slow, syrupy rush as each eyelid was dragged down and then released.

The safest approach is to announce your presence through a touch to their front or side. Most large animals will kick if surprised, and frightened horses or cows will plough right over you if approached from the front. Move carefully. Nothing sudden or surprising. Let them see you.

Dust devils of pollen still swirled around them, but the rich animal scent of her was enough to sear out the weed. Macha moved her head up and down to better focus on him. Horses struggled with depth perception, Abelard knew. Maybe it was the same for gods.

She had bent to look at him. Folded that immense body. Abelard could feel, in a dim sense, her hands hanging down on the other side, the cliff face of her blade furrowing the earth. It rained hair, stiff strands thick as ropes. There was grey in the red of her, and Abelard thought of his horse, and wondered had she ever been groomed.

'Hello,' he said.

A single gentle breath flattened a perfect circle of flowers around him.

Always leave yourself a way to get out if it becomes necessary. Try to avoid entering a small area enclosed with large animals unless it has an exit that you can get to easily. Never prod animals if they have no place to go.

'It's us trapped with you, I think,' Abelard whispered, and then cleared his throat.

'My name is Abelard Caudefoy.'

He said the words not in Answering, but in Croí. Or he hoped he did, at least. That was no comment on Netha's teaching, but they simply had not had much time to prepare him.

'I am the highest-ranking representative of the Answering left on this island.'

That might not even be true, except that Meilyr believed it, and that Macha was the Goddess of Sovereignty. Could she somehow detect it? Was there anything actually to detect? What actually made a peer a peer? Or was everyone simply judged by what they did with what they had?

What they had.

'I dedicate to you . . . er . . . Oh shit.'

Abelard had lost the bag. He'd probably lost it as soon as he'd fallen off the wall, and he somehow didn't think Macha was going to let him go get it. And he didn't know how to ask for a brief intermission in Croí.

'I . . .'

He swallowed thickly. Hearing Netha say those words had been like hearing a person as they were meant to be. Not the stilted slap of tongue on air, but a soul in flight. Abelard, by comparison, suspected his failure to win a place at Lofgeorn and Wlanc had been due not to his written submission but the interview.

'I dedicate to you . . .'

The back of his head itched. One shot would end it. Why hadn't they tried to shoot him again?

'Everything,' he said in Answering. He had run out of Croí. This would have to do. 'This will cost me my family. This will cost me the quiet, trundling life I thought I'd have. A life where I would become more and more perpendicular to what anyone needs.'

That did not seem enough, so he cast around for more.

'I dedicate the rooms I would have taken in Vildertan – our summer home, though you don't need to know that . . .'

Macha angled her head.

'I dedicate to you the empty set of chambers I was going to occupy there, full of drawings and books instead of a family. I dedicate to you a life of private and agreeable discoveries that mattered to nobody but me.'

He reached up and pulled the Caudefoy ring out of his pollen-streaked hair.

'I dedicate to you my brothers' regard. My father's respect. My mother's love. It will not follow me after this.'

Another blink, tide-slow and thoughtful. The silence that followed unstoppered him, and at last he remembered what Netha had told him to say.

'My name is Abelard Caudefoy. And on behalf of the Answering forces of Promontory, we surrender.'

41

Talasa

STORD DID NOT rush. Held out straight before him, Talasa kicked and screamed and tried to jab her elbows into him, but the soft-faced man carried her at arm's length like a dirty dress.

Then he trotted down a set of stairs to a large bay window and flung her through it.

Talasa landed hard. Spines and leaves raked her as she rolled off the flat, scrabbly back of the hedge and onto the grass, her body a mass of pain.

The sky was red and black. Smoke obliterated the stars. She squeaked as Stord picked her up again by the scruff of the neck, turning her with him to watch the fruits of her good work.

Secandeur House was a ruin. Its demise was at once methodical and distressingly quick. The outer walls charred slowly, but inside fire was racing window to window, trailing sheaves of sparks, triggering hot coughs of light that set new windows flaring, until the whole wing facing them throbbed with heat and light.

It should have felt triumphant. Talasa had *done* something. More than that, she had *meant* to. She hadn't been used, or fooled, or acted in the service of someone else. The masters of Secandeur House had threatened her, and she had burned that house to the ground.

It should have felt good. Instead, she was terrified.

What if this was what the fane wanted?

What if she had helped it? Fire was a holy thing, to some. It had been a holy thing to her, even – you lit the *gromnica* candles, you sent souls to their rest. The masters had thought they had known what they were doing, but they were children fumbling in the dark. Hadn't they been burning relics to feed it? How was this different?

It is, she told herself. If it wasn't, then why did burning mean anything at all?

She steeled herself. Stord was taking her away from the flames, pushing and shoving her up the lawn. That meant she might live. She might be able to do something. She would watch and she would listen and she would learn, and then she would escape. She would bring that knowledge to Armin Tell, or to *someone*, and they would figure out what to do next.

And the knowledge that her mother no longer made that list burned her heart to ash.

More figures spilled out onto the lawn. There was sobbing. Shouting. Arguments between those who wanted to reach out to the city, who doubtless must have seen the conflagration already, and those who feared it would draw too much attention to the work. Grown men held each other, weeping. Others raged. A fist fight broke out.

There – a young man she faintly remembered from a party in the Palace. Yerd . . . Tormley. Yes, that was it. Holdings in the New Territories, a love of rare art that had seemed almost charming and now seemed quietly sinister.

There – that was Garabon Tor. He'd been at several seances – the loudest to pshaw and harrumph beforehand, and the quietest during. How many of these academics were true scholars, and how many were men playing at such?

How far did this web stretch?

And there, a tiny, shaking figure that could only have been Master Colby, carried yowling as he fought to get back into the inferno. He was set down by his keepers, and immediately bolted towards the flames, only to be dragged back at the last second as something else ignited to paint the lawn like sunrise.

Lighting Talasa and Stord in stark relief.

The shadows from the fire made Colby enormous as he shook off his associates and strode towards her, sleeves and pointed hood forming great blades of shadow in front of him.

Stord held her out like an offering, and Colby took a long moment to regain himself before he spoke.

'Princess-Undynast. This is not what I had hoped for when I reached out to you about our work.'

Talasa looked him dead in the eye, Stord's knuckles bruising the back of her head.

'And what *did* you hope for?'

'Understanding,' he said. 'Consideration. Ambition, more than anything, for what we could achieve. All good Answering ideals.'

'Well,' Talasa said, 'I'm not from here.'

'No,' he said. 'You're not. A pity you are not more like . . .' His gaze ticked to something past her, and that smug little smile twisted his features once again. 'Your Majesty.'

Queen Kalifsena emerged from the rain-pattered darkness of the grounds as if the whole university was her seance candle, the rippling light turning her black brocade blood-dark and her eyes coal-black.

There was a smear of soot on one perfect cheek.

Talasa had been so concerned with her act of arson that she had not for a moment considered she was putting her mother in danger. Or maybe she had, and she had just known that at the first sign of calamity the Queen would have done exactly what she needed to do to be safe, without a moment's hesitation or sentiment.

At her shoulder loomed Lieutenant Gabel, impeccable in his king-scarl blacks, pistol and cavalry sabre at his side.

At the sight of them, the men of Secandcur House scattered to a safe distance, or bowed low and scraping, or hid themselves in their rescued treasures.

Only Colby stared the Queen in the eye.

'Talasa,' her mother said. 'What have you done?'

'What have *I* done?' Talasa fought Stord's grasp, but he did not let go, and the Queen did not command him to. 'Mother, I—'

Kalifsena did not wait for a reply.

'Can anything be saved?'

Colby looked sick. 'It would have taken days to move even the least of them. I salvaged my journals – the process of construction – but without matter to feed them, I do not know. I do not know. This girl has cost us years. A decade maybe. Unless . . .'

There was no expression at all on Kalifsena's face.

'That was discussed and rejected, Master Colby.'

'*Before*,' the old man snapped. 'Your Majesty. That was rejected before. The King was willing. Why aren't you, when you know what can be gained?'

It wants her.

The academics were gathering now, forming a half-circle around the Queen and her man. Talasa looked from Master Colby to her mother, hoping for any answer than the one she knew was true.

'We'll need to relocate, of course,' Colby said. Encouraging nods from the crowd. 'And if your pet Croí can provide more sites, the King could deploy in force to harvest them.'

He reached out to touch the Queen's arm, but something in Gabel's expression made him reconsider, and instead he pressed a hand to his chest.

'We can rebuild. Re-establish contact. Communion was only ever the first step. And if an expression of *goodwill* were made . . .' Something in the House collapsed – some internal upset or cataclysm – and suddenly there *were* stars, a million of them, short-lived in the sky.

'Mother,' Talasa said in a small voice. 'Please don't give me to them.'

Only if you knew her could you see the strain in those rosebud lips. That gaze fixed on nowhere, so she could convince you she saw everything.

'Mother, *please*.'

'You were told,' the Queen said, 'to stay in your quarters and *rest*.'

'It's a trade,' Colby said. 'The King was willing. Aren't you?'

A single tear ran down Kalifsena's cheek. Talasa watched it cut the soot streak in half.

Then the Queen nodded, and Lieutenant Gabel put his cavalry sabre through Stord's wrist.

The back of Talasa's head was suddenly soaked. Sopping. Something clung to her neck, a heavy spider that would not come away. Colby fell back, hands pressed to his wattled throat. Gabel's pistol barked, and a man spun as if kicked.

And the Queen held Talasa's wet face between her hands.

'I would never,' was all she said. 'I would never.'

Men were running. Stord kneeled in a pool of his own blood, holding the stump of his wrist up to his face in dreamy confusion.

'I need you to stand up,' the Queen said. 'We need to be gone from here. We can speak more when you're safe.'

'We're never going to be safe again, Mother,' Talasa whispered. 'What were you thinking? Lying to the King? Promising him—'

'What else could I do?' Kalifsena said. 'What else could I offer? As soon as I met him, I could see what he wanted, plain as day. And I knew that if I gave it to him, we would get what we wanted.'

'And what is that, Mother?'

'What we've always wanted. To be safe. To be powerful. To have our enemies confused, and our allies sated, and our bellies full. I want you to trust me. And *I want you to get up so that we can leave.*'

'No, Mother,' Talasa said. 'Offrian and I saw the fane. You'll tell me everything. You'll tell me here.'

The pistol spent, Gabel was among the fleeing, pleading men now. If they had all fought together, they might have overcome him, but they were too busy stating their names and their ranks and their families, holding them up like shields.

They were not shields. The blade flashed, red in the light. Stord had toppled sideways. Colby was nowhere to be found.

Kalifsena looked away, but not before Talasa saw more tears. She did not dare let herself believe that they were real.

'I don't blame you for being angry, child. I did not give you much of a childhood, I think. Riding from *zemlja* to *zemlja*, lying for a living, manipulating, only owning what you could put on the back of a pony. I didn't want that for you for ever.'

'I know,' Talasa said hesitantly.

'And I didn't want it for myself,' Kalifsena said, and for a moment they both laughed quietly, and everything was all right again, and it was the two of them and the wide horizon. 'Rubeo was our chance to leave it all behind. To find somewhere we could be just us. Where we could be true. Not living, walking lies.'

Her voice fell to a whisper.

'But to travel is to be new, and Rubeo . . . Rubeo became used to me. The classic methods, the old tricks. We had done our seances. We had made altars and drunk our dreamweed, and I had traced runes upon his skin . . .'

Talasa listened without embarrassment. None of these were mysteries to her.

'. . . and always he demanded more. And I didn't see the danger. He was so gentle, otherwise. I did not understand the appetite of kings.'

Would Talasa have believed her just a day ago? It seemed impossible now that the Queen could have been so naïve, but much had seemed impossible before the fane that did not seem impossible now.

'And then Colby.'

She only realised she'd said the words aloud when Kalifsena nodded.

'Master Colby,' the Queen said, her tone acid-tipped, 'is the stupidest smart person I ever had the misfortune to come across. The other academics understood it quickly enough. Asking questions can last for ever. But Colby could not leave it alone. The chance to be right, when every other culture had been wrong.'

She spat, a gesture so Shore that Talasa could not believe she'd done it in public.

'He was going to *tell* Rubeo. As if disproving obsession cured it.'

She looked up at the raging inferno.

'I thought about doing this, you know. Just to slow Rubeo's relentless collection. He was . . . becoming ugly in it. We built the embassy – that was his name for it – and that bought us a few more months of research and design, until . . .'

'Until it worked.'

'Until it worked,' Kalifsena said. There was horror in her tone too. 'I never thought it would. And when Rubeo heard it speak, he would have given it anything. They spoke one night. I was not there, and by the time I arrived, he had already left. Everything since then has been me covering for him. After he *left me*.'

The raw pain in her voice.

'The letters,' Talasa said. 'You wrote them. You called for the withdrawal. You wrote yourself *poems*.'

'That's what he would have done,' Kalifsena said. 'And I had to try and make sure there was some of Rubeo's power left to preserve. In case he came back.'

'Then why pull out of Croí?' Talasa asked desperately. 'Why give it up when doing so would so damage the Crown?'

'Because he'd given it up already,' Kalifsena said. 'And all an Answerman can do there is die.'

She stood, dragging Talasa to her feet. Talasa couldn't look at Stord, or the unclenched hand that lay behind them. Whole sections of wall were coming away from the cindering face of Secandeur House. A man in a black robe swung a scroll case futilely to try to ward away Lieutenant Gabel, but the cavalry sabre cut it and him down.

'There's nothing to salvage here,' Kalifsena said. 'There will be too many questions. Offrian suspects. Offrian hates us. And Offrian is *moving*. Making ready to be heir.'

'Mother,' Talasa said. 'I've been . . . Offrian and I have been . . .' Where to start? What to tell?

'That doesn't matter,' the Queen said, and Talasa felt something black and red as the House spider across her heart. 'We do not want to be here when he—'

'Mother,' Talasa snapped. 'He's *here*.'

They ran, hand in hand, to where Lieutenant Gabel stood over Master Colby, cleaning his blade.

The old man's eyes fluttered. Talasa fell to her knees, hands racing to find a wound, but there was too much cloth and all of it was soaked.

'My Queen,' the old man said. All the haughty knowledge had drained from his voice. Now he was just scared. 'My Queen, why have you—'

'You should have listened to me,' Kalifsena said. She did not kneel to speak to him, but stood, her arms crossed at the wrist as if waiting to be asked to dance. 'Where is the Prince?'

'It won't burn,' Colby croaked. 'Fire is the language of faith. It will survive. We will hear it again.'

Kalifsena pressed a dainty toe into the old man's chest. Colby whined like a dog.

'Offrian. The Prince. *Did you kill him?*'

And Talasa realised her mother was not concerned for Offrian.

She was making sure.

'No,' Colby said simply. 'We carried him as far as the foyer. And then . . . I remembered the journals. The blueprints. Without them . . . all the King's work would have been lost. So I sent Stord back. There was not much time.'

Kalifsena left the old man curled in a ball, mumbling. The fire was everywhere now. There wasn't a window that wasn't gold. The stone itself was dull red in places, like a coal in a grate.

'Mother, he's not dead.'

'You don't know that,' she said. 'And if he isn't, we will never make it out of the Answering alive.'

'No.'

'Talasa, listen—'

'No, Mother. *You* listen.' Talasa's fists were clenched. 'This is on you. You and the King. Colby was the first, but he won't be the last. If this is . . . real, if there is something out there, and the King is happy to treat with it, to command his own people to sacrifice to it . . .'

She couldn't finish the thought.

The Answering was bad enough. What it would become if it was alloyed to the thing beyond the fane . . .

'It asked for your *child*, Mother. You're going to let it have the Answering?'

'We can't stop it,' the Queen said. 'And we don't owe these people a thing.' She looked up at Gabel. 'Go to the stables. We need to be—'

'It isn't about owing,' Talasa said. 'It's about treating a wound.' And she bolted for the fire.

'Talasa!'

She paused, just for a second. Perhaps another mother would have sent Gabel after her. Or wept. Or begged.

But that wasn't the kind of family they were.

'Talasa,' Kalifsena said. 'I won't be here when you get out.'

Talasa nodded, and then ran into the flames.

42

Sister Wake

THERE WAS A moment, just a moment, as Sister Wake descended from the summit of Crom Dubh, when she wondered if she might be wrong.

Not about the howling Brother Caid, obviously. The piety had deserted him fairly quickly, much as it had her when her own manacle had shut. Some of the curses he threw her way when she turned her back almost made her like him.

No, as she made her way around and past the torcstone fangs, she found herself wondering whether she was wrong about Mother Promise. What was the difference between them? Yes, the old woman was lying to get her revenge on the Answering. Yes, Sister Wake's revenge had been more upfront and honest, and to save her own life to boot.

If the truth was all that stood between me and that man dead, I'd lie like a filí *with a price on their head.*

So was Mother Promise's war the same? She'd tell you it was, and lament that the Answering didn't have a single neck to wring.

Maybe the difference was in the cost. The cost to others. The cost to yourself. There wasn't a sinner alive who'd miss Brother Caid. Maybe you could do what you liked, as long as it didn't scar anyone else.

She wondered how badly she'd hurt Brother Wight.

The eastern side of Crom Dubh was semi-tame, with narrow trails scattered with stones for purchase. She took a moment, looking out upon the great dishevelled display of Umhaill – the fierce blue rivers, the rich red bog. You couldn't tell, at this altitude, if it was free or not. You just knew it was beautiful.

Worth fighting for. Sister Wake had never disagreed with that, at least.

The western side, shadowed from the island, simply fell into the sea without ceremony. The grass was mangy and blasted by the pummel of the wind, where it had managed to grow at all.

It was into that emptiness that Sister Wake stumbled and skittered and slid, clutching at stubborn tufts and ridges of hard mud. As soon as she left the summit, the only safe way to descend was on her side, pressed against the slope. To stand up was to be pushed into stepping forward by the incline and the wind, and to take a single step was to fall, end-over-end, eight hundred feet into the sea.

No such difficulty for the Cailleach, however. Those footsteps continued, in defiance of all sense, straight down the side of the mountain as if down a simple garden path. Sister Wake had forgotten how big they were – each one the length of her forearm, glittering like silver where four months' worth of dew had coated them, frozen, then coated them again.

It made an easy trail to follow, but that was the only easy thing about it. The drop plucked and worried at her, and only the cold had made the ground traversable at all. Even then, sometimes a ridge or rut would crumble under her, and there would be heartbeats of terrified, uninterrupted sliding down the slope before she could dig her hands in again.

She clung there for a minute, just gasping, the whole world the Unbeknownst Sea except for the little margin of earth in front of her, and asked herself, for the hundredth time, what the fuck she thought she was doing.

Asking for answers.

Bringing the Cailleach the names of the dead.

Listing the Answering's crimes.

Is she even going to care?

'I'll make her care.'

The words came unbidden, spoken into the dirt.

'She doesn't get to be our god if she won't.'

Hand-over-hand, one foot kicking out until it found safe harbour, and then a whole easing down, *brat* over her back, the grass tickling her nose.

'Nothing for us, nothing from us.'

Vex them, Mother Promise's voice sounded in her head.

Again and again and again.

An hour later, her foot hit empty air.

Sister Wake froze, then slowly, in strategic stages, turned herself around.

This was it – the point where the slope became a cliff in truth. Fifty feet of black stone awaited her below – sharpened and oiled by a forever of water, the sea tearing itself into white foam that she could taste in her throat.

She wasn't climbing down that with rope and picks.

Where do I go from . . .

Left was nothing but the rest of Crom Dubh, curving round to a flatter line of coast. To the right . . .

A ship. A ship moored just a hundred metres out from a scrubby scrap of beach that you never would have known was here if you hadn't completely lost your mind and decided to climb down here.

An *Answering* ship.

Sister Wake forced her *tabharthas* outwards to try to see what lay in front of her. There should have been something. Beaches were graveyards, overflowing with souls as small and quiet as the shells that held them. A gull. A fish. Anything.

It was no use. Her head was still a ditch of briars. More than that, though, there was a kind of thrumming, alien resonance that it hurt even to brush against. It was the same kind of looming, singular pressure she had felt from Mathilde's strangling fish, drowning out everything else.

Something huge was dying ahead.

Slowly, flat to the slope as if she was trying to bury herself in it, she began to ease herself closer. The fifty-foot stretch of vertical black stone beneath her became forty. Thirty. The roiling white line of surf began to break on grey sand rather than sharp rock, the hoarse roar replaced with a strange chiming.

Ice. Chunks bigger than Sister Wake, clanging and scraping off each other as the tide brought them in.

And ahead, a little beach, like the rind on a fingernail, the westernmost point on all of Croí.

Sister Wake clambered and slid until there was just six feet separating her from the colourless sand. The air was thin, as if she had somehow traded the height of Crom Dubh for an even greater peak.

Fog hung across it like downed flags. She slid, hanging by her fingers, and dropped. The sand was stiff and hard as rock.

She could see the ship better now. It was enormous – the kind of ludicrous Answering power that made you equally hate them and wonder could they ever be beaten. A floating mansion in red and banded black, with six great sails and a whole array of little doors on its side, through which gleamed the mouths of sleek bombards Sister Wake knew all too fucking well.

And she could see it was damaged. Fit to sink and listing. That soul still loomed in her head, and she couldn't help but map the great ship's wounds to the kind a strangling fish might have done. Raking slashes the length of the hull. Whole sections ripped away to reveal cross-sections like a caved-in chest.

The sunset bled out its last light, and Sister Wake saw the ship gleam with frost.

What happened here? What little war was this?

She knew. Gods help her, she knew.

That enormous soul warped and flexed in her head, and she ran towards it as if yanked, heedless of the fog, leaving broken, glassy dunes underfoot. It felt like she was racing the soul the way her terror had raced the sunrise all those months ago, death coming towards you like a hand in a mirror, like an axe to a neck.

The deep navel of the beach was still hidden from her by black rock. She placed a hand on an outcrop as she came around it, and then hissed, jerking her hand away. It was bitingly cold.

And on the beach ahead . . .

It was larger than she had initially thought. A pocket of sand a hundred feet across, cupped on either side by the sheer black rock of

Crom Dubh. Perfect for rebels or raiders who wanted to hide from the Answering. You could only see into the notched little inlet if you were further out west to sea.

In its centre kneeled the Cailleach.

Her head was bowed, her hair a messy tide of grey that broke across her white body, great licks of it stuck like seaweed to her wrinkled, knobby back. Matchlock fire had made mince of her shoulders and chest, and the chain that served her for a left arm had been severed by a cannon blast. It hung limp from her right hand as if she'd tried to jam it back in place.

The chain was not ice. Sister Wake saw that now. It had never been ice. It was a chain of torcstone, and suddenly the damage done to the ship made sense. Those lashing wounds . . .

The Cailleach's head was turned towards Sister Wake, those great black eye sockets brimming with white frost. Her soul – for that was what Sister Wake had felt, the soul of a god sawing back and forth – teetered on the brink of death.

Sister Wake ran to her. What else could she do? She had done nothing but resent the Cailleach since the god had appeared to her, but not for a single moment had she not feared her too. You didn't get a pass from that fear just because the Cailleach had spared you. It nearly made it worse.

But she couldn't just *leave* her there.

Not like this.

Not desecrated.

Sister Wake looked up into that strangely beautiful, pain-softened face, and into the sucking, horrified silence there came the high, proud laugh of an Answering man.

It took her one hundred and twenty beats of her hammering heart to circumnavigate the Cailleach's kneeling body, to walk around to the blackened headland of the old woman's toes to see what nightmare the rest of the beach had in store for her.

Beyond the Cailleach, scattered like bombard scrap, were the bodies of Answering soldiers. They had been left where they had fallen – crumpled and crushed, a fortune of matchlocks and halberds rusting in the sand.

Seeing that many dead should have been deafening. Sister Wake looked at those calm, dead faces, and should have been assaulted with who they were when they were alive.

But she could hear nothing but the dying god, lowing like a cow searching for its calf.

Between Sister Wake and the men, set up in the shadow of the Cailleach's bowed head, there was a table. A proper wooden dining table, the kind you might have found in Mother Promise's stolen manse. It had been laid with a white tablecloth, though it was not white now.

It was sticky, and red.

Sister Wake walked forward as if in a trance. Above the table, the Cailleach's bare flank was not ghost-pale but a scarlet and opened thing. Cuts had been made – neat and square at first along her side and thigh, delicate as stained-glass windows. But those were the old ones, black and scabby at the edges. As they progressed, neat cuts had become deep gobbets. Blood hung like drool from holes and gouges.

They had started with knives, she saw, in their rendering, and then gone at her like dogs.

The man at the head of the table was tall and handsome, and gloved in gore to the elbow. There was a pale circlet of metal on his brow. Sister Wake knew what that crown was, if not the man wearing it. It was on the half-scruple somehow still in the bottom of her pocket.

'Look,' the King of the Answering said, and smiled so widely flakes of blood cracked from his cheeks. 'Another mystery.'

VII

Us and Them

43

Sister Wake

SISTER WAKE HAD never seen a crown before. The *ríthe* didn't wear them in this age. That had been a long time forbidden. And now that she saw one, it struck her how ridiculous such a thing was. A special little hat for a special little man.

'But you must sit!' the King said cheerily, clapping his hands together. He wore a fine robe open over a silk shirt and tight trousers, and a coil of cloth hung loose around his neck. His accent was crisp and polished coming out of that madman's face. Rings glinted through the mash of viscera on his fingers. 'I had been contemplating some sort of sally out to a local settlement, but it seemed unwise to travel alone, and our ship is no more.'

He gestured at the table, and only now did Sister Wake notice that two men had slumped down behind it. 'My friends have been lost in thought for a long while now.'

That was probably because they were dead. Viciously, surreally dead, a kind of dead that Sister Wake, with all her blessed experience, had never seen before.

The first had simply exploded from the waist up into a bouquet of yellow flowers, the blooms all the more eye-achingly bright against the grey evening. They grew from his eye sockets, burst out of his mouth so strongly the lips had split, even peeked gaily from his nose and ears.

The other was portly, red-cheeked in the chill, his eyes still fixed upon the King's seat, as if hungry for whatever new wisdom the man might spout. Everything below his nose had turned to stone, and now his plump, flushed features sat incongruously on top of that pale, cold rock like a drawing a child had failed to finish colouring in.

They both wore those coils of cloth too.

'What happened to them?' Sister Wake asked.

'It didn't suit them,' the King said. 'That's my theory, at least. They weren't ready. We had done all the requisite preparations, of course. The meditations. Imbibed of stockwort and hannibarum.' His lip twisted in something very close to discontent. 'To be honest, I've never been sure how seriously they took it.'

His gaze brightened.

'Do you think that could be a factor?'

He asked it with such confidence at being answered that Sister Wake found herself unable to help responding.

'I think maybe you shouldn't be fucking *eating a god*.'

The King of the Answering threw back his head and laughed.

'That wonderful earthiness you people have. I have always so enjoyed it. Did you climb down here from the peak? What made you do it?'

Sister Wake said nothing. The King's firm attention was much worse than his idle politeness had been. There was cast-iron lunacy in that blood-mucked face, as bad or worse than Caid had been, and for much the same cause.

'Come on now, girl,' he said sharply, clearly unused to any sort of delay. 'I am conducting a study. Tell me what you know, and I'll see to it you are rewarded. Your family will never want for anything again.'

Casual, but hungry. His eyes searched her face.

She said nothing. A thousand smart responses came to mind and then withered on the vine. This was the *King*.

'Why would I help you?' she asked. 'What do I owe you but contempt?'

His grin remained, but there was something hurt and rat-like in his eyes.

'Bold words in the language we taught you,' he said coldly. 'Are we at least not owed for that?' He licked the tip of one of his fingers. 'If your god learned how to kneel . . .'

Another finger, worrying a bit of meat out from between his teeth, and Sister Wake sent the King's dead friends like bullets at him.

Sister Wake wasn't naïve. Killing the King of the Answering wouldn't somehow defeat them entire. Kings were like teeth in a shark's jaw. There was always another one waiting to be pushed out.

But when the ragwort man lunged off the stone to wrap his arms around the King's legs, it was worth it for the royal shock.

It wasn't easy. It was never easy, for a sparrow or a deer, even when rested, and Sister Wake was not rested now. She'd only ever raised one man before, too, and that had been the person she'd known best in the world.

So maybe it was the guilt she'd laid to rest. Maybe it was the utter blasphemy – yes, blasphemy – that had been done. Maybe this was what it was like to be Mother Promise, so furious you'd do anything for revenge.

Whatever the reason, Sister Wake *rose.*

Answermen were a bit like cats, it turned out – egotistical and complicated, but with simple hungers. Plenty of pettiness and jealousy she could use.

Guilliam Baver – whip-smart and with an ambition that had gone his whole life unfulfilled. Guilliam Baver, who read what his King read and parroted back what his King believed, but could not quell that secret, toxic root of a soul that wanted to grow beyond his station.

The flesh of the god had felt like soot and wax in his throat. Then there had been pain like nothing else, and Guilliam Baver believed he was going to come out the other side of it right until he didn't.

That was what powered him. Sister Wake barely had to touch him at all.

'Guilliam, what are you . . .'

The King reached down and grabbed the dead man's arms. Sister Wake heard and felt them come out of their sockets all at once, hanging like loose sticks in their sheaths of flesh. When Rubeo followed it up with a knee to the chest, it demolished Guilliam's torso with ease.

Flowers burst. The air smelled rank and sweet all at once.

The King flexed his scarlet hands.

'It suits me, I think,' he said. 'It suits me very well.'

Sister Wake flung out a hand, as Mathilde had done on a beach far away, and soldiers scrambled to attention. Memories, too. Lives, lives, a glut of lives, men who had indulged the King or loved the King or just liked the pay and the black coatee.

Some tried to resist, hanging back like a shy girl at a dance, the thought of raising a sword against their own King so abhorrent she couldn't get a grip on it.

Rubeo had no such qualms. The first soldier came at him clumsily, fingers like claws, and the King took him apart. He moved like Brother Able – that blurring, god-touched madness – and it took three men on each arm to halt his charge.

'It's you,' he gasped delightedly. 'You're doing this. You're like me.'

Sister Wake's answer was a halberd into his back, wielded by another set of hands. The King jerked out of the way, boneless as a worm, and kicked a man's head to paste.

'How marvellous.'

They couldn't hold him. Even with the unfeeling strength of the dead, they could not hold him. He was alive, viciously alive, and one look into his eyes told Sister Wake he would eat her, chew her and swallow her just for a *scrap* more power.

She closed her eyes against the hunger of kings . . .

And then Brother Wight flung himself between them. He came spear-first, and yet the tip *pranged* away from the King's shoulder as though it was armour, as if the Knight of the Hollow Eye had tried to stab a headstone.

Brother Wight didn't even flinch. He simply turned the spear in his hands like a quarterstaff and gave the King of the Answering the blunt end right in the jaw.

Fire-hardened ash met flesh and split, splinters flying like midges, and Brother Wight was stepping back, reversing, drawing that blade back along the other man's throat in the hope it would catch and tear.

Point. Butt. Edge. A half-heartbeat for each.

And the King simply stepped through each blow, and punched Brother Wight so hard his chest changed shape.

Her Knight flew. He hit the body of the Cailleach ten feet up and fell into the shadow of her mauled flank.

Sister Wake followed him. For once, she followed him. A thought sent the last of the men staggering towards the King. He sighed in annoyance and began to demolish their cadavers with earnest, hammering blows.

And then Sister Wake was kneeling beside Brother Wight, and he was choking around the blood on his lips.

'How did you find me?' she hissed.

'Mountain. Footprints. Screaming priest,' he gasped, somehow still managing to make her feel stupid even as he died. 'Your da . . .'

'Shh,' Sister Wake said. His chest was dented inwards like a kicked tent. He was breathing around it, but he would not be for long. 'It isn't . . . it isn't that bad. Just stay still, and I'll find a way to help you. Just *live*, and I'll explain it to you later.'

Their faces were very close. Blood had rouged his lips, but his cheeks were white. He kept blinking, as if trying to focus on her face.

She could feel him. Feel his soul draining out from between his ribs.

'Raise me,' he whispered. 'Raise me. Let me fight for you and *run*.'

'No,' she said. 'Fucking . . . no! You're not dying for me.'

'It's good. All right? It's good.' Brother Wight raised his hands and took hers. His were only warm because hers were so cold. 'Listen to me. For once. Just listen.'

His eyes fluttered closed.

'You only listen to the dead.'

And Sister Wake listened.

She listened to his pain. His silence. She listened to his fear of her. She listened to the knife wound he had taken and not told her about when three drunk warriors feared that she could bring Cailleach's eyes upon them. She listened to the times when he wanted to comfort the girl she was instead of the saint she had become.

Sister Wake knew so much now. She knew the names of his parents. She knew the shape and the sharpness of her mouth from the shape and softness of his.

'I'm sorry,' she said. 'But I've never listened to you before, and I'm not about to start.'

And she got to her feet, his wheellock pistol in her hand.

The King was advancing. He had so thoroughly demolished his own men that there was nothing workable to raise. Perhaps not all the resentment had been one-sided.

'You want to know what I know?' she asked, stepping backwards towards the sea.

The ambient roar of the goddess's pain washed over her as she moved around that bowed head, the ruin of her chest. They must have fired on her from the ship, she thought. Opened on her like an enemy fortress from afar. Only when she was weakened had the men come in with their matchlocks and nails to pin her down and harvest her.

Render her down into meat.

Why didn't you fight?

The King paced after her, fingers dripping, that damned cheery smile back on his features.

'There's nowhere to escape that way,' he said. 'Unless you swim, and I feel I could swim faster. Faster than anything. Is that how you feel, little spirit-caller?'

Gods, but he was obnoxious. The pistol was held behind her back, but Sister Wake had a shaking, horrid urge to fire it now.

'How did it happen for you?' he pressed. 'Where did you get your taste?'

'Nowhere,' Sister Wake said coolly. 'She chose me, I think. She needed me for something.'

The dead black eyes of the Cailleach did not follow her. That soul too was on the verge of departing, but like a great vessel, it took a while to empty, and though the goddess had been brutalised, she was still, fadingly alive.

Sister Wake looked up at the enormous face.

'Fascinating,' the King said. 'For what, do you think?'

'For this,' she said, and brought the pistol up. It was very gratifying to see the look of terror on the King's face.

'No!'

And Sister Wake shot the Cailleach through the eye.

44

Abelard

S*URRENDER*.

It sounded more beautiful in Croí than in Answering. Maybe that was because the Croí had more practice with the phrase. Even Abelard Caudefoy, as poor an example of the Peerage as you'd find in the empire, found the word unwieldly and foreign in his mouth.

Perhaps, he thought, *we will have to learn.*

Macha's breath was a furnace, cooking the fluids covering Abelard to dry and cracking earth. The curve of her torso was a cavern occluding the sky. She was so large and so close that he couldn't look in both her eyes at once, and his neck ached from tracking between them.

A muscle larger than Abelard twitched in Macha's cheek.

'Spare us,' he whispered in Answering. One of those colossal sail-like ears twitched. 'None of those men want to fight you. They were promised a withdrawal. Not a last stand. Not . . . not you. Let them leave and . . .'

And they'll return in force.

But that wasn't in Abelard's power to stop. One battle at a time.

'Please,' he said. 'Go.'

Macha cocked her enormous head, as if considering, and then, with a noise like a hundred cranes breaking their cables, she rose. Abelard staggered back, windmilling his arms to keep balance.

And Macha angled her whole body west, turning on the point of her blade as if preparing to bring it up against another foe.

Abelard scanned the hills to the west frantically – the little he could see at least, past Macha's massive form. A relief force of Answermen? More creatures of the Croí pantheon, come to reinforce the goddess or attack her when distracted?

With the heat of her retreating, he found himself suddenly shivering with cold.

Then, without a backward glance at Abelard or Promontory, Macha began to move. It seemed to take an age for her entire body to turn, but when it did, her momentum was shocking, lurching into a run that bounced Abelard hard against himself with every step.

In minutes, she was miles away, blade swinging out before her like a scythe, turning treetops to flat planes, sending scurfs of earth spinning skywards.

And then she was gone.

Abelard sat down hard against the dead whatever-it-was. It *was* cold, or maybe it was just the pain and exhaustion catching up with him. He was smeared in fluids even he did not want to categorise. His clothes were a stiff mass of spores and dirt.

And when Meilyr and his men found him, he was smiling.

'I'm sorry to drag you all out here,' he said. *I can do meaningless propriety too.* And the moon was out, and it wasn't as cold as before, and he felt as if he could almost manage a little snooze. It had been a long and draining day.

Five soldiers had come around the closest mound of corpses, their matchlocks up and ready, twitching between the inhuman bodies surrounding them as if waiting for an ambush. Behind them had come Meilyr, thunderous. That pleased Abelard even more.

'Get up,' the Lord Protector snarled.

Abelard did. It wasn't easy. The chill had seized his bones up some, and his clothes were stiff with gore. The Lord Protector waited patiently for him to get to his feet, and then took a matchlock from one of his men and whipped it hard across Abelard's face.

'You stupid little shit,' he hissed. 'What did you do? What did you *say*?'

Abelard didn't fall. That was something. The blow sent him staggering to the right, and his whole skull was awash with pain, but he did not fall.

'A few more steps,' Meilyr said. 'A few more, and we'd have had her.'

Was this how winning a battle felt? No wonder men became soldiers.

'Your men are alive,' Abelard said. The blow felt like it had rearranged the structure of his face, but he still found it in himself to smile politely. 'You're alive. The withdrawal can proceed now. As the King decreed.'

'That may have been our last, best chance to wound one of those things,' Meilyr said. 'We may never be able to set such a trap again.'

'Then we will never know how poorly it might have gone,' Abelard said. 'That sounds like a victory to me.'

'Because you are a fool,' Meilyr said. 'And one I thankfully do not have to suffer any longer. This is too far. Blood is no shield against outright treachery and usurpation. You had no right, and no rights. I should shoot you right here and be justified.'

'You would want to be sure of that,' Abelard said carefully. 'Before you or any of these men pull the trigger. And, for your *journal*, if you keep one, please note that I would rather be one who saves lives than spends them.'

'You've spent your own,' Meilyr said. He nodded at a soldier. 'Find a clear patch of ground. Let's do this right.'

The moon might have been high, but down amid the dead, everything was pockets of darkness, turning the headland into a lumpen, treacherous morass. Soldiers cursed and blundered. One man twisted an ankle in a rut and had to limp on. The wind whistled through the corpses.

A depression was found, ringed by swaying weeds dotted here and there by a handful of stubborn petals. Abelard was shoved to one side, and at Meilyr's gesture the soldiers took their places opposite. Abelard made himself look at each of them in turn. None looked particularly happy about what was about to happen, which he found gratifying.

'Will this change anything?' he asked quietly. He found his hands fussing over each other and ended up putting them behind his back. If he didn't look directly at the guns, he found himself almost able to be brave. 'You'll still have to answer for your failures here. Wasn't it worth it to keep Promontory intact?'

The man who had twisted his ankle cursed as his gun wobbled. Meilyr stalked over to him and grabbed the matchlock himself, sighting along its barrel. It did not surprise Abelard at all that he seemed as comfortable with it as a soldier of the line.

The Lord Protector let out an aiming breath.

'My Lord Protector,' one of the men said haltingly. 'Perhaps we should—'

'Sergeant,' Meilyr said. 'Shoot that man if he speaks again.'

Reluctantly, very reluctantly, one of the men turned to point at his fellow.

'You said you'd resisted the incivility of this place,' Abelard said. 'You know that whatever happens to me, the Rationale will question your every action. Your every decision. What does it say if you let your anger rule you now? What will they call you?'

The mouth of the matchlock looked enormous. It had more humanity to it than the black of Meilyr's eye.

'Barbarian?'

Meilyr closed one eye to sight his shot, and then closed both.

'Go.'

Abelard's eyebrows disappeared into his hairline.

'Excuse me?'

'Exile is a fitting punishment,' Meilyr said, and snapped the matchlock to parade-ready on his shoulder. 'And if I brought you back for trial, they'd question why I ever let a civilian near this in the first place. You are so fond of this benighted island and its monsters. Go to them. And if I see you again, I will make sure to have all permissions to shoot you down.'

'And Netha?' Abelard asked hurriedly. 'You should release them. They've done –'

Meilyr raised the matchlock again.

'The poet is already gone. What happens next is no longer anything you can control.'

He jerked the barrel west.

'Go!'

Abelard went. He turned his back on the Lord Protector, fully expecting the man to reconsider, for five rounds to penetrate the space between his shoulder blades. When they did not, he began to pick his way across downed stalks and body parts.

Each moment was ten moments. Each step felt like it might be his last. It was only when he had put a hundred feet and a thicket of ragwort in between him and those dead, pale eyes that he dared turn around.

The thousand torches of Promontory glowed in the distance. Beyond that was black ocean, and beyond that was his family. They would learn of what had happened here. His father's self-imposed exile was not so distancing. His brothers might lose standing in their positions, their ranks. There would be questions.

Abelard wished he had answers for them. They would have to make up their minds by themselves.

He stared at those torches until his eyes began to water. One of them might have been a boat. There might have been eyes looking back at him. He would likely never know.

West seemed as good a direction to walk as any, and so Abelard set out. The shorn and skeletal shapes of ragwort were silent company as he clambered over piles of dead or squeezed in between the bulk of slain monsters. Occasionally he would have to go around or climb into the waist-deep footprints of Macha herself.

Dawn began to redden the sky. Netha's warning about the strange summer they had passed through and what might lie in it still stuck in Abelard's head, and so he found himself moving north-west, skirting the yellow thickets. The landscape here was almost normal – Answering fields and homesteads, though most looked deserted. More than a few had been burned.

Sometimes he saw dark figures in the fields, too distant for any details to be made out. When they saw him, they hid or ran away.

Hours passed. Fields rolled beneath him. The bones of his calves became red rods of pain. He was so tired that thoughts felt disconnected, floating in prickles beneath his scalp. Dread for his friends. Anger at Meilyr. Anger at himself for not finding some sort of elegant solution that would have allowed everything to somehow be all right.

Only Macha's footprints seemed certain.

He hadn't intended to follow them, necessarily. They had just become a kind of confusing comfort, an indicator that he was making some sort of progress when the landscape seemed to stay the same.

They led him to and through an oak grove, entire trees knocked and mashed into splinters. He made his way past a mill pond, the tower of the mill itself now a broken stump, caught perhaps by the trailing end of a hoof. The little stream that fed it had been crushed into the beginnings of its own pond, and Abelard kneeled next to it to try to wipe some of the dirt from his face.

A twig cracked behind him.

Slowly he rose to his feet. His face was dripping, and stones crunched as he turned around. The forest seemed empty, but perhaps there were invisible gods and monsters too. If Netha was here, they could have sat down and written a bestiary together.

A figure stood up, pitch black against the shadowed green, and aimed an arrow at him.

Abelard opened his mouth to speak, and just like that there were two men at his sides, twisting his arms half out of their sockets. Through eyes blurred with tears, he caught the bright folds of cloaks.

Croí.

A hand grabbed his ponytail and dragged his head upright.

The woman facing him was enormous. her face a mass of pocked scars that spread like freckles down her cheeks. She had a shield on her back, hung with ribbons in a surprisingly gaudy display of colours. It didn't soften her whatsoever.

The men searched Abelard roughly, though their enthusiasm for the task seemed to wane when all they found was clotted scabs and petals.

'I surrender,' Abelard said, in hesitant, faltering Croí, and then one of the men hit him very hard on the back of the head.

45

Talasa

'THEY HAD DRAGGED him as far as the foyer,' Talasa said, her hands pressed flat on the Supplicant's Stand. 'Ten more steps, and he would have been safe.'

It was the third time she had told this story. This time, at least, she could talk through the tears.

It was a rare sunny afternoon in Dreodyrne, turning the windows bright as mercury, picking out every loose thread on every fief banner, every clump of dust and cobweb. They'd had to bring in extra seating in the galleries, and still, lesser reeves and skinny Cursors sat in the aisles cheek-by-jowl.

You wanted to be visible.

It was not half so pleasant as Talasa had imagined.

'And then the conspirators just abandoned him in favour of these . . . blueprints?' Tell asked. 'Is that correct?'

You know all this. Tell had sat with her most of the night, when the scorched carriage and its terrified horses had rattled up to the Palace stinking of soot and animal sweat. Gentle in his questioning, but not so gentle that Talasa could fool herself into thinking his concern was for her and not the Answering.

'They were obsessed,' she said softly. 'They had spent years researching. Collecting. Designing.'

She was sweating beneath the new dress they had located for her, and every trickling drop mapped a path of agony down the scalded skin of her forehead and back.

The innards of the House had been a furnace. Just being in there for the few minutes it had taken to find Offrian's prone body had cooked Talasa inside and out, parched her throat and eyeballs, dried her blood to paste.

'What they had built was more precious to them, I think, than any advantage the Prince could have delivered.'

'This device,' Tell said, wearily, over the rumble of a hundred men's sneers. 'The fane?'

That was the only time Talasa was called to speak that morning. The rest of the day became a makeshift trial.

It was quite interesting to listen to, sitting there and still smelling of soot. Reeve after reeve, hour after hour, each man stood to detail their personal discomfort with the presence of two foreigners in the highest offices of the land. Talasa had not realised that she'd been so thoroughly observed, particularly by men who were close enough to witness the Queen's manipulations and yet never be taken in by them.

Nobody had attended the seances, yet everyone knew what had been said at them.

Everyone had been just on the cusp of speaking out against the failure of morals happening right in front of them, except nobody's morals seemed to be in question but Talasa's and the Queen's.

Nobody had liked or listened to the Queen, and yet she had wielded a tyrannical amount of influence, particularly over the King, who was also not to blame.

Everything said bore so little resemblance to the truth that it was hard to focus on it, and even this seeming disinterest was commented on. Reeves loudly discussed whether the foreign girl understood what was happening at all, a thought that seemed not to contradict their accusation that she was somehow the secret canker at the heart of an entire monarchy.

Talasa spoke only once again that day.

'You have been very patient with us, Princess-Undynast,' Tell said, when the liquid mercury of the windows had dulled to gunmetal grey. He looked as tired as she felt. 'But there is a handful of details we would just like you to revisit.'

Wearily she took her place once again at the Stand. She knew which details he would like her to revisit, but kept her silence. Displaying any kind of prescience in an inquest about dabbling in occultic practice might have been unwise.

Tell combed a hand through the black curls of his beard.

'This man Colby. He told you that the King sponsored his research. Did you see evidence of this?'

I saw room after room of plundered treasure, stolen over years. I saw the kind of expenditure that might have actually made a difference in the war against the Shore. I saw men so confident in the patronage of their King, so believing in his *belief, that they fed their own flesh to it and would have fed mine.*

I saw the kind of madness only a king can devise.

'No,' she said. 'Colby believed it. But he was insane. I saw no sign of the King in that place.'

The Reeve Paramount nodded, letting those words sit for a long moment before continuing. 'So it is likely the King never knew of Colby's excesses.'

'He . . .'

Talasa looked around at the sea of faces. What would they do if she told the truth? Disbelieve her. Call her a liar. Accuse her of perjuring the King's good name, which was, when you thought about it, the only thing that kept her safe. Without that, she was just the foreign girl at the heart of a fire that might have decapitated an empire.

She couldn't risk it.

And besides, that wasn't what she had agreed to say.

She rubbed soot and sweat from her forehead. Gods, but she was exhausted.

'The King likely knew nothing. He had positioned Colby and his associates to protect his collection, but they were destroying it in their experiments. The King's interests – historical, cultural – were being burned in furnaces in the interests of wild superstition. Colby was a fanatic. Obsessed with the idea that there is something else outside what we see. Willing to kill for it.'

Tell leaned forward. 'Could they have killed him?'

Outrage and uproar, though not, Talasa noticed, from every gallery and every bloc.

That would be easier for you, too, Tell, I think.

The concern on his handsome features was expertly done. Or maybe it was genuine, and Talasa just could not tell any more.

'I do not know. They did not speak about him as if he were dead.'

'And your mother?' Tell said. That gentle, probing voice again. Talasa felt herself falter.

'I have told you . . .'

'Yes,' he said. 'You have. Tell us again, please. What was your mother's role in all this?'

'I never saw her,' Talasa said softly. 'Colby was warden to the King's collection long before she became Queen. We never spoke of his collection, and the last I saw her was when she left the Palace. For all I know, Colby killed her. Or she has gone to find the King and bring him back. I do not know where she is now.'

That, at least, was true. She wondered what lies Kalifsena would have told.

Tell let the chamber have its head on that answer for longer than any other. Eventually he raised his hands, voice effortlessly carrying over the mutters and whispers.

'A missing King. A missing Queen. A canker of superstition and forbidden practice in our own capital, at a time of great unrest. And all we have to go on is your word.' There was no accusation or prejudice in his voice as he spoke to her, but there was honest frustration. The man who liked a tidy empire, facing down an unprecedented mess.

'It is . . . inconvenient that these conspirators seemed to turn on each other when you escaped their clutches and set the fire. It is unfortunate they all killed each other before they could be put to the question. Hard to fathom, when they had worked together for so long.'

'Is it?' Talasa asked. 'Isn't fractiousness and disunity exactly what they were practising? Hadn't they given themselves over to exactly the opposite of what your Answering values?'

She might have said *our* Answering a day ago. Kalifsena certainly would. But right now, she could not bring herself to care.

Tell did not reply, and the kingscarls came to fetch her soon after. They did not go so far as to put her in a cell. There were no cells in the Bicameral Seat, as far as she knew. Reeves wouldn't countenance the thought of sharing a building with criminals.

Instead, they had found the office of some minor scribe, and chained the shutters closed. Talasa was left there without ceremony. By the time Tell came to speak to her that evening, she had read half the reports and budgets on both of the two small shelves.

'What has been decided?' she asked. There was a hollow pit of hunger in her stomach, and she couldn't help but wonder if there was a message in the fact that they had not fed her.

'Nothing yet,' Tell said, taking a seat on the scribe's desk and folding his long legs over each other. 'You understand that nothing like this has ever happened before. We've lost kings before. In war. Assassinations, even. But to lose a king, a queen . . .'

He stood, lean and disquieted.

'You could wait here. You do not need to be present.'

'No,' Talasa said. 'I want to be there.'

'You seem very resigned.'

'I don't know what else to be. I don't have anything else. It feels like everything is over. My part is played.'

'Did you have a part?' Tell asked. 'Really. Did you know anything about what she was doing? And what . . .' he had to force the words out, 'what they were trying to speak to?'

'There was something there,' Talasa said. 'You do not have to believe me, but there was. Whatever the King was trying to achieve, he did it. That's where he's gone. As for what my mother wanted, I don't know if I ever knew that. That's the thing I regret. Not knowing. Not having the chance to know.'

'I regret that too,' Tell said. 'Come with me.'

They walked through empty corridors throbbing with a kind of hesitant pressure, a waiting, sweating suspense. When they passed a window, Talasa could see that the Founders' Plaza was so crowded with people that even though it had begun to rain, it might have been the first time in the history of Dreodyrne that the stones were dry.

Tell did not stop walking, and so Talasa could not stop either. As they walked, however, she could not help but look back at all those faces, hope-empty and hunger-thin, pouring what little energy they must have had into turning out for their royal family.

You do know what faith is here, she thought.

She had assumed they were bringing her back to the Bicameral Seat for sentencing, so it was with great surprise that she followed Tell down to the Plaza itself. Two kingscarls opened the doors, and another hundred had advanced across the flagstones towards the shouting crowd, pushing them back behind a line of waiting coaches.

As they stepped out into the downpour, Talasa looked back to see reeve upon reeve depart the Seat, like rooks from a nest, finding their way to carriages in ones or twos or larger, solemn groups.

'What's happening?' she asked. Tell did not reply.

It was a long and silent ride to the Palace, and he and the kingscarl with them did not speak until they wound their way through the Palace itself, the flock of reeves ahead of them, black robes sweeping the tiles.

By the time they arrived at the ballroom, most of the reeves had vanished inside. Talasa could already hear the roaring, like children in a schoolhouse before the rhetorician walked in.

Tell bade her enter, and she did.

She stepped into the room with her head held high, ready to meet the gazes of these men who did not understand her and had never tried to. If they allowed her a chance to speak – and Tell would, she thought, he was good like that – she had already decided she would not reveal all the secrets she had heard behind their walls. It would not matter.

There was no puncturing the Answering's superiority. They took it in with their mother's milk. The world was meant for them, and the moment they proved the existence of another, that one was to be theirs as well.

Maybe you were right, Mother.

She stepped past the kingscarls at their posts, and then stopped.

The ballroom had been cleared, with rank upon rank of chairs set up for the reeves to sit. At the head of the room, on a stage where particular luminaries might have dined, there was what appeared to be an enormous canopy bed, hung with curtains of white. Talasa was walking, and then she was running, until Tell caught her shoulder and pulled her back.

'Wait.'

There was something moving within. A burgundy-dark shadow. There were other figures too, dressed in the white gloves and white robes of one of the medical academies – Talasa did not know which. They passed under the curtains and out again, holding pale sponges and long lengths of gauze.

The fingertips of their gloves were red, and red drizzled from their sponges as they squeezed them into buckets.

The air smelled like mint and pork.

The Speaker of the Bicameral was calling for order.

'Gentlemen, please! The Prince cannot—'

The voice from within the bed was wet and angry. A rose of red bloomed on the white curtain when he spoke.

'Listen to me.'

The chamber fell silent. Tell's hands were clenched on Talasa's shoulders, hard enough to hurt.

'I stand before you not as a prince, but as a wounded son.'

The blurred shape was not standing, but the damp, croaking voice was firm.

'The King is missing. Foreign predation and betrayal have taken him from us, and we cannot rest a moment until he is delivered back to the empire that loves him. The people who love him.'

Talasa's world swam as tears threatened to leak out. Faces were twisted in horror. In disgust. And in worry. Compassion. That was it, wasn't it? A king made them all feel like kings. Like a collective father was there to keep them safe.

'The family who love him.'

When Talasa had found Offrian, he had been aflame. She'd battered and pawed at him until her hands were moist with his blood and skin, trying to put the fires out. Dragging him ten paces as rafters fell and sparks flew. Ten paces that felt like a hundred, as she expected every moment for the ceiling to give way. For the fane to somehow find her with its scrabbling claws and slamming, chattering mouth.

Eleven paces had taken her screaming into open air and the wringing hands of the carriage man, who had been watching the catastrophe with open mouth.

On the frantic ride back, wincing at every shriek of pain, every bump, every shudder, all she could think to do was talk.

She'd promised she'd keep the King's name clean.

She'd promised they'd find a way to get him back.

She'd promised anything, if Offrian wouldn't die.

How much of that do you remember? she wondered, as reeves cheered and nurses fretted and Offrian coughed white cloth pink. *How many of those promises am I going to have to keep?*

46

Sister Wake

SISTER WAKE WAS used to leaving her own body to chase the souls of the departing dead, but the soul of the Cailleach was a leviathan in deep water. When it exited its body, it took her down with it.

The King of the Answering lunged towards her, hunger and horror warring on his face, and then all Sister Wake saw was blackness, and a divine kind of cold.

There was no beach. She had no body. She had no name and no memory. What she was before the cold did not matter. What she might have been without it would never come to pass.

There was just the duty.

There was just the work.

She would go and do the work until it killed her. Another girl would rise, and she would do the work until it killed her. Another girl would rise, and she would do the work until it killed her. Another girl would rise, and she would do the work until—

No.

The thought lasted the barest fraction of a second before it was numbed into non-existence. There was just the work. The cause. What gave her the right to protest, when a thousand girls had not? What gave her the arrogance to think she had a choice when no other girl ever had?

Maybe they did have a choice, came the thought. *Maybe they just hadn't been allowed to fucking make it.*

The thought was so contrarian, so absolutely herself, that it made Sister Wake remember she was alive. It arrested her descent, a single snowflake changing course in a blizzard, and she somehow found enough mind and soul to catch a couple more.

Still, though, the blizzard raged. If the soul of a wren or a woman dying was a single note, then the soul of the Cailleach was the competing cacophony of all the battles that had ever been. A memory longer than a nation's. Pain so overwhelming it had killed a body far bigger than hers. An aeon in ice that made Sister Wake's four months look like a snowflake on the tongue.

A chain that went on for ever.

But worse, far worse than the differences were the similarities.

Sister Wake delved deep into the maelstrom of thought. Sank through ages of memories. Vistas she had no words for. Emotions she was the wrong shape for. Power – *gods*, power that exalted and terrified her in equal measure.

And she saw herself through another's dead black eyes – a little stripling of a girl in a too-big shirt, clinging to her da on the mountainside. The Cailleach had looked at her the way Sister Wake had looked at Mathilde.

A broken thing you wanted to save.

A chained thing you wanted to free.

Chained the way the Cailleach had been chained long ago, when she had been naught but a little girl.

Girls.

So many girls.

Ice was a mirror, and in the Cailleach she saw herself.

Help me break it, she willed to all of them. *Help me break them.*

Rise.

The word came out of her in a little gasp, and then she was just Sister Wake again – lying on damp sand, frigid waves plashing at her shoulders.

The King of all the Answering was pushing her head underneath them.

'Wake up!' he snarled. The strength in his hands was such that Sister Wake could feel the wet sand parting underneath her, as if he planned to drown her and bury her in one move. 'I'm not *done* with you.'

A shadow fell across him.

'Oh . . .'

There was a white blur of chain, and the King was just *gone*. Had he not taken his hands from Sister Wake's neck in shock, the blow might have decapitated her, so hard did the trailing links strike. Sister Wake gasped for breath. Rolled. Spat salt.

Tried to get up, and then fell again, because she couldn't remember what body she was in.

'Get up,' she snarled. 'He's not dead, he's not . . .'

There was a hole in the mountainside where the King had impacted. A spiralling curl of scabs marked the path his body had taken.

It hadn't even come close to killing him.

'How dare you –'

He came out of the hole like a wasp from a hive, wild eyes in a blood-mired face. Fast, faster than fast – skittering forward on all fours to sweep up Brother Wight's discarded spear and fling it hard at Sister Wake.

Sister Wake didn't know which of them had the thought. She didn't know which body she was in.

It did not matter. As one, god and saint moved. Sister Wake threw herself to the side, feeling water turn to slush around her freezing skin. The spear bisected a wave, then stopped, bobbing. And the Cailleach's chain came down like a flail twenty feet long and drove the King the depth of a grave into the sand.

The goddess wasn't sure if that was enough to do it, and she didn't much care, so the chain came down again and again and again. It was only when Sister Wake spoke that the Cailleach stopped.

'We could use him. We could . . . Oh *fuck* . . .'

It was the strangest feeling. Waking any creature was a process of symbiosis. You and a soul working together in unison for as long as you could until they realised it wasn't right.

That was what it had been like, at least. Now, Sister Wake wasn't sure who was waking who. There was *so much* to the Cailleach, and she wasn't used to listening so much as she was used to having her way.

Gods, is this what it's like dealing with me? Sister Wake thought, and then found the Cailleach glaring down at her saint with grandmotherly disapproval.

'Don't look at me like that,' Sister Wake snapped, and heard her own voice from inside the Cailleach, as if speaking into a cave. 'If you're going to help, we're going to have to do things my way. Or you can die and be gone.'

The Cailleach looked at her for a long time, then reluctantly lowered her chains.

The King groaned through a smashed and bloody mouth, and then groaned louder when Sister Wake kicked him in the throat.

'Takes a lot to kill you, does it?'

She kicked him again.

'Good. Means we can do this all day.'

Another kick. He wailed.

'How did you find her? Who sent you here? What the fuck do you think you were *at*?'

'You can't do this,' the King of all the Answering squealed, trying to get up on a leg pointing the wrong way. He was hard to look at, if Sister Wake was being honest. One arm was flapping around like a bag full of blood and bone powder, and the other one was half-off beneath him.

But worse was the fact that she could already see him healing.

'I'm *owed*.'

'Owed by who?' she snapped.

'I traded for her,' he gurgled. Blood was crawling back up his cheek. A crumpled cheekbone popped itself straight. 'They picked one out for me.'

'*Who?*'

'Every herd has its herders,' he panted wetly. 'And we spoke. One head of state to another. There used to be priest-kings, did you know that? One foot in either world. That's what I've been promised, *and I have paid for it*.'

It was about eating. It was about feeding. Priests getting fat while everyone starved.

'What did you give them?' Sister Wake asked.

'What they asked for,' he hissed. 'I gave them Croí.'

That was when she remembered Brother Wight.

She bolted, leaving the King groaning beneath the Cailleach's glare, and found her Knight of the Hollow Eye lying half turned over on his side under a scattering of sand. It was blind luck or a miracle he hadn't gotten a kick or a chain.

She ran to him, skidding down onto her knees. Frost drizzled down from the god above.

Please be alive.

His eyes were nearly glued shut by sand. His mouth worked.

It was enough.

Sister Wake hesitated. Looked up at the Cailleach. And a pulse of that soul seemed like permission.

Behind her, the Cailleach scooped up the broken, spluttering body of the King, still raging at the indignity. Before her, Brother Wight convulsed as Sister Wake pushed a tiny morsel of god's flesh into his mouth.

And prayed she was doing the right thing.

Acknowledgements

I FIND A LOT of joy in writing the acknowledgements for a novel.

This is partially because I don't let myself do it until the book is done. It's a capstone. Writing for me is essentially an extended game of keep-away, where I chain myself to the desk with the promise of treats later, and there's no greater treat than the book being *finished*, and getting to look back at all the many people who were there for you when it wasn't.

Firstly, if you're interested in the history to which this novel owes so much, my constant companions for *Sister Wake* were *Medieval Ireland* by Clare Downham; *Dictionary of the Celts*, published by Brockhampton Reference; *Atlas of Irish History*, edited by Seán Duffy; *Early Irish Saints* by John J. Ó Ríordáin; *Early Irish Myths and Sagas*, translated by Jeffrey Gantz; *Early Irish Kingship and Succession* by Bart Jaski; and the works of Fin Dwyer, Liam Hogan and Sinclair Lore.

A special thanks must go to *Thirty-Two Words for Field* and *Listen to the Land Speak* by Manchán Magan, whose love for the language and the land have made me write my own weird fantasy love letter in turn. I'm also hugely indebted to the National Folklore Collection for their incredible work and generosity of time and conversation. Any linguistic mistakes and historical inaccuracies (like the giant monsters, for example) are my own.

'False Friends' by Doireann Ní Ghríofa became the epigraph very early in the process of writing this book, and I'd like to express huge gratitude to both her and Daedalus Press for its inclusion here. The full text of the poem can be found in Doireann's collection *To Star The Dark*.

I'm as always hugely indebted to my agent Clare Wallace and the entire team at Darley Anderson, who have been fantastic allies, guardians and co-schemers for not just *Sister Wake* but every book I've written. I'm very grateful for Molly Powell's expert eye, guidance and faith in this first foray into adult fantasy, and to everyone at Hodderscape for their hard work and expertise.

This book took a lot of writing, and I was aware at every step that I was drawing inspiration from something precious and crucial. Dmitrii, Cat, Jack, Devon, Nikki, Julian, Briana, Becky, Elijah, Graham, Rachael, Alex and the There and Back Again gang – I cannot thank you enough for your eagle eyes and sound advice on everything from caravels to the Cailleach.

Finally, to Sarah and Sam, my own little *túath*. I love you so much. Sword fights for ever.

Glossary

Abnetts' of Burkeshire – an Answering gunsmith famed for bespoke pieces. One of the few Answering gunsmiths successful in licensing high-quality Terod designs and gravedust.

Adake – the enormous continent to the south of the Answering. Home to many nations including the sprawling empire of the Terod Union. Trade and travel from the parochial northern nations to Adake are strictly controlled by the Union and the famed Lion Fleet.

Adhbha – the seal-haunted southernmost point of Croí.

aduantus – from the Croí word describing the fear of strange places, the *aduantus* is the collective term for indentured servants sent away from Croí by the Answering to the New Territories. Few, if any, would ever return to their homeland.

Age of Decency – a century-long period of peace during which the Answering expanded healthily into the Contested Territories, consolidated its gains and was not plagued with Erratics.

Aidhne – named for its founder, this is a *túath* and ruling family in the north-west.

Airgialla – one of the six provinces of Croí. Located in the north-east of the island. The Airgialla maintain strong connections and cultural transference with the north-west Answering, and pre-unification even had strongholds there before the First Among drove them back and consolidated their holdings in Druingill into the new Answering.

Akinidad – Ard-Ollamh of the Six-Coloured Court, master of the *filidh* and Chief Poet in Exile. A title equivalent to the Ard-Rí, or High King of Croí, if such a position still existed.

anabaster – a wiry little herb with yellow flowers. Can be served in hot water to encourage the truth.

Anfloga Dock – a minor dock on the eastern coast of the Answering, twenty miles of good sailing to the eastern shore of Croí.

Answermen – the collective term for the men of the Answering.

Anu's Scar – a mountain range stretching patchily across Croí, so named for the birthing scar proudly displayed on the belly of the Mother of Mysteries.

Attercope – the landmass on which the empire of the Answering resides. Called the 'heartland' by Answermen. While it is official record that the name of the Answering is a self-chosen reference to their central ethos of answering barbarism with reason and civility, many in the Shore say that it is simply a corruption of 'attermen' or warriors from Attercope.

Bairís Point – the northernmost tip of Croí, named for the phosphorescence that sometimes stains its waters.

Balepoint – an Answering fort along the south-western coast of Croí, erected in the first hundred years of occupation.

baleteen – a vine with hard orange berries that, when consumed, result in bad sleep and vivid dreams.

bánánach – Croí spirits said to haunt battlefields, winding down from the sky like threads of matted hair.

Banwit – a nation of the Terod Union.

barbicans – after the unification of the Answering, many minor gatehouses and military structures were converted into community halls known as barbicans, where the newly founded Order of Rhetoricians could preach the virtues, precepts and flaws of the Answering.

Bastard Cudder – a famed Croí raider and thorn in the side of the early Answering occupation. After a decade of sniping raids that steadily grew in strength and numbers, the Bastard sought to strike at the first Lord Protector, Lord Ames Salkeld, as he rode from Cusp to Promontory. Hungry for a substantial victory, the Bastard overextended himself and was crushed between the Lord Protector and a second relief force from Fort Roe.

Bay of Claws – a jagged bay on the western coast of Croí, once home to a thriving community of raiders and rebels, now wholly claimed by the Muirdris.

Bealusip white – a white wine from southern Feondhall.

Bealtaine – the Croí festival to celebrate the start of summer. Traditions vary across the island, but often involve collecting the ash from bonfires to make into protective salves, traditional dishes such as *subhais*, and pilgrimages to holy sites.

Bearm silk – one of the four old ways of weaving silk, and the one currently most in fashion in high Answering society.

Bellworth – an evacuated Answering settlement in Croí.

Bicameral Seat – the headquarters of His Majesty's Rationale, the Bicameral Seat is a sprawling mass of conference chambers, reeve offices and archives. The name of the building is often used interchangeably with the vast parliamentary chamber where the Rationale meet.

Bitanbill – an Answering fort built on the seat of the last *rí seiseadh* of Umhaill.

Black Mirandas – the colloquial name for the Tenth Regiment, named for the Queen who served when they were founded.

Blackwater – a renamed Croí town.

Blue Adelaides – the colloquial name for the Thirteenth Regiment, named for the Queen who served when they were founded.

Bluewell – a Shore herb named for its distinctive deep cup of petals. When crushed, has antibacterial properties.

Bog of Modhruadh – a bog on the southern fringe of Umhaill.

Boilg-on-the-Sea – a holy site to the Croí, where a torcstone portal tomb was erected to mark the place where Manannán Mac Lir left the world.

bombards – large iron cannons of varying sizes and specifications. The finest of these machines are purchased as licensed blueprints or imported at great expense from the Terod Union, whose technology is a century ahead of cruder, more basic Answering design.

brat/bratanna – a square, heavy cloak, usually of wool, sometimes lined with fur. Colour is often a direct or indirect indicator of rank and wealth, with the poorer Croí wearing coarser wool undyed or dyed with easy-to-find materials, while the wealthy have finer, more brightly coloured *bratanna*.

Brothers Athnach – a pair of Croí rebels who were unsuccessful in attacking Promontory. Accounts differ as to the cause of their failure, but the prevailing theory is that when the initial attack on the fortress broke, the fragile alliance between *ríthe* fractured with it.

Bulging Men – Croí demons of the oldest days, so named for their swinging bellies and voracious appetites. Defeated by the gods of the Croí and their saints in the wars of the Second Invading.

burntwine – a liquor made from grape pomace.

Bysmor – the core of pre-unification Dreodyrne, now one of its poorest districts.

Cadslina – a border fort between the Answering fief of Longreach and the Tattered Shore Grand Duchy of Salins.

Cailleach – the Croí Goddess of Death, Storms and Winter, the Veiled One, the Hammering Hag. One of the cardinal deities of Croí. Like all Croí gods, her appearance, demeanour and customs vary hugely from *túath* to *túath*, though a reoccurring detail is her long, fine hair, with which she is supposed to usher in winter by washing in the lakes of Croí.

Cailleach's Blessing – a Croí slang term for a thick, icy fog that comes upon you quickly.

Cape of Flames – the southernmost point of the continent of Adake, half mythical to the northern nations.

Cauci – the largest and wealthiest province in Croí, stretching east and south-east across the island. This wealth is partially due to its good land and partially due to the fact that its *Rí Seiseadh* Dian collaborated with the Answering King Ceolmund's first invasion of Croí.

Ceelim Bay – a large port in the south-west of Croí with regular traffic to the New Territories.

ceithearn/ceitheirne – Croí skirmish infantry, usually armed with swords and bows and bundles of fletched darts.

Ceolmund Academies – named for the first King of the Answering, Ceolmundites are the prevailing thought leaders and educators of the empire. Recognised by their distinctive red and white robes, the arguments of the Ceolmundites are said by some to have shaped the Answering as much or more as any true war.

Cichol the Wizened – King of the Bulging Men. Believed to have slain Donn, Croí God of Death, in the wars of the Second Invading, and feasted upon his body in an attempt to assuage his own maddening hunger.

Cilkeld – north-eastern Answering fief known for its iron mines and fishing industries. Its capital is the coastal city of Lindhord.

Claimwort – a Shore flower used to alleviate pain.

Codlethaf – a satellite village of Dreodyrne.

Contested Territories – the border between the Answering and the Tattered Shore, a place that has never seen peace.

Craobh Dháithí – an ash forest in the south-east, storied to be a single soul existing in thousands of trees. Now almost totally decimated by the Answering.

crithir fola – the Croí term for braxy, translating as 'trembling of the blood'.

Croghan Hills – small hills south and west of Sciáthcrann.

Crom Dubh – a mountain of black granite topped by an altar of torcstone. Storied to be the place where the Gods first arrived on Croí to share their wisdom, knowledge and power.

cruit – a Croí harp.

cuislenna – Croí greatpipes used in celebration, mourning and war.

curagh – a type of Croí rowboat with a wooden frame, over which animal skins or canvas were stretched.

Cusp – once the capital of the province of Cauci, it was built upon and expanded during Answering occupation to act as the administrative centre and capital of Croí.

Cuspwood – a carefully cultivated forest outside Cusp, where the Lord Seneschal and any visiting Peerage were known to hunt.

Dairbhreach Donn – a holy forest in the north, translating roughly to the 'Oak Plain of Donn'.

Daughters Dearg – a Croí legend. The mother of the Daughters Dearg was very beautiful and much desired by a local *rí*. When she turned him down, he slew her and turned the earth beneath her red. Her daughters, mad with grief, began drinking the blood of men. Some stories say that they save this blood for the corpse of their mother and share it with her unmoving form in the hope it will wake her.

Donn's Seat – a mountain on the south-western coast of Croí, named for the Croí God of Death.

Dornóg – a holy site to the Croí, where a torcstone portal tomb was erected to mark the place where Donn fell and was consumed at the hands of Cichol the Wizened.

Dreodyrne – the capital of the Answering. Once a relatively small city, it was chosen as the new administrative capital by the First Among precisely for its separation from previous power centres (though it must be noted that it does lie within Idegeld, the fief controlled by the Medalwyn family). Now an extensively expanded city of patchwork architecture and stubborn, pervasive ivy, it is still not the largest city in the Answering but is the beating heart of the empire.

Dreor – the river on which Dreodyrne is located.

Druingill – the north-western fief of the Answering. Its hilly and unforgiving landscape, combined with a populace with many cultural and historical crossovers with Croí, has led to minimalised influence in the Rationale, and general ostracisation by the southern fiefs.

Dunadhach – a river in western Umhaill.

Dziewona – a river in the Tattered Shore.

Ealdfaeder Gate – a private gate into the Palace, reserved for Peerage.

eating-worms – an Answering name for the Olliphéisteanna.

enrek jol – a popular sport and pastime in the Terod capital of Khoan, *enrek jol* is a martial art that prioritises holds and grappling over simply striking an opponent. With its emphasis on strategy and leverage, *enrek jol* is often taught to children as a lesson in restraint.

Érainn – one of the six provinces of Croí. Located in the relatively warm south-east of the island, Érainn has long benefited from good land and good ports, though this also led to keen interest from the Answering. As such, it was the second province to fall to the invasion and boasts the second-largest Answering military presence after Cauci.

Erratics – Answering kings who were considered to have behaved in a manner unbefitting the Crown. Though not an official historical title, and often not a popular one, the eminent Ceolmund Academies historian Joyn Taber once gave a paper in the Palace itself stating that the 'naming of Erratics is a necessary valve for historical analysis, providing enough history has passed'.

Evergreen Undercountry – the Croí afterlife. Croí depictions of the Undercountry, like Croí worship itself before the occupation, are not clearly codified between *túatha* or even families. However, most seem to agree that it is a place of plenty.

exemplars – the Rationale's most recent solution to the 'Croí problem' – offering work and land parcels in Croí to families from the New and Contested Territories. The majority of these are in Cauci, Érainn and Airgialla, but more and more appear in the west each year. Answering peers are encouraged to accept the settlers with generous grants and exemplar funds, often using mass evictions or steep hikes in rent to move the current residents to smaller stretches of land.

faewort – a Shore herb that causes pleasant feelings.

Feondhall – the south-eastern fief of the Answering. With its warm climate and favourable trade routes to the Terod Union, Feondhall is the most cosmopolitan and industrialised fief in the Answering. Its capital, Saergewinn, even boasts a small Terod enclave, which acts as a semi-sovereign state to oversee the production of Terod-licensed arms.

fidchell – a Croí board game, supposedly invented by Luige of the Oath.

fief – once a word meaning the due a king was owed by his vassal lords, this developed post-unification into the term for the sub-kingdoms making up the Answering. There are nine fiefs in the modern Answering, each easily the size of or larger than Croí, each one with its own capital and reeve representation in the Rationale.

filí/filidh – an order of Croí poets, once celebrated and now outlawed. Pre-occupation, *filidh* were part of a broad caste of lawmakers, poets, artists, mystics and advisers, often viewed as equal to a lesser *rí* or noble. Those of the *filidh* who were not slain by the invaders escaped and found refuge abroad, and a thriving community exists in the Terod Union.

Fir Glas – antlered warriors from Croí myth.

First Among – those much-lauded early kings who came together in Answering unification. Not every fiefdom was annexed peacefully, and though the names of those kings are also recorded, no statues of them will ever be erected.

Fort Domond – an Answering fort, thought destroyed by Macha in her long walk east.

Fort Roe – an Answering fort in the north-east of Croí, built after the Tumult of the Dal Riata.

Founderhall – an evacuated Answering settlement in Croí.

Founders' Plaza – the plaza surrounding the Bicameral Seat.

Four Cities – though stories differ, a popular belief is that the Gods of the Croí came from four shining torcstone cities in the Evergreen Undercountry – Falias, Gorias, Finias and Murias. Said to be seen in the skies above Croí when the *Fé Fiada*, or barrier between Croí and the Evergreen Undercountry, is thin.

Fyren – an old Answering university in the Ceolmund tradition, much respected.

geis/geiseanna – a complicated concept not easily conveyed. In modern use, particularly in the Rising, the word *geis* means a promise so strong it borders on the supernatural, the breaking of which would be catastrophic. However, it can also be used to mean a curse, an injunction or a prophecy, an immutable bond, unavoidable set of events or force of nature.

Gentlemen of the Chamber – the fraternity of peers dedicated to servicing the King's needs. In older times, this might mean guarding the royal chamber or tent on campaign. In today's Answering, the duties more regularly include providing company and counsel to the King, as well as organising entertainment.

gentry thorn – a small tree with white flowers and thorns. Often associated with death due to its musty smell.

Geslike – an Answering fort along the south-western coast of Croí, erected in the first hundred years of occupation.

giornea – a sideless overgown or tabard favoured by Answering nobility, particularly at barbican service.

Goodkeep – a renamed Croí town.

gord – the Tattered Shore term for a town or settlement.

Grand Sambia – a Shore *zemlja*.

gravedust – an explosive powder used in firearms and artillery in the Terod Union for centuries, but only more recently in the Answering. While gravedust is produced in the Answering, the powder imported from the Terod Union is of far better quality and reliability. Efforts are ongoing in the Answering to replicate the formula, but so far have been unsuccessful.

Grey Preciosas – the colloquial name for the Seventeenth Regiment, named for the Queen who served when they were founded.

gromnica – candles that sit on the chest of the newly dead in many Shore *zemlje*.

Halberd Gate – a gate separating the outer city of Dreodyrne from the inner city.

hannibarum – an Answering herb. When its leaves are ground and ingested, it provokes feelings of energy, confidence and recklessness.

Hanton – a satellite village of Dreodyrne. Known for its salt.

heart-tongue – the lyrical and long-persecuted language of the Croí. Outlawed in Answering-held territory, though the enforcement of this presents a consistent challenge for the occupiers.

Hedge-schools – roaming, secret schools set up both by the Rising and local Croí communities to teach heart-tongue, knowledge of the Gods, and other Croí traditions. Teachers in these schools risk death or indenture if discovered.

Heronry – an Answering fort in the south-east of Croí.

Highway North – one of the five main or 'trunk' roads of Croí, heavily built upon by the Answering to facilitate the quick movement of troops and supplies to Promontory.

Hillmarket – originally a Croí settlement, now renamed by the Answering.

His Majesty's Rationale – the parliament of the Answering, made up of representative high reeves and reeves from every fief. The Aetsomnes of Cauci have long petitioned to send their own representatives, but this right has not yet been granted.

hobelars – Croí light mounted skirmishers, famed for using the terrain and their nimble mounts to harry much larger foes.

houppelande – an open, flowing robe favoured by Answering Peerage.
Idegeld – a central province of the Answering, and the ancestral seat of the Medalwyn family, who formed the First Among and drove for unification of the Answering. Its capital is Dreodyrne.
Khoan – capital of the Terod Union, the Grandmother of Cities.
Kibard's Door – an entry into the Palace.
kilim – a type of pileless rug popular in the southern parts of the Shore.
Kilpick – a satellite village of Dreodyrne.
King Ceolmund Medalwyn – the Answering king who presided over the first invasion of Croí.
King Hereweald Medalwyn – while Answering historical texts state that unification was initially a joint endeavour between the then-sovereign nations of Idegeld, Longreach and Shetterling, it is also a matter of record that it was Hereweald Medalwyn's money and troops that provided its backbone. Four and a half centuries later, the family remains the first among the First Among.
King Rubeo Medalwyn – the current King of the Answering.
King's Cursors – like many institutions established in the early days of unification, the formation of the King's Cursors was as much symbol as it was expediency. A new era of cooperation required new methods of communication, and so the old, flawed system of occasional messengers, merchant caravans and hitherto surplus Peerage sons was replaced by a trained and dedicated corps of royally sponsored troops.
kingscarls – though most of the Answering's institutions have gone through a process of modernisation post-unification, particularly in their naming conventions, some retain their pre-unification monikers. One such example is the First Regiment, or kingscarls – an elite regiment that acts as personal bodyguards, force of law and a standing army in the capital. Though it has been nearly a century since any Answering king took the field in battle, the kingscarls maintain a well-deserved reputation for being the best the Answering has to offer, and it is a great honour for a serving general to be 'bestowed' a unit of kingscarls to aid his campaign.
kurvos stems – a shore tundra herb, used in cooking.
Lambent – a smaller port to the south of Cusp.
léine / léinte – a long Croí shirt of wool or linen that usually hangs past the knee. Worn by both men and women.

Leopold's Garden – a stepped amphitheatre in the Palace converted to a garden by Leopold the Second.

linden – a sweet-scented blossoming tree. Its leaves are commonly used for smoking, particularly by the Croí, who associate the tree with justice and fair conversation.

Lodemagan – the south-western fief of the Answering. With a balmy climate encouraged by the Straits of Mearc to the south, Lodemagan is a wealthy and verdant fief. Much of the Answering's wine is grown there. Its capital is Rodeorand.

Lofgeorn – an old Answering university in the Ceolmundite tradition, much respected.

Longreach – the easternmost fief of the Answering. Its capital is Ihankyle, City of Spears.

Lough Maol – a forty-mile-wide stretch of lake in Umhaill.

lucht tighe – the traditional household guard allowed by law for each *rí*, the *lucht tighe* are often comprised of family members, and are permitted to own and wear weaponry, though only to protect their land from other Croí.

Luige of the Oath – Croí God of War, the Sun and Mastery, Lugh the Beautiful, the White-Bronze King. Mastery is a distinct concept from sovereignty to the Croí, as sovereignty means control and consistent rule, and mastery means gaining a perfect knowledge of a thing from the inside. Unlike most *geiseanna* in Croí mythology, Luige is even capable of changing and twisting an oath – in recognition of the fact that nothing, not even a promise, may stay still.

Macha – Croí Goddess of War and Sovereignty, the Red Mare the Proving Ground. Sovereignty goddesses are a common feature in the Croí pantheon, as kingship is not earned once but continually. This same principle, if not the goddess behind it, also features strongly in pre-unification Answering tribes.

Macha Laws – pre-occupation, the number of female Croí warriors in any *túath* depended entirely on the culture and necessities of life in that region. It was Mother Promise who formalised the acceptance of female warriors by instigating the Macha Laws – dictating that any girl or woman who wished to fight would be trained to do so.

Mag Mell – middle province of Croí, a highly-prized breadbasket of the Answering.

Maigh Slecht – the 'plain of prostration', Maigh Slecht is one of the holiest sites in all Croí. Erected in times past by a tribe now lost to antiquity, the torcstone circle found here is the largest in all Croí, and in pre-occupation times was used as the crowning site for *Ard-Ríthe*.

Manannán Mac Lir – Croí God of the Sea, the Nine Waves King. As an island nation, Croí tell as many stories about Manannán Mac Lir as there are drops of water in his seas. These stories are not viewed as contradictory but complementary – there is no one water after all.

Marne's Bay – the bay on which Promontory sits.

menedach – a Croí savoury paste made from grains and butter. Can be served on bread or eaten by itself.

Mereweather – a Croí town, now renamed by the Answering.

Merrymain – an Answering fort dating to the time of Ceolmund's first invasion.

metheglin – a mead flavoured with rosemary.

metolves – a Shore herb with a soporific effect if smoked.

mnàthan-tuirim – Croí women who engage in a ritualistic communal outpouring of grief. The *caoineadh*, or 'crying', is made up of a combination of spontaneous sound, repeated motifs and snatches of song.

Modigmark – the westernmost fief of the Answering and the one closest geographically to Croí. Much of its wealth is derived from being 'the gateway to the west'. Its capital is Modigkaern.

Moraso's Curse – a region in the Terod Union.

Mornspiel – an evacuated Answering settlement in Croí.

Mortigern Cliffs – cliffs on the north-western coast of the Answering.

Muirdris – a terrible thing.

nawia – one of the many names for the spirit world where the souls of the Tattered Shore are believed to go after death. The *nawia* supposedly resembles the landscape of the Shore itself, albeit a more verdant one where benevolent *zmei*, or dragons, dwell.

Nemed – the Croí word for 'sacred', and the Rising's name for the various gods, demigods and craithurs returning to Croí.

New Territories – four precarious nation states along the northern coast of Adake, with strong cultural ties to the early cultures of Attercope. The Answering has long supported these nations with troops and supplies and favourable treaties with the Union, to varying degrees of popularity with the heartland.

Oauk of the Ending/Oautho the Sunset Blade – the religions of the Tattered Shore are similar in their quantity and diversity to that of Croí, though some of the western *zemlje* have instilled certain deities and representations of deities as chosen patrons and state gods. Oauk/Oautho is a war god, and one of the more common, to the point where even many Answerfolk would know their name.

Oftenord – an Answering fort dating to the time of Ceolmund's first invasion.

Ogma – Croí God of Poetry, Laughter and Lies. The Shining Man. Often described as a radiant-faced man with an enormous belly and a long, ear-studded tongue. One of the gods of skill, along with Smithing Brí.

Onchú/Hounds of Many Mothers – named for a Croí myth of a battlefield mongrel, these Croí were sent to harry Macha from horseback and lure her towards Promontory.

Oracles at Dharqesh – manipulative charlatans posing as seers in what is now the New Territory of Abelsfeld.

Order of Rhetoricians – supported and directed by the Ceolmund Academies, and led by a Rhetorician-General, Rhetoricians act as state-mandated and trained community leaders, historians and advisers to local lords.

Peerage, the – collective title for the Answering nobility. Post-unification, new titles were created to standardise the complex and sometimes contradictory piecemeal nobility of nine different kingdoms. Some of these archaic titles, such as *thegn*, remain in use, however, particularly in the hinterlands.

Peregrine, the – a gentleman's club in Dreodyrne, renowned for its exclusivity.

precepts – guiding principles of unity favoured by the Answering. Set down in the years of unification by King Ceolmund Medalwyn in his famous set of letters, *Arguing Statehood,* and proselytised since by his rhetoricians, with the argument that they are not commands to be followed but truths that stand by themselves.

Promontory – the seat of Answering military power on Croí. Relatively unique among Answering fortresses in Croí in that it has remained solely a military encampment without any settled civilian presence.

Purple Honoras – the colloquial name for the Fourth Regiment, named for the Queen who served when they were founded.

Queen Anu – Croí High Goddess, the Mother of Mysteries. Of all the gods, Anu is regarded as at once the most ever-present and the most personal – as universal as motherhood and personal as a mother. Some worshippers think of her as the island of Croí itself.

Ragwort Laughing – a monster.

Rasp – an evacuated Answering settlement in Croí.

Ratamhlagh – a village on the Cauci border where Bloscadh's family lived.

Red Grettas – the colloquial name for the Second Regiment, named for the Queen who served when they were founded. As the Second Regiment, there is a lively rivalry between them and the kingscarls, and this has earned the Red Grettas a reputation for brutal efficiency on the battlefield.

Redstone – an evacuated Answering settlement in Croí.

reeve – an Answering title equivalent to minister or senator. From the old word for 'honoured servant'. Each fief is responsible for sending a certain number of reeves to his Majesty's Rationale, where they represent the issues and interests of their people. First-born sons of the Peerage will often serve some years as reeves to learn the ways of the Rationale and make necessary connections before returning to lead their fief, while second- or third-born sons may consider it as a lifetime position.

Resist – a watchtower on the south-western coast of the Answering.

rí/ríthe – the Croí word for king. Kingship in Croí was a vast and complicated subject before the invasion, and occupation has made it no less so. While there were *Ard-Ríthe,* or High Kings of Croí, in the island's past, the power of this position varied hugely, and often lasted only as long as it could be enforced. More commonly, most *túatha* would have their own local *rí,* who would pay tribute and allegiance to a *rí seiseadh*, or provincial king of the province, though only the *rí seiseadh* of Cauci remains.

Rising, the – the name for both the Croí rebel movement and the periodic organised uprising to which it commits. Answering control of Croí has never been total, and at times in the last three centuries the Rising has waxed and waned – sometimes a patchwork network of rural insurgents engaged in theft and assassination and sometimes an extensive and public war effort.

Salins – one of the largest *zemlje* of the Tattered Shore. Shares a western border with the Answering. Its capital is Salinshrad.

Scáthach's Plain – the plain stretching across west/south-west Umhaill, named for a warrior woman of Croí mythology.

Sceir Bay – a bay on Croí's western coast.
scruples/half-scruples – Answering currency.
Secandeur House – located on Secandeur Hill outside Dreodyrne, Secandeur House is old enough to predate the Answering itself, being founded some fifty years before unification.
Second Invading – Croí has always been a land of invasions, and threats from abroad loom large in its mythology. The Second Invading is one such saga – a story cycle detailing a set of lurid battles, betrayals, alliances and even marriages between the forces of the Croí Gods and the monsters of the Bulging Men, led by Cichol the Wizened. In some stories, this war is why the Gods left – broken, battered but ultimately triumphant.
seiseadh – the Croí word for the provinces of the island. Derived from the Croí word for 'sixth'.
Seripharq of the Middle Kingdoms – an elaborate throne belonging to a now-extinct empire.
Shetterling – a western fief of the Answering. Its capital is Sceppanscealc.
Shieldwood – one of three fortresses that border Umhaill and Mag Mell, built on the Croí settlement of Sciáthcrann.
Slighe Mhór – what the Croí once called the Great Road and what the Answering call Highway West.
Smithing Brí – Croí Goddess of Smithing and Poetry and Making. First of the gods of skill, Brí was generous with her genius, and it was her who tutored the first Croí in the arts of the forge and the rhyme and the taming of beasts.
Sorbek – one of the largest *zemlje* of the Tattered Shore. Shares a western border with the Answering. Its capital is Urdur.
Spear of Luige – a spear under a *geis*. No war may be sustained against it.
St Ardgal – a saint of Luige favoured by Brother Wight's parents.
Starling King – the last true King of the Tattered Shore, whose death fractured it into the collection of city states and *zemlje* it is today.
stiffenrot – a disease in horses.
stockwort – an Answering herb that when boiled in tea causes hallucinations and lassitude.
sumptuary law – Answering and Croí laws dictating the appropriate dress for Peerage and nobles.
tabharthas – Croí word meaning offering or sacrifice or blessing.
Tamesa – a nation of the Terod Union.

Tattered Shore – the loose collection of city states that exists to the east of the Answering and stretches more than two thousand miles to the White Sea, where the increasingly frigid conditions render living impossible.

Terod Union – the vast empire covering the majority of the southern continent of Adake. The Terod Union is the most ancient empire in the world, its complexity and politics myth and mystery to the younger northern nations. Accounts and dramatisations of those who have attempted to travel or map the Union are very popular in the Answering.

Tikney – a satellite village of Dreodyrne, known for its wool.

tiompán – a Croí lyre.

Tirconaill – one of the six provinces of Croí. Located in the north-west of the island. This mountainous province is famous for its hardy, insular people, its unpredictable weather and the musical, inscrutable variant of heart-tongue that even other Croí struggle to understand.

torcstone – a bright white quartz found all over Croí, torcstone features heavily in the island's many mythologies and religious stories. Named for the traditional thick neck rings worn by Croí nobility, torcstone supposedly has one end in this world and the other in the Evergreen Undercountry. It is said that when the *Fé Fiada* is thin, the reflections you see in polished torcstone are of another place entirely.

Tornflag – a city to the south-west of Croí.

túath/túatha – a Croí word that can mean tribe or family or home, but in more modern times refers to a single geographic territory under a single *rí*.

Tumult of the Dál Riata – a failed campaign in which a number of Airgialla allied with rebellious Druingill peers and marched south to Fort Roe before being utterly wiped out.

Tur – a river on Scáthach's Plain.

Unbeknownst Sea – the western ocean. Never crossed, or at least no one who has ever crossed has survived.

Umhaill – the westernmost province of Croí. Umhaill has never fully been under the Answering's control due to its relatively poor soil and low population, and so it is here that the old traditions and religion hold most sway.

Victory – a watchtower on the Answering's south-eastern coast.

Warping Man – a Croí demigod, the Warping Man is in some stories the son of the War Goddess Macha, and in others the son of the War God Luige. What all stories agree on, however, is that behind his façade of nobility and martial prowess lurks an apocalyptic battle rage. When this rage exists, it is said, the first thing that he slays is the distinction between friend and foe, and even his own body rebels against itself in a desire to wreak havoc on the world.

wassaline – a Shore tundra herb, used to flavour meat.

Whiteseal – the Answering name for the Cauci territory most converted to the Answering way of life. Factory schools teach Answering precepts and the Answering tongue exclusively, and the first exemplar settlements have been successful.

Wlanc – an old Answering university in the Ceolmundite tradition, much respected.

Women of the Sinew – uniting the disparate cultures of the Tattered Shore is the tradition of Women of the Sinew, who act as travelling healers, midwives, political advisers and messengers. Though separate from the cultural role of priest or priestess, they share a similar worth and respect.

Wustamber – a north-western province of the Answering. Its capital is Dollowport.

Zdarind – a fertile southern plain in the Tattered Shore.

zemlja/zemlje – a territory in the Tattered Shore, the size of which can range from a single gord ruled by a local chief to a principality dwarfing an Answering fief.

About the Author

Dave Rudden is the author of the award-winning *Knights of the Borrowed Dark* trilogy, as well as multiple works in the *Doctor Who* universe and the middle-grade horror series *Welcome to Darkisle.* He has written extensively for stage, screen and role-playing games, and is the 2025 artist-in-residence at Dublin City University.